The Pentacle Pendant

By
Stephen M. DeBock

JournalStone
San Francisco

JournalStone books may be ordered through booksellers or by contacting:

JournalStone
199 State Street
San Mateo, CA 94401
www.journalstone.com

The views expressed in this work are solely those of the author and do not necessarily reflect the views of the publisher, and the publisher hereby disclaims any responsibility for them.

ISBN: 978-1-936564-27-9   (sc)
ISBN: 978-1-936564-28-6   (dj)
ISBN: 978-1-936564-29-3   (ebook)

Library of Congress Control Number: 2011937138

Printed in the United States of America
JournalStone rev. date:

Cover Design: Denise Daniel
Cover Art: Philip Renne

Edited by: Whitney L.J. Howell

For Nicolo Sturiano

Check out these titles from JournalStone:

Shaman's Blood
Anne C. Petty

The Traiteur's Ring
Jeffrey Wilson

Duncan's Diary, Birth of a Serial Killer
Christopher C. Payne

Ghosts of Coronado Bay
J.G. Faherty

Imperial Hostage, Book 1 of the Destruction Series
Phil Cantrill

That Which Should Not Be
Brett J. Talley

Reign of the Nightmare Prince
Mike Phillips

Available through your local and online bookseller or at www.journalstone.com

Prologue

Thursday, February 9, 2006
Freeport, Grand Bahama Island

On the last day of his life, Royce Williams met a woman who literally took his breath away. She was alone by the hotel pool, reclining on a chaise, an icy drink in her hand. She looked to be tall, he noted, probably close to six feet. Her hair was pale blonde, her cheekbones high, her lips full. She looked as if she could be a Swedish model. Loose-fitting white cotton slacks with a string tie around the waist were topped by a matching jacket, opened to reveal a turquoise bikini top. Brown-tinted sunglasses shaded her eyes, as mirrored ones hid his. He decided he was in love—or lust, the distinction between the two having always been somewhat blurred.

Palm fronds barely moved in the gentle afternoon breeze. The aquamarine water beyond reminded him of a bottle of Sapphire gin, and the sand sparkled like crystals of sugar. But they were nothing compared to —she took off her sunglasses and stared frankly at him. Her eyes were barely blue, so light as to be nearly gray. She squinted some in the sun's glare. His own eyes darted from side to side; was she looking at him, or was there someone else nearby?

"Hey," she said, definitely to him.

He gulped. "Hey, yourself." A swallow, then, "May I join you?"

She nodded toward an empty chaise beside her. "Please."

"My name's Royce," he said, extending his hand. The hand that took it was soft and delicate, with long fingers and polished pink nails.

"Lulu," she replied. "Short for Louise, a name I hate, by the way. You traveling alone?"

"Totally."

"Me, too."

"Beautiful women don't usually vacation alone," he said.

"Thank you for that. The beautiful part, that is. Fact is, I just finished a major case. The firm gave me a few days off to recharge my batteries."

"You're a lawyer?"

"Uh huh. What do you do, Royce?"

He was in his mid-twenties, and his head was shaved. His body—he wore baggy trunks and an open, flowered-print shirt—was as devoid of hair as his scalp, but it was much softer. Doughboy soft. Should've-left-the-shirt-buttoned soft.

Now that he saw her close up, he figured Lulu to be a little older than his first assessment, mid-thirties, maybe. That was okay with Royce. He remembered what one of his buddies back in high school had said about women of a certain age: They don't smell, don't swell, don't tell, and appreciate it like hell. Royce's naïveté hadn't matured much beyond his high school fantasies.

"I'm an executive with my father's corporation. I know, boss's son and all that. But I happen to run a very successful publishing branch—which is growing even as we speak." *That wasn't all that was growing,* Royce thought. *Down, boy.*

"Good for you." She sipped her drink and smiled at him. "And you're here for what, a seminar?"

He laughed. "I *should* be at a seminar, somewhere in East Jipip."

She arched a graceful eyebrow. "Oh?"

"I've been to enough of those, I could run them myself. Decided to sneak a few days here instead, escape the winter blahs." Lulu nodded, her smile even more cordial. He added, "By the way, may I say that you have a beautiful pair ... of eyes."

She opened her mouth—even her teeth were perfect—and paused. "Yes, I've been told that ... about my eyes. Don't know where I got them from."

"The mailman, maybe?"

"Or the milkman. Or the gardener. Or the pool boy. Any other clichés you'd like to explore?"

"Bad joke, sorry."

She touched his hand, briefly, and smiled. "Not necessary, Royce."

He nodded toward a gold star that hung from a delicate gold chain and rested just above her cleavage. "Are you Jewish?"

"No, silly," Lulu laughed and held it up for his examination. "This is a five-pointed star, see, not six. It was a gift from a friend, a long time ago. He's … gone now."

"God, this is my day for foot-in-mouth disease, isn't it? A boyfriend?"

She cast her eyes downward. "If you don't mind, I'd rather not …"

"Sure, of course." Awkwardly, Royce took a pack of cigarettes from his shirt pocket and offered her one. She wrinkled her nose and shook her head. "No minor vices," she said, brightening again as if she'd flipped her memory switch off. "Don't drink either—this is iced tea I'm holding, believe it or not—but I do, on occasion, have a nip of red."

"Does smoke bother you?" She said yes, but he lit up anyway and blew the smoke away from her. "You're upwind, you won't have to smell it. Nasty habit, I know. Probably kill me someday, right? But everybody's got to die of something."

"So they say."

He turned in the chaise to face her with his whole body, the cigarette held behind him. "Say, Lulu, would you be free for dinner tonight?"

"Oh, Royce, I'd love to, really, but I, um, I have a prior." He frowned, then cheered up as she added, "But I can cut it short. Instead of dinner, why don't we meet on the beach at, say, ten, for a moonlight swim?"

He took a breath. "Sounds great. You know, there's a full moon tonight."

"Mmm, our night to howl."

* * *

Royce practically ran from his room to the beach at nine forty-five. He had replaced his baggy trunks with a skin-colored thong, which was partially obscured by a small fold of belly fat. The hotel's towel was draped around his neck, he still smelled of tobacco, and he positively reeked of cologne.

Lulu had arrived first. She sat on a towel wearing her white cotton jacket, her slacks gone, a turquoise bikini bottom in glorious view. The bottom, Royce noticed, was a string-tied affair, like her well-filled top. Already he was breathing hard, not totally from exertion. The moon— even he knew it was another of his clichés, but it was so fitting—actually bathed her in silver light. It created highlights in her hair and made her pale blue eyes even brighter. He grinned at her as he laid his towel next to hers.

"Hi, sailor," she said with a mischievous grin. "Want to jump ship?"

"Hi, yourself, beautiful," he replied. "This seat taken?"

"Yes, it is." Royce hesitated. Then, she laughed and patted his towel. "By you, silly. Sit down before I drag you down."

He sat, and she leaned ever so delicately against his shoulder. "Beautiful night," she murmured.

"Beautiful woman," he said, congratulating himself on his clever segue. Then, he saw her wrinkle her nose. "Oh. Too much cologne, huh?"

"Yes, sorry. Very sensitive sniffer. But don't move away, okay? I'm a big girl, I can take it." She looked at his face. "Royce, why are you looking at my pentacle?"

His eyes darted back to hers. " Your what?"

"The star, on my necklace." Actually, he'd been staring at her breasts. No sagging, no wrinkles. Implants, or the product of regular workouts? Probably workouts, he decided. Probably spent ungodly amounts of hours in her law office and then worked off the stress in a 24-hour gym.

"Oh, it's just very—what did you call it?"

"A pentacle. That's what the star is called. From the Greek for five, *pente*."

He ignored the language lesson. "Pentacle. Rhymes with testicle."

"Let me guess," she said, chuckling. "You're not known for your subtlety, are you? In fact, I'm starting to think you're a real horndog." She winked at him and gave an oh-well shrug of her shoulders. "Luckily for you, I'm an animal lover." She stood, slipped out of her jacket, and reached down to take his hand. "Come on, let's go for a dip."

Royce got up and noticed something on the back of Lulu's right shoulder. "What's this? A tattoo?" She stood still as he examined it, running two fingers over the inking. "The big bad wolf. From the Disney cartoon, right?" The art work pictured only the wolf's head: shaggy, dark-furred, huge eyes, elongated snout, long yellow fangs, and an extended red tongue with a couple of drops of saliva inked in for good measure. "What's that all about?"

Lulu turned her head toward Royce's. "That's one reason I don't drink anymore," she purred.

She looked so luscious he couldn't stand it. "Lulu, you're totally different than anyone I've ever met."

"Different *from*."

"Huh?"

"Nothing, bad habit, forget it. Come on, let's go in. The water's perfect, and the beach is deserted. It's just you and me, Royce."

"Right. We've got the whole Caribbean all to ourselves."

They waded chest high into the calm, warm water. "Not afraid of sharks out here, are you?" he asked.

"Sharks don't eat me. Professional courtesy."

"Oh, right," he laughed. She looked at him through half-lidded eyes and traced her fingertips up his cheeks. This was more like it. "Well, miss lawyer lady, I'm thinking you just might get eaten tonight."

"You know, mister executive man, I was thinking the same thing about you." Lulu cupped the back of his shaved skull and drew his face to hers. Her mouth was already open as their lips met, and her tongue darted fiercely between his teeth. Royce fumbled with the tie on the back of Lulu's halter, and it finally came free. His hands roamed over her breasts— definitely natural, oh yeah—until he noticed that while he had been thus occupied she had untied her bikini bottom and draped it around her neck along with the top.

"Take a deep breath now," she said, and when he did she eased him beneath the water.

His eyes had always been sensitive to salt water, so Royce immediately closed them. He knew he could navigate by touch anyway, and Lulu was helping, guiding his head between her thighs. His first thought as his mouth made contact was that this was quality fur. His typical companions would have made him pay extra for this, which was ridiculous, because they had to love it as much as—Whoa! he thought as he felt her shudder. She's coming already. This woman's an animal!

Odd, it occurred to him as his tongue tasted her salty sweetness, her fingers don't feel as baby smooth as they did this afternoon. More like leather in fact. Her hips, clasped by his own hands, felt downy too, and that was—Ow! Her fingernails dug in behind his ears. She might have broken through the skin. Damn, bitch! All ardor gone, he pressed his feet against the sand and pushed himself up.

Just as his head cleared the water a pair of long, lupine jaws snapped shut around his throat. The last thing Royce saw before his neck was bitten through was a pair of pale, pearly eyes, eyes which gleamed ferally in the moonlight.

* * *

Lulu gorged, congratulating herself that she'd decided to skip dessert (she'd ordered dinner for two in her room and eaten both portions) and cap off her meal with this pudgy parcel instead. Blood billowed about her, and before long her heightened senses felt the change in water current that told her predators were approaching. They would pose no problem; metamorphs were recognized as alphas by all species, even the primitives. In this case, even, they would be a boon to her.

She knew to be careful about cleanup.

She bit through Royce's skull and devoured his brain. Then, she severed his spine and sailed what was left of his head in the direction of the closest triangular fin. She bit off his fingers next—no dental or fingerprint records would ever be found—and delicately held them out to the smaller scavengers. The fish plucked them from her hands like doggy treats. Then, she pushed his remains toward the sea and let the sharks consume them as she returned wholly to human form, retrieved her bikini, rinsed the blood from her body and hair, and waded back to the beach. By dawn, the crimson stain in the water would be long dissipated.

Standing like a statue in the moonlight, the woman -- whose name was neither Lulu nor Louise and who had never cracked a law book in her life—licked her lips and looked out over the rippling reflection in the water. The moon wouldn't actually be full for three more days, but it made no difference to her. She wasn't a slave to the rhythms of the moon.

Unaware of the night vision binoculars trained on her, the woman slipped on her jacket, picked up both towels, and walked back to her hotel, where she slept until noon the next day.

PART ONE
LUNA

FOUR YEARS EARLIER
Chapter One

Friday, May 3, 2002

Criterion University, home of the Catamounts, nestled itself in New Hampshire's White Mountain wilderness, some fifty miles, as she'd say, from Upper Nowhere, USA. The faculty, with few exceptions, were undistinguished. But judging by the standards they set, well, the undergrad would think he was in Harvard—which was well to the south, well to the east, and well up in crust. But it did have one redeeming value, this school, it was relatively cheap. Claire had to watch her funds since her parents' deaths had left her orphaned at seventeen.

Her inheritance didn't amount to much, but it paid for tuition and room and board without necessitating an on- or off-campus job. Proceeds from the sale of her family home were socked away in a money market fund on the advice of her parents' attorney. He was her nominal guardian until she became of age, at the end of her first year of college. Being relatively free of monetary concerns, she could concentrate on her studies—which was ironic, considering the current state of her studies. The irony she was contemplating as she sat alone in the town's only bar: What do you do with a BA in English?

She had just finished her second Seven-and-Seven and stubbed out her third cigarette of the evening—Seagram's and ciggies, perfect together—when she saw him approach. If her mood had been other than what it was, she'd have seen him as attractive, if a little on the older side, with his wheat-blond hair, blue eyes, and shoulders wide as a refrigerator. As it was, she turned her head and hoped he was headed for somewhere (translate, someone) else. It wasn't to be.

"Hello," she heard over the twang of the jukebox and the white noise of the crowd. "And happy birthday." What was that? "I'd sing it to you, but trust me, you wouldn't want to hear me sing. When I sing in the shower, the tiles fall off the wall."

"How do you know it's my birthday?"

"Bartender's one of my students. He ID-ed you tonight."

"And you're accosting me because?"

"Not accosting. Greeting. You're alone, and from the frown on your puss, you're not all that happy. You should be celebrating with your friends."

"All right," she said. "If this were a romcom movie I'd be walking out of the theater about now."

"Why?"

"Come on. It's too contrived, too pat. Two strangers meet in some cutesy fabrication. She's caught shoplifting, and he pays for the loot. He's injured in a car wreck, and she's an EMT. His son plays with her daughter in the park, and they just happen to meet on the playground. Or," she said, "he sees a girl alone in a bar, and the bartender tells him it's her twenty-first birthday. It's cliché; it's passé; it's … no way."

"A versifier, too. Must be an English major, right?"

"Look, if you're a teacher trolling for trollops, I'm not interested. Why don't you go home to your wife and kids."

"Wow, you really know how to hurt a guy. I'm not married, I'm not a teacher, and I'm not trolling. I'm a TA, I'm in line for my master's, and I'm here because the bartender is one of my undergrads who missed class today and needed some handouts."

"How old are you?"

"That's pretty direct. Twenty-four."

"Oh. I thought you were … never mind."

"I get it. Happens all the time." He extended his hand. "Lukas. Lukas Ehrlich."

She almost begrudgingly took his hand. His grip was strong. "Claire."

"Claire de Lune, perhaps?"

"No. Delaney, if it matters."

"Jewish then?"

"Right: Jewish as Paddy's pig. So what kind of name is Ehrlich?"

"German. It means honest."

"Uh huh. Cutesy again."

The jukebox fell silent and another song began, one about a cheating husband who left his wife and now wanted to cheat on his new love to return to her. The title was "Two Wrongs Don't Make It Right."

"God, I hate country music," she said.

He smiled. "You're not alone there. But you are alone here."

She rolled her eyes. "Cute. Maybe bordering on clever."

"So why aren't you out celebrating?"

"I am celebrating. Can't you tell?"

She noticed how deeply blue his eyes were. Her own were so pale as to look gray.

"Claire, if you want me to leave you alone, I will. I don't pretend to be a wolf in TA's clothing. You just looked unhappy sitting here, and … I don't know. It didn't seem right."

She took a breath and stared at him. "Want to buy me another drink?"

Lukas smiled and motioned for a refill. For himself he ordered club soda. As the bartender filled her glass, Claire lit another cigarette. She noticed moisture forming in Lukas's eyes.

"You upset about something?"

"No. Smoke just makes my eyes water. Gag, too. Another reason I don't like to come in here, besides the country music. As I said, if it weren't for the bartender … but that's too cutesy, right? I'll just shut up now."

She stubbed out the smoke, although why she did was unclear.

"So Claire, if it's not too personal, why are you here? You've got to have friends on campus who'd want to celebrate with you."

"I do, but they don't know. I never mentioned it. Listen: I came here to do what tradition says I should do to celebrate my twenty-first birthday. And my upcoming graduation. And my continuing slide in GPA. I know I shot down my *summa* this year."

"Wait, you're a senior? At barely twenty-one?"

Claire sipped her drink. Careful, she thought, you could get seriously buzzed, and who knew what this guy was up to? Really?

"I graduated high school at seventeen. Skipped sixth grade back in the day."

"Really. How did that work out for you?"

"Okay, I guess. Even then I was taller than most of the seventh-graders, so I fit in all right."

"Did you slouch to make yourself look shorter?"

"Very perceptive. Yeah, I did, at first. Then my teacher pulled me aside one day and told me to stand tall. He meant it both literally and figuratively. I got it."

"Must've been a good teacher."

"A great teacher. So how about you? What's on your agenda -- the academic one, that is."

"I'll have my master's when you get your bachelor's and begin my doctoral studies in genetics in the fall."

Small talk evolved: he told her his parents were both deceased ("So are mine"); that politically he leaned liberal ("I'm definitely conservative— which explains why I don't have that many friends on campus"); that his grandparents emigrated from Germany ("I'm a fifth-generation Jersey girl, born and bred at the shore"); and that he neither drank nor smoked, nor did he even experiment with pot ("I only started smoking after 9/11. Figured I could be dead tomorrow, so what the hell. Thing is, my mother died of lung cancer. She was a nurse ... and a chain smoker. Go figure. You'd think I'd know better too.")

"You heard what the tobacco honcho said once? Someone remarked that he didn't see anyone who worked at the company smoking. The honcho said, and I quote, 'We don't smoke that shit, son, we sell it.' Big tobacco man said that smoking was reserved for four groups of people: the young, the poor, the black, and the stupid."

Claire glanced at the ashtray. "Hm. Guess I fit three of the criteria. Shoot me with melanin, and I meet all four."

"Nah. You've only been smoking for eight months. There's hope for you and your lungs yet, Luna."

"What?"

"Oh, jeez. Sorry, it's just that your eyes look silver in this light, like they're reflecting the moon. I'm still seeing you as Claire de Lune, I guess. You mind?"

Claire stuck two fingers into her mouth and made retching sounds. "Pet names after one meeting? Puh-leeze. Too gooey cutesy-poo, gag reflex kicking in."

"You don't like it, then."

"Well, let's put it this way, there, honest Lukas Ehrlich. If you want to call me Luna, how about I just call you ... Lucy? Nah, forget it. Lukas it is."

"Luna and Lukas: perfect together."

"There you go again."

* * *

They left the bar at closing time, with the juke box blaring a ditty about a couple who were expecting their first baby, called "One Plus One Makes Three." Two hours later they were in his bed. Three hours later she was lying on sweat-soaked sheets wishing for a cigarette while Lukas was in the bathroom with the door closed. He offered to let her go first, but she insisted that he be the one. Mainly because she couldn't have moved if she'd wanted to. He had pounded her so hard she thought her pelvis had separated from her spine.

He had begun slowly enough, gently disrobing her and exploring her body—"Elegant," she remembered he'd whispered—with his hands, his lips, and oh yes, his tongue. Then, he began nipping at her, tenderly at first, then just hard enough to leave tiny marks. When he entered her, he filled her completely, and soon his slow, measured strokes began to grow faster and more urgent. He held himself above her, supported on his outstretched arms, and thrust his hips forward and back as his eyes locked onto hers.

A drop of sweat fell from his face to her chin, and he lowered his lips to lick it up. Their mouths locked on each other and their tongues danced deep inside. His hips slammed into her harder, and the image of an automotive piston powering into a well-lubed cylinder popped unbidden into her mind. She arched her back as he drove her over the edge, and he came at the same time, throwing his head back with a cry that reminded Claire of a wolf's howl.

Wow, she thought as she heard the water running beyond the bathroom door. I think I'm in lust. Sure beats my high school "graduation present" from Jimmy—at a time in my life when I was most vulnerable emotionally—in the back seat of his father's Merc: all grunts, groans, sweat, and quick carnal consummation. What was the big deal, she'd said to herself. The guy was a fumbling fool; I've been porked by a dork.

But Lukas—no Lucy, he, definitely no Lucy—took his slow, sweet time. This time it was all about her, about his pleasing her; next time—and there would be a next time, she promised herself—she determined to do some pleasing of her own. Did that make her a fornicator in the eyes of the church? Claire had had a typical Catholic upbringing but railed at confession: she felt she didn't need a middleman to communicate with God. And, judging by the attitudes of her young peers and their parents, church attendance had been an obligation, not an opportunity to worship; a club for Christians, not a hospital for sinners. She had stopped attending when the church would not allow her father to be buried next to her mother in hallowed ground. But the ingrained guilt from her catechism remained.

The gift that keeps on giving.

Occasionally she would pray, but Claire also railed against begging God for favors. It felt as if she were a brat asking for candy. She remembered the time her parents had taken her to Monmouth Park for a summer's day at the track. There she spotted an elderly woman saying the Rosary before the first and second races, then tearing up her tickets when she lost and storming out of the stands. Claire wondered if she had gone to change her religion; maybe she'd have better luck in the future if she were a Protestant.

Young Jimmy had been Claire's first sexual experience; Lukas, tonight, had been only her second. Oh, not that some of her classmates hadn't tried, especially the jocks, but Claire remembered her father's warnings when she'd begun dating. Jimmy had proved him right. Slam, bam, thank you ma'am. If she hadn't been so tipsy tonight, she might have resisted Lukas's advances, too. But don't blame it on the booze, she cautioned herself. Lukas was gorgeous, true, but it was only after their initial verbal sparring had run its course that she had felt some sort of psychic bond which hinted there could be a genuine relationship ready to form.

If she were to stay in New Hampshire after graduation, that is.

What was she going to do with her life? What does one *do* with a BA in English?

I really ought to give up smoking, Claire mused as the synapses in her brain screamed for their nicotine fix. She knew firsthand how stupid the whole deal was, knew she wasn't immune to the addiction, and considered that maybe Lukas himself could provide the motivation to kick it.

The toilet flushed, the door opened, and he emerged. His face might look older than twenty-four, she thought, but his body was as toned as a Greek god's. And he was an inch or two taller than she was, unlike most of her peers. This guy she could look up to in more ways than one.

"Your turn," he said and helped Claire out of bed.

Fifteen minutes later, with steaming water pelting their bodies, Claire gave in to the desires she'd denied herself for four years and showed Lukas what she herself was capable of—thanks to the "instructions" she'd gleaned from the occasional bodice-ripper that served as a break from her assigned readings. When Lukas finally stood her up and pressed her against the wet tile wall, with the shower steaming and her legs locked around his hips, they both cried out in mutual climax.

* * *

"We're both orphans, and we both have no siblings. We're alone in the world, Luna. Except for each other, that is."

They lay naked on top of the bed, she on her back, he on his side. Lukas supported his head on one hand and with the other caressed her curves. Claire's eyes were closed, her lips parted in a smile. "Except for us," she murmured, as if in a dream, and wondered what he was thinking: was she an easy lay, or could she be a prospective soul mate....

The sun was just beginning to color the treetops outside his small cabin. They still hadn't slept. Good thing today was Saturday. "You are amazing," she said. "No, insatiable. It's like you were born to rut." His fingers found her labia. "Please, no more, I'm really sore," she said.

"There you go again, a natural versifier," he replied, but moved his hand back up her belly and rested it there.

"Lukas, how did you know I'd be so … easy to get into bed?"

"I never associated you with the word *easy*."

"All right, mister semanticist. You know what I'm saying."

He sniffed. "Let's just say for now that I have a nose for certain things."

"Like who wants to boff you?"

Lukas kissed the tip of Claire's nose. "Something like that. Now, let's get some breakfast. I'm starved."

"I'm tired. Leave me alone."

"If I don't get some bacon and eggs inside me, I'm going to have to eat you instead."

"Maybe I could stay awake for that."

"Come on, I'm cooking." He slapped her on the hip.

"Ow," Claire cried as he sprang from the bed. "Take it easy with the spanks, there, buddy. I'm not into pain."

"Sorry," he called over his shoulder. "I should've forewarned you that I don't know my own strength sometimes."

"*Forewarned*? Redundancy alert."

He stopped. "Huh?"

"Damn. Sorry, bad habit. English major, remember. I tend to correct people's grammar, whether they want me to or not. It's become automatic. I've got to learn to control myself, because it really tends to piss people off."

Lukas thought for a minute. "*Fore*warned. As in, what other kind of warning is there, right? But we do say 'Forewarned is forearmed.' What's that, a double redundancy?"

"You can say that again."

* * *

Lukas's cabin was a two-room affair: bedroom and all-purpose room; plus bath, of course. Now that the smell of bacon had overcome her need for sleep, Claire got up, found one of his clean shirts to put on, and appraised her surroundings for the first time in daylight. Plain, utilitarian, woodsy — appropriate for a cabin in the woods. Far enough from campus so as not to be confused with an outbuilding, close enough that on a nice day he could walk to his classes.

"About time, lazy," Lukas said as she stood behind him and slipped her arms around his waist. She looked over his shoulder and frowned.

"Okay, cookie, what U.S. Army regiment is coming over for breakfast today?"

"Just us two," he answered. I do have a rather strong appetite."

"Mmm. Tell me about it."

"How many eggs for you?" he asked as he fished the last of the pound of bacon out of the grease.

"Two, max. Over easy, if you can do that."

"Like to see the nuclei bleed when you pierce them?" he asked.

"Nice image, bio boy."

"Sit down and let me cook. Coffee's ready on the counter."

The coffee was rich and strong, and when Lukas put double her egg order and nearly a quarter pound of bacon in front of her, along with two thick slices of toasted Italian bread bathed in butter, Claire didn't object. But she did stare at his plate, which contained eight eggs, the rest of the bacon, and four slices of toast. "Eat," he said and began to wolf his own down.

"Hate to have to pay your grocery bill," she remarked.

"Yeah, it's pretty steep. That's why I can't afford to rent more plush surroundings."

She speared a yolk and sopped it up with a corner of her toast. "You must have quite the metabolism, there, Lukas. You eat like that and yet you're as buff as G.I. Joe."

"Look at yourself," Lukas said. "Not an ounce of fat on your body, and I've explored it enough to know. Well, except of course those glorious globes on your chest."

She looked down. "Great. I've never heard these things referred to as glorious globes of fat before. Sort of takes the romance out of it, doesn't it?"

"Not for me. Can't help it if I'm a science major. And I like the way they fill out my shirt. Although I'd like it more if you unbuttoned it some."

"Shut up and eat." But she unbuttoned the shirt to the bottom of her cleavage before picking up her fork again.

* * *

"So why are you failing your senior year?" asked Lukas as he washed the dishes and Claire dried.

"I'm not. I mean, my grades are slipping, that's all. My first three years' GPA will let me sail through, but as I mentioned last night, not with a *summa*. Maybe I'm scared. I just can't motivate myself to excel any more. Not the faculty's fault, mine. I'm wondering what I'll do once school's over, where I'll go, how I'll manage to earn a living ... with a freakin' degree in English. I could never teach. I hate kids." She put their breakfast plates into a cabinet. "No, I don't really hate kids, I just don't relate to them. I mean, I was so eager to get out of high school, and all that teenage angst, I can't tell you. No way I'm throwing myself back into that den of wolves."

Lukas smiled. "Interesting choice of words."

"Meaning?"

"Oh, nothing. So, what you're saying is that the University is your cocoon, right? You've been a safe little caterpillar here for four years, and you don't think you're ready to be a butterfly."

She put the dishtowel on the countertop and leaned on it. "All right, genius, no need to patronize me. How do *you* cope? Just continue with school? Finish your master's and then on to a doctorate? And then what? Back to the classroom to teach? The vicious cycle continues. The circle of shi— oh, I'm bad."

Lukas lifted her chin with one finger, forcing her eyes to meet his. "Listen to me, my dear Claire de Lune. I think I can help you out of your funk. My faculty advisor is a guy named Gabe Zeklos. His specialty is hematology. Anyway, he happened to mention to me that a friend of the family, a book publisher, is looking for someone..."

"Hematology. So he's a blood boy."

"Distinguished blood boy—Gabe, that is, not me. Romanian descent, I think. He was a big deal in Boston for a while, but he got fed up with the politics and what he calls the AMA's closed-mind collective, and kind of retreated into academia." He continued: "The University made him an offer he couldn't refuse in return for lending his pedigree to the faculty roster. Now he does research and mentors grad students, most of whom teach his classes about half the time while he buries himself in his lab. I'm one of those TA's."

"So he's not Doctor Frankenstein, I presume."

"Hardly. Great guy." His eyes twinkled. "Kind of hot, too."

"Hey! You work both sides of the buffet line, mister?"

He laughed and gave her a slap on the butt—ouch—and kissed her full and hard. "Just wanted to see if you were listening, my little vixen. I'm strictly a one-woman man. Operative word being *woman*." He drained the sink. "Dishes are done, let's take a walk. Monday I'll call Gabe and ask about his friend."

She looked down at his shirt -- which for now served as her blouse — and smiled as he slipped his hand inside. "Doesn't seem like you're in the mood for a walk right now."

His Adam's apple bobbed once. "Maybe we could take that walk a little later?"

Claire guided her fingers into the waistband of his jeans. "I'm not all that sore any more."

Chapter
Two

"My friend's small publishing house has grown faster than he'd anticipated. He brings in good talent, and his success rate in the field is quite impressive. He's not one of the big dogs, but he likes being small. His managing editor told him she could use another junior on staff. Does an entry level editor's position interest you?"

Claire and Lukas sat across the desk from Professor Zeklos, she leaning forward, hanging on his words. Lukas was right, she thought upon meeting him. He is kind of hot for a guy somewhere in his fifties. Full dark hair, olive complexion, and nearly black eyes that could easily compel one's attention. They'd fixed on her like magnets. His hand, when he took hers, was cool, but his grip was firm. His voice was a rich baritone, with just a trace of an eastern European accent. That, combined with his urbane mannerisms and good looks, made him almost devastatingly attractive—or would have, if she had been in the market and if she went for older men.

As it was, Lukas, although just three years older than she, with the same fair hair and pale eyes, looked more like an older brother than a lover. Hmm, she thought with an inner smile, would that make his cabin an incest nest? She had tightened her thighs when she sat down. Yes: still sore from the weekend. Sore but sated, sensation rendered sensational.

"Radu is second-generation American," the professor continued, "as am I. His last name is Jones. The coupling of a common Romanian name with a common American one is amusing, don't you think?" He chuckled. "We met in grade school in Boston and have been fast friends ever since. His classmates Americanized his name to Ray, and that's what he goes by today. As for me, Gabriel went down well with them, named as I was after an angel.

Now, Miss Delaney, about yourself. When Lukas called, he told me that you are very witty, you have a knack with words, and that you will brook no nonsense from others. Does that fairly well sum you up?"

"I'm amazed that Lukas could size me up in such a short period of time. We just met last Friday."

"I've known Lukas long enough to trust his instincts." Zeklos smiled at Claire, whose eyes darted about the room. "Why the curious expression on your face?"

"Because it would look ridiculous anywhere else." Claire grinned, then grimaced. "Faux pas, professor, sorry, sometimes I'm just a wiseass. No disrespect intended."

"None taken."

"I was just—just looking around your office. Most of my profs have their diplomas and awards framed like trophies. Your walls are empty. Well," she continued, "except for that display case and those beautiful black-and-white landscapes up there, but no ..."

"No," he said. "I do not need any reminders to feed my ego. The photographs, by the way, are by Ansel Adams, and I keep my classic gun collection in the case. They are all serviceable, by the way, but I have yet to fire one. I am intrigued by how items meant solely to destroy are rendered so lovingly exquisite by their makers."

Lukas interjected: "Gabe has so many diplomas and awards that there isn't room enough for all of them. And that's the truth."

"Don't listen to him," said Zeklos. "This conversation is not about me. So, Claire, would you like an introduction to the esteemed Mr. Radu Jones? I can arrange an interview for you after you graduate next month."

* * *

That evening found Claire back in Lukas's cabin, and because it was a school night they only managed a two round interlude. After classes the next day, she moved her belongings over from the dorm. A month later, with her in-person interview with Radu Jones on her calendar three days hence, Claire and Lukas celebrated their graduation with a round of lovemaking followed by champagne. Cheap champagne, but it got them both sufficiently buzzed. Afterward, they wandered downtown, hand in hand. They stopped at a well-lit shopfront, just about the only place beside the tavern that was still open: a tattoo parlor.

"I've got an idea," said Lukas as he scanned the designs in the window and fastened his eyes on one. "Let's get that one, right there."

"What're you, nuts, laughing boy? Why would I mutilate my beautiful body?"

"Luna, my love. Don't you see what it is?"

"Yeah, a freakin' cartoon. So?"

"Remember that night we met? When you thought I was a lone wolf 'trolling for trollops'? I haven't forgotten that. But neither of us is a lone wolf, we're more like a pack, you and I. What say we get that put on us? Anywhere you want, I don't care. His and hers tattoos. Mates. Shows we're committed."

Claire giggled through the champagne haze. "Sweetie, there are more conventional ways to show that we're committed." She waved her left hand before his face and held out her ring finger. My God, what am I doing, she wondered. We've known each other, what, thirty days, and we're talking serious commitment? Is this guy too good to be true? Would I be a fool to put him off? Should I have drunk so much champagne?

Lukas said, "Rings come off, love; tattoos are permanent."

A few hours later they returned to their cabin with gauze taped behind their right shoulders, covering their freshly-inked tattoos of the big bad wolf.

*   *   *

"I'm starting in a month," Claire reported after her interview. "That would be the first of August. The managing editor is really nice, even gave me a list of affordable flats I can look at. Course, affordable in Boston means exorbitant up here, and living expenses are high, too. They don't call it Taxachusetts for nothing. Good news is, my salary will be enough to cover it. Barely, but enough."

"Outstanding," said Lukas, sitting beside her in their bed and enjoying simply watching her nakedness. "And it's only a few hours away. I can make the weekends, as long as my trusty Jetta holds out."

She grinned. It was just what she'd wanted to hear. "You know, I'm feeling much better about my English degree now. No prospect of sitting at a decrepit desk, facing a roomful of jumpin' juvies for me." She snuggled up to him. "So that gives us a month of bliss before the prospect of work rises to bite us in the ass."

"I'll bite your ass any time. On another topic entirely: what's Mr. Jones like?"

"Seems nice. Short, say five eight or nine. Gray hair, dark eyes like Gabe's. A little paunchy. No wedding ring."

"Hey," Lukas interrupted. "You noticed he's not wearing a ring? Getting ready to stake a claim, are we? Making plans to seduce the boss?"

"Please. That's so cliché." She pressed her mouth onto Lukas's. "You're my old man," she said, and added teasingly, "operative word being *old*."

Before she could kiss him again, Lukas turned to her and held her hands to his chest. His expression was serious. "Claire," he said, dropping his pet name for her. "I need to tell you something."

Her expression changed, and her body stiffened. "Uh oh, this isn't one of those 'We need to talk' things, is it?"

"Oh, God, no," Lukas said. "I'm so sorry. No, love, it's actually just the opposite." Unseen by him, Claire unconsciously flexed her ring finger. "I want to share something with you; something I've never shared with any living soul before." Except for Gabe, he thought, but that was for another reason entirely.

"You're serious, aren't you, Lukas?"

"Never more so."

"So, share. I can't wait."

He swallowed. "When you were in Boston interviewing, I ..."

Claire held her breath. "Don't tell me you bedded down another woman. I'll kill you."

"That's almost funny," he said, his eyes downcast. "Claire, listen. I -- wait. Let me put it to you this way. I want to share something with you. A gift. My gift."

She knelt on the bed and straddled his legs. Looking down, she remarked, "You've shared that gift with me a lot, there, Lukas."

"Please, be serious for now."

"Sorry."

"No other way to say it but to say it." A breath. "I am ... what I would prefer to call a metamorph."

Her expression was blank. Finally: "English major, remember? Not science."

"Then you should be able to figure out what the word means."

"I remember from seventh-grade science—when I should've been in sixth grade, remember—that when a caterpillar changes to a butterfly it's called metamorphosis. That what you're talking about? You're a butterfly?"

His eyes belied the absurdity that came from his mouth. "No. I'm a ... a shape shifter. To be specific ... a werewolf."

Claire looked deep into those eyes. Then, she laughed out loud.

"I'm serious, Claire. That's why I hate that word. It's like a bad Lon Chaney, Jr. And *lycanthrope* isn't much better. This isn't a joke."

"Do you change into a bat, too, and suck virgins' blood? Because you're a little late there, buster." She was still smiling.

"No, I don't. There are no such things as vampires."

"Oh, but there are werewolves. Right. And you're one of them. Halloween's not for three months yet, you know."

Lukas spun her onto her back, her legs splayed, and in the same motion he covered her with his body. Her arms wrapped around his waist, but her face still held that damnable smirk. "I want to give you the gift," he breathed. "The gift I inherited from my parents. Do you understand?"

Her grin broadened. "I've got the feeling I'm in for some kinky sex here, Lukas, old man. Hey, if you want to play, I'm game. Just don't hurt me, okay? Because I'm definitely not into S and M, know what I mean?" An old joke occurred to her. "Know what a sadist does to a masochist? Answer: nothing."

Lukas shook his head. He seemed about to cry. "Close your eyes," he whispered and lowered his face to the junction of her neck and shoulder.

"Okay. Eyes closed."

He bit her.

She screamed.

* * *

Gabriel Zeklos, MD, Ph.D., stood up and slammed the palms of his hands so hard against his desk that the telephone receiver nearly jumped off the hook. "You ... stupid ..." He searched hard for the proper word and found one that he absolutely never used. "... *fuck!*" he cried. "You insensitive, unthinking, stupid *fuck!* How could you *do* that? *How?*" His eyes burned; spittle sprayed onto the desktop; he hurled the student thesis he'd been reading against the wall, breaking the binding and scattering the leaves across the floor.

Lukas Ehrlich jumped to his feet and took a sudden step backward. "Gabe, I ... you don't understand, I really love this girl, I want to share my life with her. Don't you see, I had to give her the gift."

"Gift? Gift? You've given her a *disease*, not a gift!" He slumped into his chair. Lukas remained standing, fear and defiance fighting for control of his face. "I thought your parents had instilled some sense of ethics in you. What happened to that? To your promise to refrain from hunting, to your promise of confidentiality about our research?"

"I didn't tell her anything about our research."

The professor's voice grew calmer; the heat was replaced by ice. "What exactly did you tell her?"

"Nothing at first, I mean, she passed out from the shock of being bitten. That was when I made the exchange and bandaged our wounds. When she came to I told her that her life, our life, was changed forever. She was like me now, the next stage in human evolution. Nietzsche's *Übermensch.* For real." He took a breath. "She didn't want to listen. She screamed at me and tried to rip my eyes out. I had to nearly choke her to make her calm down."

"Well, there's a shock," Zeklos said, his voice dripping venom. "Did you tell her about your parents?"

"Just that I inherited the gift from them. And that as metamorphs they did some really good work. Gabe, they never killed children, and they never killed people who didn't deserve to die."

"No, they lured thugs into mugging good people, and then they tore the thugs apart. Let us nominate them for the Nobel *Pieces* Prize."

"Those people were scum, all of them. They weren't victims, they were victimizers. You know that."

"At that point in their lives, perhaps. But were they beyond redemption? Your parents and I argued about that constantly. And what happened to your parents eventually? How they died? What, Lukas?"

"You know what. You watched it happen."

"And for all my research I was unable to save their lives. Just as I fear I am no closer to being able to save yours. My latest attempt, the one we had such hopes for, became unstable yesterday. And now there's the matter of another innocent life. But does the girl know?"

Lukas sat down again, somewhat tentatively. "No."

"Why not? Is your relationship so prone to deception? Already?"

"Jeez, Gabe, it was hard enough just to tell her the basics, you know? I mean, she freaked. She believed it but then again she didn't. Finally her eyes just kind of rolled back into her head, and she passed out. She was still asleep when I left this morning."

"So she doesn't know how your parents died? And why?"

"No."

"Have you looked in the mirror lately?"

"I'm telling you, I might not be able to control the one, but I can control the other. Absolutely. And Claire will be able to, too, I'll make sure of it. And you'll keep on experimenting ..."

"Lukas, listen to me. I know you can control *it*. What worries me is whether you can control *you*. And now you've infected the girl, I'm doubly worried. Are you going to continue your parents' tradition, clear the world of scum, as you call them, like some noble but flawed comic book superhero?" Zeklos rubbed his fingers through his hair. "Have you at least cleared her mind of the myths?"

"No. She wasn't exactly in a listening mood."

Suddenly: "Why are you here? Why are you telling me this?"

Lukas sat back as if struck. "Well … I knew you'd want to know. I thought you'd be happy to be able to expand your research."

"And you thought not to ask me first. How considerate of you. Get out of here. You need to be there when she wakes up."

* * *

Claire paced back and forth in the empty cabin. Despite the summer's heat she had closed the windows against the forest sounds and scents. She imagined she could hear insects crawling and birds breathing, smell a varmint's scat and the stench of skunk cabbage by the pond—the pond that was over a hundred yards away. But that was impossible. Sealed inside, she thought she could hear the dust settle on the furniture.

From her purse she fished out a cigarette, the last of her pack. She had rationed herself to one after each meal, and she'd vowed to give up the habit completely the day Lukas offered her a ring. What the hell, why bother now? She flicked her lighter and felt the heat of the flame, sucked in the hot smoke, and (surprise!) tasted not only the tobacco but also the myriad chemicals the manufacturer had spiked it with—benzene, formaldehyde, arsenic, even cyanide, for God's sake; she tasted all of them and more—and nearly threw up. The smoke burned her eyes and made them tear. She threw the cigarette onto the wooden floor, ground it out viciously, and spat into the sink. She turned on the faucet and held her head alongside, sucking in the water, rinsing her mouth, spitting it out, drinking in more and swallowing it greedily.

Thirst slaked, Claire realized she was starved. She ran to the refrigerator (how did I get here so fast, she wondered) and yanked it open. Then she spun, food forgotten, as she heard the front door open behind her. When she saw who it was, she hunched her shoulders, jutted out her jaw, and growled. Growled! What am I doing, she thought in panic. What have I become?

"Easy, now, love," said Lukas, arms outstretched and palms forward. "Easy. You were asleep when I left. I thought you'd still be asleep when I got back. I should've left a note, I'm sorry. Please. Listen to me, and I'll explain everything."

Claire's eyes bored into his as he eased the door shut without looking behind him. "You. Son. Of. A. Bitch," she snarled. She twisted her mouth into an angry grin. "Hey. It just hit me. You really *are* a son of a bitch," she said. "Your mother *was* a werewolf. Am I right? Isn't that what you said last night - - *right before you took a chunk out of me*?" She reached into the refrigerator, grabbed a bottle of milk, and hurled it at him. It crashed -- exploded -- against the door. Had Lukas not ducked at the last instant, it might have been his skull that exploded.

"What have you done to me?" she said, holding up a cautioning hand lest he try to approach her. "And how can you undo it?"

"Please, Luna..."

"Don't call me that! My name is Claire! Claire Delaney! Not Luna, not Claire de Lune! Got it?"

"I wish it were Claire Ehrlich," Lukas mumbled to himself. But Claire, her sense of hearing enhanced, heard it.

Her jaw dropped. "You can't be serious. After what you did. You're sick!"

"Lu—Claire—it's why I did what I did. I told you the truth, you agreed to the gift."

"Oh, that's pure bullshit, and you know it. I thought it was some kind of game..."

"Listen to me. You are now a metamorph. To explain it simply, my blood carries the mutation that makes me what I am. Legends aside, it's not the saliva in a werewolf's bite that turns another. It's his blood. Look." He rolled up his sleeve to expose his wrist. A ragged patch of red showed through the gauze, a match to the one on the junction of Claire's neck and shoulder. You have my blood inside you now. I did this because I love you. Because I wanted to give you the most precious gift I could. Myself ... my inheritance."

"Modest, too, in addition to being a sonofabitch." She plopped down at the table, and he sat opposite her. He placed his hands on the table, but she put hers in her lap. "More, I need to know more. What am I, really? What does all this mean? I don't remember one thing about what you told me last night. All I knew was I wanted to kill you. I still do."

"You know a little of what it means already. You hear and see and smell better than a human. You can move faster. You're stronger."

"I feel like I could tear you apart with my teeth."

"You could. But I'd hope you wouldn't."

She stood suddenly, knocking the chair over, and returned to the refrigerator. "Bacon," she said, and pulled out a package. Returning to the table, she slapped the package down and peeled off the slices, eating each one raw. "Hungry," she said.

"Claire, listen, you now have the power to change your form into that of a wolf. At will. No full moon nonsense. Daytime, nighttime, full moon, no moon, makes no difference. And it won't hurt. It feels ... almost orgasmic when you do. Your whole body seems to cum with the change."

Claire sneered at him. "Stop. You're making me hot." She swallowed another rasher of bacon, barely chewing it first.

"And, you will be able to control the degree of change. That is, you don't have to morph fully into wolf form if you don't want to. It's wonderful when you do, the sense of freedom and absolute oneness with the wild, but it's not, like, one minute you're human and the next you're on all fours. How can I explain it?" He paused. "I'll prove it. Put your hands on the table."

Claire drew her lips back. "Don't touch me." She snapped as she placed her hands palm down before her. "Now what?"

"Make your fingernails grow."

"Duh."

"No, really. Make them grow into claws. Like this."

Her eyes bugged as Lukas's fingernails darkened and ... grew. In seconds, they were black and pointed, and his fingers and hands were covered in light fur. "*How did you do that?*"

"The same way you will. Think it. There's a mind-body connection. When you were a baby, you had to learn how to control your fingers before you could grab anything, right? Well, you're like a baby again. Go ahead, try to make your nails grow. Like mine."

Claire stared down at her fingers, squinted, and concentrated. Nothing happened.

"Harder," Lukas prompted.

"I am, I am," she muttered through gritted teeth—teeth that seemed to fill her mouth—and gradually her fingernails became claws, her hands became paws, her nose and jaw became a snout ... and she threw her head back and howled.

Lukas jumped up and raced behind her, wrapping his arms around her chest and holding his face next to hers. "Too much!" he said. "Calm down! Go back to human form! Don't try to bite me, I'll have to protect myself, and I could hurt you!"

Claire struggled for a few seconds, and then her breath became more controlled. Her wolfish tongue retreated from where it lolled by the side of her jaw; her snout shortened; fur pulled back beneath her skin; and she was once again a beautiful, if terrified, young woman. Lukas released her and backed off. "You'll learn to take charge of that," he said. "You'll learn, and you'll rejoice in the knowledge. Claire, you'll be a ... a goddess among women. Claire? Talk to me."

Claire swiveled her head slowly from side to side, examined her hands, ran her fingers over her face. She looked at her maker, her expression unreadable. Her answer, when it finally came, took all of three words: "What happens now?"

His reply: "We hunt. Small game for starters. Then … larger, more dangerous game. You'll see."

* * *

"It won't be safe to hunt when you're in Boston, obviously, unless you like the taste of sewer rat," said Lukas. "And you won't, I promise. You'll have to hold off until the weekends, when I can drive down to see you. I've found a spot back here in New Hampshire, near a village called Francestown, which is surrounded by woods and has lots of game."

"You're serious."

They were eating a brunch composed of a pound of sausage and a dozen eggs. Claire was still dumbstruck—but the realization didn't stanch her appetite. Her appetite was another aspect of her condition that amazed her.

Lukas took a long pull from the half-gallon milk carton (each had one, but Claire used a glass) and as he drank Claire asked him if he were the seventh son of a seventh son. He almost choked on the milk.

"Seen a few too many horror movies?" he asked. "Short answer: no. Longer answer: it's all crap, and I don't know where it came from. Silver doesn't hurt us—any bullet will do the trick—and we're not controlled by the full moon. Oh, and we're not particularly parthenophagous either."

That brought her up short. "What? What's that word?"

"Aha!" he cried as he stood and broke some more eggs into the frying pan. "Got the grammarian. How many more can you eat?"

"Three, four maybe. And put a few more of those brown-and-serves in the pan too, will you?"

"Parthenophagous," said Lukas as he stirred the eggs. "Can you figure it out?"

"Stop showing off."

"All right. *Parthénos* is the Greek word for virgin. You've heard of the Parthenon, where virgins were dedicated to Athena. And *phage* means to eat."

"Okay, given some time I could've figured that out. So I guess the story is we're supposed to eat virgins. Where does one go to find virgins these days? We could starve to death."

Lukas spilled some eggs onto her plate along with some sausage links. "Here, feed on these. Virgin eggs."

As they ate, Claire asked what other tidbits of werewolf-dom he could tell her. He asked if she'd ever heard of Peter Stubbe.

* * *

The most infamous werewolf in all of Germany lived in the latter years of the Sixteenth Century, Lukas began. At the age of twelve, he supposedly made a pact with the Devil. In return for his soul, Satan gave him a wolfskin belt which, when worn, would turn Peter Stubbe into a wolf. On the night of the full moon, Peter would climb a hill, etch a pentagram in the dirt, stand in the center, and mark the territory by urinating in a circle around the pentagram. Then he would don the belt, become a wolf, return to his village, and kill.

Livestock were the first of his victims—sheep, goats, cattle. He'd rip their throats out, drink their blood, and eat their organs.

Peter grew into a man, took a mistress, and fathered a daughter. Meanwhile, he continued his killings, having graduated from animals to young women and children—hence the genesis of the eating of virgins. He would typically bludgeon or strangle them, then disembowel them with his teeth and hands, and feed. The village and its environs lived in terror of this monster, and the superstition that prevailed in the 1580s convinced the villagers that the killer was a werewolf.

Stubbe's most heinous act came after he fathered a son by his own daughter. He took the baby into the woods, tore him apart, smashed his head with a rock, and ate his brains. At his trial later, he declared they were the greatest delicacy he'd ever eaten.

Twenty-five years into his reign of terror, Stubbe's luck ran out. He had disemboweled a pregnant woman when he was discovered by a hunting party and chased into the woods. The trial records indicate he was in wolf form at the time. He disappeared into a thicket, and when he emerged he was in human form and was easily caught.

Stretched on the rack, Stubbe confessed to having been a werewolf, implicating his mistress and daughter as his accomplices. He then, according to the records, begged to have his death be made as excruciatingly painful as possible, in order that his soul might be purified and worthy to stand before God in judgment. The authorities were only too happy to oblige.

Stubbe's mistress and daughter were simply burned at the stake. He himself was strapped to a wheel, and red-hot pincers were used to strip away his flesh, which was then tossed into the flames. Those same tongs pulled off his fingers and toes. Then, with the blunt part of an ax head, his arms and legs were crushed. Finally he was decapitated, his body burned, and his head erected on a stake as a warning against any and all who would do commerce with the Devil.

Claire's fork lay forgotten on her plate, eggs and sausage untouched. "Lovely mealtime story, Lukas. Thanks."

"You asked. But now you know what we're up against."

"Come on. Stubbe wasn't a real werewolf, he was a madman, and a serial killer to boot."

"But that's what attaches itself to us. To our kind, if there are any more of our kind out there, and if there are I don't know about them. We are not demons, Claire, we're not in league with the Devil. We're good people. Although I will admit to being a lunatic: that is, mad about my Luna."

"Careful. You're not out of the woods yet. But seriously, no one today believes we exist. I'm still having trouble with it."

"And we have to keep it that way. That's our best defense against the real lunatics."

Claire picked up her fork, hunger forcing down her revulsion at the story of Peter Stubbe. Lukas downed his second helping with the rest of the milk. After they had cleaned and put away the dishes, he faced her, held her shoulders, and looked into her pearl-gray eyes.

"It's a beautiful day," he said. "Care to go for a drive in the country?"

Chapter Three

Claire's first kill was a rabbit.

It was late afternoon on the last Saturday in July. Lukas had driven her to the woods near Francestown and led her deep into the forest. He had her remove her clothes but kept his own on. She asked him why, wouldn't she attack and try to kill him?

"Again, too many old movies, dear. Thing is, even though you'll be in wolf form, your brain will still be human. You'll have the urges and abilities of a predator, but they'll be under human control. Now, remember how your hand morphed into a paw, how you controlled it with your mind?" She nodded and began to tremble. "Let me explain. One of my undergrad professors proposed a mind-body connection. He said the mind has the ability to make you sick and also to make you well. All it takes is belief. Some of the class rolled their eyes, so he asked how many people do not believe that the mind controls the body. About half the class raised their hands. And he said, 'How did you do that?'"

"I understand," Claire said, "but I'm not sure ... no, I am sure, but I'm scared, Lukas."

"Of course, you are. Let's start with the small stuff. Let your fingernails become wolf claws. Just tell them to with your mind, and let it happen."

She closed her eyes and tensed her body. Her fingernails turned dark, grew thick, and extended as her fingers retracted into hands that were becoming leathery paws.

"Excellent. Now your feet."

They had begun to turn even before he had finished the sentence. Claire's body hunched as she dropped gracefully to the ground. Her back above her shoulders humped, her face began to change into a wolf's, and pale golden fur started growing from her entire body. Her ears flattened against her head as the auditory canal shifted up toward the wolf's ears that were sprouting from the top of her skull. Her breasts retracted flat against her barrel chest, and four more nipples appeared on her abdomen. Her spine extended into a tail covered with bushy fur.

The wolf looked up at Lukas through pale blue eyes, the only part of her body that did not undergo the complete metamorphosis. She looked around, taking in the sights from her new perspective, inhaling the scents, hearing the whir of insects' wings. Lukas looked down and nodded. Suddenly, she reared up on her hind legs and placed her front paws on his shoulders and began licking his face. He hugged her furry head to his cheek and then let her down gently.

"Now, you can hunt," he said. "What's out there for you?"

Claire bolted into the woods, where she found the rabbit munching on a small bush. She was upon it before it knew what was happening. Her jaws closed on its body, and the rabbit shrieked. Its cry meant nothing to her; in human form she would have felt pity, but she was no longer in human form. She was a wolf, a predator, and the rabbit was her prey.

She remembered the story of Peter Stubbe and crushed the rabbit's skull. The tiny brain was the most delicious morsel she had ever tasted.

When she returned to Lukas, her muzzle reddened, he congratulated her and stroked her fur, then told her it was time to return to human form. "Do it the way you did before," he said.

A few minutes later she stood before him and threw her arms around his shoulders. "What a thrill!" she cried. "I have never felt so free, so alive. Oh, Lukas, I know I must sound like a little girl, but this was—this was ..."

"I know," he whispered into her ear. "I know." But behind his words were the ones he could not bring himself to utter. Gabe would eventually find the remedy, he believed. There would be plenty of time.

Claire put on her clothes, put her hair in a ponytail, and washed her face in a nearby stream. It was time to refill their larder, and on the drive back to Criterion they stopped at a small local market to buy milk and meat. Once inside, they heard from the next aisle a barrage of insults in a man's deep and twangy voice.

"What do you wanna buy that shit for? It's too expensive, and it ain't no good anyways. Now I know where my money goes, you buyin' all this crap. You get the condensed soup, you add water, and it's just as good as this frozen expensive shit. And look: get the no-brand cereal, it's the same as the fancy stuff and a hell of a lot cheaper too. Man, have I gotta go to the store to supervise you every time instead of doin' what I should be doin', relaxin' at home with a beer? I swear, you are fuckin' useless!"

Claire and Lukas looked at each other, and then he poked his head around the aisle. He looked back at Claire. "He's waving his arms at a tiny woman who looks as scared as a mouse. She won't look into his eyes; she looks like she's trying to melt into the floor."

"My God," said Claire.

"I've got to do something, I'm sorry."

Lukas walked around the displays to the next aisle as Claire bit her lip.

"What're you lookin' at, pretty boy?" demanded the voice.

"Nothing," Lukas said. "Absolutely nothing."

"You a smartass sumbitch, boy?"

"No. But I think you may not want to harass your wife and embarrass yourself in front of the other customers."

"I don't have to explain myself to you or anyone else. She is *my* wife, and I'll treat her any way I damn well feel like. Now why don't you be a good little boy and beat it before I open up a can o' whup-ass on you?"

Lukas returned to the aisle where Claire waited. "Discretion's the better part of valor," he noted. "But if I got him alone in the woods, he'd be meat."

As they paid for their groceries, the cashier, a plump woman in her fifties wearing what looked like a house dress, said quietly, "Thanks for not makin' Dink get physical, mister. He can be mighty mean when he gets riled up."

"He's done this before, then," said Lukas.

"All the time. Poor woman just takes it, too. Sometimes I see her come in with bruises, and I just know he hurts her somethin' terrible."

"Don't the police ..." began Claire.

"No, honey, she won't press charges. Dink might not be much, but he's all she's got. They got kids at home, and she needs the money he brings in to take care of 'em. She told me once she looks forward to Saturday nights, because that's when he goes to the bar and leaves them alone. Though sometimes he comes home drunk and slaps her and the kids around some. It ain't pretty."

"No, it's not," said Claire. "I'm so sorry."

"That's very kind," said the cashier. "You're nice people."

From behind a stack of groceries, the man called Dink continued to berate his wife.

They carried their groceries to the car and pulled back onto the road. "Son of a bitch doesn't deserve to live," mumbled Claire as she shook her head and looked down at her lap. Her hands were clenched into fists.

Lukas nodded but didn't say a thing. Claire would be moving to Boston in a couple of days, and while she was occupied with her new job he'd be back here ... doing some research that was not at all related to academics.

* * *

On Monday, July 29, Lukas drove Claire to the studio apartment she'd rented in the Beacon Hill district. The trunk and back seat easily accommodated Claire's clothing and personal effects. After she'd sold her parents' home and furniture, she took to college only the necessities and some family memorabilia. She knew they'd fit comfortably in her one-room efficiency. The apartment manager had graciously offered her three days' rent free, as the apartment was already vacant. For Claire, it meant she'd have extra time to furnish the place and settle in before reporting to work.

When they arrived, Rowena Parr was standing outside the building. She looked exaggeratedly at her watch. "Ten minutes late," she admonished Claire. "If I were still in college and the professor were ten minutes late, that would be our excuse to leave the room. How lucky you are girl, that I'm feeling especially lenient today. Besides," she added, "I wanted to get a good look at your boyfriend. I'd say he's worth the wait, mmm hmmm." She extended her hand to Lukas. "Hi, I'm Ro, Claire's slave driver-in-chief. Welcome to Bah-ston."

Lukas took her hand, introduced himself (unnecessarily), and thanked her for offering to help Claire get settled. Claire shook Rowena's hand and thanked her again. The managing editor of Jones Publishing brushed their thanks aside and said, "Let's get you unpacked."

Rowena Parr was in her thirties, Lukas guessed, and perhaps the most striking woman (except for Claire) he'd ever seen. The product of a marriage between a black Marine and a Vietnamese woman, she displayed the finest physical traits of each ethnicity. Her skin was the color of coffee and cream, her facial features made her look Eurasian, and she stood midway between her mother's and her father's height, say somewhere around five eight. Her hair was long, pitch black, and her figure reminded him of a grown-up Barbie doll's.

They got the apartment set up in no time, and then it was off to shop for a bed, linens, kitchenware, blinds, café table, and chairs. Not much more would comfortably fit, but for Claire the apartment suited her fine. She was in her first place and starting her first real job, and that thrilled her.

"Lukas, you know we've got you here for the grunt work, right?" asked Rowena as they climbed into his Jetta. "Claire, honey, can you slide your seat forward a little? Thanks. I know a place that sells furniture on consignment. It's used, but it's in serviceable shape, and best of all, it's cheap. Let's try there first. We can bring the furniture back to the apartment and then head out for the smaller stuff. If we need to, I know a guy who can lend us his pickup."

"That's fine. Oh, and for that stuff, I think we'd better look at Walmart rather than Bed Bath and Beyond Our Means."

"Understood, my dear. Lukas, get those mice under your hood moving on that treadmill they call an engine. We have places to go and things to buy."

* * *

At the end of the day Rowena left them, saying she had to get home before her husband reported her missing.

"I have to greet him in Saran Wrap," she added. When they said nothing, simply stared dumbly, she said, "Come on, now, kidding. My honey and I are married ten years, do you think we do that stuff … still?" Her eyes sparkled as she teased. "Now you, on the other hand …"

"Get out of here, you," laughed Claire, "and thanks for all you've done."

"Make it worth my while, girl. See you bright and early Thursday morning. And Lukas, don't know if Claire here told you, but our boss is taking us to dinner two weeks from Friday. He does this with all his new hires, gets to know them on a more personal level. My husband Bill will be there, and you're invited, too. Don't try to beg off, this is a command performance. And yes, the boss picks up the whole tab. Won't even let us peons put in the tip."

"That would be … be great. Thanks."

She pecked him on the cheek. "See you in two. Bye, Claire."

* * *

Lukas stayed with Claire Tuesday, mostly putting the finishing touches on the apartment with her, doing grocery shopping, and giving the squeaky springs in her second-hand bed a workout. They also checked out bus schedules and found the Concord Coach had regular service from Boston to New Hampshire, where Lukas could meet her on Fridays and return her on Sundays. They planned to alternate weekends between Boston and Lukas's cabin on the Criterion campus. The first weekend they'd spend alone, as it would follow Claire's first two days on the job and his first two days preparing for his Ph.D. work. The weekend of August 9-11, she would take the bus north, and the following Friday she would drive south for the introductory dinner with Mr. Radu Jones along with Rowena Parr and her husband.

On Wednesday, Lukas left for New Hampshire, citing a meeting with his doctoral advisor, a meeting that had not, in fact, been scheduled for this week but for next. His first stop was the market where he'd run into the abusive husband and his cowering wife.

He reminded the cashier—not that she had needed reminding—of the incident they'd witnessed the week before and asked what she could tell him about the man called Dink. Apparently he worked for a lumber company and told him where they were currently located. Lukas drove to the site and parked near the office trailer.

Inside, he inquired about a job—for a cousin from out of state—and learned that not only was the salary good (probably better than Dink had let on to his wife), but so were the benefits. Benefits that included a hefty life insurance policy. That was what he had come to find out.

Lukas drove away and parked on the shoulder of the road where he could see the lumbermen's cars as they drove home from work. Dink he recognized immediately. He drove an older Mustang convertible with the top down. At a respectable distance, Lukas followed him to a mobile home park, where he parked in front of a double-wide and stormed through the door shouting orders. That was all he needed.

Back in his cabin, Lukas e-mailed Claire that he had arrived safely—her orders—and that he couldn't wait to see her on the 9th. He concluded his message by telling her he had a surprise planned for Saturday night.

* * *

Dink had a day's worth of beard stubbling his lantern jaw, and already his eyes were half-lidded thanks to the drafts of beer he'd consumed. Dark, greasy hair tumbled down from his cap, but at least he was wearing it with the bill in front. His breath reeked of brew, and sweat stained his checkered shirt. The ashtray in front of him was full, but the wooden pretzel bowl on the bar was empty.

"My friends call me Dink," he said to the tall blonde who had zeroed in on him, ignoring the stares of the loud and crowded bar's other potential suitors.

"Hello, Dink. I'm Lucy," she said.

His grin grew, and he affected a Desi Arnaz/Ricky Ricardo accent: "Loosee, you got some 'splainin' to do."

"Like I've never heard that one before. But you're cute, so I forgive you."

"Don't remember seein' you here before. And I would remember, darlin'. New in town, right?"

"Uh huh. Just passing through, thought I'd catch some of the local night life before heading to my motel."

"Is that right? Your motel, you say?"

"My motel, I say." She licked her lips. "I don't drink alcohol, Dink, but I sure could use some club soda, if you're buying."

"Well, Lucy, I sure am, although I must say, you're a cheap date."

She sipped from the glass of sparkling water and wrinkled her nose at the bubbles. "So what do you do, Dink? For a living?"

"I'm a lumberman."

"Really. Big and strong, I'll bet."

"You'd win that one, darlin'. Say," he said, grinning, "I've got a joke for ya. Why did the lumber truck stop?"

The blonde grinned. "I give up, Dink, why did the lumber truck stop?"

"To let the lumberjack off!" He roared with laughter, and she tossed her head back and joined him, although her laugh was much softer, seductive even. Forced for sure, but he didn't notice that.

"You're quite the comedian," she said. "I like a man who can make me laugh."

Dink pulled a pack of cigarettes from his shirt pocket. "Smoke?"

She shook her head. "No minor vices, Dink." Her gaze, her smile, were direct.

"Lucy, darlin'? You didn't say nothin' about major vices, now, did you?"

"*Anything*, and no I didn't," she said, her words barely audible over the din of the jukebox and the chatter of the mostly male clientele of this roadhouse, which was more honky-tonk even than the one fifty miles to the north—the one where in another life she'd once gone alone to "celebrate" her twenty-first birthday. "Major vices, those I do happen to have, in spades." She slid a hand over his. "I like strong men, Dink. Just how strong are you?"

"Oh, my," he said, his mouth suddenly dry. "I can make you cry uncle if you want."

"What if I want to cry Dink?"

He gulped. "Just say the word, darlin'."

"Word. Now, how about we, blow this joint."

The pun wasn't lost on him. He left a dollar on the bar—first time he'd ever left a tip—and followed the blonde outside into the pine-scented night. "Want me to drive you to your motel?" he asked.

She turned and pressed herself to him. "Dink, I don't think I can wait that long. She took his hand and slid it down the front of her jeans. "Feel me." Her panties were already damp—from the thin film of petroleum jelly she'd smeared on earlier. "Where can we go that's close? I don't need comfort. I need cock."

Dink stood behind her and cupped her crotch with one hand and squeezed a breast with the other. "Lucy, darlin', you are one hot mama."

"Dink, you are about to learn just how hot this mama is. Now, where can we go where no one from inside can see us?"

He led her into the woods about fifty yards from the tavern. Moonlight filtered through the trees. From somewhere far off an owl hooted. A boulder, left by retreating glaciers eons ago, stood near their path. "I figure we can lean against this, that okay with you, darlin'?"

"Perfect," she replied. "Now, you just stand by that rock and watch me while I make you hard."

"I'm already hard."

"I'll make you hard as that rock you're standing against."

"Darlin', I'm harder than that rock. I'm so hard I coulda pole-vaulted out here, and that's no joke."

"Neither is this, baby."

As if moving to a song only she could hear, the blonde began swinging her hips and unbuttoning her blouse. Her bra was a front-fastening model with lacy white cups. When she unfastened it and cast it aside, Dink gaped at the perfection of her breasts in the moonlight. For a girl tall enough to be a basketball player, she had impressive sweater meat, that was for sure. And now she was unfastening her jeans and sliding them down. He could see the moisture darkening her panties, and seconds later he was seeing her lightly-furred triangle. "Oh, my," he whispered as if in prayer. "You do look good enough to eat."

The blonde smiled and kicked off her loafers before flipping off her jeans and panties with her foot. She stood stark naked before him, and her effect was obvious by the tent pole in his trousers. "I'll be happy to start the festivities," she said. "But be advised, mister lumberman, I do intend to eat you up." He gulped. "And Dink, just so you know, I swallow."

"Omigod, Ms. Lucy, omigod," he said as his trembling fingers fumbled with his zipper. "Baby, you're gonna fly me to the moon, aren't you?" His pants were bunched at his ankles now, his drawers as well.

"The moon's just for starters," she replied as she walked toward him, licking her lips. She stopped inches from him and leaned her face close to one ear. The scent of booze and tobacco that clung to him was almost too much to bear. "Before we begin," she whispered, "you might want to look behind you."

Frowning, Dink turned and looked up. Staring down at him from atop the boulder, its eyes glinting, stood a wolf, the largest one he'd ever seen. Something in its eyes looked unnatural for a wolf, and Dink would know, he'd killed many a one, just for the hell of it. Saliva, hot and slick, spilled from its mouth and onto Dink's face. A growl nearby him made him spin. Where the girl had been stood another wolf, golden maned, head low, fangs bared. Its eyes were so light blue they could've been gray, just like Lucy's—

The second wolf leaped, paws pinning him to the rock, and he felt its jaws close on his throat. Fangs pierced his neck on both sides, and with a tug of the beast's head his throat was ripped out in a scarlet spray. As the animal chewed, its maw inches from Dink's face, the panicked man clutched his hands around the wound, trying to stop the bleeding. He couldn't yell, because his larynx was somewhere inside the predator's chomping jaws. He inhaled, his lungs filled with blood instead of air, and he felt the panic of a drowning man. He tried to blow out and heard a gurgle from deep inside his chest. Then, his head was smashed against the rock as the wolf drove its muzzle into the wound and bit cleanly through his spine.

When the lumberman fell to the ground, the other wolf, which had been watching the whole time from atop the boulder, leaped to the ground and tore open the man's belly. He pulled out the liver and shared it with his mate. The fur around their muzzles was mixed crimson and brown as they chewed and swallowed. The heart was next, but they left the stomach and the putrid lungs alone. At the last, the male took the man's head in his mouth and carried it to the rock. He pressed the man's face against the boulder to hold it steady. Then, biting down with fierce force, his teeth breached the bone, and the skull gave up its contents like a broken egg. The pair dived into the brain, their teeth plucking pieces out, tongues licking up the blood and scraps until the cranial cavity was completely clean.

They stared at each other for a moment, each one scenting another signal, equally primal. The bitch raised her tail and splayed her legs as the male mounted her from behind and drove his red hardness into her, furiously and fast, until they both collapsed in a panting heap. It took every ounce of will power not to howl when it was over.

* * *

The depth of the crash matched the peak of the high. Claire's tears flooded down her face as she sat at Lukas's table later that night, fingers fisted in her hair. Blood matted her blonde locks, blood crusted the creases in her hands and fingers, splotches of brown colored her clothes where she'd held them while getting dressed, her mind in some sort of stupor. She had said no words on the drive back, nothing when they arrived at the cabin. Now, seated and still, with the memories of what she'd done squeezing in on her until she thought her brain might burst, she let them out in fierce sobs.

Lukas stood back, remembering his own first human kill, knowing he was powerless to help. Softly, he walked to a drawer and removed a long narrow velvet box. He put it in his back pants pocket and sat across the table from Claire.

Finally, her grief found a voice, small and almost hiccupy. "I hate you."

He reached a hand to cup her face, but she brushed it away, almost savagely. "Claire. I love you. You must know that."

"Bullshit," she sobbed. "If you loved me, you wouldn't have turned me into—into this. You wouldn't have made me hunt with you. Lukas, don't you realize what I—what we -- did? We killed another human being—and ate him! We're murderers, and we're cannibals, and, and ... we're *inhuman*!"

Lukas kept his voice soothing. "Not inhuman; superhuman. And as for that creep, we did the world a favor. You know that. Claire, my Luna, remember it was you who said the son of a bitch didn't deserve to live."

She looked up, her eyes still stinging from the tears. "That's another part of it. It was so ... so *calculating*. It's like you're some sort of vigilante weeding out the dregs of society. And, you're good at what you do, Lukas. You convinced me. When I walked into that bar and saw him, I was ready. It was like I was the big bad wolf, and he was Redneck Riding Hood. But that's not what I do, Lukas." She took a faltering breath. "That's not me." She wept anew.

He took her hand, and this time she didn't rebuff him. "You were more like the woodsman in the story, love. You saved a woman and her children from something worse than the big bad wolf. Look, I told you the lumber company has life insurance on its employees. They'll get by. You've given some innocent prisoners their freedom. They can make a good life for themselves now."

She whispered, "I still can't believe what I did. How I did it. I'm a cold-blooded killer."

"No. You're a hot-blooded killer."

She took a breath. Her expression changed from grief to anger. "And, you're a full-blooded asshole if you think I'm ever going to do that again."

He looked at her, silent, something in his eyes ...

"I mean it. Who am I to decide ..." She turned her eyes upward, then down to the table, toward Lukas's hands holding hers. Her tone softened. "I don't know what I am any more."

The teakettle whistled, and he got up and poured hot water over teabags in two large mugs. He returned to the table and placed one in front of her. The steam rose into her nostrils, and she inhaled deeply. "Claire," he said, "tell me what you felt ... then ... at the moment of the kill. And afterward."

Claire cupped the mug between her palms and took a breath. She looked him directly in the eyes. Her expression was profoundly sad, seeming to belie her words. "I felt wonderful. All-powerful. And afterward ... afterward ... I've never known sex could be so intense. God, Lukas, I never had a climax like that before. My whole body felt like it was plugged into an electric socket. And it lasted! I mean, no oops, guess that was it; it was like a jolt that kept on jolting.

"But now. Now the guilt ... I'm ashamed, Lukas, I'm more than ashamed. I'm damned!" Her eyes gleamed grey behind her tears.

"Tell the truth. Tonight was a high to end all highs. Am I right?"

Softly: "Yes." What she couldn't bring herself to say was that the kill itself was almost as thrilling. Which only intensified her ingrained Catholic sense of shameful remorse.

"Love, I feel the same, always have. But in all the years I've been a metamorph—I changed for the first time at eighteen—I've never killed wantonly. My parents taught me that. They were good people, and they followed my grandparents' example. Listen, my German ancestors took out many a Nazi during the war; but never a Jew nor a Romani did they harm. Nor, for that matter, an intellectual or a homosexual. They were tolerant, loving people, enemies of the State maybe, but not of the pawns purged by the State in places like Oswiecim—Auschwitz to you. They weren't playing God; they were doing God's work, doing what He should've been doing all along.

"Claire—Luna—we live in this world, we're a part of it, and we do good by it. Forget what you've seen in the movies. We ... are not ... monsters."

He took a breath. "How's your tea? Cooled enough yet?"

Claire lifted the mug to her mouth and sipped. She ran her tongue around her lips and sipped again. "Good," she said. "How's yours?"

"Fine."

"Lukas, how many of ... us ... are out there?"

He looked at her matter-of-factly. "Only two that I know of, as I told you before. And both of them are sitting at this table enjoying a cup of tea, just like any other happy couple."

What was it in his tone?

She saw him reach behind and produce a small, elongated box. When he slid it across the table toward her without a word, she hesitated opening it. "A necklace," she said, her voice small. "A star pendant."

"A pentacle," Lukas said.

"To commemorate our, our, what, our werewolfy-ness? Like the tattoos aren't enough?" Her voice carried that hint of sarcasm he loved, which implied the old Claire was returning.

"To commemorate something deeper, I'd hoped," Lukas responded. He lifted her chin with his fingers, leaned across the table, and kissed her. She didn't resist. "I think we should finish our tea, put our clothes in the washer, and take a shower," he said, standing. "What do you think?"

Without a word, Claire stood and turned her back to allow him to fasten the gold chain around her neck. Then she faced him again and began unbuttoning her blouse.

At slightly past noon on the following day, she boarded the bus for Boston. She folded her hands on her lap, closed her eyes, and bowed her head.

Anyone noticing would have assumed she was praying.

Chapter Four

From: cdelaney@jonespub.com
Subj: Missing you
Date: August 13, 2002
To: lehrlich@criterion.edu

Dear Lukas,

Back in Boston, US of A, birthplace of the Revolution, home to Old Ironsides, and to some of the best restaurants in the world. Rowena and I have gone out to eat a few times now, and she always apologizes for making a pig of herself. "Rehearsing for when I'm eating for two," she says. "Bill and I have been trying to get pregnant for a year now." Then, after we say goodnight, I have to hit the fridge to fill up, because even the jumbo portions the restaurants serve here aren't always enough. My being a (fill in the blank) makes me hungry all the time. No weight gain, though. Metabolism must be working overtime.

As you can tell, I'm adjusting, or at least trying very hard to adjust. It isn't easy, though. There are times I feel like a fraud. I am totally conflicted. (*Conflicted*: is that a legitimate word, or a verb made from a noun to make it sound impressive? Like *prioritize*, for Pete's sake. What's wrong with *setting priorities*?) I still have nightmares about you know what. Guilt is a terrible thing to waste, or something like that.

My job for now is to attack the slush pile, the unsolicited manuscripts that come in, as they say, over the transom. Some of them are real trash, pure amateur-hour stuff. Some are okay, and occasionally one comes in that's decent. The decent ones I forward to Ro, and if she likes it, on it goes to Mr. Jones. He makes the decision as to whether the piece is worth publishing. All this takes more time than you might think.

Mr. Jones explained that, with regard to certain contemporary subject matter books, by the time they see print their information is already obsolete—which makes the public libraries that get them, in effect, storehouses of misinformation. He's been very supportive and patient. He likes my being a stickler for grammar, and sometimes he'll "turn me loose" on an MS that's already been accepted just to clean it up grammatically. Hey, extra hours, extra overtime. OT is nice, especially considering how expensive it is to live in Beantown. The locals never call it that, by the way.

I wish I were interested in sports. If you don't know anything about the Red Sox here, you're a pariah. Rowena took me to a game at Fenway Park, and I had to pretend I liked it just so she wouldn't think I was descended from Benedict Arnold. The hot dogs were okay, though; we both pigged out

The closest I've come to appreciating professional sports is Abbott and Costello's "Who's on First" routine. I can't afford cable, so I can't veg out in front of TV Land or Nick. I miss my Lucy and Gilligan and Addams Family. And as for the Munsters, well, don't even go there. I don't think I could ever look at Eddie in the same way again.

(You've asked why I gravitate toward the old TV shows, and at the time I wasn't sure. But I think I've figured it out. First, we agree that the new ones are junk—the reality shows are the most unreal of all—but the main reason, I think, is that these old programs are the shows my mother and father used to watch when they were growing up. Watching these shows kind of connects me to my folks. I see them and imagine hearing Mom and Dad laugh with me. Make sense? Please don't say I'm just hanging on to the past because I'm not ready or willing to embrace the present.)

Anyway, Ro says that she and Bill are looking forward to Friday's dinner with Mr. Jones. I am, too, and I hope you are, as well. Can you get here a little early on Friday? Hint, clue.

Speaking of (how do I put this in an e-mail?), I'm feeling certain … urges, and they seem to get stronger as I approach my monthly cycle. I noticed them last month, and here they come again. Next week is the full moon. Uh oh. Did your mother ever sit you down and have a talk with you about that? Can you fill me in (pun intended) when I see you this weekend? Yes, I guess I am adjusting.

BTW, I've not taken the pentacle pendant off, not once.

Love,
Claire

* * *

From: lehrlich@criterion.edu
Subj: Re: Missing you
Date: August 14, 2002
To: cdelaney@jonespub.com

Hello, Luna my love,

To answer your burning question: no, Mother never had "that" talk with me, but I will be happy to "fill you in" anyway. (Wink back atcha.)
My Ph.D. advisor is a woman. Her name is Dr. Daciana Moceanu, another Eastern European type like Gabe. She's a geneticist, and my thesis is going to focus on genetic mutations. Kind of hits home, doesn't it?
Back to your question, does your cycle coincide with the full moon? I don't know, but that could explain where part of the myth comes from. We'll talk more about this when I see you. I can't wait. Two more days, seems like two years. Maybe when we get together we can do some planning for the future …

Love,
Lukas

* * *

From: cdelaney@jonespub.com
Subj: Re: Missing you
Date: August 15, 2002
To: lehrlich@criterion.edu

Darling, about that "planning for the future" remark: how else could we plan? Does one ever plan for the past?

Sorry, sweetie, couldn't resist taking another swipe. Forgive me? The "planning" sounds "intriguing." See you tomorrow.

Your loving Luna

* * *

From: lehrlich@criterion.edu
Subj: Planning for the future
Date: August 15, 2002
To: cdelaney@jonespub.com

No one likes a smartass.

Chapter Five

She captured his scent before he even knocked on her door. One rap, and she was there, swinging it wide and opening her arms wider. No word passed between them, just an embrace that threatened to snap each other's spines. Finally, Lukas spoke, his voice a guttural whisper:

"I want to take you to bed, right now."

"Um ... don't you think we should close the door first?"

Lukas kicked the door shut, and he forced Claire back onto her bed, a short distance in her very small efficiency. She'd been prepared: a bathrobe was her only garment, and she spread it wide as Lukas fumbled with his trousers and veritably leaped upon her. Their mouths opened, and their teeth ground against each other as their tongues thrashed. His hands were all over her, and soon his mouth joined them. Then, before Claire could think to reciprocate, he was inside her. She felt his saliva drip onto her face, felt her jaw jut, felt her claws dig into his furry back as he drove down again and again and passion drove them both to the point of release.

It was over almost before it had begun. Panting, they lay side-by-side on her bed. When she'd caught her breath, Claire looked down and frowned. "You nipped my nips," she said, her voice pretend-petulant. "Look, there are teeth marks all around them. You animal."

Lukas turned onto his side and kissed her breasts. "I'm sorry, Luna. I did get carried away. And so did you, I'd say."

Her face turned serious. "Lukas, did we, did we really begin to *turn* when we were making love? I don't know, it's a kind of blur. All I remember is letting myself just, just go."

"It's true. Something I should've prepared you for. Sometimes in the heat of passion we can lose control and release ourselves to the change. The change itself adds to the orgasm ... doesn't it?" She shuddered, nodded her head, smiled weakly. "It's ... I'll admit it, it's kind of addictive in its way."

Then she said, "We didn't change fully, did we?"

"Impossible, considering how we were linked." That brought a laugh from them both.

Claire slapped his thigh—and he jumped. Her strength was the equal of his now. "Come on, get up. Time to get ready for dinner."

"Well, all righty, then. I'm so hungry I could eat a horse."

"The whole horse, I'd bet. Try to control yourself in the restaurant, okay? Don't embarrass me in front of my boss and my friend."

"Um, pot, kettle?"

* * *

They all met at a seafood restaurant and raw bar in Cambridge: Rowena, her husband Bill, Radu Jones, and Lukas and Claire. Rowena's exotic good looks were complemented by a vivacity that befitted a cheerleader. Bill, on the other hand, was pure white bread. He worked as a financial advisor for Fidelity, which was about as far removed from Lukas interest-wise as polar bears from penguins. But Bill was affable and made the perfect complement to Rowena's natural effervescence. He more or less let his wife do the talking, and she teasingly refused to let him interject financial nuggets whenever an opportunity arose. Jones ("Call me Ray, please") may have been the boss, but he deferred in conversation to his female employees as if he were beholden to them. A gentleman to the core, he opened the door for them, held out their seats for them, and insisted they place their orders with the waiter before the men.

"What is making you frown, Lukas?" said Jones as he watched Lukas study the menu.

Lukas tried to hold back a grin. "I'm just looking at this appetizer: crab balls."

"Uh-oh," said Claire. "Fasten your seat belts."

"No, I'm just wondering, um ..."

"How they're harvested?" asked Rowena, her mock-serious face a match for Lukas's.

"How big they could possibly be?" added Bill.

They turned to Jones: your turn, boss. He sat back and with the air of a most pretentious professor said, "Surely, my friends, you've heard of the Vienna Crab Choir."

Their laughter caused the other patrons to stare at them; some might even have wished they could join them. Jones signaled the server, a young, fresh-faced collegian, and called out, loudly enough for the rest of the room to hear, "Waiter: crab balls all around!"

Without missing a beat, the server closed his legs tight, bent over at the waist, and said, "Ouch!" And as the house joined in laughter, the elegantly dressed middle-aged hostess, standing at her podium, simply shook her head and smiled. Boys. Do they ever grow up?

The appetizers were the size of golf balls, lightly breaded and deep fried, delicious but not something one would find in a health food restaurant. As they studied the menu prior to ordering, Bill said almost to himself, "So far, this has been salmon chanted evening."

The others looked at him. "What's that you said, honey mine?" said Rowena.

"Hm? Oh, nothing, just that earlier I had a haddock ... but I feel fine now."

"Oh, no," his wife cautioned the others. "Don't get him started on puns."

"Don't be a crab, dear."

"Stop it."

"Shall I clam up now?"

"I'm going to punch you if you don't."

"She's strong," Bill said to the table. "You should see her mussels."

"That's it," said Rowena, standing and affecting a hurt expression. "I'm going outside to check the air pressure on the tires." She winked and walked out, her purse over her shoulder.

"Tire pressure?" asked Lukas.

"Code. She's going outside to grab a smoke."

"Alas," said Jones, "the lady's only flaw—if I may say so, Bill."

"Say away, Ray. I've been trying to get her to quit, but she just says anything in moderation. At least she doesn't stink up the house."

"I have an idea," offered Claire. "Ro's told me you're trying to start a family. When she's pregnant, she'll stop. Then after the baby's born, it should be easier to stay stopped—if for no other reason than the baby's health."

Bill took a breath. "So I have to get her pregnant, huh? Looks like I've got my work cut out for me. Oh, and by the way, I love my work."

Soon Rowena returned. "Air pressure's fine," she said as she sat. "What did I miss?"

"They were talking about you," Lukas said.

"No fair. My smoking, I bet." Claire looked at her sympathetically. "What?"

"Not my business, Ro."

"Come on, out with it." Her tone said she'd heard it all before, but it wasn't defensive.

"Some day you'll have children, Ro. And if you go back to smoking, well, some day you will cause your children the most intense emotional pain they could imagine when they watch their mother die in agony from emphysema or some form of cancer." She took a breath, remembering. "And even as they love you, they'll hate you for depriving them of all those extra years they would've had with you if only you hadn't decided to mortgage your life to a bunch of legally-sanctioned drug pushers so you could have the privilege of an early and excruciating death." She paused, suddenly self-conscious. "Whoa. Sorry, guys. I'll get off my soapbox now."

The men looked at each other.

"Wow. Where did that come from," said Rowena softly.

"I'm sorry, Ro. Really am. It's just ... well, I know."

"You know?"

She nodded. "My mother. And the stupid thing is, even knowing that, I still gave in and smoked for almost a year. It was right after 9/11, and I was feeling pretty fatalistic for a while. Then along came Lukas. He persuaded me to quit." She looked at him directly, her expression unreadable. "I ... I just don't want your kids to go through what I did with my own mother. Understand? Still friends?"

Rowena placed her hand over Claire's. "BFF, as the kids say. And I'll think about it, Claire, I really will."

Good, Claire thought, because that cloud that's clinging to you really reeks.

"So," Jones said, changing the subject, "How are your crab appetizers? As for me, I'm having a ball."

Everyone groaned.

* * *

With coffee after dinner—all agreed they were too stuffed for dessert, although in two people's case it was a lie—Jones asked Lukas what was new with his childhood friend Gabriel. "Still elbow deep in blood, is he?"

"Eww," said Rowena. "Nice image, boss."

"Pretty much. He's devoting a ton of time to his research. TAs pretty much teach his courses. I did myself for much of my master's work, but now I'm buried in research for my Ph.D., and I don't see him much at all. My doctoral advisor keeps my nose to the proverbial."

"Understood. Well, when you do see him, tell him I send my best. And thank him for sending me Claire."

Claire said, "Thank him for me, too."

* * *

They returned to Claire's flat, raided her small refrigerator, tore off each other's clothes, and fell into bed, this time resisting the urge to change during lovemaking. Later, they talked.

"I'm trying to reconcile myself with what I've become," said Claire. "And adjust to some kind of normal life with a normal job in a normal world. But I'm not normal any more. Lukas, there are times I love you for what you mean to me and times I hate you for what you've done to me."

Her head rested on the crook of his arm, and he rolled toward her to kiss her. His lips grazed her forehead, her cheek, the tip of her nose, and he nuzzled his own nose against her neck. "I am sorry for those hate times, really I am. You know I love you, Claire de Lune. And when I realized I love you I also realized that you couldn't love me until you knew who I really am. That's when it got confusing, that's when I jumped the gun, that's when I figured that if you were like me, if we were the same, then maybe we'd be linked in a way that ..."

Claire gently pushed his head back so she could look into his eyes. "What made you think I couldn't love you as a plain old human being? No matter what you are?"

"I don't know. Maybe I was afraid you'd think I was some kind of monster. And you'd give me up."

"You mean to the police?"

He shook his head. "No, you know how that'd turn out. I meant you might give me up, as in run away as if your life depended on it." He chuckled. "It wouldn't, I wouldn't hurt you, but you'd probably live in fear of me, thinking I'd kill you to keep my secret safe."

"Paranoia is one of your many weaknesses," she observed. "Now, if you really want to get paranoid, consider this. Now that I'm a werewolf— excuse me, metamorph—like you, if I ever catch you tossing me aside for someone else, then *you'll* have something to be afraid of."

She kissed him, and they snuggled for a bit. Finally she said, "You have a scent about you when you want to have sex. Which is pretty much all the time, by the way."

"Uh huh. Pheromones. You do, too," he said, "and that's how I knew you'd go to bed with me the night we met."

"That's an unfair advantage, you know."

"Only if you're dating a metamorph."

"Did your nose tell you how vulnerable I was at that moment?"

"No, and if you think I exploited that vulnerability, I sincerely apologize. I would never try to take advantage of you or anyone else. You do know that, right?"

"So tell me about these urges I keep having, Lukas. Since you changed me, just before my period, I've been wanting to turn into wolf form. I want to change, I want to hunt, and I want to have sex. It's like a nicotine fit, but more intense. Last month, after -- you know, that lumberman -- that was right before my period. This month, well, if you hadn't been here I'm afraid I'd have had to mount the building superintendent. But if last month is any indication, after my period comes in a few days I should be fine again. And, to answer your question, next week is the full moon. What's going on, biology man?"

Lukas nodded and kissed her forehead again. "To put it bluntly, you're going into heat."

"Heat? My God, I *am* an animal!"

"Let me be melodramatic here: you're not an animal, but you're not human either. Does that sound like a line from a grade B movie?"

"Yes, but seriously, I'm going into heat? And this will continue until, until, oh God, menopause?"

He just stared at her.

"What do I do about it? See, Lukas, what I also want to do is not only change but hunt. I want to become a wolf, bring down prey, and howl at the moon. Did you know this would happen when you changed me? Because if you did ..."

He put up his free hand. "I truly had no idea. I mean, I'm not a woman, I didn't even think about that." She called him a pig. "I know. Male chauvinist metamorph type. The worst kind."

"Would you have changed me if you did know? Watch out, it's a loaded question."

"Right. Like there's no correct answer."

The question went unanswered.

PART TWO
RIGHTEOUS
KILL

Chapter Six

When, during channel surfing, she heard Kermit the Frog sing "It's Not Easy Being Green," Claire said to herself, "You don't know the half of it, Kermie. Try being a werewolf." She had been at home suffering through the first day of her period, taking a break from the stack of manuscripts she'd brought to the apartment to veg out for a bit in front of the television. (Some day, she thought, when I have most of my evenings free, I'll get cable and start looking at TV Land and Nick at Nite again. Hi, Mom, hi, Dad. Miss you.)

Memories of Dink had begun to fade; she knew the family she thought of as Mrs. Dink and the Dinkies were far better off without his daily abuse, and privately she wished she could visit them or at least monitor how well they were doing. But Lukas had warned her against it, sternly so, and she assured him it was only a whim.

Claire and Lukas had spent New Year's Eve partying in Boston with Rowena and Bill (a sip of champagne at midnight, sparkling water before), and the week earlier had spent Christmas by themselves in New

Hampshire, snuggled up in his cabin. They even allowed themselves a few times to make love—to mate—in partial wolf form. The campus was deserted during the holidays, and no one was nearby to hear their howls. They also frequented the woods to the south, near Francestown, where Claire, under Lukas's tutelage, learned to bring down more formidable game than rabbits, squirrels, and possums. The first time they took down an aging doe brought Claire an appreciation of life's relentless cycle of kill or be killed, eat or be eaten.

She had to shake her head when she heard the complaints of animal activists whose idea of nature was anchored in *Bambi*. Claire loved animals—Ro and Bill's retired racing greyhound, appropriately named Greycie—was absolutely adorable. She railed at the LD-50 chemical tests (how much exposure is lethal to half the population) performed routinely on animals from lab rats up to and including monkeys. But that was different from killing animals for one's own survival. Animal rights groups routinely decried the "inhumane" killing methods of food animals.

But which was worse, she reasoned: a blow to the head or slice to the throat; or being torn apart by a pack of predators and eaten while still alive. (One of the MS's she'd had to read described how the female tarantula wasp paralyzes the tarantula with her sting and then injects her eggs into its body. The eggs hatch, and the young wasps eat their way out of the helpless spider. Claire still shivered when she thought of it.) Show me an animal that dies peacefully of old age, Claire thought, and I'll show you an animal in a zoo or a household pet.

Claire had had no desire to hunt the most dangerous game and swore to Lukas that Dink was both her first and last human kill. He'd only looked at her obliquely and changed the subject.

They saw each other on weekends, alternating between Boston and the Criterion campus, and they'd compare their weeks: Claire's graduating from the slush pile to agented material, up one rung of the ladder, Lukas's dedication to his Ph.D. research under the watchful eye of Professor Moceanu. Life was full of promise—so long as their identity as metamorphs remained a secret.

* * *

Saturday, the ninth of August, three days before the next full moon, found Lukas in Boston and Claire itching for a hunt. The couple decided on a change of venue that weekend and headed westward to where the Appalachian Trail meandered through that part of the state.

They drove for two and a half hours, mostly along I-90, in Lukas's old Volkswagen (the Wolfsburg Edition, he pointed out for the hundredth time. The car now sported his new vanity license plates, reading LUNA. This time she joined him in his childish *Yip, yip, hwooooo!*), and exited the Interstate at Great Barrington. They parked the car at the access to the Appalachian Trail and hiked the Berkshires for about a half hour. They had brought backpacks filled with water bottles, a blanket, and some power bars. They carried no other food.

This was beautiful country in the peak of summer. Trees shaded the trail, with sunlight freckling the couple as they hiked and laughed and swatted at flies. They passed another couple heading in the opposite direction, middle-aged, she huffing a bit and he striding like a stallion, urging her on. They stopped, exchanged greetings, and drank water, the wife eager for a breather. Then, at her husband's prompting—"Only a little ways to go now, Toots"—they said goodbye and parted. Next they crossed paths with a fresh-faced teen-aged girl and her surly boyfriend, she absorbed in nature, he oblivious between his earphones. To them, the couple afforded a nod and a smile, which the girl returned, and the boy didn't acknowledge.

When they arrived at a tiny man-made shelter, Lukas opined that their choosing the Appalachian Trail for a hunt might not have been the best of ideas. Too many people, for one, and two, that could mean too little game. Reluctantly, Claire agreed. "We need to go off trail if we're going to find anything." They had thought small animals would be abundant here, but such was not the case, unless one counted the squirrels chattering in the branches high above.

"The deer come out at dusk," Lukas reminded her and checked his watch. "Which is around eight o'clock these days. It's only four now." He raised his eyebrows, Groucho style. "What do you think we can do in the meantime?"

"Down, boy. I think for now we should scout around for a clearing, kind of far from the trail. Set up shop at the edge. Then"—she arched her eyebrows in return—"maybe we can give your blanket its rut test."

"You so have a way with words."

"Hey, it's my yob, mon."

Deeper into the woods they walked, and after about an hour they stopped dead. The breeze had shifted, and with it came an unmistakable odor: the coppery scent of blood. They flared their nostrils, sniffed again and again. Something had made a kill, and they could track it easily—as Lukas had said, just follow your nose.

They walked stealthily, their sneakers silent, avoiding fallen twigs, and soon they came to the edge of a small clearing. Crouching behind a concealing bush, they stared in shock as a man dragged a woman, obviously unconscious, inside a small tent. Seconds later he emerged, looking furtively from side to side. In one gloved hand he held a fierce-looking hunting knife. Its blade dripped red.

* * *

"Assholes," Junior Puglio laughed to himself as he wiped his blade on the canvas of the couple's tent. The water-repellent material didn't absorb the blood on the blade; it simply smeared it. "Shit." He ducked back inside and found a piece of underwear in a backpack and used that. Sheathing his knife, he brushed aside the tent flap and stood in the sunlight, counting the bills he had taken from the man's wallet. "What was wrong with these asshole campers," he mused, "carrying all this cash." He'd been stalking them since they left their Beemer at the Brush Hill Road in Sheffield. Its plates told him that they were from New Jersey. "You from Joisey? I'm from Joisey!" he had said to himself as he watched them disappear into the woods, laden with camping gear. The trail itself, he knew, was about a three-hour hike, with at times spectacular views west to New York's Taconic Mountains.

Junior was making his annual pilgrimage to the AT, as hikers referred to it. But he never came to the same place twice. One year he might be in Georgia, the next in Virginia, the next in North Carolina. Never in Jersey, though, where the Trail crossed the state's northwest corner. Too close to home, even if home was as far removed from nature as Heaven was from Hell. Junior knew all about Hell. He was spawned there. And, he loved it. It was home.

Newark, the Roseville section. Garden spot of the Garden State. Hah.

Just a few steps from his parents' run-down home on a one-way street, where the houses were separated by three-foot-wide alleys and gang wars were as commonplace as fender-benders. There he could look across the lake in Branch Brook Park and see the famed Cathedral of the Sacred Heart. He never went though. Every Sunday he'd been coerced by his burly father (Alphonse Senior) and his scrawny, chain-smoking mother (Maria, no *Ave*, please) to attend St. Rose of Lima on Orange Street. Al Senior never went, of course. But Junior and his brother Angelo (a misnomer if ever there was one) had had to get duded up on Sunday mornings and walk with Mama to church. They'd dip their fingers in holy water (How do they make it holy? Boil the hell out of it), cross themselves (spectacles, testicles, wallet, and comb) and listen to the priest chant (Get-ta dose Guineas off-a da grass) until they couldn't stand it any more. They never went to confession; mass was penance enough for their sins.

Ah yes, their sins. Like the time they found the stray black cat and saw she was about to pump out a litter. They took it in, put it inside a box, and watched her birth the little shits. Cute little pussies. Kind of felt like Rosie Rottencrotch's down the street. First thing they did was go back into their pool-table-size back yard and drive a stick into the ground. They tied up the mother, bound her back to the stick so that she was forced to stand on her hind legs. Then they piled tinder around her, proclaimed her to be a witch, and did unto her what they'd heard had been done to witches in the old days. They never thought such a small animal could shriek that loud. It made them laugh.

Next they climbed out the window of their second-floor bedroom onto the kitchen roof and lynched two of the litter of four. The remaining two they tied to the tracks of the City Subway System and high-fived each other when the trolley rumbled through.

Their mother, looped on Guinea red, never knew. She'd spend her days either in the sauce or making sauce, so their father could come home and rage, "Macaron', macaron', that all you know how to make, macaron'? Useless bitch!"

Angelo, the stupid shit, OD'ed when he was in high school. Junior wouldn't touch the stuff himself. He got high in other ways. The kittens had taught him that he really liked torture.

Course, he couldn't torture people and get away with it, although he did once when he curbed the spade he saw talking to Rosie after school one day. He got a real charge when his heel connected with the back of the kid's head and his teeth went flying across the sidewalk. Rosie, the dumb twat, didn't appreciate it one bit. "We was just talkin'!" she protested.

Junior was, oh yes, a Boy Scout. His troop met in the basement of the James A. Garfield Elementary School, and to the scoutmaster he presented himself as a natural leader, believer in the Scout Oath and follower of the Scout Law. The occasional weekend campouts were what he lived for -- primarily because in the woods around the Boonton campgrounds, he could steal off with some like-minded buddies, look under rocks for salamanders, and torture them. Over time, he became rather proficient at woodsmanship and found he somewhat enjoyed that, too.

After high school, scouting long behind him, Junior began running numbers and became known to certain influential people from downtown. He would never rise higher than a soldier in the organization, but that suited him fine. He took a certain pride in his reputation as The Enforcer. Kind of like The Terminator, but he didn't terminate anyone; he just made sure they paid their bills. He saved the terminations for his vacations.

This couple was easy, no challenge at all. Once they got themselves settled in, he "just happened" to saunter on by and wave hello. They were a cute couple, early twenties, probably a few years younger than he, and totally in love. Couldn't keep their hands off each other, friggin' yuppies in lust. They asked why he wore those cotton gloves, and he told them he'd gotten burned at work. He was a restaurant cook, and—dumb ass—he'd stumbled in the kitchen and fallen hands first against the hot grill. The guy mentioned that they'd brought some wine with them, and would he like to share a canteen cup.

The girl said she thought it was too early to start drinking, it wasn't even five o'clock yet. But the guy laughed and said that it's always five o'clock somewhere in the world and went inside the tent. That was when Junior cold-cocked the girl. When her husband came out, Junior was standing beside the tent flap and drove his Bowie knife into his neck. He went down with a gurgle, falling back through the bright green canvas opening, his blood pooling on the ground tarp.

When the girl came to, she was spread-eagled on the grass, wrists and ankles tied to tent stakes. Her jeans and panties were gone, and Junior was kneeling beside her. She opened her mouth to scream, and he shoved a wad of cloth inside. It was blood-soaked cloth cut from her husband's shirt. He fastened another strip of shirt around her head to tie the gag fast.

Junior had found a bottle of K-Y Jelly in one of their backpacks, and he now applied it between her legs, shoving his fingers roughly between her labia. The girl pulled and kicked, but the stakes were too deep, and Junior knew his knots. She twisted her head from side to side, eyes coursing with tears. "Prob'ly wonderin' where your hubby is, right? Don' worry, he won' be interruptin' us."

When he was finished (he knew enough to spew his seed into another strip of cloth he'd cut for the purpose, and which he would burn later), he figured he'd had enough fun for one day and decided not to torture the girl—any more, that is. It was a long drive up from the city, and he'd want to be well out of the state before the bodies were discovered. He knocked her out again, dragged her into the tent, and casually slashed her throat.

Standing outside now, Junior looked around. The meadow was still. He sheathed his knife, spread his arms to the side, and stretched. A good day. He'd be back on the trail in no time, right after he made a small fire and destroyed any evidence of his having been there.

Then he saw the dog walking out of the woods toward him.

* * *

It looked like one of those German shepherds, but it was a lot bigger, and damn, it was fucking beautiful. Its coat was like a silver blond, and as it got closer he could see a thin collar around its neck. Probably lost. Maybe its owner was nearby, in which case he'd better get going, but then again, if there was somebody nearby he might have to off him too, just to be safe.

Friendly damn dog, Junior thought, the way it's just trotting up to me, tail wagging and all. He crouched down. "Nice doggy," he said. He'd always had a soft spot for dogs. He'd never hurt one of them. Cats? Another story altogether. Too friggin' independent, like they'd as soon flip you the bird as look at you. Who the fuck did they think they were?

The dog came up to him and sat down, tongue lolling, as if waiting. Junior noticed that its collar was really thin, it looked like gold, with a little star hanging from it. Never saw a license tag like that. He took off his right glove and reached out his hand, and the dog lowered its head for a scratch. "Good dog," he said as he ruffled its thick fur, and he imagined he heard a grateful little whine coming from inside its throat. "That's a good doggie," he said and brought his hand around so the dog could sniff it.

A few snuffles later, the dog extended its tongue and licked Junior's hand. "Dogs like me," he said to himself. And then the animal's jaws snapped on his wrist like a hunter's leg trap. A scream burst from him as iron-like spikes pressed through skin, flesh, blood vessels, and then crunched through bone. The dog shook its powerful head once, twice, and Junior's right hand was ripped from his wrist.

He wobbled to his feet, staring dumbly at his spurting stump, when a growl from behind him made him spin. It was another dog, just like the first one, except—holy shit, these weren't dogs, these were wolves! Fuckin' wolves! It cocked its head to the side, the way dogs do when they don't understand, but this one understood. It fuckin' knew!

Pain bit into his left ankle. Pain like fire. The other dog—other wolf, the first one. He felt the vise grip, heard and then felt his ankle bones splinter, and now he was on the ground, his left leg a stump, just like his right arm.

Junior brought up his left knee and tried to dig his stump into the ground, seeking pressure to stop the bleeding. His left hand he held to his right wrist, his white cotton glove absorbing the blood, quickly becoming saturated with it. I'm fucked, he thought, Mother of God, I'm fucked!

Wait. What was happening?

The wolves weren't attacking him, they were looking. The second one turned its head toward the tent, like a sideways nod, and the first one disappeared inside while its partner stood guard. Junior whimpered, the pain really powerful now, driving up his arm and leg. That happens when the shock wears off, he'd been told.

And now delirium was setting in. He knew it must be delirium, because instead of the wolf coming out of the tent, it was a woman. Oh God, a beautiful naked blonde, with that same collar—no, it was a necklace—around her neck, and blood—his blood, he knew—splotched on her cheeks. She stood over him, and pink foam fell from her mouth onto his face.

"Just so you know that we know what you did," she said. "And that you will pay."

As he watched, the woman's nose and jaw extended. Pale fur grew from her body. Her breasts retracted into her chest. Her back arched, and her arms and hands became forelegs and paws. And she was once again the wolf -- standing over his face, her head low, her eyes—still that pale grey-blue, the only part of her that hadn't changed—boring into his, her snout inches from his jaw, her lips drawn back to show teeth that went way beyond wicked.

She snapped her jaws, and a piece of Junior's cheek disappeared into her mouth. "Oh God, no!" he cried, but his words sounded strange as the air escaped through the side of his face. A tug at his shirt drew his attention to where the other wolf was almost delicately pulling it away from the buttons and exposing his belly. He let go his stump and tried to push the wolf's head away, but he was too weak, and the sight of the blood spurting from his wrist made him woozy. He grabbed his wrist again as he felt the second wolf's jaws close on his belly and begin to tug. His skin yielded, and his bowels, pink and gray and steamy, lay exposed for legions of flies. The wolf's muzzle probed inside the cavity. Junior could feel it inside him, as if searching. Suddenly—a pain, unlike any other, worse than anything he'd inflicted upon anyone in his line of work. Something ripped away, and when he looked down he saw the second wolf with something brown in its mouth, something soft and dripping.

His liver.

"Hail Mary, full of gra—" were his last words as the blond wolf's jaws tore out his windpipe.

* * *

They didn't make love after. Unlike before, there was no rush, no thrill of the hunt, no rapture in the kill. This was vengeance, pure and simple. Revenge for those who couldn't avenge themselves. They knew nothing of Junior, nothing of his past or his proclivities; they only knew he had killed a pair of innocent people, in cold blood, and their takedown of him was equally cold.

They ate because they needed to, and they crushed his skull to get at his brain, but they found no sweetness in the deed or in the organ itself. They were full, glutted even, but they weren't satisfied. When they were done, they tore his body to shreds, furious again at the memory of the two in the tent.

The wolves morphed into Claire and Lukas once more, and they took the couple's bottled water, washing the blood from each other's body. The bottles they wiped clean with their clothing and buried them at the edge of the clearing. They pulled their clothes on quickly and just as quickly departed, leaving the scene and what remained of Junior to the bugs and the carrion feeders circling overhead.

They drove back to Boston in silence, under the waxing moon. When they got back to her flat, Claire bolted to her tiny bathroom. She came out a little unsteadily, fingers clutching her pentacle. "My period started early," she announced. "And, it's a doozy."

* * *

Rowena stopped short when she popped into Claire's office Monday morning. "Honey," she said, "pardon my French, but you look like you've been shot at and missed, and shit at and hit. What's the matter?"

She wasn't exaggerating. Claire Delaney had seen far better days. Lukas had left after breakfast yesterday following a long and unsatisfactory discussion of what they'd done, leaving her alone with her regrets and the memory of his rationalizing.

"I don't want to go all Sweeney Todd here," she'd said. "I can't keep on doing this."

"Another meat pie, Mrs. Lovett?" Lukas responded, far too glibly.

"I'm serious, Lukas, don't patronize me. We killed—and ate—another human being yesterday."

"He deserved it." He restrained himself from voicing Sweeney's justification for his murders: They all deserve to die.

"I know he deserved it. Even more than Dink, this guy was pure evil. What he did to those poor people! But still, who are we—"

"We're the star chamber, Claire. Or we're doing God's work, if you prefer. We see evil, and we root it out."

She stared at him for a full moment across the dinette table. "How much evil did you root out ... before you met me? And, did you in fact actually seek it out?"

He took another moment before saying, "I'm my parents' son. I acted upon their guidance. And Claire, I'm being serious now, I will not have you or anyone else judge them. End of discussion."

They sat in stalemated silence, then Claire stood and brought their dishes to the sink. She washed and Lukas dried, maintaining silence, He then announced that he had work to do back at Criterion before meeting with his professor first thing tomorrow. "Will I see you next weekend?" he asked after he went to kiss her, and she turned her cheek to him.

"Yes, of course. I'll just need some time to get over this."

"We are what we are, love."

Claire had spent the rest of the day fighting her cramps, both the physical and the emotional. But inwardly she couldn't stop thinking, debating really, about what she and Lukas had done on Saturday. The moral implications still staggered her. On the one hand … but on the other … Great, now she was Tevye.

She thumbed through a manuscript she'd brought home, and after a few pages found herself able to concentrate on its text. Soon it became compelling, and for the next few hours she found blessed relief buried in its pages. This, she decided, was a winner.

But when she finally surrendered to sleep, nightmares assaulted her.

Now this morning her dear friend and mentor was looking at her with a concerned expression that had nothing to do with Claire's efficiency and everything to do with her welfare. "Shit at and hit," Ro had said. She wasn't far off the mark.

"My country cousin's really giving me hell today," Claire admitted, her voice soft. "Do I really look that terrible?"

"Well, let's see: your eyes are red around the rims and there's more shadow under them than above; your mascara is lumpy; your lipstick is sloppy; and your complexion is as pale as your eyes. And girl, that's the nicest thing about how you look. Come on, you and I are going right to the ladies' room, right now, and get you straightened out."

Fifteen minutes later, Rowena gave the nod to Claire's reflection. "Human," she said. "Barely, but human." Claire grimaced. "Hey, honey, we did a major makeover here, and in record time. No sour puss, all right?"

"I'm sorry, Ro, it's not a reflection on you."

"Pun intended?" she asked, looking into the mirror. "Are we getting back to normal now?"

"I guess we are; thanks."

"You know, you can call in sick, right?"

"Uh huh. You'll remember, I've done it before. But I wanted to come in and show you this manuscript. Got a minute?"

Rowena retrieved the MS from Claire's desk and skimmed the first few chapters as Claire stared hopefully at her. "We'll take this to Ray," she said.

"You really do love him, don't you, Ro? Platonically, of coure." said Claire as they walked down the hall.

"Sure do, sweetie. He's a prince. And a role model, too, if I can tell you without your following it up with a lecture."

"Meaning?"

"Back in the day, Ray was a three-pack-a-day smoker. After his latest heart attack, he gave it up cold turkey. I figure if he can do it, so can I. But I do intend to get pregnant first."

"Did you say his *latest* heart attack?"

"Uh huh. His second. Doc said the next would be the last. He blamed it on the pressures of the job, the deadlines, the bills, whatever. I mentioned to Ray about maybe taking the company public and delegating some of his authority to others, but he said never. He said small means he's responsible to his staff and his authors; big means he's responsible to his shareholders, and that means the bottom line. Ray Jones is the last of his line—his parents left him enough money that he never needed to work at all—and he took up publishing simply because of his love for language and literature. And disseminating it."

"A real idealist. You never told me that."

"He's modest, he doesn't want it known how sweet he is. Opens one up to be taken advantage of by people less scrupulous than him. Oops, I mean than he. Anyway, zip your lip, sweetie. This conversation never took place."

* * *

Many a business owner or administrator will tell his employees his office door is always open to them, but it's usually just another in a string of well-intentioned lies. Radu Jones's door was never open—because his office didn't have a door. True, it had the corner view, and true, there was a small conference room adjacent to his office that did have a door for private meetings with authors and their attorneys. But the person who spent the most time in it was the custodian. Jones didn't even have a private lavatory.

The office of the president, or CEO, or owner of the company (there was no sign indicating his title next to his nameplate screwed beside the jamb) could have been a veritable Taj Mahal, a tribute not to lost love but to self love. It could have been, but Radu Jones's office was spartan: not even an anteroom with a private secretary. A large desk, a phone with multiple lines, a computer, floor-to-ceiling bookshelves, a plasma television (always tuned to a cable news station but nearly always muted), and a sofa and chairs comprised its furnishings and appointments. Those, plus the walls with Jones's collection of new still lifes and landscapes by an artist who painted under the name of H. Hargrove.

"He's not a native-born American," said Jones when Claire remarked about them. "He's from Sicily. Came here as a young man to work as a chemist in an upstate New York winery. He painted on the weekends, and the owners displayed the paintings in the public tasting room. When the visitors showed more intereset in his paintings than the wine, the die was cast, and young Nicolo Sturiano crossed the Rubicon. He built his reputation with depictions of Americana, so he gave himself an American pseudonym. I met him once at a gallery show, and we talked for quite a while. Very nice gentleman and completely self-made. Never had an art lesson in his life, can you believe it. Yet, he's managed to become world famous in spite of it."

Claire said. "You're both self-made men, and you're both successful. It's reasonable that you'd get along so well."

"These paintings here happen to be giclées," Jones said as he made a sweeping gesture. Claire frowned. "Puzzled me, too, until he told me they're museum-quality reproductions, made from the originals using computers. You can't tell them from the originals. That said, I had to have a few originals to hang in my house."

"Boss," Rowena said, "sorry to interrupt the lesson, but Claire here has a manuscript she thinks is worth a read. Based upon a quick scan, I tend to agree."

"Sit down, ladies, and let me see it."

Claire handed him the MS, and he sat on the edge of his desk and began speed-reading. "I think you're probably right, Claire," he said. "I'll take it home tonight. Can't say much for the title, though. *Memoirs of a Seventh-Grade Teacher* hardly stirs the blood. What in particular struck you about this?"

"Okay, full disclosure here. My best teacher ever was in seventh grade. He was warm, and he was funny. But he was probably one of the most demanding teachers I ever had. He taught English, and I guess it was there that I picked up my love for grammar. I loved his love for precision in writing and in speaking. We even had to learn 24-hour time— the kids called it army time—so there would be no doubt as to whether we were talking AM or PM. There was no confusing 0730 with 1930, for example."

"Sounds to me," Jones said with a smile, "that he might have been your first adolescent crush, too." He raised his eyebrows. "Claire, are you blushing?"

"All right, Ray, you got me. But anyway, back to this book. The author, Gene Franks, is retired now, which means he finally has time to write for pleasure. I know his title is nothing, and he admits it. His cover letter confirms it's just a working title that tells what the book is about, and if the MS looks promising he'd be happy to come up with something better. Or he'd let the publisher decide."

"Oh? And has 'the publisher' decided?"

"All right, I'm blushing again. But I thought we could capitalize on another best seller and call it *All I Really Need to Know I Learned in Seventh Grade—from My Students*."

Jones tented his fingers and pursed his lips as Rowena grinned. "That is a shameless steal, Claire. Shameless. But I like it. Have you already stricken the manuscript with your deadly blue pencil?"

"Yes. There wasn't that much to strike, actually. I did rearrange some paragraphs for flow and ask for some expository information here and there, but grammatically speaking, this guy seems to know his stuff. And it gave me some insight into what it's like to sit at the big desk. There used to be a saying in the school I went to: 'The Lord made the bee, and the bee made the honey. We do the work, and the teachers get the money.' If people really knew what teachers do, or at least what some teachers do —because I had some real duds along the way, too—they'd be paid a heck of a lot more."

"And seeing how you turned out, I'd like to pay your old teacher a handsome bonus myself. All right, Claire," he said. If I agree with you as to its potential, we'll call the author and set up a meeting." He glanced up. "Hello, what's this?" He picked up the television's remote and clicked the mute button. The banner on the bottom of the screen screamed BREAKING NEWS.

"—a grisly discovery this morning along the Appalachian Trail near Great Barrington," the breathless male announcer intoned with an urgency that suggested an erection just below camera range. The bodies of two campers, along with the savagely dismembered body of a third person ..."

Claire put her hand to her mouth. "Excuse me, sir, but I think I might be sick." And she bolted from the room.

Chapter Seven

Saturday, September 13, saw Claire and Lukas driving south from Criterion to Francestown, having promised each other on the day of the "grisly discovery" never to visit the Appalachian Trail again. Lukas had missed seeing Claire two weekends, citing pressure from Professor Moceanu to schedule meetings on the occasional Saturday or Sunday. Truly, he thought, the woman doesn't have a life. Which made him wonder, because his faculty advisor was really a handsome lady—all right, make that distinctively attractive. She favored dark clothing that hugged her slim form, and her nearly black hair framed her pale face with its dark lips, Roman nose, and subtly lined black eyes. She wore no wedding ring; clearly, she could or should be spending her weekends with any number of eager suitors. Then again, maybe she didn't have a life by choice. And that meant she didn't consider others needed to have a life either.

They arrived at their traditional hunting spot just as the sun was going down. "Listen!" said Claire as they left the car. "Wolves!"

Lukas said, "Surprise. This is why I wanted us to come here. I heard them one night last week. Didn't approach them, though." He began walking. "Come on, let's go."

It was three nights after the full moon. As it rose, its cold light replaced the warm glare of the sun. On they strode through the forest, along familiar trails, and after a few minutes they found themselves in a clearing, upwind from a pack of wolves tearing at a kill. The animals lifted their shaggy heads and stared at the intruders. The largest of them, his muzzle red and his belly distended, stood off to the side as the others of his family froze in position over the body of the doe.

"The alpha," whispered Lukas. "Watch." He took two steps toward the wolves. The large male lowered his head and took two paces toward the human. They continued in this two-steps-then-halt routine until they were within arm's reach. Lukas stared into the wolf's intelligent eyes and nodded, whereupon the great beast rolled over upon its back, legs extended. Lukas crouched and scratched the wolf's belly, whispered soothingly in its ear, and stood. The wolf regained its feet, turned, and walked back to the others, tail high. One or two of them made low growls, and the alpha snapped at them, sending them back—sullenly, if wolves can be sullen—to the fallen doe.

Lukas backed up to where Claire stood. "We're the alphas here," he said. "Long ago my parents told me that among all predator species, metamorphs are acknowledged to be alphas."

"All right, Lukas, I'm impressed. But you know, in the movies and the like, dogs and other animals are afraid of werewolves. They bark and back away, and..."

"And it's the movies, my dear Luna, the movies."

"But what I'm getting at is that Ro and Bill have adopted this retired racing greyhound, Greycie they call her—"

"Spell that." She did. "Cute. What you'd expect from a word maven. So, anyway ..."

"So, anyway, when I go to their house for dinner, Greycie comes right up to me. When I first saw her, I got spooked, wondering what would she do? But she didn't do anything. She came up to me the way that wolf did to you, lowered her head, and rolled onto her side for a rub. It was beautiful, like we connected."

Something nudged Lukas's leg, and when they looked down they saw a young wolf with a piece of meat in its mouth. It dropped it at their feet and walked back to the kill, the alpha male watching intently.

"Protocol," said Lukas. "That little one is the omega." They removed their clothes, morphed into wolves, and shared the gift. It was the doe's heart.

* * *

The following Monday Claire sat in Rowena's office, clearly anticipating her first in-person meeting with Gene Franks. Radu Jones had green-lighted the book last month, but Claire's attempts to reach the author by phone and e-mail failed.

"Turns out he and his wife were on a cruise," she said. "On a Princess ship bound for the Caribbean out of New York. When I finally reached him and told him Jones Publishing was considering his book, he started stammering, just couldn't believe it. I think he thanked me a dozen times at least. He's driving up from Jersey for our two o'clock meeting. Calls me from every rest stop with a progress report, assures me he'll be here on time."

"I like him already," Rowena said.

"When we spoke initially, his voice and his inflections reminded me of my own seventh-grade teacher. How weird is that? Not only that, but he lives down the shore, a stone's throw away from my old town. It'll be like old home week, right here in Boston."

And so it was. Gene Franks and Claire hit it off as if they'd known each other all their lives. And in terms of manners, he and Radu Jones were a match. Neither used even the mildest of expletives; each stood when a woman entered the room; and each seemed to compete with the other when holding a chair out for the junior editor, treating her like—if not royalty—the VIP she definitely was not.

The meeting went so well that Jones insisted, if the teacher had no other appointments, he would be delighted to invite them both for dinner at his home.

"I live not so opulently as one might expect, but I do indulge myself in a housekeeper and a chef. Emma is a stout German woman who may look unfriendly but is the sweetest person in the world. And neat as a pin. When she cleans a house, the dirt is afraid to come back. Benjamin is her husband. They drive in together, and while she cleans he prepares dinner. I'll call him and ask if he can expand the menu for this evening. What do you say, Gene? Claire?"

"Are you sure it's all right?" asked the teacher. "I don't want to intrude."

"I assure you, you are welcome. Benjamin loves cooking for company. It's his chance to show off his talents to someone besides me. How about you, Claire?"

"I'm game," she replied, and wondered if that were precisely the right word.

* * *

Radu Jones lived in a brick two-story center-hall colonial about a half hour west of Boston, with a fenced in yard and a view of the Charles River from the back deck. Emma greeted them at the door, and although her normal expression might have been a scowl, her smile was positively beatific. Benjamin, in suit and tie and possessing a head of thick white hair complemented by a neatly trimmed mustache, welcomed them all with a bow and a sweeping gesture. He offered a tray of crudités, cheeses, and fruit and asked what they would like to drink.

"Wow," said Gene Franks, "this is a little more elaborate than the old faculty lounge."

"Maybe just a little," Jones replied. "Come, Gene, Claire, let me show you around."

The living room was deeply carpeted, with Mediterranean-style furniture and walls adorned with those original Hargrove paintings her boss had mentioned. Jones told Gene the artist's story while Claire browsed the bookshelves and found some of her own favorites, along with some first editions she dared not even touch. Jones noticed her and called her attention to one in particular.

"That *Alice's Adventures in Wonderland* is a facsimile of Carroll's original, in his own handwriting," he said. "It's charming. There are photos in the introduction of Alice and her three sisters as children, and also Alice on her visit to New York as an octogenarian back in the 1930s."

Claire found the photos as Gene looked over her shoulder. A tall, balding, somewhat spindly type, he could've passed for Ichabod Crane but for his unassuming and modest air. Ichabod, if she remembered correctly, was an obnoxious boor.

"I see Alice is a brunette," Claire said. "How come she's a blonde in the books and the Disney movie?"

"I can answer that," said Gene, looking toward Jones, who nodded. "When Lewis Carroll presented the manuscript to the publisher, it included his own drawings. He was a talented artist and photographer as well as a writer, you know. And a math teacher by day, kind of like yours truly. But much more gifted. Anyway, the publisher accepted the manuscript, but he hired John Tenniel, who was *the* political cartoonist of the day, to do the illustrations. He figured attaching Tenniel's name would guarantee more book sales. When Tenniel drew her as a blonde, Carroll was furious, but there was nothing he could do."

"He was at the publisher's mercy," added Jones. "But don't worry, Gene, there are no illustrations in your book for us to fiddle with. That said, why don't you engage the services of an entertainment lawyer for when we prepare a contract for you."

Gene grinned like a youngster who had just learned the biggest gift under the Christmas tree was his.

Claire looked at another photo and remarked, "I can't imagine Alice as anything other than a little girl. In this photo, she's in her eighties. I feel a sadness for her." She returned the book to its place on the shelf.

"We all grow old, my dear," said Jones.

Gene said, "I decided not to." When they frowned, he added, "Nope, early on I decided I'd refuse to grow old. So I can stay young 'til I die."

Claire smiled. "No wonder your kids loved you."

* * *

After dinner (Claire wanted to eat everyone's portion of the rack of lamb, it was that good), they retired to the living room, where Benjamin served brandy to the men ("I'll never get used to this," said Gene) and iced club soda to Claire.

"I never asked," said Jones. "How was your drive up from New Jersey?"

"Fine, until I got to Boston. I didn't know this was a kamikaze training ground."

They laughed.

"You and your wife live in Manasquan, right?" Claire noted. "I'm from just up 71 in Belmar."

"Is that Exit 71?" asked Jones with a wink.

"Ha ... ha," said Claire. "It's Route 71, smartass—oops, smart alec, oops, sorry, boss. But let me tell you, contrary to popular belief: New Jersey is a lot more than the Turnpike. It has the best beaches, some beautiful lakes and mountains, and even a ski area or two. And if Chef Benjamin goes to a supermarket up here and sees Massachusetts tomatoes next to Jersey tomatoes, which do you think he'd buy, Miss-ter Jones? Huh? The defense rests."

"Hear her?" asked Jones. "I think she's getting defensive, don't you? She calls her beloved employer, pardon me, a smartass. Which could be interpreted as impudent; insubordinate; even subversive. Think I should fire her?"

"Oh, please, no. At least not until the book is published."

They sipped their drinks. It was turning into a lovely evening. Until Gene mentioned the hikers killed on the Appalachian Trail.

"That girl had been one of my seventh-graders," he said. "We remained friends for years. My wife and I went to her wedding. Beautiful day." He paused, eyes staring at something the others couldn't see. "Lovely, lovely girl. Married a good man, too. And to have that scum do what he did to them both ..."

Claire held her breath.

"This is personal for you," said Jones.

Gene nodded. "Very personal. They were sweet kids, just starting out. I'm still in touch with her parents, we've become closer since ... since."

"The police identified their killer."

"Through his vehicle registration. He was a dirtbag from Newark, a mob enforcer who evidently offed innocent people on the side for his own amusement. There are unsolved murders up and down the coast involving hikers, and the FBI's starting to examine DNA evidence to see if there's a link."

Claire sat stone-faced.

"Any idea what did him in? Officially, that is?" asked Jones. "The newspapers just speculate."

"Right. Wild animals, maybe a pack of wolves. The question is, why they would take the trouble to eat him while leaving the other two bodies untouched? That, no one seems to understand. I mean, they were freshly killed and already bloodied—Claire, am I upsetting you?"

"No, no, I'm just a little squeamish is all."

"Sorry. I can tell you this, Ray," he said, leaning forward and lowering his voice. "One of the detectives working the case is also one of my former students. He swore me to secrecy, so maybe I shouldn't be telling you this ..."

"That's entirely up to you," said Jones. "But I have never been known to break a confidence. And I believe I can vouch for Claire." Claire nodded weakly.

"They did DNA tests on the bite marks. Lots of saliva, as you can imagine. The coroner was stumped, and he sent it on up the line to the FBI, and from there it went to some agency the detective had never heard of. The forensics people found animal DNA, which they expected. Specifically, it matched that of a pair of wolves."

Jones said, "That had been expected, although wolves in that area are unheard of."

"But here's the odd part. It's what I'm not supposed to tell anyone. Mixed in with the saliva, kind of homogeneous with it, they found human DNA, as well. DNA that didn't match the killer's or either of his victims. And that little bit of forensic evidence, well, they simply can't explain."

Chapter Eight

Claire phoned Lukas as soon as she got back to her apartment, waking him up. "Lukas, listen to me. Forensics found our DNA at the scene of the camper killings."

"I know that. It was on TV and in the papers. Wolves, they said. They were right. So what?"

"Listen to me, Lukas. Our DNA. They also found *our* DNA, our *human* DNA in the wounds."

"Oh, shit."

"What's that sound?"

"Sound? Oh, the bed creaked. I'm sitting up now. You've got my full attention."

"Do you have your DNA on record anywhere?"

"No … wait a minute, when I was doing my master's work with Gabe he took some samples of my blood, but those are long gone. There's nothing on file with any government or law enforcement group. You?"

"No. Listen, are you absolutely sure there's no record of your DNA?"

"Claire, Luna, listen to me. Pay attention to the voice of reason. Why would anyone come all the way to Upper Nowhere, USA, looking for evidence to link anyone to anything? Most people in the country don't even know Criterion University exists. Meanwhile, we'll swear off people, no matter what, stick with game animals instead. No one ever checks them for DNA."

She pondered a moment. "I don't want to do this any more. I'm done, Lukas."

"No, Luna, I'm afraid you're not." His tone carried a sadness that was almost palpable.

"What do you mean?"

"Neither of us will ever be done. That's the price we pay for the gift."

"A gift I didn't ask for, I would remind you."

"I'm sorry if you still think I tricked you, Claire. I'm sorry that I acted on impulse. I'm sorry that I acted out of love for you."

"Hey. Don't turn it back on me. I feel guilty enough for what I've done. I don't need you to make me feel worse. Or try to."

"I think it'd be best if we hung up now. I'll see you this weekend."

* * *

In Rowena's office the next morning, Claire told her about having had dinner with Ray and Gene, focusing on the instant camaraderie and omitting everything about the murders. "Great work, kid. You're gunning for my job, right?"

"Right. And I'm going to seduce the boss to clinch the deal."

"You are? How exciting." The voice came from the doorway behind Claire. Rowena chortled as Claire spun around, her face already aflame.

"Oh my God!" cried Claire, her hands pressed to her hot cheeks. "Mr. Jones, Ray, I swear to you. I swear, I would never ... oh, God, please don't fire me. I was just teasing Ro, honest, we tease each other all the time."

Jones looked at Rowena, who deadpanned him back. "Not true, boss, we never tease. Don't get along at all. Point of fact, she hates me."

Claire spun back. "Rowena!"

The two burst out laughing as Claire collapsed into herself. "Sit down, Claire," said Jones as Rowena wiped away tears. Claire fell into a chair, still shaking. She looked down at Gene's edited MS in her lap, still too embarrassed to look up.

"I think you've got a sexual harassment case on your hands, Ray," said Rowena. "I'd recommend you dump her. And leave the field open for me."

"Please stop," Claire murmured to her lap, but the corners of her mouth were beginning to turn up.

Jones perched on the edge of Rowena's desk and lifted Claire's chin so their eyes could meet. The skin around his crinkled. "Claire, there's nothing to be embarrassed about. And if you want me to be completely candid, if I were twenty years younger, and you were not already romantically involved, and—most importantly—if you were not in my employ, I would seriously worship you from afar."

Claire knitted her brow. "From afar? What—why would you do that?"

"Speaking frankly, because your brains and your beauty would have intimidated me. I'd have been afraid to approach you."

"Oh no, you've got me blushing again."

Rowena stuck two fingers in and out of her mouth and made gagging sounds. "Stop right there, boss, I've got first dibs, remember? And when it comes to chicks like us, you prefer dark meat, right? You know what they say, 'Once you have black, you ain't goin' back.'"

To which Claire tentatively responded, "Once you have white, you're good for the night."

And Rowena countered with, "Once you have yellow, you're a real mellow fellow."

"Not fair. You're multi-ethnic!"

With the banter dead-ended, Jones turned to Claire, and she noticed for the first time the large clasp envelope in his hand. "Claire, Mr. Franks's contract is ready." He handed it to her. "It's standard issue, standard royalty rate for first-time authors. It won't make him a millionaire, but I think he'll be pleased. If his lawyer is the greedy type and demands more, remind him ..."

"Excuse me, Mr.—excuse me, Ray, but what are you saying?"

"Well, I thought you might want to present the contract to him in person. You used to live nearby, you said; I simply thought you might like to take a few days to visit the old homestead. Maybe enjoy a day or two on one of those lovely beaches you touted. I know it's not the summer any more, but still ..."

"Jeez," said Rowena with mock scorn. "Talk about sucking up to the boss." Claire suddenly looked uncomfortable again. "Hey, kidding, sweetie. Ray gives good perks, know what I mean? Keeps morale up and loyalties strong." She looked at Jones. "Should I tell her you've already promised to double my salary if and when I ever get pregnant?"

"Yes, why don't you do that?"

"Nah, it's none of her business."

Claire looked from one face to the other. "If you two jokers will excuse me, I need to call Gene Franks and then check on the train schedule from Boston to Point Pleasant. And by the way, the fall's the best time at the shore. The Bennies have gone by then."

"Bennies?"

"Tourists, Ro. They come for the benefits of shore life, then leave their litter behind."

"Why don't you drive, Claire?" asked Jones.

"Hmm, let's see. Oh, right, because I don't have a car?"

"You don't? Well, we can't have our representative be seen on a train," Jones said. "Rent a nice car, one that does justice to the prestige of Jones Publishing"—he smirked at his pretended pretentiousness—"and voucher the bill. Don't sleep in a fleabag, either. Treat yourself as someone important. If you feel important—and you are—then you will be better able to represent yourself properly to Mr. Franks's attorney should he, as I mentioned last evening, come across as greedy. I like Gene, but he and his lawyer must be made to understand that as an unknown author with no name draw, he is in no position to negotiate. Understood?"

* * *

Gene Franks understood without having to be made to understand. Meanwhile, his attorney took the contract home with him to study and returned it the next day with no suggestions, corrections, or revisions— but with a bill for his services. Gene was happy to write him a check on the spot.

Upon Claire's arrival in Manasquan, Gene and his wife Nina insisted she stay with them. "We're empty nesters now," Nina said, "and we'll be happy to put you up. Lots of room, don't even think of a hotel. I forbid it." Claire gratefully accepted. She liked Nina immediately. She looked to be a good complement for Gene: some tartness to balance his sweetness.

Between their two meetings with Gene's lawyer, Claire repaired to the Manasquan beach, a short block from the Franks' home. It was unseasonably warm, and she fully enjoyed the heat of the sun on her body, the cold rush of the surf on her legs, and the scent of salt in the air, stronger now that her senses were so acute.

"Season's over, no beach badges to buy," she said upon returning to find Gene in his garage. "Only in New Jersey do they charge you to swim in the ocean."

"Tell me about it," said Gene as he examined an unfinished bookcase. "Wait a minute, young lady. A few days ago you were defending New Jersey to your boss; now you're criticizing it?"

She returned his grin. "Absolutely. I can do that since I'm from here." Only a Jerseyite can make fun of Jersey. Everybody else, hands off." Claire watched as Gene ran his hand down an edge of the case, feeling for any roughness. "You made that, I assume?"

"Yup. Never tried woodworking before. When better than in retirement? I have time now to putter. And you know what's nice about this, Claire? Instant gratification. You know right away if you did it right or wrong. You don't get that in education. Kids aren't wood."

"But they can be shaped and molded like wood."

"Ah, touché. In fact, I remember having taught some whom I thought were made of wood, at least between the ears."

Nina stuck her head into the garage. "Know what else is nice about Gene's woodworking? It keeps him out of my greying hair."

Gene shot a smile at his wife and turned to Claire. "Know what she calls retirement? Twice the husband, half the pay."

Claire looked from one to the other. "You both look like you're suffering so very much."

* * *

"You're originally from Belmar, Claire?" asked Nina at dinner. They were celebrating the signing of the contract at one of the area's most elegant restaurants, Jones Publishing's treat.

"Yes, I left after high school and never came back."

Nina studied Claire's face and opened her mouth as if to ask a question, but unsure of how. Finally: "Do you have family in the area?"

"No. My mom died when I was sixteen, lung cancer." Nina looked as if she'd intruded into forbidden territory. "No, I'm okay talking about it. My dad was a sheetrocker. This was during the building boom at the shore, and he was almost never home. So, Mom smoked herself to death, and he died a year later."

"I'm afraid to ask how. He must've been young."

"He turned on the car with the garage door shut. I found his farewell letter in a large inter-office-type envelope tied to the front door when I got home after school. The whole house stunk from the fumes. I ran next door and called the police."

Gene said, "What a lousy thing. You poor child. I'm sorry."

Claire took a drink of iced tea. "I'm fine now, really. And before he 'did the deed,' Dad made sure I'd be okay financially. Even wrote down the name and number of a realtor friend so I could sell the house for college money after I graduated."

Nina leaned forward. "Are you all right now, Claire? Is there any way we ..."

"And they say I'm a bleeding heart," said Gene.

Claire smiled. "Nina, my life today is perfect, absolutely perfect. I have a great job, a great boss, and a great boyfriend. What could be better?"

Except, she said to herself, *that I'm a freakin' werewolf.*

PART THREE
DACIANA

Chapter Nine

In May 2004, Claire turned twenty-three, and the next month *All I Really Need to Know I Learned in 7th Grade—from My Students* became an instant best seller. Jones confided to Claire it was the title—her title, he stressed—that piqued buyers' curiosity. The book certainly had merit, but without her title it probably would have collected dust in the remainder bin.

Gene Franks's royalties would handily supplement his pension and make his retirement "twice the husband, more than twice the pay," for which Claire was immensely grateful. She genuinely liked both him and Nina and saw in them what her parents could have been. Plus, she remembered, he hadn't raised any objections at all to her editorial suggestions, one of which involved the controversial Oxford comma.

"But explain to me why it's not redundant," he'd said as she pointed out his omission. His voice held no challenge, as if he were still learning, as if this kid less than half his age, this wet-behind-the-ears whelp, could actually have something to teach the teacher. "Strunk and White say that you should use the comma after each item in a series *except* before the conjunction; because the *and* takes the place of the comma."

"Ah, well, let's take a look. Your text here says that on Fridays the cafeteria served, and I quote, pizza, a veggie platter, spaghetti and what the kids called mystery meat, unquote. Later you mention that the mystery meat was usually hamburgers; in other words, not part of a meat sauce for the spaghetti. Putting a comma after *spaghetti* removes the ambiguity; it's no longer spaghetti and meat sauce but 'spaghetti, comma, and what the kids called mystery meat.' Two different choices. Or, let's say the choices included corned beef and cabbage. Without the comma, it's a combo dish; with a comma, it's two separate offerings. The kids can take the corned beef without the cabbage." She thought back. "Not that they would take either, by the way."

"I stand both corrected and enlightened. Thank you, Claire." Not a trace of irony in his voice. "Maybe you should've been a teacher."

"If I had," Claire countered, "you wouldn't have had the great good fortune to have me as an editor, poised to make you a publishing superstar."

Little had she known that was exactly what he would become. Nor would she know that as a result, a coveted parking place in the garage would have her name painted above it, right next to Rowena's.

"It's very touching, but Ray, I don't even own a car," she protested, and he smiled and presented her with a small jewelry box. She frowned, almost afraid to open it. Inside was a key, a blank one from a hardware store. "What?" was all she could think to ask.

Her boss sat behind his desk, looking like the Cheshire cat. Claire looked up from the box, her head tilted to the side.

"It's symbolic," said Ray. "Gene Franks's book is headed for its second printing, at triple the first run. I felt it only proper that you should share in his success and in the company's profits."

"Meaning? I think I know, but I'm afraid to guess."

"Buy yourself a car," he said. "I wouldn't presume to choose one for you; that would be patronizing. Just please don't go whole hog and buy an Aston Martin or a Maserati; I insist you keep it under fifty thousand. Remember, this is a bonus, and you'll be taxed on it."

Claire sat back in her chair, stunned. She brought her fingers to her pentacle as she held the key blank in her other hand. "I … I don't know what to say."

"Perhaps you should call your boyfriend, and tell him that you'll be driving north to see him this weekend instead of taking the bus."

"I could kiss you, no sexual harassment or any other offense intended."

"None taken, and thank you for managing to resist my irresistible charms. No door to the office, remember."

Suddenly blushing—her boss had a talent for making her blush—Claire excused herself and retreated to her own office, where she made that phone call, left a message, and then flew to Rowena's and asked if she wanted to go car shopping with her after work. After some serious haggling (she knew she'd still overpaid), Claire wound up with a champagne-colored Toyota Highlander she dubbed the Golden Goose.

A bit bigger and better than Lukas's Wolfsburg, she thought. And a much less ironic name. She phoned Lukas again, got him on the line, and told him she'd be driving to Criterion on Friday, and that he could put his Little Wolfie to bed for the weekend. He made the remark she'd been sure he would. He followed it up with the news that he was nearly finished with his dissertation, that he'd be called upon to defend it next, and that meant he could see the light at the end of the tunnel—and it wasn't connected to a locomotive.

When she parked in front of his cabin on Friday night, Lukas went ecstatic over the car and was as eager to have Claire show it off as she was. On Saturday they got up at dawn, and she drove him here and there, from the Interstate to the blue highways to the backwoods trails.

Eventually they happened upon a greyhound track.

"I wonder if Ro and Bill got Greycie from here," Claire noted. "I love her to death, she's such a sweet dog. What say we take in a race or two?"

Greyhound racing wasn't what they'd expected. There was something in the air that puzzled them, something unpleasant. Their noses picked it up, mingled among the smells of the beer, the dust, the sweat of the crowd. It was the scent of fear, the acrid scent that stung their nostrils, and it was most noticeable when the dogs, chasing the artificial rabbit around the rail, sped by them. The dogs should be exhilarated, and that was part of it, but it was underlain with fear. They determined to find out why.

The kennels backed up to the woods, and leaping the cyclone fence was no problem for Claire and Lukas. Once there, they hid and watched what happened after the races were done and the crowds had left. The dogs were confined to metal crates, some too small for the larger ones. The animals lay down on their sides, heads on their forelegs, silent, eyes fixed on the handler who walked out from an outbuilding with a bucket of slops. This he emptied into a trough, and when he did the dogs stood in their crates and began to salivate. Their tails curved between their legs in a narrow C. All of them trembled.

Being downwind, Claire and Lukas could smell the food. It was spoiled meat.

The handler walked by the crates and opened them one by one. The dogs flew to the trough and began gorging themselves. By the time the last hounds got to the trough, it was empty. They looked to the handler, a stubble-faced man in a red-and-black-checked flannel shirt and filthy jeans. Their noses turned up to him and then down to the trough. They shook like leaves in a windstorm.

"Don't you get it, asshole?" whispered Claire. "They're starving."

The other dogs, meanwhile, gathered around a communal tub of dirty water and hurriedly slaked their thirst. The hungry ones still buried their noses in the trough, searching for any scraps that might have been left.

"Back in your crates," barked the handler and started grabbing the dogs from the water tub, yanking on their leashes. He forced them inside and fastened the doors. One dog was left, licking the trough, desperate for nourishment. The handler grabbed it by the leash. "You snooze, you lose, shitferbrains." The dog whimpered, and the handler kicked it soundly. Claire and Lukas both flinched at the blow. "Move!" His muddy boot connected again with its ribcage, and the dog cried as it tried to back away, but the handler held tight to the leash and kicked it again. Something cracked. With a yelp, the dog went down and lay still. It was barely breathing.

The handler dragged it by the leash to its crate and picked up the clipboard that lay on top. He looked at it and shook his head. "Yer a fuckin' loser, shitferbrains," he muttered. "You was gonna be whacked anyway."

In the woods, and without a word, two people shed their clothes.

A dumpster stood nearby. The handler removed the collar and leash from the greyhound and placed them on top of the clipboard. He then picked up the dog, sixty pounds of muscle and bone, as if it were a child's stuffed toy. He heaved it up and over the dumpster's top where it fell among the garbage inside.

The handler shuffled over to the empty crate, picked up the clipboard, and made a note with the pencil attached to it with a string. The other dogs suddenly stood in their crates and pressed their bodies against the sides. The handler turned and dropped the clipboard.

Standing three feet from him was a couple who looked like they'd just stepped out of the Garden of Eden. The guy was good looking; but the blonde was a knockout. Their expressions were blank; they just stood there looking at him.

The man spoke. "What's your name?"

"Chuck. What's yours, and who's your friend?"

The woman remained silent. The man said, "It looks like you're fucked, Chuck."

Chuck glowered at the man. "You want a kick in the nuts, smart boy?"

"That's what you'd go for first, eh, Chuck? Well then, maybe we should, too. You want an introduction to my friend? Her name's Luna, and she can do tricks. Show him, Luna."

Before he could move, Chuck found himself held from behind. How'd that bastard do that? He was just standing over there a second ago … what was the blonde doing?

Luna walked toward Chuck, and when she reached him began unfastening his belt. She licked her lips, but it wasn't sexy in the least; in fact, her teeth looked kind of weird. The blonde squatted to pull down his pants and drawers. All he could really see of her was her mane of pale yellow hair. Then she looked up, and what he saw made his bowels release. The guy behind him backed up, dragging Chuck through his own waste, his hand clasped over his mouth so he couldn't scream.

The woman's face had a downy coat of fur. Her jaw was extended, and her brow ridge drew down over her grey eyes, eyes which contained not one ounce of mercy. She snarled, and when she did her lips drew back to expose the most frightening fangs he had ever seen. Curved cutlasses they were, and he watched as her snout extended, the tip of her nose turning dark. Her taloned fingers crept up his naked leg.

The handler couldn't move, couldn't scream. His arms were locked behind him, his legs were ice, and he could feel his testicles retract. "Luna can't talk when she's like that," the man said calmly, so I'll explain for her. See, Chuck, you didn't give these puppies enough to eat, and what you did give them was rotten. We could smell it all the way over there in the woods. So we're going to make sure they all get fed. And this time, maybe for the first time in their lives, the meat will be fresh."

Chuck's eyes nearly popped out of his head as he felt the woman's claws clamp around his testes. Then came the pain: the most agonizing pain, pain beyond anything imaginable. It shot from his groin to his gut.

His intestines felt like they were being pulled out of his crotch. He tried to scream like a pig in a slaughterhouse. He knew what that sounded like, because he used to work in one and really enjoyed it. His scream never escaped his mouth. He felt the fire of torn flesh, felt blood rush down his leg, and then he watched with renewed horror as the woman-thing fed his nuts to one of the starving dogs. It accepted the morsel without showing any fear of the thing, and it licked its lips as if asking for more.

The woman returned, ripped off Chuck's shirt, and tore off a patch, which she shoved into his wound. From behind him, he heard the man: "Don't want you to bleed out on us, Chuckles, now do we?"

Luna paused before Chuck and looked to Lukas. She glanced at the dumpster, and he nodded. Chuck wasn't going anywhere. She leaped atop the dumpster and dropped inside. The mortally injured greyhound was not the only dog in there, but it was the only one still breathing, albeit barely. Its rib cage had been kicked in, and it lay there looking up at her, tongue lolling, blood flowing from its jaws and frothing at its nostrils. Its gentle, intelligent eyes stared at her without fear; pleading, perhaps. Unable to speak now, Luna was able to think, and to feel, and tears dripped from her eyes as she held the dog's head gently in her own leathery hands. *I'm so sorry*, she thought, and snapped the animal's neck.

When she returned from the dumpster, she saw Lukas pressing Chuck's face into his excrement. "Bad Chucky, bad dog," he chided. Then he flipped him onto his back. "Bite-sized pieces, I presume?" She nodded her lupine head. "Then I guess I'd better join you. The dogs are hungry." He tore another patch from Chuck's shirt and forced it into his mouth, without bothering to wipe his face first. Then he and Luna both morphed fully and tore the handler apart.

When they had finished, they returned to human form and placed the pieces in the trough. Claire got fresh water for the tub as Lukas released the crates' doors. The dogs bolted for the trough as their liberators washed at the spigot that fed the tub. The hounds had never eaten so well in their lives.

* * *

The next morning, watching the news on Lukas's small television, Claire groaned when she learned that all the dogs had been put down after the carnage had been discovered. The spin, of course, was that the greyhounds had gone wild and for some unknown reason had attacked their trusted and beloved handler, Mr. Charles Conklin.

"As if those gentle, helpless animals could ever go wild. They were more like abused children, too frightened even to look you in the eye. Where is the Humane Society? How come you can't so much as kill a cockroach in a movie without the ASPCA on your ass, but you can commit this—this *obscenity* to dogs and nobody says a word? Those sweet, beautiful animals, they're—they're our *kin*, Lukas. Do you realize that? And we got them all killed."

Claire cried openly, continuing to blame herself for not thinking beyond simple vengeance, for not seeing the unintended consequences. Lukas countered by telling her matter-of-factly that the dogs were better off dead, and the world was better off without the beloved Mr. Charles Conklin. Then he drove home the most damning message of all. "Come on. Admit it, Claire. You loved being Luna. You loved making the kill."

"I never knew you could be so cold," she said, the bitterness in her voice joined by a certain dreaded acknowledgment. Because somewhere deep inside her, she knew that Lukas was right. Did the predatory instincts of the wolf, she wondered, have the power over time to overcome her humanity? Or was she simply plumbing her own psyche and discovering that within her did lurk a killer? "I swear. I swear before you right now," Claire whispered with an intensity that almost made it seem a shout, "that I will never hunt another human again."

Lukas looked at her and shook his head. "Sure. Like you've never said those words before."

A moment passed in which neither spoke. Then Claire stood, the dried tears marking a trail on her cheeks. "I have some other words for you. Go fuck yourself."

He watched her without speaking, hurt, knowing he'd said exactly the wrong thing and knowing he deserved her scorn. Claire hurriedly stuffed her clothes, toiletries, and whatever else she had stored at Lukas's into her duffel and stormed out without so much as looking at him.

* * *

Tears fogged Claire's vision as she drove south toward Massachusetts. Tears for the dogs, tears for the thousands of other greyhounds being abused at who knew how many dog tracks around the country, tears for

Lukas and for herself. What had he been trying to say to her back in his cabin that made her drop the F-bomb, a word she never used? Was he really so cold, or was he simply a realist? She feared each possibility equally.

After a kill, after they'd filled their bellies with the organs of their animal prey, they felt an indescribable feeling of power, of freedom, of being an unstoppable force of nature, at one with the wild. And the sex after their meal was a part of that, whether she and Lukas were in human form, wolf form, or somewhere in between. Afterward, for days and even weeks, she would feel no compulsion to hunt, but as the moon waxed and her monthly cycle drew near, she would experience urges that were definitely beyond human, urges both sexual and predatory. Going through the change itself was a kind of electric foreplay.

And she was never totally human now, anyway. Her hearing and sense of smell were acute, her night vision was enhanced, and she was stronger than any normal person, woman or man, had a right to be. In fact, she had to be careful not to give her strength away. She could leap her own body height, run like a thoroughbred, even break a man's spine if she were to hug him too hard. And then there was the matter of her appetite. Her grocery bill was twice what it should have been, and most of it went for meat—most, but not all of which, she cooked.

She believed she loved Lukas, but there was something in his voice, the last words he'd spoken to her that morning, that shook her to her core. Not only what he'd said, but his tone when he'd said it. As if there were something he hadn't told her yet, something important, about her being a metamorph. About their both being metamorphs.

Then there was that other bomb, the one he'd dropped without thinking the morning after he'd turned her, about wishing that her last name were his. He'd said it in response to her anger; had it been spoken out of conviction or of weakness? He hadn't mentioned it since, but the question still hung there, waiting for her reply.

Her mind raced. What if? And, oh, my God, what about children? Lukas had been born to werewolves; he'd had no choice as to what he was. Do I even want children … now? Could I dare nursing one without risking a nipple? Should I get myself spayed? Spayed? *Spayed*? Come on, Claire. But, well, if I don't marry Lukas, could I have children with someone else? More to the point, do I even *want* to get married? I always assumed that one day I would, but now …

That's it, she thought. I'm making a one-eighty and sorting this whole thing out. Never go to bed mad at each other, so says the old cliché—strike that, all clichés are old. *God, now I know I'm stressed. When I make a grammatical mistake* ... and on top of the F-bomb, well. It's a beautiful day, why not kiss and make up and make it perfect. Yes. Let's get things sorted out, get some questions answered, make up ...

Claire exited the Interstate and doubled back.

* * *

The woman walked into Lukas's cabin without knocking. Of medium height, slim, dressed in a loose black pullover and long black skirt, she seemed to glide across the floor to where Lukas sat at his dinette table. Her hair was long and dark, her complexion pale, her eyes coal. Her age would have been hard to determine: she could have been thirty-five; she could have been ten years older. What was not hard to determine, though, was her power to attract. And, perhaps, intimidate.

"Hello, Lukas. I thought I would get to meet your friend today. Didn't you tell me she would be spending the weekend with you?"

"Daciana," Lukas said, standing. "You surprised me. Lu—Claire and I had a bit of a row, I'm afraid. She's already left. I'll call her later when she's back in Boston. And hopefully cooled off some. I mean, if you want, you can meet her another time."

"I see. Well, these things happen, don't they? So. Down to business then. You have something for me?"

Professor Daciana Moceanu, Lukas's faculty advisor, sat down at the table and waited for him to present the last chapter of his dissertation. She thumbed through the pages, nodding and hmm-ing here and there. Putting the pages aside, she stared at him. Her eyes were somehow compelling.

Her voice carried a faint trace of Eastern European accent, much like Gabe's. Lukas assumed she probably knew his graduate advisor, but she never spoke of him. In fact, she never spoke of anything personal, except for her casual interest in his relationship with Claire. At every meeting, the topic of discussion was always his progress.

A knock at the door interrupted their discussion. Excusing himself, Lukas opened the door to find Claire standing there. Her expression changed immediately when she saw his visitor. She took a breath and said, "I didn't know you had company. I'll leave."

"Don't," Lukas said hurriedly. "Come in. Daciana, I'd like you to meet Claire. Claire, this is my Ph.D. advisor, Da—"

"Doctor Moceanu," the woman said, turning her head but not extending her hand. "You are the young woman Mr. Ehrlich has been seeing." Her tone was matter of fact, neither friendly nor hostile.

"So, I can see you're studying," Claire said to Lukas, annoyed at how awkward, how *duh!* she sounded. "I'll leave you to your work."

"No, Claire, let me fix us some lunch, and—"

"No. Your work comes first. You two are busy, and I'd be a distraction." No word of protest came from Dr. Moceanu. "Call me later tonight if you think of it."

If you can get away from Morticia Addams, that is, she thought moments later as she flew the Goose south toward Boston.

*   *   *

Silence filled the cabin for a moment after Claire left. Lukas stood in the open doorway, and for a long moment his mind went blank. He had seen the tension in Claire's face; he couldn't miss it. *What did she believe,* he thought: that as soon as she stormed out this morning I called in a replacement?

She tells me to fuck myself all because of some dumb damned dogs, and I'm supposed to come whimpering at her feet, begging her to pet me, throw me a bone? Not in this lifetime, Miss Claire de Lune.

All right, that was his asshole speaking; his mind knew better. And he did feel sorry about the dogs.

His thoughts returned to Daciana. She respected him, treated him like a colleague, an intellectual equal. She knew his intellect, yes, but she had no idea of *what* he was. That secret was his ... and one other's only; two, if he counted Gabe.

Lukas closed the door and became aware of movement behind him. He turned to find Daciana standing close. Her eyes picked up light from the windows, and a half smile played about her lips. His nostrils flared at an unmistakable scent, a scent which triggered an unmistakable and sudden reaction. *Oh my God, I've got wood,* he thought. Not wood, more like a titanium pipe. What's going on?

"You feel it, don't you, Lukas?" she asked.

He backed against the door. "Daciana, Claire ..."

"Is a child. You saw how she looked at me, you heard what she said."

"She barely spoke."

"But in her body language, she betrayed herself. In her voice, she betrayed her possessiveness, her need for control. I make no such demands upon my lovers."

He gulped. "Lovers? Plural?"

"Don't be naïve, Lukas. I am not chaste, but I am discreet. No one need know."

The pressure in his pants was hard to bear.

"Besides, I have something that I think you will find very attractive."

"Daciana, you are totally attractive, and I'm flattered—honored— that you might want …"

She kissed him, and her tongue darted into his mouth. Lukas's palms pressed back against the rough wooden door, but she could feel his need and pressed her hips to his. With a will of their own, his hands reached behind her and cupped her buttocks, cupped her hard.

"That's better," she said, her lips brushing his. "But when I said I had something you'd find attractive, I was not referring to my sex. Although you will soon see that I am a formidable partner." She backed away at arm's length, looked down at the bulge in his trousers, and smiled. "I believe you may be able to match me, however. Soon. But first: Lukas, I am fully aware of your little secret. Yours and your friend Miss Delaney's."

He went cold. He thought he should say something like, Yes, a grad student with a hard-on for his advisor, but her eyes told him that she knew. She really knew.

"I have studied Gabriel's notes."

His knees went weak.

"I know fully of your curse. Not the *loup garou*, that is no curse at all, that is a gift."

What I told Claire, he thought, and she cursed me. And Gabe called it a disease.

"I am talking about the curse that took your parents, the curse that is in the process of taking you. I can lift it, without any help from Gabriel and his experimental potions."

Lukas's jaw went slack. "I need to sit down."

"Yes, sit."

She led him, without resistance, to his bed. He sat with his back against the headboard, and Daciana unbuttoned his shirt. He looked at her, unspeaking, as she took off her top. Her breasts were small. He could see her nipples pressing against the cups of her bra. I can't, he wanted to say, but more, he wanted to know what she knew, how she'd gotten to Gabe's notes—was he one of her lovers?—and, most important, how she could cure him, just like that, when Gabe, after years of research, was unable to crack the code. And what did she want in return?

She answered that question first. "When we make love, Lukas, I want you to turn me. I want to become what it is you call a metamorph. It's a silly term, I think, descriptive yes, scientific yes, but oh so dry, no romance, no glamour to it at all. I want to hunt as you hunt, kill as you kill, make love as you do, as a wolf. That is what I want. In return, I will remove from you the sword that hangs over your head even as we speak. Yes, I can do that, and I can do that today."

He watched a smile play about her lips as she unzipped her skirt and stepped out of it. She radiated sex, and her pheromones swarmed into his nostrils like a rush of hornets. She wanted to become like him. She wanted the power. She was a natural predator, unlike Claire, who rebelled against the change. Daciana would embrace it. And now she was crawling onto the bed, straddling his legs, kneeling before him, her hands on his shoulders.

"I will give you freedom from your fear, freedom from the curse," she said, her voice husky. He could see flecks of saliva at the corners of her mouth. How, he wondered, how could she do that, how could she be so sure, having just read Gabe's notes? No analysis, no hypothesis, no experiments, no testing? It's illogical, absurd. Impossible.

Daciana saw the doubt in his face. She would resolve that doubt, now. She placed her palms against his cheeks, comforting him as if he were a child. Her smile broadened. "You give me your gift ... and I will give you mine."

And Lukas understood.

* * *

Hours later, Daciana Moceanu left Lukas's cabin and walked across the campus to her own home, the one she shared with her husband. The wound at the junction of neck and shoulder was nearly healed. Before she walked in, she leaned forward and tore holes in her skirt and ripped her panties. She squeezed some blood from the wound and spread it along the inside of one thigh. She spit onto her fingers and smeared her mascara. It trailed down her cheeks like black tears. Then she threw herself against the door and opened it.

Gabriel Zeklos dropped his glass of wine. It shattered on the hardwood floor, but he didn't notice as he ran toward his wife. "Daciana! What happened?"

"Oh, Gabriel," she wept. "Look at me. Look. He … he raped me."

"What? Who?"

"It was … it was that student, Lukas Ehrlich."

"Lukas? But I can't understand …"

"I was in his cabin, going over his dissertation, and from out of the blue he began telling me that over the time we've been working together he'd become attracted to me, and …"

"But the Delaney girl, he told me he intended to marry …"

"He said she's a child, she doesn't understand what love is."

"She's a metamorph, like him! He turned her, he can't just desert her!"

"Don't shout, it's me you should be concerned about."

He took her in his arms. "Oh, my darling, you are all I am concerned about. Are you hurt? Did he hurt you?"

"He hurt me very much. He's so strong, Gabriel."

"I'm going to..."

She put a hand on his arm. "No, dear, you mustn't. If you confront him, I think he might lose control and kill you. Please, just let me collect my thoughts." She took a breath and nodded. "I'm going to be all right, darling. Listen. I'm going to throw these clothes away and take a hot bath. A long hot bath. When I'm done, we'll sit down over a cup of tea and discuss, calmly, what we're going to do about this. All right?" She kissed his cheek, and they embraced.

Daciana stripped off her clothes and put them in a black plastic garbage bag. She gave her husband a weak smile, blew him a kiss, walked into the bathroom, and closed the door. Soon he heard the sound of water running into the tub.

Gabriel Zeklos stood watching the bathroom door, immobile, for what seemed like a long time. Then he spun around and left the house. He headed toward his office in the science building. In his hand he carried the key to his gun locker.

* * *

When midnight came without a phone call, Claire put down the manuscript she'd been half-reading, set the alarm, and turned out the lamp. She unconsciously stroked the pentacle around her neck as she tried to give herself over to sleep but never fully succeeded. The next morning she reported to work with luggage under her bloodshot eyes.

Chapter Ten

"Well, if it isn't Miss Shot-at-and-missed," quipped Rowena from behind her desk when Claire stopped by to say good morning. She put down the *Globe* and cocked her head.

"Sleepless night."

"Must've been a good weekend. Or a bad one. How's Lukas?"

"Oh … Lukas's fine."

"Well, there's a ringing endorsement. Listen, Claire, I'd love to delve into your love life, but I think you might want to see this." She turned the paper around. "Your school: Criterion, in New Hampshire, right?" Claire nodded. "There are no real details yet, it's too soon. Reporters are probably swarming over the place now, getting in the police's way."

"I'm sorry?"

"Here." She pointed to a headline.

NH PROFESSOR SLAIN IN VICIOUS ANIMAL ATTACK
Remains Found in Grad Student's Cabin; Student Missing

Claire fainted.

* * *

What was I thinking, she wondered as her mind mucked its way back from wherever it had been. *Animal attack* doesn't mean Lukas. *New*

Hampshire professor doesn't mean Morticia. *Grad Student's cabin* doesn't mean Lukas's. But if you put them all together … circumstantial evidence … where am I? What's that cold drippy thing on my head?

She awoke on the sofa in Radu Jones's office, a wet hand towel over her forehead. Jones knelt beside her, looking helpless. Rowena stood a few paces back. "Claire?" said Jones. "Are you all right?"

Claire blinked her eyes—they were so heavy—and then snapped them open wide. She tried to sit up, but her boss's hand on her shoulder urged her to stay put. She couldn't summon the will to resist. His face was so concerned, so kind … "I didn't sleep last night," she murmured. "Didn't eat breakfast, guess I'm just weak."

The telephone rang. Claire stiffened as if jolted by an electric shock. "Only the phone," Jones said. "Relax, Claire, stay still. Please don't try to get up just yet. Rowena, maybe some water?"

"Gotcha, boss," Rowena replied and headed for the lavatory.

Claire heard Jones's voice in the background, but she didn't listen to his words.

Think, Claire, what kinds of wild animals are up there near the campus? Certainly not wolves, they wouldn't come near the place. Bears? Possibly. Yes, probably a bear. Maybe some doofus prof saw a bear foraging and decided to offer it something to eat, maybe a candy bar, and maybe she—he—was even dumb enough to try to hand-feed it. Or maybe he saw a bear, got scared, and ran. You don't run from a bear, that incites it, everyone knows that …

But she kept coming back to what she intuitively knew was the truth: that for some reason her boyfriend had morphed into a wolf and killed his doctoral advisor. But why?

Rowena returned with a glass of water. Claire got herself upright, thanked Rowena, and sipped from the glass. She placed the hand towel on the arm of the sofa. Her forehead was still damp, but her skin wasn't so clammy anymore. They both looked to Radu Jones, whose face was pale and lined with sadness. "Of course, of course. I'll be there. And if there is anything I can do in the meantime … Yes. I'll see you soon. Goodbye."

Somewhat unsteadily, Claire got to her feet and stood beside Rowena. Two pairs of eyes zeroed in on one. Jones leaned against his desk. "That was Daciana Moceanu," he said, so softly that Rowena strained to hear.

Claire's grip tightened on the glass.

"The funeral will be in three days. Claire, perhaps you would like to accompany me. You knew the victim, after all. Rowena, can I leave you in charge?"

"What—what's going on?" Claire had to fight to keep from stammering.

Rowena eased Claire back on the sofa. "She didn't read past the headline before she fainted," she explained. Jones nodded, his expression grim.

"I don't know quite how to explain, Claire. The police are calling your friend Lukas Ehrlich a person of interest, as the body was found in his cabin near the campus, and he has apparently vanished."

"Lukas? No, impossible. But wait: the body?"

"Was of the gentleman who referred you for employment. Daciana's husband, and my dear old friend, Gabriel Zeklos."

The glass shattered in Claire's hand, drawing blood and flooding her lap with water. Which camouflaged for a few seconds the fact that her bladder released at the same time.

* * *

"Thank you again for asking me to join you," Claire whispered three days later as they stood behind the fully occupied chairs at the graveside service. More were standing than sitting: college kids in casual wear, some neat, some grungy; older men and women, faculty, she supposed, most dressed in dark suits or ensembles, one or two Asian women in mourning white.

Radu Jones nodded, eyes fixed on the mourners, the canopy, and the coffin beneath it. "You're welcome again."

"I don't know if I should have come, what with Lukas's being a 'person of interest' and all."

Another nod. "I asked you to come as much for me as for Gabe."

She looked at him. His expression was inscrutable. "You did?"

"I'm no tower of strength. I need the support."

"Then I'm grateful you think I can provide it."

The day was bright, not a cloud in the sky; no drizzle to enshroud the mourners; not an umbrella in sight. Daciana Moceanu sat front row center, under the canopy, sunglasses hiding her eyes. She sat still as a stone throughout the priest's homily and the tributes of fellow faculty members and friends.

There was no other family.

"I only met Professor Zeklos that once when he advised me of your job opening. He seemed awfully nice; intense, but not aloof. Does that make sense? I think I'm rambling."

"Gabe was intense, that's true. He was dedicated to his work and to his students. And to his wife. I was best man at their wedding."

"I never even knew he was married. Lukas never mentioned it."

"He probably didn't know. Gabe was private in his personal life. I don't think any student ever knew anything about him that wasn't related to academics."

Claire thought back to her days as a student. "They probably never asked. Not interested in their teachers beyond what they could learn from them." She grimaced. "Or how they could wrangle a grade."

"I wonder..."

"Yes, that's by way of admission. Maybe confession would be more appropriate."

"Thank you for that. You've grown, Claire."

In more ways than you know, boss, she thought.

* * *

Finally, everyone filed past the closed casket containing whatever remained of Gabriel Zeklos and placed a flower on top. His widow stood amidst a small knot of colleagues and accepted their condolences. Most of the students and some of the adults held back, talking amongst themselves and looking uncomfortable. Daciana looked outside the group, saw Jones and Claire, and excused herself. She hugged Jones lightly and accepted Claire's hand. The professor's hand felt cold. Her eyes were hidden behind her glasses.

"I'm so sorry," Claire offered.

"Thank you, Miss Delaney." Daciana looked down. "Your hand."

Claire glanced down at the bandage. "Broken glass," she said, dismissing the bandage. "A few stitches, nothing serious. Just a klutz, I'm afraid."

"So you do have an imperfection. From the way Mr. Ehrlich spoke, you had none. I am glad to see that you are in fact human ... like the rest of us."

"About Lukas ..." Claire began and realized she didn't know how to continue.

"Nothing need be said."

Jones broke the suddenly awkward silence. "So, no word of Lukas then."

Daciana shook her head. Claire wished she could see her eyes. "His car is gone. That's all we know. I know what the authorities are probably thinking, I know what I am thinking, and I can guess what you are thinking. But there is no evidence to support any of those thoughts."

Claire said, "When I met you …"

"We were discussing Lukas's dissertation. I apologize if I seemed aloof; I was deep in concentration on his text and became temporarily disoriented when you walked in. No, don't apologize, it was not your fault. Anyway, I left shortly after you did; Lukas seemed distracted, and our time together wasn't so productive as I'd have liked. When I returned home, I discussed his project with Gabriel, and he said he needed to speak with him. He left the house, and when he didn't return for dinner I called Lukas's cabin. When I got the answering machine, I decided to go there myself."

Jones said, "So you discovered …"

"I'm afraid I did. And I called the police immediately."

Claire stared at the woman. Her voice sounded dispassionate, as if she were lecturing a class, or recounting what she had told the autorities. She wondered, for the thousandth time: why would Lukas kill Gabriel Zeklos, and worse, in his own cabin, where he was sure to be implicated once the body was discovered? Did Gabe even know about Lukas's being a metamorph? Odd, they'd never discussed it, she and Lukas; she'd never thought to bring it up. No, not so odd, she reflected. Gabe was a teacher, after all, and therefore irrelevant—so she'd have thought, as a student then herself. Where was Lukas now? He'd fled, his car hasn't been spotted. He'd probably panicked—which was totally unlike him—and took off. But where would he go?

At least he'd had the sense not to head for Boston. The police had interviewed Claire yesterday and seemed satisfied that she'd not been complicit. Maybe he'd also had the sense not to call before they did, so that she couldn't give anything away. Maybe he'd call her soon, when it was safer, to explain what had happened.

Her stomach lurched. Would the authorities do a DNA test on Gabe's wounds? Find Lukas's along with the wolf's, and then tie it to their killing of that punk Puglio on the Appalachian Trail? Would the FBI or that other unnamed agency Gene had referred to, the one his detective friend had mentioned, take over then, and ask Claire for a sample of her own DNA?

A cold hand brushed against her arm. "Miss Delaney, you look ill."

Claire looked into black lenses. "I'm sorry, my knees went a little weak there."

Jones took her elbow. "Maybe we should go."

Daciana shook her head. "Please stay. The faculty has a small reception planned. You'll need to eat before returning to Boston." She looked directly at Claire. "You could probably use some food in you. I admit I could. Even now, in spite of all this, I still eat like my namesake."

"Sorry, I don't understand."

"No, of course you wouldn't, why would you?" She glanced at Radu Jones and then back to Claire. "In the Romany language, *Daciana* translates as *wolf*."

* * *

An hour later they were back on the road, heading south. "You're quiet," said Jones as he glanced from the road ahead across to Claire. She had been mostly silent, hands clasped, eyes downcast.

She looked at him, her face a mask. "I don't get it," she mumbled. "I've been trying to piece it all together, what happened. I mean, listen, boss, what's wrong with this scenario? Lukas and I had a fight last Sunday. I said something hurtful and left. On the way home, I decided I needed to apologize and drove back to campus. I found Lukas and Mor -- Professor Moceanu sitting at his table, with his papers spread out on it. I hadn't met her before. She was professional, kind of cold, really."

"She tends to give that impression upon first meeting. I felt the same thing years ago, but we've since become friends. Through Gabe. I suspect, given the chance, you'd eventually warm up to each other."

Claire looked at Jones. "Anyway, it was awkward. I couldn't apologize to Lukas with her sitting there, so I left and told him to call me later. He never did. Next day I learn that her husband's been killed, and in Lukas's very cabin. Lukas is gone. His car's gone. It's obvious what happened. Isn't it?"

"But it was an animal attack, Claire. A bear, maybe? An angry bear could probably break down the door."

"But the local black bears aren't all that aggressive. And if the door had been forced open, wouldn't the paper have reported it?"

"I assume so. So to answer your question, I don't know what to make of the scenario either."

"I know, I know, and I'm just repeating what we went over on the way up here. You're so patient with me, Ray. More and more I appreciate why Rowena says she loves you."

"I am irresistible, aren't I?"

"You're being self-deprecating now."

"I can't take myself seriously, if that's what you mean." He tapped his heart. "Life's too short for that." He paused. "As the events of the past few days have borne out."

Claire saw the sadness creep into his eyes. It seemed to mirror her own. She took a breath as she turned her face back to the road. "There's a diner up ahead," she said quietly. "Would you mind?"

"Of course not. But didn't we eat just a little while ago?"

She looked at him, her expression distraught. "It's not that. I think I'm going to be sick."

* * *

Moments after the pair entered the diner, a gray sedan pulled into the parking lot and stopped, its hood pointed toward the windowless side of the building. The car had New Hampshire plates, and on both bumpers were stickers proclaiming *Go Catamounts*. On the rear window was a decal that read *Criterion University*. The driver shut the engine down and got out. He was wearing a dark suit and carried a screwdriver. In seconds he had unscrewed the bolts and lifted the plates off to reveal Massachusetts plates beneath (and in the trunk was another set labeled U.S. Government). The bumper stickers were taped on and came off easily. From inside the back window, he peeled off the plastic decal, then shrugged out of his jacket and replaced his shirt and tie with an unbranded short-sleeved polo. From the glove box he produced a minor league Harrisburg Senators baseball cap and put it on. Then he returned to the front seat and waited.

* * *

Friday, July 2, marked the next full moon, and Claire needed to hunt. There was plenty of light left after work to let her drive to southern New Hampshire before sundown. She parked the Golden Goose in a familiar patch of woods well off the road—thank heaven for all-wheel drive—and waited for sunset. The first time she'd been here had been two years ago with Lukas. They'd returned many times since.

Francestown. More a village than a town, really, surrounded by forests rich with game. Somehow she felt as if she could find her way here from anywhere else in any direction, the way those animals in *The Incredible Journey* remembered how to get home, though they had been hundreds of miles away when they started out. To her wolf self, to Luna, these woods were home.

She had heard nothing from Lukas since she'd left on a Sunday morning early last month, the day after they'd killed the greyhound handler, the day the innocent dogs themselves had been put down by the powers that be. The day she dropped the F-bomb on him, had returned to apologize, and seen him with his professor. Dr. Moceanu had appeared distant then, but at Professor Zeklos's funeral she had been more solicitous to Claire than Claire could bring herself to be with her. First impressions weren't always the right ones, she reminded herself.

She missed Lukas terribly, but she hated not knowing the circumstances around Gabe's death and his own disappearance even more.

Claire was hungry. Ravenous. She could probably have found one of Dink's friends in that dilapidated old bar—no, what was she thinking. "Thou shalt not kill," the Good Book says, and Claire had broken that commandment three times already in the past two years. Fortunately, Dink's death didn't draw attention past the local area. But forensics people had found her DNA in that Newark thug's wounds, and the only reason they didn't find it in Chuck's was because they assumed the dogs had killed him. Not that there was all that much of Chuck left to analyze anyway. For practical reasons if for no other, she had to keep her kills restricted to animals. Other animals.

Claire took the key from the ignition and got out of the car. She locked the door and began walking toward the woods, her nostrils flaring as she tried to pick up a scent. She stepped on a piece of flat metal but didn't look down: junk some hiker had discarded. Deeper into the woods she walked until she found a young tree sprouting low branches. She placed her keys in the crotch of two limbs, then removed her clothes and draped them on top. Her hiking shoes and socks she left at the base of the trunk. Naked now, she looked up at the darkening sky, and although the trees blocked her view of it, she could tell by the fairy light that the full moon was on the rise.

Claire took a breath ... and changed.

Her nails were always the first—maybe, she thought, because that was how Lukas had begun her morphing lessons—and they grew dark and pointed. Not talons like a raptor; after all, she needed them to run, not to capture prey. It was her jaws that caught the prey, and she felt the sublime thrill as her face extended into a snout. She snapped and felt her long, curved canines slide down over her lower jaw. Hair grew like pale yellow grass over her entire body as she sank to all fours. Her spine extended from her pelvis to form a tail, furry as a bottlebrush but infinitely softer. Her breasts compressed against her barrel chest and two nipples were joined by four more.

Were a wildlife biologist to see her in this state, he would marvel at her beauty. That is, until she snarled and drew back her black lips to reveal the scepters within, saliva dripping onto the ground.

The wolf sniffed. Nothing. She turned in a circle, nose to the ground, seeking any scent to pursue. Still nothing. No sign of animal life, except for the gnats that buzzed around her head and the early-season mosquitoes that found the inside of her ears fascinating. The human part of her brain remembered something Lukas had told her, that only the female mosquitoes sucked blood, not the males. Isn't that universal, he'd joked: it's the females who are the bloodsuckers. Where are you now, Lukas, she wondered. Why haven't you come to me, why haven't you called at least, let me know you're all right? Are you all right? People, even werewolves, don't just disappear without a trace.

A scent brought her back to the moment. A mammal, a small one, prowling, rooting. Not a threat -- as if anything out here could be a threat. Criterion University's unremarkable football team was called the Catamounts, but no mountain lions had been seen here for decades. Her ears pricked forward, her head lowered, and she crept along, belly to the earth. There it was, an obscenely fat opossum, pale as chalk dust, with its rat's tail and pointed snout. It was upwind of the wolf and had no idea that its hour had come.

The wolf leaped, ran some fifteen feet, and snapped her jaws around the opossum's back and belly. Her teeth first puckered, then punctured the skin, fat, and flesh. Her head shook the animal from side to side as it squealed once, twice, three times—and then went limp. She bit through the spine—insurance against its playing possum—and released it. She placed a paw upon the opossum and began tearing through its skin to get at its innards.

Later, when nothing was left of her prey but skin, bone, and tail, the wolf backed off and licked her chops. Her appetite was satisfied, if barely, but another yearning would go unfulfilled.

The moon was visible now above the trees, and its light silvered the scene as a lupine body became human once again. Claire's keen eyesight led her directly to the tree where she'd cached her clothes. She tossed her keys into a shoe and tied the laces together. She looped the laces in one hand and held her clothes in the other, relieved of tension again as she walked barefoot toward her autombile.

As she neared the car, she stubbed her toe on something metallic and swore under her breath. The moon illuminated a New Hampshire license plate. Claire caught her breath and dropped her clothes. She stared, rooted.

It was a vanity plate that read LUNA.

Beneath the word was embossed the state's motto: Live Free or Die.

* * *

Downwind from her and hidden by brush, a black wolf fixed ebony eyes on Claire. It watched her pick up the license plate, look around her, and heard her utter a low, keening sound. It was, unmistakably, a whimper. She stood holding the plate, as if unsure of what to do next. Finally, she returned it to the ground where she'd found it. "Lukas?" she cried. The wolf's ears pricked up. "Lukas, what's happening? Where are you? Why did you leave this here, right where you knew I'd find it? Why won't you call me? Come to me? Let me know you're all right? Lukas, Lukas, can you hear me? Where … are … you?"

The woods remained silent.

Claire hunched over, picked up her clothes, and dressed. She swept the area once more with her eyes, drew in a deep breath, let out a long sigh, and walked back to her car with tears trailing down her face. The wolf watched her leave, heard the engine start. Still it didn't move. Only when it heard the car drive away did it enter the clearing, pick up the license plate in its mouth, and move, wraith-like, deeper into the forest.

* * *

Now returned to human form, Daciana Moceanu Zeklos, nee Ibonescu, nee Milosovici, nee Stanga, nee Tugurian, nee Gori, nee a host of others dating back to her original surname Corvinus, carried the license plate deep into the forest to where her own clothes lay in a pile. She thought it very satisfying to be able to torment her young rival this way, though rival she would be no more.

Gabriel's funeral had been a week after last month's full moon. Lukas had told Daciana of Claire's fixation on hunting during the full moon, that it happened to coincide with her period, and that this place was their "Werewolf Walden." Placing the license plate where Claire would have to find it during her hunt had been a touch of sadistic genius. As for Daciana's own monthly cycle, it was but a distant memory, something for which she was infinitely grateful.

Daciana's original lover, whom she still remembered with devotion, had been decapitated in battle against the Turks—some accounts suggested by his own soldiers—and his head sent to Constantinople, never to be rejoined to the rest of his body. No more would he steal softly into her chambers at night, no more would he lavish his love upon her. Cruel he might have been to others, but to her he had always been gentle as the breeze of the Balkan spring.

Her lover did not possess the Gift himself; that came from her first husband, the fool Dobos, whom she destroyed when she discovered his infidelities. She had been young then, naïve, but thanks to the insistence of her father, the king, and her own sense of practicality, ever so skilled with the sword. Dobos never suspected that their private picnic—in a secluded grove known only to Daciana—would end with his being drugged, bound to a tree, and methodically dismembered before she severed his head from what was left of his body. She had burned it down to the skull before grinding it into dust beneath her boot.

Daciana tossed the license plate onto the ground and put on her clothes: undergarments, denims, turtleneck, socks, hiking boots, and leather gloves -- all black. She leaned against a tree and looked up at the full moon. It bathed her pale face in its reflective light.

Gabriel Zeklos: now, Gabriel was no fool, nor was he a cuckold. In fact, he was an honorable man, serious and principled. She had loved him—once—to the degree that she was capable of love. But time had dulled their marriage, and when she finally told him why she never seemed a day older than when they had first met, he had reacted with shock and a palpable fear. She couldn't blame him, but she realized that he might now, however unwittingly, however unwillingly, become a threat to her.

That was where Lukas had come in. He was a handsome boy, strong and no doubt virile, and—best of all—a metamorph. She had never met a werewolf, had in fact dismissed their existence as legend, just as most people dismissed her own Gift as the stuff of campfire tales. But Gabriel's notes had proved conclusive, his research flawless.

Lukas presented new possibilities, new adventures, and frankly Daciana had become bored. Perhaps it was time, or would be soon, to move on. But first, she would have Lukas's Gift; and in return, she would give him hers. The events of that Sunday in early June proved to be a marvel of serendipity. Her husband's and her lover's reactions were exactly as she'd hoped, nay, planned, they would be.

But Lukas, hidden since Gabe's killing in the basement of Gabriel and Daciana's home, could not dissociate himself from the girl he called Luna. Daciana had insisted that he never see her again, that it was for the girl's own safety (as if she cared a whit about that). The authorities would be monitoring the Delaney girl's movements, after all, and it would be no time before they tracked her to him. His DNA was doubtless in Gabriel's wounds. And Lukas's new Gift would not stand against a gurney and a needle. So much of the folklore associated with Daciana's kind was false, had in fact been created by them specifically to mislead, to make their very existence seem preposterous. Gabriel had even refused to acknowledge the name given them; steeped in his science—and perhaps more than a little fearful should he utter it—he instead referred to her as a hemophage.

Daciana had asked Lukas where he and Claire hunted for game, and he told her about the forest outside Francestown. She insisted they visit late one night when she could sneak him out of the house unobserved. Lukas was nervous, distracted, and, she thought, unwilling for now to bestow upon her the devotion that he'd shared with Claire. But Daciana would replace Claire in his affections, of that she was certain.

Claire, after all, would eventually die, and much sooner than she'd thought; Daciana and Lukas would never die.

They entered the woods and disrobed. Half-heartedly, Lukas coached Daciana through the change, her first time to assume total wolf form. Her coat was sleek and black, as shiny as the hair on her human head. Her snout and eyes were coal. She was darker than a shadow—except for her yellow fangs, which dripped sticky saliva.

Daciana nudged Lukas and licked his muzzle, then rubbed her cheek against his. He turned his head to the forest, from which came the sound of stealthy pads that a human ear would never be able to hear.

The wolf pack with which Lukas and Claire had become familiar stood at the edge of the clearing, eyes glinting. One or two gave out a soft whimper. The alpha stepped forward and cocked his head, scrutinizing the two motionless wolves—one of which looked familiar, but its scent had changed to match that of the new wolf, both strange and confusing. The yellow bitch was missing.

Lukas took a step toward the alpha, and the latter took a step back. Then he turned and fled into the woods, the pack on his heels. Lukas lowered his head, knowing that he had lost something he could never regain.

Daciana, thinking that her mate was sniffing for a spoor, lowered her head to the forest loam and finally picked up a scent: a rabbit. She tore off, her nose guiding her like a missile, and the rabbit shrieked as her fangs cleaved its spine. She bit through its skull and was about to draw out the brain when she saw Lukas watching her. She took the rabbit's head between her jaws, holding it as tenderly as a baby, and dropped the carcass at Lukas's front feet. She lifted her muzzle to nudge Lukas's, then lowered it toward the rabbit, as if pointing. Lukas lapped the inside of its skull clean as Daciana watched, satisfied. She was simulating submission, a skill which had proved effective with lovers past.

When he was finished, they stripped the rabbit's flesh and organs from its bones. The two wolves stared at each other, and the bitch caught a glimpse of a red shaft protruding from the male's penile sheath. She slid her head beneath his abdomen and licked at it. The shaft grew longer, and she turned away and offered herself to him. He mounted her and drove himself inside, his hips pistoning against her.

Daciana had never experienced such sensation. It was frantic, urgent, powerful, and when he shot his seed she could feel the force of it splashing against her insides. She sang with joy, her howl reverberating through the trees, and then she fell to her belly, her eyes lidded and her tongue lolling from between her jaws.

A few moments later she heard a sound behind her. It was Lukas, in his human form, naked and looking like a Greek statue. "We need to go," he said. That was it. She didn't know what she'd expected his first words to be after their lovemaking, but those were farthest from her thoughts.

Daciana stood on four legs. The fur on her body began receding into her skin. Her tail, devoid of its bushiness, retracted above her bare buttocks. Her back lost its hump as her spine straightened with a series of barely audible pops. Her paws became hands and feet, her claws became nails. Her snout pulled back into her face as her fangs retracted into her gums. She was now a slim, ebony-haired, attractive woman of indeterminate age, kneeling on all fours.

Lukas reached down his hand and helped her to her feet. Daciana hugged him, her cheek pressed against his chest, one hand sliding between his legs and feeling limpness there. It was all right, though; human sex couldn't compare to what she'd just experienced in lupine form. She closed her eyes and sighed. She could not see the pain on Lukas's face.

* * *

"You must not entertain seeing her again," said Daciana the next night as she snuggled next to him in her bed. Lukas stared at the ceiling, ashamed and yet somehow proud of his lack of response to her sexual advances.

"I can't do that," he said. "Daciana, you have to realize that last night it was the wolf, not the human, who mated with you."

"Interesting word, 'mated.'"

"You know what I mean."

"No, Lukas, I do not."

They lay still for a few moments.

"I said I do not know what you mean."

"In wolf form, animal instinct sometimes trumps the human. But still, as we—made love—I knew I was betraying Claire once again." He turned and met her coal-black eyes. "Daciana, I still love her."

"Listen to me, Lukas. I cannot hide you forever. Plus, I've been here at Criterion long enough. I must change locations periodically before my associates realize that I do not age as they do. I plan to leave Criterion before too much longer, citing continued grief over my husband's murder. And you must come with me, for your own protection. We will start a new life together somewhere far away, with new identities. And if, over the years—or decades, or centuries—we tire of each other, we can simply move on."

"Witness protection," he said, rolling his head from side to side. "I don't like it." He took a breath. "But I see your point." He turned onto his side and propped himself on one elbow. "Listen, I'll do as you say. But I have one condition."

"Condition? You have a condition?"

"Just one. I need you to arrange a meeting with Claire, someplace safe for both of us. I'll tell her everything, tell her about the metamorphs's curse, and give her the chance for me to turn her as you turned me. I'll explain why we can never meet again. She'll understand. And then we'll say goodbye."

Daciana was silent, pretending to think about Lukas's proposition. But she was no fool, and he was playing her for a love-struck one. She knew that after the Delaney girl was turned immortal, Lukas would desert Daciana and take up with her rival again. It was a scenario that Daciana could not abide. Hate came easily to Daciana Moceanu, and she decided that she hated Claire Delaney.

And she would do something about it.

"All right," she said with saccharine sweetness. "How about if I set up a meeting, just the three of us, in the woods outside Francestown?"

"That would be perfect."

"Good. Give me her e-mail address, and I'll send her a message tomorrow from one of the campus computers."

"Thank you, Daciana. I owe you big time."

"Yes. You do."

*　*　*

The full moon was now a week away. Daciana, lying, informed Lukas that Claire had been thrilled to get her message and that she would meet them at the designated spot that coming Sunday. On the Friday prior, Daciana canceled her classes and without informing Lukas drove to Francestown, taking with her certain items she would need later. On Sunday night, June 27, she drove them both to the forest. He had planned to go alone, but she said it would be better if she were the one to turn Claire, as the condition of her blood was "more mature" than his, thus making the change quicker, less painful, and more efficient.

Lukas couldn't argue. Despite the discomfort of two women, rivals for his affection, meeting under these circumstances, he knew it would be best for Claire in the long run, and he agreed -- not that he ever had a choice.

"She wrote in her reply that she wants to hunt with you one last time," Daciana said as they stood in the clearing. "Of course, I deleted her message immediately. I will remain in human form, Lukas, so as not to appear a threat when she arrives about an hour from now."

Anticipation clearly written across his face, Lukas began disrobing. He tossed his shirt to the ground and reached down to untie his shoes. As he did, Daciana took a few steps backward and drew a sword from its hiding place behind a tree. "She's early," she said, and Lukas stood up.

Daciana's ancient sword, razor sharp, cleaved cleanly through Lukas's neck, sending his head tumbling from his shoulders. "I'm truly sorry," she said, and she meant it. She considered Lukas's face as his eyes bulged and blinked, as his mouth opened and closed before growing still. It was reflexive, she'd been told years before by a headsman -- the victim always died the instant his spine was severed -- still, despite what she knew would be Lukas's later attempt at deceiving her, she hated having to do this to him. And -- were it not for her hatred of Claire -- she would never have done what she did to his body next: a small, non-sexual mutilation designed, like the license plate she'd stripped from his car, to make a game of taunting her.

* * *

Daciana wiped the plate down with a handkerchief plucked from her pocket. Then she stuck it edgewise into the ground, just below a zipper-locked plastic food bag she had earlier tacked to the tree.

She assumed Claire would return during daylight, searching for signs of Lukas. She would find that the license plate had been moved — and deduce correctly that she had been observed. That in itself should be enough to spook her. Then she would use her metamorph's senses to sniff out the spoor (note to self, she thought: wear perfume if you expect to be in Claire's presence, to drown out your scent) and find herself at this spot.

Find the license plate again. Find the present that had been tacked to the tree. Daciana's smile was mirthless.

Claire would never notify the authorities instead of returning; that would signal some kind of involvement in Lukas's disappearance. But if, in some irrational panic, she did notify them, they would find the plate and discover what was in the bag above it. DNA would be tested. Lukas's identity would be confirmed, as would his complicity in Gabriel's death. Which would leave another mystery: who had done this to him; where was his car; and where was the rest of his body? They would find the car, eventually, where she'd abandoned it; as for the other, no one would ever find that. She'd had to kill him, but that did not mean she didn't, in some way, still have feelings for him.

Daciana walked out of the woods and continued north for a mile more in the chill air before leaving the road for a forest trail that led to her small black sedan. She lowered all the windows -- the night air was cool, and besides, she hated air conditioning -- before driving leisurely back to the Criterion campus. The moon was so bright she almost forgot to turn on the headlights.

* * *

"What are you doing?" Claire said to herself after an hour on the road. "You have to go back. You can't just walk away. Lukas could be out there, somewhere in the woods. Maybe in trouble." She made a U-turn and headed back toward Francestown.

Returning to where she'd found the license plate, Claire was shocked to discover it gone. She bent forward and sniffed the ground. She detected a new scent, one she couldn't identify. Familiar in some subtle way, but otherwise alien. She took off her clothes and changed, nose to the ground. Her padded paws made no sound as she glided over the soft earth, her nose guiding her deep into the forest. She was so intent on the scent that she almost bumped into a tree trunk before she saw the license plate before it.

The plate was stabbed edgewise into the ground, obviously on purpose. Claire looked around, saw nothing, smelled nothing but that strange spoor. Looking up, she spotted something tacked to the trunk of the tree, above her reach as a wolf. She returned to human form and plucked the transparent plastic bag from the trunk. She moved to a patch of ground where moonlight provided illumination enough to see what was inside.

For a moment she simply stared, barely breathing. Then with a whimper that turned into a cry, she held it to her breast and lowered her head as fresh tears flowed down her face. Without thinking, she morphed into her wolf form once more, the bag falling to the ground as she lifted her snout and howled her despair to the moon—whose cold, white light revealed inside the plastic bag a slice of human skin, on which had been tattooed the black, furry, slavering, cartoon head of the Big Bad Wolf.

PART FOUR
Music

Chapter Eleven

The gossip at Jones Publishing, strictly confidential and strictly between Rowena and Claire, was that the boss was seeing someone. Rowena had noticed a subtle change in his behavior and teasingly asked if he were cheating on her. He replied, in the same vein, that he would never cheat on her, but it was the way he'd said it that sparked her curiosity. He kept regular hours at work, but once Rowena had called him on a Saturday to invite him to dinner the next day, whereupon she learned from Emma that he'd be away the whole weekend, as was becoming his custom these days. *Well, good for him*, she thought. When he's ready, he'll tell us.

Rowena never asked Claire any more about Lukas, not since the day last year when she'd stated through tears she "just knew" her Lukas was dead. *When she's ready, she'll tell me.* It was 2005, and their friendship had grown rock solid.

Claire herself had accepted her loss—the evidence she'd found in the woods had been irrefutable—but kept her own counsel. Eventually, she thought, the weight would lift from her shoulders. She had said nothing to the authorities, and she never returned to the Francestown woods to hunt.

It was Wednesday, May 18, that she received a call at home that initially sent a chill through her. When she answered, the first thing she heard was heavy breathing, more like a wheeze. She wished she had a police whistle at hand. Finally, a voice came through the receiver.

"Hello? Is this Claire Delaney?"

"I'm on the Do Not Call list, so—"

"No, no, Miss Delaney—may I call you Claire?—my name is Ronny Music, and I teach at the same school where Gene Franks used to work before he retired ... 'n stuff." Claire frowned, glancing back at her half-finished family-sized portion of microwave dinner. "I teach art. Kind of funny, isn't it, a guy named Music teaching art?" He chuckled. She picked up a hint of the South in his voice, not the Deep South, but a kind of easy drawl. "Anyway, Gene and I are great friends, and when I saw how good you did with his book"—*well*, Claire thought, gritting her teeth—"he said he was sure you'd want to work with me on mine."

Something's not right, she thought. "You're telling me that Gene Franks gave you my home phone number? Without asking me first?"

There was a brief pause. "Well, not exactly. But your number's not unlisted. I just kept the four-one-one operator busy giving me all the C. Delaneys in Boston. There's a lot of you up there! But I persevered, and here we are. Can I tell you about my book proposal?"

Claire closed her eyes and bit her lip. A friend of Gene's. For Gene's sake, be polite. "Listen, Mr. Music ..."

"Ronny, please ... Claire."

"Mr. Music, Gene has my telephone number, both at work and at home. But I have to tell you, in all the times he's called me, he's never used my home phone. I would appreciate it if you would observe the same courtesy. I will be in my office tomorrow and Friday from eight until six. Now if you'll excuse me, I'm expecting an important call."

As she replaced the receiver, she heard, "And what is your work number again?"

Click. Not *again*, I never gave it to you the first time. And I wonder if Gene ever did. Must call him tomorrow.

The phone rang again. "How you doin', sweetie? Rough day?"

"Ro, thank goodness, a sane call for a change."

"Say again?"

"I just got off the phone with some weirdo who claims he's best buds with Gene Franks. Says he wants me to look at a book proposal of his own."

"Called you at home. Where'd he get the number?"

"Four One One. I know Gene never gave it to him."

"Okay, my opinion of Mr. Franks has just bounced back up out of the toilet. So what'd you say?"

"Hung up on him."

"No you didn't. You told him to call you at work. Didn't you? Huh? Huh?"

"Bitch. How do you peg me every time?"

"Ah, that's my girl." Rowena continued: "Well, listen, kid. How'd you like to join Big Bill, Greycie, and me for dinner Friday night? Just one sweet guy and we three bitches."

* * *

First thing the next morning, Claire was on the phone to New Jersey. Nina picked up. "Claire, sweetheart, how are you? You've dropped off the face of the Earth. Don't be the kind of person who only visits during the summer so she can use the beach. Did you ever know people like that when you lived here?"

"Now that I think of it, yes, I did. Mom and Dad had relatives they never even knew they had 'drop by to visit' during the summer, just so they could use the beach. Used our resident beach tags, too; wouldn't spring for a day badge. And their 'visits' amounted to a Howyadoin' followed hours later by a Nicetaseeya and S'long."

"So you're not going to be one of those, then? Because you know our house is always open to you."

"I know, and I love you for it. I've been busy, but some weekend -- before the summer, promise—I'll take the Golden Goose to Manasquan and bore you to death will all my projects."

"Summer starts in a month, you know."

"Gotcha."

"And Gene has a project of his own, I think you'll be happy to learn. But I'll save that for him to tell you."

"Actually, I'm calling to check on something with Gene. Is he around?"

"As the song says, gone fishin'. But you wouldn't remember that one. He's down at the surf, trying for some early season blues. Everyone knows they bite on bait this time of year, but Gene insists on casting his Hopkins and reeling it in, over and over again. Does it as much for the exercise as for the fish, I guess. Says he can't stand still and watch the tip of his rod and wait for it to twitch. Of course, I've said that about him too, once or twice ..."

"Nina!"

"Don't you dare tell him I said that. Oh, dear. Anyway, anything I can help you with?"

"Well, I got a call last night from a guy named Music, said he taught with..."

"Ronny Music?"

"Uh huh."

"Oh, honey, don't lend him a dollar, you'll never see it again."

"Say that again?"

"I'm sorry, sweetie, that's not very Christian of me. Let's just say that whenever Ronny Music calls for Gene, it's only because he wants a favor. He always ends the conversation with 'We'll have to get together,' but the invitations only go one way. I've yet to see the inside of his place. Not that I'd want to."

"So I can assume he and Gene aren't best friends, and Gene never told him to call me about a book Mr. Music was working on?"

"What? That's the most ridiculous thing I've ever heard. I don't think Gene even knows Ronny is writing a book. But you know, come to think of it, I'm not surprised. I'm thinking what's going through Ronny's mind is if Gene can write a best seller, he should be able to, too. He's always trying to upstage everyone he knows. *I* could write a book about that."

Claire let out a long breath. "Nina, you've made my day."

"Wait, honey, you're telling me Ronny told you Gene said to call you?"

"That's what he said."

"Bastard. Oops, sorry, sweetie, that's not very Christian either. Listen, if you want the scoop on Ronny Music, you'll need more than a long-distance phone call charged to your company. How about you come down here this weekend, and we'll have a good old-fashioned gab fest, just us girls—and Gene."

It's Thursday, Claire thought, maybe I could use a couple of days to clear my head -- as well as be forewarned—make that warned, Miss Grammarian—about Mr. Ronny Music. "Nina, can you hold for a sec while I clear something?" She pushed the intercom button and said, "Ro? Can I take a rain check for dinner tomorrow night? I've got the chance to go to Jersey to get the scoop on the creep who called me last night."

"No prob, Claire. How's about you come Sunday night instead? The long drive back should work up an appetite—not that you ever lacked for one."

"You're a prince."

"Thanks for that."

"And tell Greycie I'll be bringing her a nice big boiled marrow bone, all the way from the Belmar Shop Rite."

* * *

"You must have the world's best boss," said Gene Franks the next day as he and Nina welcomed Claire with bear hugs. "Come on in, and drop your bag. We can get it to your room later."

"He is, no question," said Claire. "I mentioned this morning I'd be driving down to see you after work today, and he pronounced my work day officially over, told me I could use some time for myself -- a mental health day, he calls it. And what's even better is I don't have to field what would be a very uncomfortable phone call from Mr. Ronny Music today. I left an 'Elvis has left the building' message on my machine. It'll be interesting to pick up his voice message when I get back."

"Forget Ronny for a minute, Claire. Have a seat, kick off your shoes, eat some goodies, and relax. You look great. It's been too long, little lady."

"Little? She's hardly a little girl, Gene."

"Figure of speech, my love," he said with forced sarcasm. Nina stuck out her tongue, made for the refrigerator, and returned with a tray of iced tea. "She knows her place," Gene said, which got him another stab of the tongue. "So, how have you been? How's work going?"

"Never mind me. I'd love to hear what you're up to, Gene," Claire said. "Nina told me you've got a new project."

"Oh, that," he replied dismissively. "It's just that the *Asbury Park Press* has asked me to write a weekly column for their Sunday edition. No biggie."

"No biggie?" said Nina. "No biggie? You'd think they'd offered him the moon. A lousy fifty bucks a week, and …"

"To start," Gene interrupted. "Enough to keep me in lures and lumber."

"That's fantastic," said Claire. "Who knows? Get an audience, and you could get syndicated, and then you might find yourself busier than you ever were in the classroom."

"I'm already that. I wonder when I ever found time to work."

Claire's stomach growled. "Oops. One of life's embarrassing little moments."

Nina said, "I love your appetite. I'll get some cheese and crackers, I think there's some pepperoni in the fridge, too."

"You're a doll. Oh, and Nina, could I ask you to do something else for me?" Claire picked up a tan plastic bag and from it produced a wrapped foam tray. "These are marrow bones. Could I ask you to boil them up and put them in the freezer after they cool?"

Nina raised an eyebrow. "For your midnight snack?"

You've no idea how true that could be, Claire thought. "I'm going to dinner at a girlfriend's house Sunday night. I promised her I'd bring her dog some marrow bones. She's a greyhound—the dog, that is—and she loves sticking her needle nose into the bone to lick out the marrow. Takes her all night. Then Ro—that's my friend—stuffs the empty bone with peanut butter and refreezes it. She gives it to her when she and her husband leave for work in the morning, and Greycie—that's the dog—is happy as a lark sitting in her crate. They—listen to me rattle on, like all this matters to you. It's just so good to be with you two again, you're like …"

Claire looked at the couple, suddenly speechless.

"If you were going to say 'like parents,' Claire," said Nina softly, "that would be the sweetest thing you could say to us. But you don't have to if you don't want to."

"I think I do want to. Whenever I vist, I feel like I've come home again. And it's not just because you live down the road from where I grew up."

Nina stood up. "All right, group hug!" she demanded.

* * *

"So you want the scoop on Ronny Music," said Gene after dinner. "I'll try to be diplomatic, he's really not the ogre Nina probably painted him out to be."

"No pun intended," said Nina. "Get it? Art teacher? Painted? Gene does it without even thinking."

Claire grinned. If it weren't for the fact that she was getting close to her period, with all the accompanying werewolf-y urges, she would have been perfectly relaxed. She wiggled her toes under the table and sipped her coffee as it steamed in its mug. If home is where the heart is, this was home: there was certainly plenty of heart here.

"I should probably tell you the nickname the kids used to call him behind his back; probably still do, I'm just not there to hear it any more. Ready? They call him Runny Mucus."

"Clever kids!" said Claire. "And these are what, seventh-graders?"

"Five through eight," said Gene. "We used to be a strict middle school, six through eight, but with population growth, fifth graders were brought over from the elementary school. So we've got ten-year-old children on one side of the building, hiding from the fourteen-year-old gorillas on the other. Anyway, I don't know who gave Ronny the name; I just overheard some kids in my class talking after they came back from art. I also heard, from more than one source, that the kids knew he was a good artist, they just wished he didn't spend the first half of each period telling them how good he was before turning them loose on their own projects."

"One of those, huh?" Claire said.

"Full of himself," added Nina. "Full of something else, too, if you ask me."

"Not very Christian," reminded Claire.

"Hush, you. Tell her about the car, Gene."

He took a breath. "When Ronny came on board—he'd been teaching at another school down around Norfolk, I think—why he left Norfolk in the first place, no one asked. Jersey's no cheaper to live in than Virginia, that's for sure."

Nina said, "Didn't his wife have family here?"

"I think she did, does, somewhere out near Cherry Hill. Anyway, I was selling my car and put a notice on the faculty room bulletin board, and Ronny asked for a test drive. He and his wife had just had a baby, and they needed something bigger than a Beetle."

"You should have seen him getting out of that Beetle," snickered Nina. "Ever seen those clowns?"

"He's kind of heavy," explained Gene. "All right, Nina, he's fat, okay? She has no truck with that man. Anyway, Ronny asked me if I could sell him the car on time, let him make the payments to me, as he didn't have the cash on hand to qualify for a bank loan."

"And good old Gene says sure, why not? So Mister Mucus takes the car, and he promises that every payday, the first check he'll write will be to Gene. Well. What do you think happens? Payday comes. No check to Gene. Next day: no check. Next day: Gene has to ask for the check, and then he gets it. But he has to beg for it, like he's asking the guy for a favor instead of collecting what he's due." She looked at the table. "I need more streusel cake. How about you, Claire?"

"You think I'd refuse streusel cake, Nina? And more coffee, now that you're up?"

"I can eat one piece and put on a pound; you could eat the whole cake and not put on an ounce. How do you do that?"

"Metabolism, I guess. Just lucky."

"Not eating for two, are you?"

"Bite your tongue." But in a sense, she thought, I am.

"Gene, you tell the rest."

"Well, thank you, mother. This went on for about a year—he'd paid off about half the car by then—and then one payday he said he couldn't pay me, that the baby was sick, and he wouldn't have family health coverage until he got tenure, so would I mind if we just added another two weeks to the loan? I said fine, but after a few more months I realized he must have had one sick kid. I questioned him, and he put on a hurt face and swore he was trying his best. Meanwhile, he was into some other teachers for money, too, which I didn't find out until later. Not a good thing."

Nina plopped the plate of crumb cake on the table, along with the coffee pot. "Not a good thing. An understatement. He even borrowed gas money one day from the mother of one of his kids after a parent-teacher conference. Bet she never got it back, either." She took a bite of cake and followed it with a gulp of coffee. "You know, sometimes I think Gene's a doormat; other times I think he's acting out of Christian charity."

Claire said, "So what is he with regard to Ronny Music?"

Nina cast a look at her husband. "I think I'll practice some Christian charity myself and just keep my mouth shut."

"Thank you," Gene said, continuing his story. "With one or two payments left, Ronny totaled the car. Not his fault, he wasn't injured, and fortunately his wife and baby weren't with him at the time. But he needed another car, and he asked me to defer the rest of the loan until he'd paid for another used car."

"And when did he pay you, Gene?"

"Um, when? I'm retired now, I guess he figures I don't need the money."

"Wow, and this guy wants me to work with him on a book?"

"Hey, he might make enough off of it to pay me back."

Nina said, "And if bullshit were money, he'd be a millionaire. Oh dear, that's—"

"Not very Christian of you!" called Claire and Gene.

* * *

After breakfast on Saturday, Gene said it would be a shame to waste the day on anything but fishing. He had a couple of extra surf rods and reels, and Claire was welcome to join him. Nina shooed her out, said she had some volunteer work to attend to at the hospital—"It's the Christian thing to do"—and moments later the two were headed to the beach, fiberglass rods resting on their shoulders, looking for all the world like Tom and Huck on their way to the fishing hole.

The sun was hot, the surf icy. They stood knee deep to cast their metal lures, and the water's ebb and flow between calves and thighs sent more than a shiver through Claire. It was like a cold caress. And she was getting those urges again. Tomorrow night she'd be at Ro and Bill's. Maybe Monday night after work she'd head somewhere to hunt. Animals, only animals.

"So Gene," Claire said, "you're telling me Ronny Music never got my name from you?"

Gene cast his lure, watched it splash, and began to crank the reel. "Nope. He called me once after the book came out to congratulate me, or so he said. But he spent the rest of the time asking me about how I went about the process: drafts, queries, you know."

"And before he hung up, did he say you'd have to get together sometime?"

"You've been talking to Nina. Yeah, he did. It's just the way he signs off, nothing more."

"He didn't ask you for a loan, did he?"

"He's not stupid, Claire. And I figure he got your name from my acknowledgments page—you know, where I thanked everyone from God to my new best friends at Jones Publishing."

"Oh, duh. How come I didn't connect with that? Okay, so why did he tell me that you recommended him?"

"As I said, he's not stupid. Just a bit manipulative, maybe. But I try not to judge him."

Claire watched her metal lure wobble in the wash of a wave, reeled it to within a foot of the rod's tip, flipped the rod back and forward, and sent the Hopkins seaward. It took a long time to splash down.

"How do you do that?" asked Gene. "I've been surf fishing all my life and never learned to cast that far."

Oops. "Oh, maybe it's just how I use the rod's springiness to get it out there. Hey, guy, I'm no stranger to fishing. I grew up near the surf, remember?" She made a mental note to keep her strength in check. "You tend to cast from the side, as if you're playing baseball. Try bringing the rod back over your head, and when you feel the pull of the lure behind you, snap the rod forward."

"I'll try it," Gene said, and when he did his lure sailed out in a graceful arc and hit the water perhaps five yards farther than before. "Excellent," he said. "Not so far as yours, but still, not bad." He began to reel in. "You know, Claire, if there's anyone from my school who should write a book, it's a guy named Dale Keegan. He taught in the next room to mine for three years."

Claire cast out again, not so far this time. "Oh? Why's that?"

"I'm not talking about school topics now. Dale was an Army ranger. He quit after his hitch was up and earned his teaching degree up the road at Monmouth. I bet he'd have some stories to tell. About his adventures in the military."

"Maybe he can't tell them? Classified, maybe?"

"I think he's just naturally reticent to talk about himself. I do know the kids loved him. Especially the girls. He looks like GI Joe: tall, buzz cut, green eyes, chest out to here, handsome in a rugged kind of way. He ran his class like boot camp. You wouldn't believe how disciplined his kids were. But they loved it. Loved him."

"*Esprit de corps*," Claire said. "Not restricted to the Marines, I guess."

"I guess."

"You're talking past tense," Claire noted.

"Yeah. Education's loss. After 9/11 he either re-enlisted or was called back up, I don't know which, and applied for an indefinite leave of absence from school. The Board of Ed, in its wisdom or lack of it, said they had no policy to address that, and they were afraid granting him leave, especially with an indefinite return date, would set an unwise precedent. So, he had to resign. Of course, after he left the board replaced him with a brand newbie right out of college and saved themselves a boatload of salary money."

"I hear you. So this Dale, he's no longer around."

"He was gone for about a year, maybe a little more. Came back once to visit us in the faculty room, and all he'd say was that he'd been 'vacationing' somewhere in Afghanistan." He smiled to himself, staring out at the breakers.

"What?" Claire demanded.

"Oh, nothing." She glared at him. "Okay, something. And I'm not being judgmental, remember that."

"Be as judgmental as you like. I won't tell Nina."

Gene cast his lure and began reeling in. "While Dale was oohed and aahed over by the single women on staff, Ronny Music joined the conversation and started expounding on his experiences as a Boy Scout at Philmont. That's some kind of camp in New Mexico. And when that got him no notice, he started telling stories about his security cop days at the racetrack, Monmouth Park. Oh, and about his marksmanship on the pistol range."

"Playing Can You Top This, was he?"

"Uh huh. Very insecure, I'd say."

"Very much an a-hole, I'd say." Claire stuck her rod between her legs and spread her hands. "On the one hand, Army ranger in a war zone." She looked to her other hand. "And on the other, a Boy Scout? A rent-a-cop? Come on!" She laughed and picked up her rod, tossing her lure beyond the breakers.

"Well, the other teachers ignored him, they'd heard it all before anyway. As for Dale, he just nodded politely, then after a few minutes more he shook hands all around and left. He's still attached to the military, but he wouldn't—or couldn't—say in what capacity. I told him to call me when he was back in town, and he said he would. Like I said..."

"As I said."

"*As* I said, smarty, if someone could pry his experiences out of him, there'd be some stories to tell."

"Are you suggesting little old *moi*?"

They cast again, and as soon as Gene's lure hit the water it was snatched. His rod bent into a C, and he gave a shout as he began cranking his reel. Then Claire's line went taut, and both of them were pumping. Suddenly the water's surface came alive with ripples and silver flashes, and just as suddenly the few other fishermen dotting the beach were hurrying toward Claire and Gene. Seagulls seemed to appear from nowhere, hovering over and diving into the melee, shrieking and spearing baitfish driven to the surface.

"A blitz!" cried Gene as he backed up, dragging a three-pound bluefish through the wash. He hefted it onto the beach, and soon Claire had its schoolmate on the sand beside it. "Careful, those teeth can take your fingers off!" Gene said. "And watch out for those spines ahead of the dorsal fin."

"I know, Gene, I know." They exchanged indulgent smiles, like father and daughter.

Gene threw a rag over his blue's back to protect his hand and carefully reached down to disengage the treble hook from the fish's jaw. He didn't notice that when Claire squatted to take the hook from her own catch, the bluefish—one of the most vicious sport fish in the ocean—suddenly stopped thrashing. Its piranha-toothed mouth relaxed and opened, as if inviting Claire to remove the hook, presenting it, and itself, as a gift to her. Thank you, she said silently. Then she took a knife from Gene's tackle box and stabbed it through the head.

That Gene noticed. "You don't want to kill it right away," he admonished. "Nothing spoils faster than a bluefish. Let it live as long as it can." He tossed his fish flopping onto the sand.

"Couldn't let it suffer," Claire responded. "Sorry."

"That's okay. We'll just catch what we can eat tonight. Blues don't freeze so well either. Get real oily-tasting." He looked at her and shook his head. "But you know that already, right?"

They reclaimed their place in the surf and immediately tied into two more fish. Then, leaving the other fishermen to rake in however more they could, they gutted the fish, tossed the entrails to the gulls, and waltzed home, visions of a fresh fish dinner dancing in their heads.

Chapter Twelve

Claire walked through the door of Bill and Rowena's house waving a plastic freezer bag filled with marrow bones. Hugs and kisses for them were followed by a bow from their greyhound and a rollover onto her side. Claire scratched the dog's tummy, told her what a beautiful, beautiful girl she was, then opened the bag and offered a bone.

Greycie looked at the prize, then at Claire, as if asking for permission. She smiled and nodded, and the dog took it delicately between her teeth and trotted off to her crate.

"Greycie's getting some real gray around her eyes and nose," Claire observed as she watched the dog's tongue burrow into the center of the tasty delight. Greycie was overall white, with a brown patch around one eye which went back through her ear, a matching saddle mark on her back, and a few ticks of black at her hind quarters.

"Getting old, you know," said Bill. "Dogs do that quicker—sorry, ladies, more quickly—than humans. What is it, seven years to one?"

Rowena extended a glass of iced tea to Claire. "So sit down and tell us all about your weekend. By the way, your friend Ronny Music never called."

"Oh, that's a shame. If he had, he'd have gotten a message. Or he'd be routed through to you, which would really give you a treat."

They sat around a coffee table in the living room, where Rowena had prepared cheese and crackers, along with cantaloupe wrapped in prosciutto. Claire made an effort not to devour them all. "Well, Gene and I caught four bluefish yesterday."

"No," said Rowena. "Another skill you've never told us about. So how many did you eat yourself, kid?"

Claire flushed. "Two."

"Figures, Miss Piggy. How you keep so skinny I'll never know."

"You don't want to," said Claire.

Bill said, "Maybe she's got a portrait in her apartment that gets fat instead."

"Now you're on to something, hubby mine." Ro pecked him on the cheek, then said, "Come on, Claire, give me a hand in the kitchen. You can tell me all about what you've learned from Mr. Franks about your mystery caller."

"You mean, Runny Mucus?"

Rowena laughed. "What?"

"To the kitchen, woman."

*   *   *

Dinner had been ample and delicious, and breakfast on Monday had been its usual over indulgence. Still, by the time noon rolled around, Claire was more than ready for lunch. The spring day was brisk and breezy, and she threw on a light jacket before heading outside. She was so preoccupied she almost ran over the little man coming through the door.

"Oof," he said as they collided. He looked up as Claire looked down.

"Oh, I'm sorry," she said as she backed off. "I wasn't looking where I was going. Are you all right?"

"Fine," the man said. "Now that I've got your attention," he continued with a chuckle, "I wonder if you could direct me to Claire Delaney's office."

She stared at him a moment, trying to remember if she'd made an appointment she'd forgotten. He was a full head shorter than she but more than twice as big around. He had thinning ginger hair and a beard to match. The beard was short and circumscribed his round face, leaving his double chin exposed and exaggerated. His eyes were green, with laugh lines at the corners, and he wore a wrinkled tan sport jacket with a green tie. He reminded her of a leprechaun. A roly-poly, sweaty leprechaun. With a briefcase.

"Um, I'm Claire Delaney," she said.

He brightened. "My, you're a big one," he said, his voice a rich baritone. "I'm Ronny Music, and it looks like I'm just in time to take you to lunch … 'n stuff."

Claire stammered a few words, ultimately couldn't think of a polite way to say no, and directed him to a local luncheonette she liked, a short walk from the office.

"I'll have my usual," she told the waitress, a young woman whose curves didn't go unnoticed by the man sitting across from her.

The server smiled. "Two burgers, make 'em moo, no bun, cole slaw, iced tea. You, hon?"

"Let's see. I'll have a double burger, medium, large fries, and one of those vanilla shakes in the sign on the wall."

"Want some malt in your shake?"

"No, I'm on a diet," he said, winking at her. She looked at Claire with a you-can-do-better-than-that face and retreated to the kitchen.

Claire returned Music's stare. "Well, this is a surprise."

"I like surprises."

"Isn't this a school day, Mr. Music?"

"It's Ronny, and, um, achem, achem," he said, holding a pudgy hand to his mouth and feigning a cough. "I've still got some sick days left, and this late in the year the kids aren't in the mood to learn anything anyway."

"So you take all your sick days, whether you're sick or not."

He shrugged. "Use 'em or lose 'em. Why work when you can get paid not to? Anyway, I didn't drive up here today all the way from Jersey to talk about me." He winked. "Well, actually I did, but more about my book."

"Your book proposal," Claire corrected.

"Right. I call it *The Art of Music*. Pretty catchy title, huh?"

She nodded. "I'll give it that. But what makes you come to us?"

"I came to you. Specifically. Not *us*. You edited Gene Franks's manuscript, and it turned out great."

"That was Gene's writing, not mine. I just cleared up a couple of grammatical points and made one or two changes for clarity's sake. I'm sure you've told Gene how much you liked his book." Music smiled, and Claire knew he hadn't. She also knew she wouldn't tell him of her visit this past weekend with Gene and Nina. "But that was a memoir. You sounded on the phone like you want us to publish a book on your art. That's really not in our field."

"Yes, well, your company did come out with a coffee-table book on some guy named H. Hargrove, am I right?"

Caught. He had done his homework. "That was a special case, Ru—Ronny. Our publisher, Mr. Jones, is an avid collector of Mr. Hargrove's art, and it was he who solicited the artist for the chance to create that book. I had nothing to do with it. Maybe you'd like an appointment to talk with Mr. Jones ..."

The waitress returned with their orders, and Music dug in. Wiping ketchup from the side of his mouth, he said, "I think you're probably prettier than Mr. Jones."

Claire wrinkled her nose. His sweat mingled with another scent, one that would have been welcomed from, say, Lukas ... she forked a piece of meat and placed it in her mouth. "Pretty doesn't get one published," she said after swallowing. "Talent does."

"I have talent. Believe me, I have talent. More so, I daresay, than Mr. Jones's friend does. Listen, I have my portfolio in my briefcase, and I'd like you to see it. Then maybe we can discuss it ... 'n stuff ... say, later tonight?"

"Whoa. Slow down, Ronny, will you? My head's spinning. Listen. Leave me your portfolio and I'll get back to you."

"Well, I have to drive back home tomorrow."

"Only a few sick days left, I take it."

He missed the sarcasm. "Yup."

"I can't promise to get to it this afternoon. I have other manuscripts to work on. You've got to understand I can't drop everything."

"I know." He reached across the table, as if to put his hand over Claire's. She drew hers back and picked up her iced tea. Ronny took a slug of his shake. "Do you have a boyfriend, Claire? I notice you're not wearing a wedding ring."

Claire coughed and snorted tea through her nose. She grabbed a napkin and held it to her face, only her eyes visible, shooting arrows across the table. Even were she inclined to answer, she wouldn't know how. Instead, she lowered the napkin to the table. "I'd bet you're divorced."

He grinned. "Bingo. You must've seen the pale stripe where my wedding ring used to be. Very good. Yes, I'm divorced. She took my kid and went home to live with her parents. Took me for every dime, too. That's why I've put on so much weight. When I'm stressed, I eat. Normally, I'm about one-fifty." He looked double that, at least.

In an ironic voice, she said, "When I'm stressed I eat, too."

Ronny gave her another once-over. "You must not be under any stress at all."

"You'd be surprised. So, Ronny, why the divorce?"

Now it was his turn to squirm. "I made a mistake or two … 'n stuff," he said.

"Let me guess. Women?"

"I'm an artist. Sometimes women commission me to paint them. Full body. Nude … 'n stuff. And sometimes they, well …"

"Come on to you."

"I'm only human, Claire."

And I'm not, she thought. And I'll bet your flesh is beautifully marbled. Careful, Claire, don't drool. "So she couldn't forgive you for your 'mistakes,' Ronny, that's what you're telling me."

"That's right," he said, finishing his shake with a noisy slurp.

"And what mistakes did she make?"

Music stared at her, this time without words to offer. Finally he said, "I'll leave you my portfolio. Promise to get back to me soon?"

"I promise to give it the attention it deserves whenever I can, that's all I can do."

"Okay." The waitress brought the check, and he reached into his jacket pocket. "Um, Claire, would you mind if we went Dutch on this? I'm, uh, a little short."

It was all she could do not to laugh out loud.

* * *

Claire stormed into Rowena's office and slammed Music's briefcase on her desk. "He ambushed me," she said. Rowena asked who. "Music, Runny Mucus. He was downstairs, insisted he take me to lunch, then made me pay for mine, and had the nerve to…"

"Girl, chill," Rowena said. She looked at the briefcase. "So, it sounds like you've met the living definition of chutzpah. What's in the bag?"

Claire took a breath. "His portfolio and MS. I couldn't put him off."

"Well, let's take a look." She opened the case and took out a large bound portfolio. When she opened it, Claire walked behind Rowena's desk and looked over her shoulder. "Stuff's pretty good," Ro said. "Likes the ladies, I'd say."

The figure studies were, to say the least, exquisite. "Likes the boobs, too, I'd say," Claire added.

"Yeah. Some of these look like Vargas girls. From the old *Playboys*," she added, noting Claire's puzzled look. "Bill used to subscribe. For the articles, of course. But that was before we got married. Then he graduated to the genuine article." She winked at Claire and turned pages. "The portraits are nice, too." More pages. "Still life's just okay; landscapes are, I don't know, treacly, too much like Kinkade's. Hargrove's are much better."

Claire rifled through Music's manuscript. "Can't spell worth beans, I'll tell you that. Huh."

"What?"

"According to his bio, autobio really, he's the most beloved teacher in his school. Right. If he only knew what Gene told me. Oh, and the parents love him, too. Sure, they—oh, my God."

"What? Give, girl!"

Claire had been rifling through the pages. "He notes here he painted the mother of one of his students. Figure study. Nude."

"Don't tell me the kid walked in."

"No. Too cliché, right? Besides, if the kid had walked in, I'm sure the guy'd have been fired the next day. I'm guessing he took a sick day and painted her while the kid was at school. He mentioned at lunch that he'd done nudes, but he didn't mention this. I'd bet this was one of his dalliances …"

"Dalliances? Ooh, I so love it when you talk dirty."

"Shut up. His wife found out about his catting around and divorced him."

"He's a hunk?"

"He's a troll."

"Isn't that a bitch?" said Rowena. "No matter how homely a man is, he still has no trouble getting women. He's got character, they say. But a woman? Hah. If a man goes out with a homely woman, they say if Moses had seen her, there'd be another commandment."

* * *

Rowena insisted that Claire join her and Bill for dinner again tonight, saying she had something she wanted to share with her outside the office. She offered no hint as to what it might be, and furthermore she filled the dinner conversation with small talk. Claire knew better than to press her. Ro would broach the subject when she felt like it and not a moment before.

An hour after they'd finished dessert, Bill excused himself to prepare notes for a week-long seminar he'd be leading next month in New York—"He just found out today. Can you believe he's sweating the details already? But he says it could lead to a promotion, so I say go, boy"—and the two women began cleaning up the kitchen. "We wimmens knows our place," Rowena joked. "As in, 'Yassa, massa. I's be wit chew soon's I shuffles up fum de back o' de bus.'"

"That'll be the day, when you take a back seat to anybody. Where does this serving bowl go?"

"In the cabinet above the microwave. How many times have you been here, and you still can't remember?"

"Steep learning curve."

"Right."

There was a casement window above the kitchen sink, and on the ledge below it Rowena normally kept a pack of cigarettes and an ashtray. It was convenient for her to blow the smoke out the window and then empty the ashtray into the trash can. Suddenly Claire noticed that neither the cigarettes nor the ashtray were to be found. Not only that, but she realized that the scent of tobacco that normally clung to Rowena's hair wasn't there—and at dinner tonight she drank only ice water. She hadn't had one drink of wine all evening. Claire held the serving bowl and stared at her friend.

"I was wondering when you'd notice," Rowena said.

Claire put the bowl on the counter and hugged her.

"Not sure yet, so don't say anything. I am six weeks late, though."

Claire's congratulations were cut short as she doubled over and muttered an expletive. "Oh man, I wish I could say that—but not for the reason you have. This one's going to be rough." She grabbed her purse and bolted for the bathroom.

* * *

"Rowena, there's a man here to see Claire, but I told him she's not in today. Says his name is Ronny Music."

"Really. I'll see him, Jacqui. Send him down, please?" Rowena replaced the phone in its cradle. "Looks like I'll get the chance to meet the famous Runny Mucus after all." She knew that in being absent today,

Claire would see a silver lining in her monthly. Poor kid really suffers with it, Ro thought. She needs to get pregnant, get some nine months' respite. Of course, she'd need to have a husband first, and that doesn't appear too likely at present. Okay, let's see, the guy's portfolio is on the side table, and if Claire's right about his ego, he'll be pitching each painting as if it were a Picasso. From his realism period, of course.

The word *period* brought her back to thoughts of Claire and her legendary first-day cramps. She turned her eyes from the portfolio to her office door and stopped. Standing there, immobile, was a three hundred pound bowling ball, with ginger hair and wispy beard, just staring at her with his mouth open. *How awkward is this*, she thought.

Ro stood and extended her hand. "Mr. Music? Hi, I'm Rowena Parr. Claire's out today. What can I do for you?"

Ronny walked in and took her hand, held it a second or two longer than she'd have expected, and shook his head. "Aida."

"No, Rowena."

"No, Aida. I must've seen you in the opera."

"Come on."

"I'm serious, you look like a genuine Nubian princess." He shook his head again, as if to clear it. "I'm sorry, it's just that—well, I'm an artist, as you can see from my portfolio, and I'm finely attuned to beauty ... 'n stuff." He motioned toward a chair. "May I?"

Rowena nodded and sat down herself. "Claire told me she met you. Shouldn't you be back in New Jersey teaching school?"

He faked a cough and winked. "Just stopped in to see if you'd decided to publish my book yet."

She leaned back in her chair. "If only the process were that easy. There's a whole chain of command the manuscript has to go through before the boss can pass judgment on it. And, to tell you the truth, most manuscripts never make it to the final step."

"But mine? Did Claire say anything about mine?"

Rowena reached for his portfolio. "Actually, she showed it to me. Your work is very impressive."

Ronny's expression told her that this was nothing less than he'd expected. In fact, he'd expected something more effusive. He nodded toward the portfolio. "May I show you something?"

"Of course."

He stood and almost reverently turned the leaves until he found what he was looking for. It was a portrait of a beautiful woman sitting on a wooden stool. She sat in three-quarter rear view, the left half of her back exposed down to her buttocks, the right half covered in a red satin sash which tucked under her right butt cheek and from there fell nearly to the floor like a crimson curtain. The sash draped over her right shoulder and swirled down to the side of her breast. The woman's arm crossed her body beneath her breast, pushing the satin folds up over her nipple but leaving the curve of its upper half exposed. She peered over her right shoulder directly at the viewer. Her eyes were dark, her lips the color of the sash, and playing over those lips was a Mona Lisa smile. The background was a gentle wash of soft grays.

Originally, Rowena and Claire had simply flipped through the portfolio; today, upon looking at it, she had to admit that this was probably one of the most sensually alluring figure studies she'd ever seen. "It's beautiful," she said, her voice soft.

"Do you know why I wanted you to see it?"

"No."

"Because when I saw you from the doorway, I saw you in this pose."

Rowena sat back. "Don't you think you're being a little forward, Mr. Music?"

Ronny sat down again, his expression abashed—or pseudo-abashed. "I'm sorry," he said. "Look, I know how I sounded just then, but I don't mean anything by it. I just feel you have the kind of face that belongs on a portrait … 'n stuff. The woman in the painting had that done as a present for her husband. He absolutely loved it. Are you married?"

"Yes, I'm very happily married, thank you. To a martial arts instructor with an impressive collection of samurai swords and other deadly instruments." She giggled inside. Bill didn't even belong to a gym, and he was a devout gun control freak. The only blade he owned was in his razor.

"Well, in case …" He reached into his pocket and handed her a card. "I've got summer vacation coming up. I could do you in a week."

Oh, she thought, now there's a choice of words. But she took his card, told him Claire would get back to him on his manuscript, shook his damp hand, and wished him a safe drive back to New Jersey. She returned to her desk and sat down. The portfolio was still open to the portrait of the lady on the stool.

* * *

The next morning, Claire looked into Rowena's office before heading for her own desk. Ro looked up, and her sarcastic tone couldn't mask the concern in her eyes. "Welcome back, Miss Melancholia. God, girl, you look grim."

"Nice alliteration," Claire noted. "Tough day yesterday, sorry I couldn't be here."

"Ever thought of seeing an OB/GYN about it? I mean, some discomfort is normal, but the way you look today..."

"I'll be okay," Claire assured her. "I think the worst is over, and I should be good for another twenty-eight days or so."

"I met your friend Runny Mucus yesterday," Ro said.

"What was he doing here? Wait, I can guess. So tell me, is he a troll or what?"

"That's a very apt description."

Claire said, "I'll ship his portfolio and MS back with a rejection slip today."

"No, Claire, you're going home. I'm doing the honors."

"But I have other stuff to do ..."

"Take it with you. You still look like hell. I appreciate your work ethic, but I don't believe you for a minute that the worst is over. Doctor Parr here prescribes another day at home. Uh uh, don't argue."

Claire took a breath. "All right, doc, I will." She turned to go. "And thanks for understanding." While saying to herself, You don't understand the half of it.

"No problem, girl. We sisters have to stick together."

Claire looked at her. "You are like a sister, you know."

"No need to brown nose me, kiddo. My own nose is naturally brown anyway."

Claire forced a laugh. "Considering the literal meaning of brown nosing, your imagery is way off."

"Hell, girl, you're not that sick. Now get out of here before I change my mind. And don't worry about Runny Mucus."

"Thanks, Ro. Just thinking about that guy makes me want to wash my brain out with soap."

After Claire left, Rowena pulled the portfolio from her center desk drawer and opened it.

* * *

Even today, nearly three years later, Claire's period brought with it not only a profuse flow of blood but also her memories of Lukas, his obvious (to her) murder of Gabe Zeklos, and the fact he himself was undeniably dead. None of which she could share with anyone, not even her closest friend Rowena or her surrogate parents Nina and Gene. Driving through Boston was bad enough even when you were alert, and here she was barely even looking at other traffic. She called up the who, what, where, when, why, and hows from her high school journalism course, and could only come up with the undeniable what: Lukas was dead.

And she was alone. Alone in what she knew. Alone in what she feared. A lone wolf, the only one of her kind. Time had not eased her burden; it had only intensified it.

The tears began once she was inside her flat. She tossed her briefcase on her bed and lay face down alongside it, her mind still trying to wrap itself around the events in the Francestown woods on the night of the second of July, 2004, almost a year ago.

Lukas's killer, or someone affiliated with his killer, had to have been observing her while she was hunting in the woods, and her sensitive ears and nose hadn't picked him out. Clearly, he had known she was a metamorph. He also knew that she would eventually return to her hunting territory and placed Lukas's license plate where she could not help but find it. He was not only watching her, he was purposely tormenting her. With the patch of Lukas's tattooed skin. The Big Bad Wolf. Twin to the tattoo behind her own right shoulder. Bastard!

Claire had known since that night she was in danger, absolutely vulnerable. But from whom? From a blackmailer? From a vigilante? Was someone watching her movements even now?

Paranoia, it'll destroy ya.

All right, she thought as she turned over and lay on her back to stare at her flat's popcorn ceiling, reviewing her situation for the umpteenth time. She knew the what. Now postulate the why. Lukas had killed Gabriel Zeklos and in his wolf form. But why would he do that? The two were friends; all right, not drinking buddies, but they certainly shared a strong respect and regard for each other. What had transpired between them to cause this?

She thought briefly of the professor's wife, Daciana, whom she'd met the day she'd dropped the F-bomb on Lukas—the last day she'd seen him alive. Talk about a Morticia look-alike: compared to Claire, she was a wisp. A fragile academic who, when they'd met, had figuratively looked down her nose at her. But the woman displayed a certain warmth, if not affection, at her husband's funeral. If Claire remembered correctly, she said she'd been home when Gabe was killed. She contended she couldn't be certain, despite overwhelming circumstantial evidence, that Lukas had been responsible for her husband's death.

She was a scientist. That hypothesis, like all others, demanded facts to back it up. She did not accept circumstantial evidence as proof.

The professor's assertions aside, the evidence against Lukas was incriminating, to say the least, and the authorities thought so, too. Naturally, forensics had taken DNA samples from Gabriel's wounds. They'd have found a wolf's genetic code, as well as a human's. Identical to one of the codes taken from that thug Puglio, who was a real monster.

Gene had mentioned his detective friend's hinting there was some kind of shadow organization involved in that case whose authority eclipsed that of the FBI. That worried her, too.

Back to Puglio. Had he had an accomplice in the woods, a lookout perhaps? Someone who had been stationed nearby to make sure he wasn't spotted when he slaughtered that innocent young couple in their tent? Had he seen Lukas and Claire morph into wolves and been too frightened to warn Puglio, too scared to try to intervene? And was he now planning his revenge for his friend's slaughter at their hands—er, fangs?

Claire got off the bed and brewed herself a pot of coffee, extra strong. Her body craved sleep, but she couldn't allow that. She had to think. The black brew was so hot it nearly singed her throat, but she gulped it down with a … vengeance.

Where? Where had Lukas been killed? In the woods? In his car? He had probably been shot; certainly, no one could overpower him physically. That would answer the how question, too. The thought of Colonel Mustard in the library with a candlestick flitted through Claire's mind, making her wince.

She wondered if Lukas's killer were even now observing her, through a telephoto lens, from somewhere across the street. She lowered the blinds and nearly screamed seconds later when the telephone rang.

Chapter Thirteen

"Claire, how are you? Rowena told me you were home sick."

She exhaled, still trembling. "Hello, Ray. I'm fine, really. Well, no I'm not, but it's nothing to be concerned about. I'll be in tomorrow, promise. And I did bring a couple of manuscripts home." Which was the truth, although up 'til now she hadn't given them a second thought.

"You just take care of yourself, young lady. Listen, I'm sure you've had your suspicions, and I'm sure you've been discreet, but it's true: this old hermit has a ladyfriend, and I'm entertaining her at my house for dinner Saturday. I've invited Rowena and Bill, and I'd like you to join us."

"Really? That is, yes, I'd love to."

"Then I'll see you Saturday."

"You'll see me tomorrow, bright-eyed and bushy-tailed. And thank you for calling, Ray. I swear, if Ro didn't have first dibs on you, I'd be staking a claim on you myself."

At last, she thought, we get to meet the mystery woman.

* * *

Claire drove to Bill and Rowena's home late Saturday afternoon; they would drive to Jones's house together in Bill's new Benz. "Boys and their toys," Rowena said.

"Hey, the old Volvo with the torn leather seats won't cut it if I have to take some high-level suits golfing during the seminar next month."

"How about that? Is this going to be a seminar or a schmooze fest? Only in corporate America. Okay, Claire, down to business: you're just in time for Greycie's walk." She gave Claire the leash while she herself picked up the requisite plastic bag.

"Look at this," Ro observed as they strolled the neighborhood. "When I walk Greycie she walks alongside me, but when you walk her, she stays a half a length behind you."

Claire smiled. "She defers to me as the alpha bitch—don't you, Greycie?" The greyhound trotted happily behind them. "Getting a little more gray there, Ro. The dog, I mean."

"No spring chicken anymore, she is."

"Well, thanks for that, Yoda."

"Not like us."

Claire leaned close. "So ... any news?"

"Fingers still crossed."

* * *

Emma beamed as she opened the door. "Mr. and Mrs. Parr, Miss Delaney, welcome. Come in. Mr. Jones is in the library."

"Whoa." Claire stopped short, her nose twitching. "What is that aroma?"

"Ah, that is Benjamin's famous prime rib roast."

"Well, I hope he's prepared something else for the rest of these people, because I'm going to eat the whole thing myself."

"Miss Delaney, this is why my Benjamin loves you." She ushered the party into the library, where Radu greeted them with drinks: a 20-ounce pint of English lager for Bill, a French Bordeaux for Rowena, and iced sparkling spring water for Claire.

"Ray, what Claire's drinking looks good to me. Do you mind?"

"No, not at all." He looked at her obliquely. "Rowena ... do you have something you'd like to share?"

She lowered her head and shuffled her feet, then slowly looked up. "The EPT shows positive, and even though it's not a hundred percent accurate—"

"You don't want to take a chance." Jones hugged her. "I am so happy for you, Rowena, so happy. Oh, and don't worry, my lips are sealed."

Rowena eased him back and held him by the shoulders. "We've got a doctor's appointment next week to confirm it. But speaking of your lips being sealed, you've been pretty secretive yourself, young man. Time to fess up to Mama."

The doorbell rang. "Good. That cuts off further discussion. Time to meet our mystery guest." He beamed as Emma escorted the lady into the library.

She was dressed stylishly in a sleek black dress, perhaps just a shade darker than her hair, which was long and glowed like a shampoo commercial. Her make-up was artfully applied, her jewelry delicate. She smiled and extended her hand to Jones. "Radu," she purred as he offered her what had been Rowena's wine. She kissed him chastely on the cheek.

"Let me introduce you," Ray said. "This handsome couple is Bill and Rowena Parr. And I believe you remember Claire."

She extended her hand. "I do. Hello, Claire. So nice to see you again."

"Hello, Doctor Moceanu."

* * *

"Benjamin, I have never tasted roast beef this good!" enthused Claire as she finished her second medium rare slab and inwardly wished she could ask for more. "What's your secret?"

Jones had called Benjamin from the kitchen at Claire's request. Emma stood to the side, beaming.

"You have to buy the second through the fourth ribs," the elderly chef explained. "I told the butcher, I said two prime ribs from the same steer, second through fourth on each side. That's the secret. Plus the seasonings," he added, "and those will remain my secrets."

"All right, then," said Bill, "but can you tell us about your Yorkshire pudding? It's so light it almost floated off the plate. I had to hold it down with my knife and fork."

"Ah, that's no secret at all, Mr. Parr. I place the ribs directly on the middle oven rack and put a roasting pan on the rack below it to catch the drippings. After the beef is done, I take the roast out to rest for a few minutes. I remove the middle rack and pour the pudding batter into the hot drippings. It rises like you see it, but it has to be served immediately, else it falls."

Rowena said, "This is a work of art, Benjamin."

"Men make the best chefs," interjected Emma with a nod to the guests. "That's what I keep telling him."

"Hear that, Bill?"

"Hey, I cook."

"You sure do … but not in the kitchen. Ah, Jeez, folks, now my hubby's blushing."

"No fair. No one can see it when you blush."

"I never blush."

Benjamin excused himself to prepare dessert. Once he was gone, Jones said, "Emma, I've said it before, you chose well."

"As did he, sir," replied Emma. "Now if you'll excuse me." She left to join her husband in the kitchen.

"You see why I love these two," said Jones.

"So, Daciana," said Rowena, turning the conversation, "tell me how you happened to meet Ray."

"Radu and Gabriel were fast friends growing up. They went to high school together here in Boston, and even though one was what you would call a science nerd and the other was a literature buff, they had much in common besides a love for the Red Sox."

Jones nodded. "We went our separate ways after high school but still managed to convene at Fenway Park when the Sox were playing at home. Gabe met Daci when he joined the faculty at Criterion. I was best man at the wedding." He looked from Daciana to his guests. "And she looks as lovely today as she did when she was a bride."

"Stop it, you."

Claire said, "So, I have to ask, are your intentions toward our boss honorable?" She tried to keep her tone light, but there was an edge to her voice. Maybe it had something to do with Daciana's perfume, which might have been subtle to the others, but to her was overpowering.

"Very, I assure you both," Daciana said. "Gabriel, after all, has been … gone … for just a year, and I still pine for him. Radu has been an island of familiarity—and comfort." She added, "If only he didn't live so far from the college." She turned her attention to Claire. "So, Claire, I know this might still be a sensitive subject, but have you heard anything, anything at all, from your friend Mr. Ehrlich?"

Before she could sputter an answer, Benjamin entered the room. "Emma, the table needs clearing; dessert's ready."

* * *

On the drive home—Daciana had left first, citing the long drive back to Criterion—Claire asked from the Benz's spacious back seat, "So, what did you two think of Morticia?"

"Who?" asked Bill.

Rowena said, "What do you mean, Mor—oh, I get it."

"Doesn't she look like she belongs in the Addams Family?"

"That's not kind. You both should be ashamed of yourselves," said Bill. "I think she's kind of hot."

"Down, boy. You're spoken for."

"Besides, I'm not being totally fair. When I first met her she was an iceberg. But tonight she was almost charming. Maybe it's Ray's influence."

Rowena said, "Well, what was that about, her asking about Lukas? I mean, that sounds pretty callous. Or maybe just naïve?"

"I kind of wondered about that, too," said Bill. "Obviously, she knows Lukas is a person of interest to the authorities."

"Say it, Bill: a suspect. It's okay," said Claire. "It's been a year now, and I'm used to it. But I know in my heart he wouldn't kill Gabe. I mean, it was an animal that did it, right?"

"Or made to look like an animal."

"Well, even if it were Lukas—and again, I'm sure it wasn't—why would he kill him in his own house? That part absolutely doesn't make sense."

"Agreed. But if Lukas happened to come home and find the body there, why didn't *he* call the police instead of just disappearing like that? That doesn't make sense either."

Claire nodded. "Maybe fear took over. I don't know. The whole thing is crazy."

Rowena turned to look at her friend. "It's still driving you nuts after all this time, isn't it, babe?"

"You have no idea."

* * *

Claire had forgotten about Ronny Music by mid-June. She hadn't thought to ask Rowena if she'd returned his portfolio with a letter of rejection. But Rowena hadn't forgotten. When she was alone, she would often thumb through his portfolio, stopping at the figure study of the woman on a stool. Finally, she took out her cell phone and made a call to New Jersey.

"I know we haven't gotten back to you in a while, and I'm sorry to have to inform you the news on the publication front isn't good. Normally, we'd send you a form letter, but I wanted to tell you personally —and talk to you about a possible commission. My husband will be away on business for a week later this month, and I thought I'd surprise him …"

* * *

Ronny arrived at Rowena's front door with a folded easel in one hand and a suitcase in the other. When he noticed her puzzled expression, he explained that if he'd had to book a hotel (and try booking a hotel in Boston during the summer for less than two hundred a night), he'd have to charge her even more.

From her talk with Claire, Rowena knew Ronny was either perpetually short on funds or a total cheapskate. Maybe alimony and child support had drained his bank account. "We have a spare room," she finally said. "At the far end of the hall."

"Great," he said and proceeded to make himself at home. Once settled in, he retrieved from the trunk of his ten-year-old Nissan Sentra a thirty-by-forty-inch canvas, pre-stretched and stapled to a wooden frame, a paint-spattered easel, and a set of oils in a hardwood box. "Before we start—" he began.

"I know. It's lunchtime. I'll fix us something."

Ronny smiled. He reminded her of a ginger-bearded snowman. "Where did you say your husband was again?"

"I didn't say. But he's in New York leading an investment seminar."

"Outstanding. And you did arrange to have the week off from work, right?"

"Uh huh. In the real world, we call it vacation."

"Then we can get started this afternoon."

Across the kitchen table, munching on his second chicken sandwich, he said, "What about your dog over there?"

"Greycie? Well, I'll have to take her out for her walks, but otherwise she'll just watch. Greyhounds are couch potatoes. Sometimes I think they're more cat than dog. She won't be interrupting anything, if that's what you're thinking. She's an old timer now, spends most of her time sleeping."

Ronny nodded and wiped a touch of mayonnaise from his mustache. "Excellent." He fidgeted. "There is one thing," he said as Rowena brought the dishes to the sink. She turned and leaned against the counter, regarding him. "I don't want to make you uncomfortable, but before I apply the paint, I'm going to have to sketch you first in charcoal … in the nude."

She arched an eyebrow as she asked, "So … why do you have to be nude?"

Ronny blinked. "No, you—oh, I get it. Good one."

"I understand why. Proportion and all that. But I warn you, my daddy was a Marine, and he taught me some tricks with a bayonet that you wouldn't want me to demonstrate."

"This is totally professional, I assure you," he said. "The woman in the portrait you like was also nude at first." He smiled back, the skin around his eyes crinkling. "And I promise to keep my distance from you. That's best anyway, it avoids distortion."

She took a breath. "So let's get started. Set up your canvas and easel, and I'll get ready."

Even in a white terry bathrobe, Rowena looked stunning. Her cocoa-colored skin, her large dark eyes, her glossy black hair now down around her shoulders made Ronny gasp as she entered the living room. She walked to the kitchen and brought out a stool, placing it across the room from him.

"Aida," he said to himself, just loud enough to be heard.

"You wouldn't say that if you heard me sing," Rowena replied. "So—what do you want me to do?"

"Sit on the stool with your back to me … and take off your robe … 'n stuff."

"There's no other 'stuff,' Ronny. Just me."

"It's a habit. Fills dead air." He watched as she turned her back, shed her robe, and perched on the stool. She doesn't have the stereotypical BWA, Ronnie thought, admiring the gentle curve of her buttocks. "Now turn a bit to the right. Good. Maybe you could put your right heel on the lower rung of the stool, and place your right hand on your knee." He knew he wouldn't use that pose, but he did want to see the shape of her breast and the color of her nipple. After a moment's "study," he had her resume her first pose. "Look over your right shoulder at me," he directed. "Perfect. Now hold still. Just like that." He picked up his charcoal stick, and his hand flew over the canvas.

"You are good, very good," Rowena said after he was done. She had her robe on again, the sash cinched around her waist, looking at the finished figure study. Ronny stood alongside, admiring Rowena almost as much as his charcoal work.

Ronny didn't thank her; she was simply acknowledging a fact. "What background would you want?"

She thought a moment. "I don't know. What would you suggest?"

"How about the one in the other painting?"

"I like that. Subtle, and it didn't compete for your attention. It looked almost like a photographer's backdrop."

"That's what I would've chosen, too. You have a good eye," Ronny said. "And the rest of you looks pretty good, too."

Rowena stepped aside. "Careful there. Remember my bayonet training."

"Just kidding," he said. "I found if I make a woman feel beautiful it comes through in her facial expression when I paint it … 'n stuff." He noticed her look. "Not that you're not already beautiful, because you are. I'm just … habit again."

"I'm going to change into my clothes now, Ronny. Then I'll fix dinner."

"Um … would you like to go to a restaurant?"

She thought back to Claire's description of their lunch together. "I'm a good cook," she said. "Beauty, brains, and a dynamo in the kitchen."

"Your husband's a lucky man."

"I remind him of that almost every day."

* * *

The days passed and the painting took shape. Ronny painted the background first, in a wash of oils that was darker at the edges than in the area that would halo Rowena's body. Then he painted her body, nude, filling in every detail from memory. When she asked if it were necessary to show the parts that would be covered by the sash, he insisted it was.

And after they'd said goodnight, he came back from his room with a digital camera and photographed it.

When the time came for Ronny to position the drape around his subject, she once again perched nude on the stool. He was very fastidious about its positioning, running his hands over each fold, smoothing it out here, tucking it in there, his fingers occasionally and "accidentally" sliding over Rowena's skin. She glanced at his face as he worked the drape.

"Is the AC set too warm?" she asked, the picture of innocence. "I notice you're sweating." Like a pig, she said to herself.

"No, it's fine," he replied, sneaking a look at her nipples. "Okay, that's perfect. Now look over your shoulder at me but don't worry about your facial expression. I'm going to do the drape first, then I'll do you."

"Excuse me?"

"Your face," he amended. "I know, it came out wrong." When he was satisfied with the drape, he told her to look at him and put a half smile on her lips. She might want to relax her eyelids too, give them a come-hither look. "That's perfect," he said.

"Shouldn't I have put on some make-up first?"

"No. I'll do that in paint. I've seen you in your make-up, you know, when we met, and I can duplicate it. Maybe even enhance it a little." He caught her look. "I mean, it's perfect for work … 'n stuff. You know, tasteful, understated, and all that. But for intimate moments, you might want to enhance it just a tad."

When Bill and I are "intimate," Rowena thought, I'm usually not wearing any make-up at all. It smudges the linens. She chuckled to herself. When we were newlies, we didn't worry about that at all. She took a breath, and her smile became genuine.

"Perfect," Ronny said. "Hold that look."

* * *

The week ended, and Ronny proclaimed the painting complete. And he turned it to the wall, refusing to let Rowena look at it until the next day, when it had dried. That night she took him to a neighborhood pub where comfort food was the specialty. She ordered fish and chips with malt vinegar. Sparkling water to drink. Ronny ordered an appetizer of nachos followed by a cup of chili con carne, a Delmonico steak, two baked potatoes, and stir-fried zucchini. Rowena finished her meal with coffee, Ronny with death by chocolate.

"It's going to be the death of me yet," he said, grinning.

"Well, if you're dead, that makes your art even more valuable, doesn't it?"

He laughed.

The bill was placed on Ronny's side of the table. He made no move to pick it up. Rowena finally reached across the table and took it.

* * *

When Rowena awoke the next day, she walked into the living room and saw that Ronny had placed a drape over the finished painting. She stood there in her pajamas, wondering if she dared lift the screen.

"Don't do that," came a voice from behind her. Ronny, dressed in shorts and a polo shirt that might have carried a Michelin stamp embossed at the waist, left his room carrying his suitcase. "Let me put my stuff in the car. Then I'll be back, and we can look at it together."

When he lifted the drape, Ro inhaled audibly. The painting was beyond beautiful. She was speechless for a full minute, studying every detail, as Ronny preened.

Finally, he took a piece of paper from a pocket in his cargo shorts. He unfolded it and presented it to Ro. It had spots where his sweaty fingers had held it. "My bill," he said.

It was exactly as he'd quoted her—no surprises. But considering the way he'd eaten her out of house and home this past week, the painting had cost her double. Bill would love it, though. She would have it framed and hung on their wall—living room? Bedroom? Hmm.

"I'll get my checkbook," Ro said.

Ronny placed a hand on her arm. "Wait," he said.

"Yes?"

"It's been a good week."

"Yes, it has."

"You're a beautiful woman. Aida, my Nubian princess."

"Not Nubian, not a princess, and definitely not yours, Ronny. Please don't ruin a good thing by taking this any further."

She tried to pull her arm back, but his hand tightened around her sleeve.

Ronny's forehead was glistening. "You are so beautiful. You've got to let me at least kiss you."

Her face clouded. "I don't, and I won't. Now leave. I'll mail you your check. But right now, I sincerely need you gone."

Before she could react, he pulled her toward him. He cupped one hand to her buttocks, reached up with his other hand, and pulled her face to his. His lips smashed against hers, the mustache and beard scratching her face. He forced his tongue into her mouth—and she bit it.

"Ouch!" he cried, pulling back.

"I could've bitten through it, Ronny. Consider that a warning."

"I've got to have you," he cried, advancing on her.

She backed into the kitchen, where he cornered her against the granite counter and pressed himself against her. He pushed his hips forward, grabbed her buttocks with one hand and a breast with the other. He didn't hear her slide a drawer open, but he did feel the point of a blade under his armpit. It pierced his skin, and he shrieked. Ronny took a step back, felt a trickle of blood run down his side, saw it begin to stain his shirt. His mouth opened wide, his eyes wider.

"A little prick for a little prick," Rowena said through clenched teeth. She assumed a fighter's stance, a slight crouch, her feet spread shoulder-wide, left arm forward, and the right—the one holding the nine-inch knife—back by her side. Her hand didn't grip the hilt, but the blade itself, halfway down, as her father had taught her. "Now if you don't leave I'm going to cut your balls off and shove them down your throat."

Ronny ran from the kitchen, past the painting, to the front door.

"Stop!" Rowena called, and he did, turning to face her, one hand on the knob. "Here's your bill." She crumpled it up and threw it at him. "And here's something else for you to think about."

"No!" he cried, watching in horror as she plunged the blade through the upper left corner of the canvas and sliced it down to the lower right. "No! No! No!" Tears sprung from his eyes.

Rowena took a step forward, knife at the ready, and stopped as Ronny fumbled with the doorknob. Her eyes were tearing, too. "Now, either prepare to eat your nuts or get out of here before you drip blood on my carpet."

He flew off, leaving the door open behind him.

Rowena slammed and locked the door behind him. She leaned against it, breathing hard, sobbing. She looked at the painting, the slash an obscene gap in what until a few moments ago had been a masterpiece. She walked—staggered—past it and back to the kitchen. She ran the tip of the knife under the faucet, dried it, and put it away. Her legs and hands were trembling. She stood at the sink, looking down at the drain, wishing for a cigarette to calm her nerves.

Retreating into the prosaic, she put on a pot of coffee and waited for the first cup to drip down. She sugared and creamed her coffee and drank it too quickly; it burned her mouth. She poured another cup and with shaking fingers picked the wall phone from its cradle.

*   *   *

Claire arrived as soon as she could after work. She looked at the painting, at Rowena—still in her pajamas—and listened as they sat at the kitchen table while Greycie napped in her crate. "I just put on a robe and slippers to take her for her walk. Neighbors must've thought I was nuts. Or drunk."

Then she told her friend exactly what had happened.

"But the painting," Claire protested. "Did you have to ruin it? It's gorgeous."

"Babe, every time I looked at it I'd be reminded of the vermin who painted it."

"So what will you do with it?"

"Shred it. Put it out with the trash. Along with his bill. Just let him try to collect—although I don't think he will. I pretty much scared him. Scared myself, too. I never thought I could threaten a person like that … and mean it." She paused. "I'm not sure I like what I learned about myself today."

Claire covered her hand with her own. "Ro, you did great."

"Don't mention a word of this to Bill, okay? This week never happened."

"Understood." She made a zip motion across her lips.

Rowena took a breath. "I think I could have killed him, Claire."

"I know I could." Claire looked into her friend's red-rimmed eyes. "In fact, I think I'd enjoy it."

Chapter

Fourteen

"Claire, dear, I know this is sudden, but Gene and I would like to invite you to spend this weekend with us. Fourth of July is Monday, and you know there's nothing like the fireworks over the ocean. Please say yes." When she heard no immediate response, Nina continued: "Dale just called; he'll be staying with us, too. You'll remember, he's the Army ranger we told you about, he taught with Gene until 9/11. I'm sure there's a book inside him waiting to be written."

Nina couldn't see Claire's smile from the telephone, but she could hear it in her voice. "Nina, I think you're up to something. I'll seriously have to think about it." And without waiting a beat, said, "All right."

They laughed, and then Claire winced at the thought of the holiday traffic. Today was Friday, it was barely nine o'clock, and the traffic would have started already. It would be bad enough normally with people flocking to the Cape or the Vineyard. But that barely mobile parking lot couldn't hold a candle to the crawl heading for the Jersey Shore on Independence Day weekend. Oh well, she was committed. "What can I bring?"

"Just your sweet self, dear. We'll gorge on the typical holiday fare, maybe do some fishing from the surf—well, you will—and watch the fireworks over Point Pleasant."

When she hung up, Claire thought the timing was perfect. Still paranoid that someone might be watching her every move, what she needed was a few days relaxing among friends, friends who had become more like parents, on her old stomping grounds. As for this Dale person, well, he was an unknown. She was more interested in seeing another man at the moment, also a New Jersey resident: one whom all of them knew to some degree, but none more intimately than Rowena Parr.

*   *   *

"Well, it's about time you got here," said Gene, his arms open wide as Claire climbed out of the Golden Goose wearing shorts and a loose-fitting top. Her fair blonde hair tumbled from her Red Sox baseball cap, and dark sunglasses hid her sensitive eyes from the too-bright sun. She ran into Gene's embrace, then hugged Nina, as well.

"Hey, when I told Mr. Jones I'd be visiting you he told me to get out of his office and hit the road. How's that for a boss?"

"I'll get your bag," said a deep voice. Claire looked up at the speaker, a man who at first glance reminded her of GI Joe on steroids. He stood a couple of inches taller than she, and his light brown hair contained a trace of gray at the temples. It was cut short on the sides, what servicemen called "high and tight." His face gave the impression it had been chiseled from stone, all angles and sharp definition: high cheekbones, Roman nose, square chin. His eyes were pale green, his chest reminded her of a beer keg laid on its side, and his waist looked like she could wrap her hands around it and have her thumbs and fingertips touch. He was a walking recruiting poster.

"You're Dale, I presume."

"Dale Keegan, and if you're not Claire Delaney, well, that's okay by me." His voice was a touch raspy, his smile disarming.

"Dale just got here himself," said Nina. "Gene picked him up at the airport."

"Newark?"

"No, Monmouth, right next door in Wall Township; they renamed it Allaire since you've been gone. Dale flew his plane in for the weekend."

"I'm impressed."

"No big thing," said Dale. "It's a puddle jumper, on loan from our rich uncle; you know, Sam."

"But you are a pilot."

"I'm learning." His grin told her he didn't take himself seriously.

They adjourned to the screened porch and enjoyed tall glasses of iced lemonade. "You must be a baseball fan," said Claire, starting the conversation with small talk. "That cap you're wearing. Harrisburg Senators. Would they be in the American League or the … other one?"

Dale smiled. "They're a farm team for the Nationals; you know, Washington?"

"Oh."

"My sister lives in Central Pennsylvania; or as she calls it, Pennsyltucky. She bought me this when she dragged me to a game. I'm sorry to say that I couldn't care less about professional sports."

"Why sorry?"

He nodded toward her cap. "You're obviously a Red Sox fan."

"Hah. No, I just live in Boston. If you don't support the home team, you're ranked up there with Benedict Arnold." She pointed toward her cap. "A friend bought this for me when she took me to my one and only game at Fenway Park. To tell the truth, as if you haven't guessed already, I don't even know how many hits equal a touchdown."

"You are kidding, right?"

"Not by all that much."

Nina excused herself to fix dinner, and Gene decided to join her, something Claire knew he was unaccustomed to doing. Cleanup yes, preparation no.

"So you're in the Army, Gene tells me."

"Uh huh. Reactivated after the terror attacks. I was perfectly happy teaching little kids history, but such was not to be." He took a sip of his lemonade and saw her watching him. "I don't drink alcohol, and I don't smoke either. Weird for a soldier, huh?"

"Neither do I. And no, not weird. So where did the Army send you when you went back in? And how long before you can go back to teaching school?"

"Second question first. I'm in for the duration. And after the Army gave me a refresher course in Ranger training, they sent me on holiday to Afghanistan."

"Some holiday. What was it like?"

"Cold."

"Pardon me?"

"I know, it doesn't fit with what you've heard. I was sent there in the winter, to the area around Khost. Lots of mountains, lots of snow and ice."

"What were you sent to do, if you don't have to kill me after you tell me, that is?"

"Afraid I would, Claire." Another grin. "And I wouldn't want to do that."

She narrowed her eyes. "Have I seen you somewhere before?"

"Not that I'm aware of. And I think I would be aware if I'd seen you."

"Silver-tongued devil," said Nina through the screen door. "I heard that."

Claire fidgeted in her seat. She sniffed a certain scent about him that was nearly covered by the tang of salt air, one that was vaguely familiar. Pheromones? Experience had told her to expect that from men, but this was subtly different. Hard to tell, competing as it was not only with the salt air but also with the smell of frying fish wafting from the kitchen. Whatever it was, it seemed to call up a memory of Lukas.

"Soup's on," came Nina's voice from inside. "Come and get it."

* * *

Dinner conversation was mostly small talk, with Gene and Nina contributing most of it. Until, that is, Claire mentioned that she had finally gotten a cable TV connection and could now watch her favorite programs from the 1960s and '70s. Dale's interest was piqued.

"Really. I watch those, too, when I have the time," he said. "What are your favorites?"

She rattled off a few, and he nodded as Gene and Nina exchanged pleased looks. "I've always loved the *Get Smart* shtick Max would spout in every episode. Have to laugh, even though you know what's coming."

Dale cocked an eyebrow and twisted his mouth to the side. *"Would you believe,"* he quoted, "that at this moment, the entire Naval Sixth Fleet is steaming up the river on its way here to smash your illegal shipping operation and rescue me?"

Claire picked up, deepening her voice and affecting a Russian accent: "I would find that hard to believe, Mr. Smart."

"Then ... would you believe a forty-two-foot Coast Guard cutter?"

"I don't think so."

"How about ... two cops in a rowboat?"

They laughed together.

Gene said, "Would you believe ... that Don Adams was a Marine who fought in the Pacific during World War II? Guadalcanal, I think."

"Mister Trivia," Nina said. "I keep telling him he should be on *Jeopardy*."

"You mean Maxwell Smart was a Marine?" asked Claire.

"He was, and quite the hero. When I started teaching in 1970, the show was in its final year. I enjoyed telling the kids about actors who had served honorably. Expanded their perceptions. Lee Marvin, you know, also fought against the Japanese. Earned the Purple Heart."

"Him I'd expect. Tough guy."

Dale said, "Then would you believe … Captain Kangaroo?"

"What?" Claire said. "What's next: Mr. Green Jeans was really Douglas MacArthur?"

"No, but it's true that before he became Clarabelle the Clown and Captain Kangaroo, Bob Keeshan was an enlisted man—Marines again—but before he could ship out the Japanese surrendered, so he never saw action."

Claire held up her right hand and formed a V between her second and third fingers. She arched an eyebrow. "Fascinating, Captain."

"Staff sergeant, actually."

Nina said, "Dale was offered a battlefield commission while he was in Afghanistan, but he refused."

"Thanks, Nina. Last time I tell you anything."

"No kidding," said Claire. "Why did you refuse?"

Dale shrugged his shoulders. "Figured I'd rather work for a living."

Nina said, "Listen, you all. There's plenty of light left, so why don't you three take some fishing poles and head for the surf? These are the last of the fresh fish." Her eyes twinkled. "After all, Gene and I are poor pensioners now, and we need to live off the land—or in this case, the sea—as much as we can."

"Poor pensioners my foot," said Claire, laughing. "I've seen your royalty statements, and we're getting ready to gear up production for your next printing."

* * *

The three of them, dressed in bathing suits, waded into the surf and cast their lures. Other fishermen lined the beach, but no one seemed to be catching anything. With the sun lighting their backs, Claire couldn't help but notice the roadmap of scars on Dale's body. Some formed a series of parallel lines, others pale circles in closely spaced pairs. She said nothing, but they convinced her, as if she needed convincing, that if they'd been recently earned, his Afghan "holiday" was no vacation at all.

"Speaking of trivia, I have a question for you, Claire," Dale said as they stood in the wash.

"Shoot."

"What's the first thing you know?"

She frowned. "Okay, that's not the question I'd expect. What is it again?"

"What's the first thing you know?"

"You're serious?"

"Serious."

They cast their Hopkins lures past the breakers as Gene called over to tell them to stop casting so far out. They were making him look bad. The surf swirled around their calves, and pink-shelled sand crabs bumped against their ankles, carried by the wash.

Claire thought for a minute. "First thing you know. Okay, what it's like to have a doctor hold you upside down and slap your behind."

"Good guess, but no."

"What it feels like to be floating inside the womb?"

"Nope."

"All right, genius. When you're a freshly fertilized egg."

"No again. What's the first thing you *really* know?"

"Is this some kind of metaphysical question?" He didn't reply. "All right, I give up. What's the first thing you know?"

"I'll tell you tomorrow, before I take off."

"You fink."

As the sky darkened, Gene pronounced them skunked, and the trio returned to the house carrying only their rods and Gene's tackle box and bucket.

* * *

The fish weren't biting Saturday or Sunday either. Gene wasn't deterred, but Claire and Dale finally gave up and spent most of both days swimming in the sixty-degree surf. The ocean was at its warmest in September, but these crowds didn't seem to mind the cold. The water was clean and green, the breakers were perfect for body surfing, and the sun dried their bodies almost as soon as they emerged from the wash. Nina brought picnic lunches to the beach both days, and the four of them presented a picture of proud parents and happy children.

After dinner on Sunday, Dale announced that he'd be leaving the next day.

"But it's the Fourth. You'll miss the fireworks," said Nina.

"Tell the truth, I'm not all that fond of fireworks any more. And I do have work waiting for me on Tuesday."

Claire looked at Dale and thought that his dislike of fireworks was logical considering where he'd been and what he'd probably experienced. He seemed stoic, but she wondered about his scars, both the physical and emotional. Maybe Gene was right; maybe there was a book inside Dale waiting to be written: a book about his mission in Afghanistan, about whether he suffered from battle fatigue, or shell shock, or PTSD, whatever they called it these days. Maybe, too, Gene would be the one to write it.

* * *

For breakfast Monday morning, Nina fixed a whopping meal of bacon, Taylor ham, sausage, and eggs—three eggs for Claire, four for Dale. They noshed with gusto. "Look at them go," said Nina. "How do they stay so slim?"

Dale wiped his mouth. "Got to have my protein."

Claire looked up. "Hey. You said it right."

"What?"

"Pro-te-in, not pro-teen. How many other people know how to pronounce that word?"

Dale considered and said, "Pro-teen. Doesn't that refer to someone's advocating on behalf of adolescents?"

Gene advised Dale never to engage in a grammar contest with Claire.

Claire said, "Okay, here's your final exam. Pronounce P-I-A-N-I-S-T."

"P-I-A—"

"Stop it."

"All right. Pee-AN-ist. That okay?"

"Bingo. How many people pronounce it PEE-in-ist? Answer: most."

"Well, the instrument is a pee-AN-o, not a PEE-an-o. Just seems to make sense. Besides, I would think that PEE-in-ist refers to the person who drank the most beer."

Gene looked to his wife. "I think these two make a good team, yes?"

Dale said, "My turn. How do you pronounce M-A-C-B-E-T-H?"

"Gee, that's a tough one. How about MacBeth?"

"Very good. Now try M-A-C-D-U-F-F."

"As in, 'Lay on, MacDuff'?"

"Okay, last one: M-A-C-H-I-N-E."

This was too easy. "MacHine?"

"Excellent. Next time I'll teach you how to say *machine*."

She crumpled up her napkin and threw it at him.

After breakfast, Dale insisted Nina let him do the dishes. Claire said she'd dry if he washed, and he replied he'd call her when he was ready. He cleared the table, and before long they heard the water running. But he didn't call Claire right away, so she walked into the kitchen to check on him.

Dale had already packed his duffel. It lay in a corner of the kitchen. Claire saw he already had most of the dishes washed and resting on the drainboard. "It's really more sanitary if they air dry," he explained.

"Right," Claire said. "Not trying to avoid me, are you?"

"Why would I do that? You planning to attack me with another deadly napkin?"

"Maybe, you know Nina told me your life story would make a good book, and maybe I'd try to finesse a book deal out of you."

"Nah. Here's my life story, and it's not remarkable at all. To begin with, I was born at a very early age."

"Stop it. Now."

"Okay. I was born in Point Pleasant, other side of the inlet. After high school I enlisted in the Army, went to airborne and Ranger school, did some assignments stateside and overseas. And no, don't ask. Anyway, I discovered I'd rather win the hearts and minds of children than deprive them of their fathers. So when my hitch was up, I went back home and took teaching courses at Monmouth. I got a job at Gene's school and had three great years ... until the terror attacks. Then I went back on active duty. And, after my vacation in Afghanistan—"

"Which wasn't a vacation."

"All right. After my tour of duty, I was reassigned to conduct training exercises back here at home."

"Uh huh." She decided not to press him on Afghanistan. Not yet.

"And that's about it. Oh, my parents have retired and moved to the Pacific Northwest to their new digs on Puget Sound. Seems they can't get away from the water, and Mom loves her garden. Weather's much more conducive to planting. And Dad? I remember his telling me when I was a kid that he couldn't wait until he was old enough to putter." His eyes looked at Claire but were focused on something beyond. "Now he has his workshop, and he putters all day long. Good for him. Good for them."

"How old are you?" Claire asked.

"Beg pardon?"

"You've packed a lot of experience into your life. I'm just wondering how many years that is."

"Oh. I'm thirty-three. You?"

"Got a few years on me, Gramps. I'm a mere twenty-four." She grinned. "But I'm old for my age."

"You're twenty-four?"

"Yes, why?"

"No reason. I just thought you might be older."

"Ouch. You mean I look older."

"No offense, but I thought you were closer to my age. Guess I should've kept my mouth shut, huh?"

"Too late now, the damage is done."

"Maybe it's time for me to leave before I put my foot deeper in my mouth. Gene's driving me to the airport. I don't suppose you'd want to come along?"

* * *

The drive to Allaire Airport took less than a half hour. "There's my plane," said Dale, pointing beyond the fence. "It's a Cessna 172, about as old as you are, Claire. With an upgraded powerplant." When she appeared surprised, he said, "Planes don't age like cars, and they don't become obsolete. Some DC-3s built in the 1930s are still earning a living."

"No, but I mean it's tiny. And it has just one engine."

"So does your car."

"Yes, but if my engine stops, I can pull over to the side of the road. You can't park on a cloud and call AAA."

"True."

"So you wear a parachute, in case?"

"No. If the engine were to quit—very unlikely, by the way—I'd just have to find a place to put down."

The three of them walked into the administration building. Dale greeted the man behind the desk, who handed him the keys to the plane. They walked through another door and onto the ramp. Claire said, "But isn't a crash landing more dangerous than bailing out?"

"Claire, my first responsibility is to make sure I don't injure any innocent civilians or damage any buildings on the ground. I couldn't guarantee that if I left the plane to crash wherever it happened to fall. Oh, and by the way, we don't call it a crash. We refer to it as an off-airport landing."

"Well, that's comforting. Ever happen to you?"

"No."

They reached the aircraft, and as Gene stood to the side, Claire followed Dale as he opened the doors to let the summer heat escape, placed his duffel in the luggage compartment, and then began his pre-flight inspection. He examined the plane as if he expected every rivet to fall out.

"So: where are you headed?"

"Frederick. That's in Maryland."

"Is there an Army base there?"

"No. But the airport isn't far from my duty station."

"Which is where?"

"Thurmont. Little town just south of Gettysburg."

"Have I heard of it? The name sounds familiar. Thurmont, I mean."

"It's a pretty small installation. But it's on mountainous terrain, which makes for an excellent training environment." He motioned to Gene and shook his hand. "Next time, brother."

"Next time," Gene replied.

"Claire, really nice to meet you." He extended his hand. "In spite of my gaffe about your age."

"Next time," she echoed. Dale nodded, closed the door under the right wing, and walked to the the pilot's side. "Wait a minute," she called. "You forgot something."

"What's that?"

"You promised to tell me the answer. You know, what's the first thing you know."

"Oh, right, the first thing you absolutely know, beyond any reasonable doubt." He leaned his head forward, gripped an air guitar, and affected a country twang as he sang, "First thing you know, ol' Jed's a millionaire."

Her eyes bugged. "You—!"

"And you call yourself an old-time TV buff. Shame on you."

"Hey, wait."

"What?"

"Some day I want a ride in that thing."

"You got it." He tossed her a casual salute and climbed aboard.

They watched him fire up the Cessna's engine, taxi to the runway, and take off to the northwest on Runway 32. "Very cool," Claire said to herself, without bothering to question whether she was referring to the plane or to the man flying it.

* * *

"Turnabout's fair play," Claire said when they'd returned to Manasquan and she'd packed her car. "You both have to come to Boston for Thanksgiving. That's an order. I'm negotiating right now for an apartment with two bedrooms."

The couple looked at each other, then back to Claire. "You've got a deal," said Gene.

"Claire," said Nina, "you dried the dishes. Where'd you put the juice glasses?"

Claire thought a second. "With the others, in the cabinet next to the sink. Why?"

"I set the table with four. Only three made it back. Oh, well."

Claire shook her head and shrugged.

Gene glanced at Claire and said to his wife, "I hid it. I'm trying to drive you slowly insane."

"What do you mean, slowly?"

"Was it the Fred Flintstone glass? Your favorite?" Nina stuck her tongue out. "Looks like you're just going to have to buy more jelly."

Nina shook her head. "Hopeless." Then, "Claire, you drive safe now."

That would be *safely*, Claire thought but kept her mouth shut, wondering why she couldn't shake that damnable habit of correcting others' English, even if only in her own mind.

"Love you both," she said, hugging and kissing them. "Oh, by the way, have you heard anything from Ronny Music? He didn't seem happy when he learned Jones Publishing was probably not the venue for his book."

"Haven't heard a word," said Gene.

"Good riddance to bad rubbish," said Nina, adding, "but that's not very Christian of me, is it?"

"Ronny's probably at Monmouth Park as we speak," Gene said. "His summer job, I think I mentioned it to you."

"Oh, right."

"Race track rent-a-cop," said Nina as if she'd bitten into a lemon.

"Just curious. Some people don't handle rejection well. I'm glad he didn't come around demanding to know why you got published and he didn't."

"Just let him try," muttered Nina.

More hugs, more kisses, and Claire was on the road. She took Route 34 North and picked up the Garden State Parkway at Exit 98. But instead of staying on the GSP to connect with the Turnpike, she got off at Exit 105 and headed east on Route 36.

Toward Monmouth Park.

Chapter
Fifteen

There he was, chatting with a girl who looked half his age, wearing a white shirt and a black tie that hung half the distance to his belt, his wrinkled black trousers valiantly struggling to stay up around his waist. Claire thought he'd gotten even heavier since she'd seen him. He'd said he ate when he got stressed, she remembered. Maybe Ro and her kitchen knife were responsible for the extra heft.

The girl had shiny chestnut hair that fell to the top of her low-rider jeans, and her midriff was bare up to the bottom of her modest breasts. *Modest*, Claire thought, might not be the best choice of words; the neckline of her halter-top was scooped nearly to its elasticized bottom. A jeweled chain descended from her navel. She had a cigarette in her hand, and Ronny was making a show of checking her driver's license, ostensibly to make sure she was twenty-one.

He didn't see Claire as she approached from his rear quarter, all attention focused on the girl's photo ID, her face, and her neckline. "You are definitely legal," he assured her in his most authoritative voice. "But you look so young—that's a compliment, by the way—that I had to check you out."

The girl stood a couple of inches shorter than he, even in her high-heeled cork-soled sandals. She took a slow drag, pursed her lips, and blew smoke into his face. Then she turned on one heel and walked away toward the rail.

"Can't win 'em all," Claire said. Ronny jumped and spun around. "Maybe you'd have better luck if you set your sights ... higher." She smiled down at his astonished face.

"Claire. Claire Delaney. What—what are you doing here? You're supposed to be in Boston."

"I was visiting friends. Just thought I might stop in at the track and catch a race or two before heading back to Boston. And *voila*, look who I run into."

He stammered a greeting, and Claire decided to let him squirm a bit. He has to be wondering if I know about his week with Rowena, she thought. Was she a threat to him, or might she be a prospect? Time to put his mind at ease, for now. She put out her hand and took his.

"Great to see you again, socially that is. I want you to know I put in a plug for your book proposal, but I'm just a lowly editor, and it was nixed higher up on the food chain." She forced a sweet smile. "I really tried, Ronny. I believed—still believe—you have a lot to offer." She lifted an eyebrow. Lordy, she thought, am I vamping this guy or what?

The bell clanged, the crowd cheered, and the speaker blared, "They're off!"

"Um, I'm on duty until the track closes. But would you want to, uh, get together ... 'n stuff ... later?"

Claire pursed her lips, as if in thought. "I guess I can book a hotel. Don't have to be back in Beantown until the day after tomorrow anyway."

"Claire, you've been away from the area too long. This is the Fourth of July. Every hotel at the Jersey Shore is booked, I guarantee it. But ... if you need a place to crash ..."

She gave him a half smile. "You devil, you. But ... why don't we see what happens, okay?"

His Adam's apple bobbed. "What would you like to do after I get off work?"

"Well, this may sound stupid, but when I was a kid I always loved going to the boardwalk at Seaside Heights. Play the arcades, people watch, go on a few rides. Is the merry-go-round still there?" He nodded. "Good. Why don't we meet there at, say, eight o'clock? Meanwhile, I'll see if there are any hotels that haven't booked up ... you know, just in case ... and I'll see you later in Seaside."

* * *

Ronny arrived at the carousel a half hour early and watched the young riders go around in circles as the recorded organ music competed with the squeals of children and the loud voices of older boys trying to impress their dates with their knowledge of all things Jersey Shore—the best arcades, the best cheese steak stands, the best pizza. Guidos, he thought. He wore white shorts and a blue short-sleeved shirt, unbuttoned halfway down to expose a scattering of curly orange hair. A heavy gold crucifix descended from a thick gold chain and rested just above the deep crease where man breasts met belly. On his finger was a gold lion's head ring. Its eyes were inset with ruby chips. He jumped when Claire appeared at his side, as if by magic.

And she would be hard to miss, he thought, at nearly six feet tall, with that pale blonde hair falling over her shoulders, that shapeless red and white sundress doing nothing to steer attention from her breasts. Her lips were glossed pink, her nails painted the same shade, with French-style tips. Ronny's palms were already beginning to sweat.

"Scare you?" she said.

"I'll say. How do you sneak up on a person like that? You did that at the track today, too."

"I walk on padded feet, like a wolf on the prowl," she said. "And be careful, because I do bite." She laughed, and he joined her.

"Um, first things first, did you happen to find a hotel room for tonight?"

She shook her head, put on a sad face. "No, I didn't. And I confess, I gave up after Howard Johnson's. When I told the desk clerk I wanted a room, she laughed at me. That was after the Holiday Inn booted me."

Ronny beamed, reached into his pocket, and pulled out a key. "I kind of hoped you'd say that. Here, I had this made for you. It's to my condo in Toms River. The address is on the tag there."

"Well, Ronny, aren't you sweet. But why give me this, when you can unlock your own door for me?"

A touch of color came to his pasty cheek. "Maybe you'll want to visit me from Boston every now and then? If I'm in school ... 'n stuff ... you can let yourself in. Take it?"

"But wouldn't that start the neighbors gossiping?"

He put his hand to the side of his mouth, as if imparting a secret. "I've lived there a couple years and haven't met one neighbor. Listen: Their automatic garage doors open in the morning, and they drive off to work; around six o'clock their garage doors open again, they pull inside, and that's the last you see them until next morning."

"Perfect," Claire said and slipped the key into a pocket of her sundress. "So, now that that's settled, we're at the south end of the boardwalk. Let's go north, and stop at every booth." She offered her cool hand, and he took it in his clammy one. "Look, Kohr's frozen custard. I haven't had one of those in years. Come on."

Ronny actually paid for their cones, and they laughed as the custard melted down the cones and onto their hands. When they were done, Claire grabbed a handful of napkins and wiped Ronny's hands as well as her own, stroking his fingers slowly and pretending not to notice her effect on him.

They strolled on, the human beach ball and his blonde eye candy, past a busy sausage and pepper stand. "Want to get a sandwich?" Ronny asked. "I know, shouldn't have dessert first, but I haven't eaten since lunch."

Claire nodded toward the stand, where a cook sweated over a hot grill that fronted the boardwalk. Her acute eyes discerned a certain movement, and she thought she knew what was coming. "Watch," she said.

The cook rolled the sausages with the flat of his spatula and flipped the chopped green peppers on the greasy grill. The fly Claire had seen landed on the counter next to it. With a deft and practiced swipe, and cook slammed the flat of the spatula onto the fly and then returned it to the sausages and peppers.

"Still hungry?" Claire asked.

"How did you know that was going to happen?"

"Remember, I used to come here as a kid. Nice to know some things never change. Let's get a pizza instead. Any living thing on that will be sterilized to a crisp in the oven. Any preferences? I like the meat lover's pie myself."

The meat lover's pie it was: pepperoni, sausage, and ground beef. They ordered at a sit-down stand and polished off an extra large. "You do have an appetite," he observed as they licked the grease from their fingers.

"You have no idea. Oh, look, there's the fun house ride. I haven't been in one of those since I was a little girl."

"You were never a 'little' girl." He Groucho'ed his eyebrows, the way Lukas used to do. Claire hid her repugnance behind a come-hither smile.

They stood outside the fun house and watched the individual two-occupant cars creep along the rails through one door and, finally, out another some twenty feet away. Most cars were empty, but they traveled the course regardless. The wheels clacked on the tracks, and eerie music and deep ominous laughter blared from loudspeakers. Dracula, the wolf man, the mummy, and Frankenstein's monster, all designed to look like the Universal Pictures horror icons of the 1930s and '40s, were painted rather amateurishly on the façade. The ride was operated by a skinny, acne-scarred teen-age boy who looked like he'd rather be anywhere other than here, watching the rest of the world go by.

"Business slow?" asked Ronny of the boy.

"It's dead," he replied. The boy's tongue bore a stud, and his left eyebrow sported a gold ring. He checked his watch. "An hour to go, then I'm done. Just in time for the fireworks."

"Then you get to howl," said Claire. "Well, we'll give you some business. How much?"

They climbed into the next car, and the door opened as it rolled into pitch blackness. The first thing they felt was some gossamer strands strung from the ceiling to simulate spider webs. From either side of the tracks came a metallic chittering made to sound like rats. A double door in front of the car opened, and they entered a dim red-lighted chamber with an upright coffin to the left, a plastic skeleton standing inside. On the right, a spring-loaded Dracula lurched for the car and then pulled back. Rubber bats with battery-powered red eyes hung on monofilament fishing lines from the ceiling. Ahead, a mummy stood with arms outstretched and unmoving. Around a curve the car went, and there was Frankenstein's monster, locked in motionless combat with the wolf man, complete with recorded growls and howls. No wonder this ride is so unpopular, thought Claire. It wasn't even scary when she rode it as a child with her father. But then, its paucity of riders was what made it so attractive to her now.

The car wound through the last set of double doors, and they were back among the flashing lights, the whirr of the wheels at the games of chance, the hawking of T-shirts bearing obscene messages.

"So this was where you spent your misspent youth?" Ronny asked.

Claire twisted her mouth, looking at the T-shirt stand. "Some things have changed. For the worse. But look, Skee Ball." They entered an arcade, bought tokens—Claire's treat—and played a few games. Ronny racked up higher scores on every game, unaware that it was by her choice. "Man, I'm so rusty. Oh well, you win. Bravo, my hero."

"Aw, my aim's excellent is all. You should see me at the firing range."

"I noticed the gun at your hip today."

"Uh huh. It's not just for show …'n stuff. I took a … friend with me to the pistol range awhile back, and when she saw the pattern I put in the target she said she hoped she never did anything to get me mad." He laughed.

"I'm impressed. You're not packing now, are you?" As if he could hide a gun anywhere inside his clothes.

"Why? Should I be?"

"One never knows … does one?"

They reached the north end of the boardwalk and began walking south. When they approached the fun house, her sensitive ears picked up a conversation human ones would have to strain to hear: the bored attendant, speaking to another young man who could have been his clone. Perfect timing.

"'Bout time you got here."

"Dude, I had a date."

"Yeah, well what if I have a date, too? Waitin' for me, you know?"

"I'll be back in a sec. Gonna get me a shake at the custard stand. Hang tight, bro."

"I ain't your bro."

Claire turned to Ronny. "Let's go through the fun house again."

"Again? Why?"

"Because I want to have some fun. You know, real fun." She winked. "They're going to start the fireworks soon. I want to make some fireworks of our own. You game for an adventure in the dark?"

By way of answer, he hummed a tune. Claire recognized it as "Walkin' My Baby Back Home." She told him she liked the old songs, and he told her he liked his own version of the lyrics better. He sang:

"Gee, but it's great
After eatin' your date,
Brushin' your teeth with a comb."

He looked at her and winked. She winked back.

Once again they climbed into a car and clacked through the curtain into the darkness.

"So, when does the fun begin?" Ronny asked. He was breathing hard already.

"Into the next room. We'll get out there."

"Get out?"

"Uh huh. We'll toss Mr. Bones out of his coffin, and … well, you'll see."

He almost tripped over the edge of the car as they climbed out and briefly watched it continue, empty, down the track. Claire led the way to the upright casket and faced Ronny.

"All right," he said. "How do we do this?"

"Simple. I'm going to eat you first."

"I like it when a girl takes the initiative."

"Oh, I'm taking the initiative all right. Give me your hands."

He extended his arms, and Claire's hands encircled his pudgy wrists, holding his hands up, palms toward her. She could feel the change beginning, but she held it in check.

Ronny prepared for her to guide his hands to her breasts; she didn't. He tried moving them in that direction; she held him firm. "Claire?" he said. "Let's get on with it, before a car with people in it comes through."

"I agree," said Claire. "Let's get started—by my telling you that after you left Rowena's place with your hands grabbing your balls, I was the first person she called. Told me everything. Beautiful portrait, by the way, and it would've made a great gift for her husband." Through clenched teeth she said, "Too bad you had to go and *fuck it up*."

Ronny's jaw went slack and the whites of his eyes grew large. In the pale light they reflected red. He tried to free his hands, but her grip was too strong. "Claire, I can explain. She, she came on to me. Like, to thank me for such a beautiful job. Kind of like a bonus, yes? It happens … 'n stuff. What's a guy supposed to do?"

"A bonus, you say? A boner is more like it, there, Runny Mucus." He gasped at hearing the name his students called him behind his back but wouldn't dare utter to his face. "And I'm pleased to tell you you'll never have another boner as long as you live. Which, by the way, won't be that much longer."

He pulled, he pushed, but her grip was relentless. He felt tighter pressure on his wrists, followed by punctures, and saw that her thumbnails had become claws, and those claws were digging into and through his veins. Blood trickled, then ribboned down his arms to fall from his elbows.

"Ronny," Claire said, "I noticed your cross. Do you believe in the Bible?"

He nodded, whimpering, whispering her name.

"Remember 'Thou shalt not commit adultery?' And 'Thou shalt not covet they neighbor's wife?'"

"Oh, God."

"Do you believe it when it says, 'Vengeance is mine, saith the Lord'?"

He mewed like a kitten, uttering a word that might have been *yes*.

"Then behold the instrument of the Lord's vengeance ... 'n *stuff!*"

Golden fur sprouted from Claire's face. Her brow lowered, and her nose and jaw extended into a snout. Fangs grew and drool dripped over her lips, lips now black and splotched here and there with small patches of pink lipstick.

"No," Ronny cried. Spittle flew from his mouth and speckled his mustache and beard. "No, please! This isn't happening!"

From behind him came the clack-clack of a car's wheels—and voices. He had hope! "Help me!" he screamed. "Help me!"

The metamorph's mouth clamped around Ronny's throat. Her ears twitched as she heard a little girl's voice: "Look, Daddy, over there! That's like scary cool!"

A man's voice replied: "Hey, baby, looks like they've finally hired some live actors. It's about time." He called over to them: "Looking good, folks!"

Claire nodded her furry head in the direction of the father and daughter, Ronny's neck still stuck in her maw.

"No!" he shouted. "We're not—! She's a were—! She's going to—"

The car clanked on, and Ronny's voice was cut off as Claire bit through his fat neck. He staggered back against the upright casket, mouth opening and closing silently as he watched the woman who was a wolf swallow his larynx in one gulp and run her tongue along one side of her jaw to the other. Blood gurgled from his neck. His hands clasped at his savaged throat; his body convulsed as blood flooded his lungs, and he tried to cough it back up. Claire angled her head to the side, opened her mouth again, and sandwiched his face between her jaws. She applied pressure, gentle at first, then firmer, demanding, and with hungry satisfaction heard his skull crack and felt it collapse as her fangs broke through. With a sudden twist, she tore away the front of his head, spraying her saliva mixed with his blood, and when he collapsed to the fun house floor she buried her muzzle in his brain.

When Ronny's skull was empty—she'd had to hurry, but she did manage to lick it relatively clean—Claire reverted to human form, took his condo key from her pocket, and stripped off her sundress. Beneath it she wore shorts and a tank top. She used the dress, which she'd bought that afternoon along with the clothes she was wearing beneath, to wipe the blood from her face and fingers, and wedged it between Mr. Bones's ankles and his casket, where it assumed the appearance of something that belonged there. Finally she walked to the exit curtain and hopped into the next empty car. In seconds she was outside again. The car stopped, the replacement attendant helped her out, and wished her a good night. He admired her backside as she walked away. "There's gotta be a law against lookin' that hot," he muttered.

Claire strolled down the boards to the south parking lot and noticed that she had a few minutes left on the meter. Cars to either side, whose meters showed red in their windows, bore tickets courtesy of the Seaside Heights Police Department. She sat inside the Golden Goose and reapplied her lipstick using the mirror in her sun visor.

I've taken yet another human life, she reflected.

And this time, I actually enjoyed it.

The other times—the redneck, the punk, the dog handler—their deaths I could at least justify. The world was a better place without them. But what exactly did Ronny Music do? He may have been a scum-sucking dirtbag who preyed upon gullible women, using his art to seduce them, but consensual sex isn't the same as rape, and certainly not a capital crime—not even when the intended victim is your best friend. The scare that Ro put into him with the kitchen knife, and the slashing of his painting in front of his vain, piggy eyes, should've been enough to make him rethink his priorities.

But evidently it hadn't been, as evidenced by his hustling the girl at the track earlier today. Claire recalled Rowena's mentioning to her during their day in Fenway that not only did Babe Ruth score the most homeruns of any player of his day, but he scored the most strikeouts, too. The guy just kept swinging.

And so did Ronny; but did he deserve to die? Killing him, Claire thought ironically, "wasn't very Christian of me." Still, part of her reveled in his death.

She recalled her fear that maybe she was becoming more wolf than human. More predatory than compassionate. It chilled her to the bone.

Lukas had claimed his parents, and later he himself, never took down innocent people, just the dregs of society. That might have been so. But who got to make that judgment? Who gave them—and who gave her—the power to act as judge, jury … and executioner?

Which brought her to that "instrument of the Lord's vengeance" bit. Where had that come from? Seeing the cross around his neck? She hated it when people wore their religious symbols as costume jewelry. Wasn't religion supposed to be a private matter, not something to be flaunted? She remembered in catechism as a child, learning you should pray in the closet, not on the street corner.

And speaking of judgment, she wondered anew how she herself would fare on the day of final judgment—if in fact there were one. She ran her fingers over the pentacle necklace Lukas had given her, and which she never took off: not exactly a religious symbol, but not exactly not one either.

Am I beyond the power of prayer to save my soul? she thought. I am a killer, after all. But "Thou shalt not kill" applies only to humans killing other humans; in the animal world, killing other animals is necessary to survive. Spiders kill flies. Owls kill mice. On the African veldt, a man-eating lion kills people. It's in their nature; certainly God wouldn't damn them for acting upon the very nature He gave them. And when she hunted, when she killed, when she feasted, she wasn't Claire, the human. No, she was Luna, the wolf.

Stop right there, she thought. Now I'm going schizo. Problem was, schizophrenics didn't know they were schizo; since she did know, that excuse just wouldn't work. It was just rationalization, and rationalization burned her. Besides, even though Luna had the instincts and hungers of a wolf, she still thought and reasoned as Claire. And which identity was she when she only partially morphed? The father and daughter who saw her attacking Ronny believed she was a performer wearing a "scary cool" wolf mask. Who—what—was she then?

The big question … not did she have a soul worth saving, but did she have a soul at all? Years of religious instruction had told her yes, and even though she was no longer a churchgoer, even though thoughts of religion were so rare today as to be nearly nonexistent, she never entirely forsook the concept of a higher Power in the universe. She realized she still believed in God, but no less than she believed in Darwin—after all, what if it was a superior *Intelligence* that *designed* evolution? Darwin, she remembered having read, had himself been a devout Christian.

A certain brand of Christian would call Claire an instrument of the Devil.

She thought back to her first human kill, Dink, the philandering wife-beater she'd picked up in the bar, the one they had decided was worth more to his family dead than alive. His offense was far greater than Ronny's. But did he deserve to die? She remembered feeling remorse afterward, no matter that he was an abuser. And the way she did it: seducing the man had run counter to every one of her moral standards.

Puglio, on the other hand, well. That was a case of monster versus monsters, and may the best ones win. They had. There was nothing good in him, nothing. And she put no credence in the "difficult childhood" excuse that was currently so popular among the psychological cognoscenti. He was the embodiment of pure evil (now there's an oxymoron, she thought), and every moment he lived on Earth was an affront to God.

She thought of Chuck, the guy who had abused the greyhounds. Was he as evil as Puglio? Her biggest regret regarding killing him seemed to be learning the dogs had been destroyed because of it. That was when she'd promised never to hunt humans again. But it was because of the dogs, not the man. Was that the first sign of her predation's beginning to take control?

Tonight it was Ronny Music. No capital offenses on his record. Boiled down to the basics, he was a moocher and a scumbag, plain and simple. As for the women he had taken advantage of, hey, it takes two to tango, right? Ro didn't fall for his pitch, why should they have?

But the big question, at least for the moment, was why did she feel absolutely no regret, no remorse, at being—call it what it is, she thought—a calculating murderer? Was Hyde really assuming dominance over Jekyll?

She felt a headache coming on.

A red marker flipped up in the window of her parking meter. Claire started the car and left the lot, bound for the Barnegat Bay Bridge that led to the mainland and Toms River. At the next red light, she keyed

Ronny's address into her portable GPS and turned on the radio. She heard an announcer's voice: "This is Oldies 100, WJRZ, Manahawkin," followed by the Platters singing "The Great Pretender."

That's more like it, she thought, as she drove west on Route 37, anticipating a good night's sleep inside the condo of the man she had just killed.

Chapter Sixteen

Rowena was sobbing when she opened the door to let Claire in and wept openly when she saw the bag of marrow bones her friend carried. Beyond her sat Bill, his eyes nearly as red. Greycie's crate was empty, the door open, her furry squeak toy lying in the corner.

"Don't tell me," said Claire as Ro stepped aside to let her in.

"It's true," Rowena whispered. "Just this morning."

Bill said, "I'm the one who gets up first to take her on her walk, and when she hears me in the bedroom getting dressed, I can hear her tail whapping like gangbusters against the side of her crate. When I let her out she jumps up on me and can't wait to get the leash on. Lately, she hasn't been jumping, but then, she'd gotten old. Her tail hadn't given out, though.

"But this morning I didn't hear anything. And when I came out of the room …" His eyes teared and he choked up. "Sorry."

Claire hugged Rowena and sat next to Bill. She kissed him on the cheek. "It's okay, let it out."

Ro stared at the crate. "Bill took her to the vet, even though it was obvious she was … gone. Vet said he could do an autopsy, but there really wouldn't be any point. There was no doubt she died of natural causes. She was no youngster, Claire. But we've had her since she was retired at three years old, and that's a long time. It hurts. It hurts so much."

"I'm ready to bawl myself, and I've only known her for a couple of years."

"That's not all the bad news, Claire," said Ro. "Were you listening to the radio on the drive up?"

"No, I had CDs on all the way. Why?" Actually, she had listened to the news throughout the trip and knew what Ro was going to tell her; it had been the lead headline on the New York and Boston newscasts. She had prepared herself to play ignorant.

Ro darted her eyes toward her husband and then back to Claire: clearly a caution, Bill knew nothing. "You remember a guy named Ronny Music? He intercepted you on your way to lunch a while back. With a book proposal."

Claire nodded almost imperceptibly. "I remember, yes. Short, heavy-set guy, orange hair, right?"

"Well, he's dead. Murdered."

"No."

"In a fun house in Jersey."

"A fun house? Talk about irony. Did they get the guy who did it?"

"No. The body was found this morning by the manager, and he called the cops. TV says there was a father taking his daughter on the ride, they witnessed it."

"They witnessed it? Then why didn't the father call the police?"

"He thought it was a couple of live actors, pretending to be a werewolf and her victim."

"*Her* victim, you said?" Play it cool, Claire thought.

"Uh huh. See, the werewolf was wearing a dress. The face he figured was just a mask. Very realistic, though."

"I guess."

"When they got to that part of the ride and saw this—fun house werewolf—she had her jaws around Ronny's throat, but he was still very much alive. Said he was screaming for help, like some guy he'd seen in the haunted mansion at Six Flags. Said he even gave them the thumbs up as the car went by."

"Wow. So what do the cops say? Do they actually believe there's such a thing as werewolves?"

"Be serious." Rowena sat in a chair next to Greycie's crate and lowered her voice. "But you mentioned bizarre? Ronny's face was actually ripped off. And his brain was missing. Gone, as if his skull was scooped out."

"That's horrible, Ro." Claire took a breath. "Pardon me, but this sounds like a scene from a bad horror movie, one that's shooting for black humor. You know, the dumbest kid in the crowd is killed like that, and one of his buddies sees his head is empty and says, 'That explains a lot.'"

"Only you, Claire, only you."

"Yeah, pretty lousy taste. But you've got to admit …"

"Funny, I know. You familiar with Seaside Heights? That's where the fun house is. On the boardwalk."

"Oh, sure, I know Seaside. My parents used to take me there when I was little."

"How far away does your friend Gene live?"

"I don't know exactly, ten, twelve miles, maybe a couple more."

"Oh."

"Oh?"

Ro shook her head and looked at Greycie's crate. "Just … oh. That's all. Nothing."

Claire stood and leaned over Rowena and hugged her. "So sorry about Greycie."

* * *

In the faculty lounge in the biology department of Criterion University, Daciana Moceanu sipped at her coffee. She used to take it black, but now that her tastes were enhanced, she had to dilute it with milk, lots of milk. Were it not for the presence of Charles and Lewis sitting on the lounge across from her, a bit too close to each other for Daciana's liking, she would have been drinking something more to her taste—refrigerated, true, but the cold kept the smell down, and it could easily pass for tomato juice as long as she kept it in an opaque mug.

"Daciana, dear, why don't you stop correcting those papers, get up from the table, and relax for once?" said Charles. "We'll make room for you here." He patted the sofa cushion next to him, the side not occupied by Lewis.

"Thank you," she said, "but I'm, what do the kids call it today, on a roll. I told my students I'd have their papers done by our next meeting, and that's in"—she checked her watch—"two hours."

Lewis said (and why did he have to lisp? Was it real or an orientation affectation?), "I think it's great that you've taken on the undergraduate intersession. Keeps your mind off, you know."

"That was thirteen months ago, Lewis. Gabriel's death was tragic, and his murder is still unsolved, but there is nothing I can do about it. I've resolved myself to the situation and refuse to let it dominate my life. I don't mean to be blunt, but I've moved on."

"That's very … practical of you." He lit a cigarette and blew smoke toward the ceiling. Daciana wrinkled her nose and tried not to breathe. "Smoke bother you?" he asked.

"As a matter of fact, it does."

"It never did before."

"Before what?"

Charles said, "Why don't you put it out, Lewis? We're a smoke-free facility now, remember?"

Lewis grumbled and stubbed the cigarette in his hand-held ashtray. He released a button, and the lid closed.

"Those things'll kill you one day," his partner said.

Lewis mumbled "Bitch" under his breath, but Daciana picked it up. She wondered if the word applied to Charles or to her. Maybe both. *In my day*, she thought, *in my youth, you two would be impaled. In my lover's garden of stakes.* Lending to the term "anal intercourse" a whole new dimension.

Charles stood, walked around the table, and put a hand on her shoulder. She refused to flinch. "I admire you, Daciana. Some of the folks around here think you're a little cold, but I know there's a genuinely warm person inside."

Only if I ate you, she thought. "I appreciate that, Charles. Thank you."

"Time for our next session—class, that is," said Lewis, standing and casting an eye at Charles. "See you later, Daciana."

"Later," she said, not looking up from her papers.

They had not even noticed that she had been looking at the same paper the whole time they were in here and had not made one mark on it. She had in fact made no promise to her students to return their papers today, although she could easily have whipped through them before class.

She pushed the coffee away. It was tepid now. She had eaten her lunch, a pound of raw ground beef, in her lab before heading to the lounge, so she wasn't hungry. At least not for physical sustenance.

Emotional, though, that was another matter.

Lukas. She still thought of Lukas.

She had become acquainted with his uniqueness through Gabriel's research, which he readily shared with her—before he learned of her own proclivities. She had become acquainted with his intellect through her husband, as well, and recognized his promise. She had spied him on campus and noted his physique, the way he carried himself, the way some of the coeds stared at him as he walked by. Hitler would have called him the perfect Aryan.

Hitler, of course, was a fool. The true Aryans were Persians, small and dark like Hitler himself, not tall and fair like Lukas. It was during Hitler's ascendancy, in fact, that the country of Persia renamed itself. *Aryan*, translated into Farsi, becomes *Iran*. But that was a long time ago, in a far different world. Daciana had fed upon both Germans and Jews, and their blood tasted basically the same, even those who kept a Kosher household. She had never visited Persia.

Gabriel had intellect, but his sudden fear of her—a "hemophage," in his euphemistic terminology—made him a liability. Lukas, she felt, would embrace her identity, and would leap at the chance to partake of her Gift, almost as much as she wanted his. Unfortunately, Gabriel would have to go, and Lukas would have to be the one to send him on his way.

She had envisioned the two of them, she and Lukas, joining a pack of wolves, his curse lifted, they the new alpha male and female. Saw their pack encircling a panicked doe or buck, savoring the smell of its fear, the bulging of its eyes, the froth flying from its nose. She saw herself and Lukas lunging for its soft underside, gripping tight with yellowed fangs soon to drip red, tearing it apart, watching its steaming entrails falling free and plopping wetly onto the ground. Saw them burying their noses into the deer, sharing its still-beating heart, savoring its soft liver, then backing off, satisfied, to allow the rest of the pack to feast.

She had envisioned them expanding their territory from New Hampshire farther north, to Maine, or west to the Upper Peninsula of Michigan, even father west to Yellowstone and the great forests of northern California.

Hunting game and occasionally hunting hunters.

Humans were the most dangerous game, and humans would also be their prey. Which put Daciana and Lukas at the very top of the food chain. They were the ultimate in evolution.

She had envisioned themselves in human form, too, changing identities and living unrecognized among two-legged society. They could teach. They might even take lovers from the student body now and then; monogamy, after all these years, was not Daciana's style, and she would forgive Lukas occasional trysts for his own amusement—but only for purposes of amusement. His loyalty would necessarily remain with her.

Daciana had amassed considerable wealth over six centuries, mostly in Swiss accounts, keeping enough on hand for fluidity's sake in small local banks. They would never suffer for want of material things.

At times she had daydreamed about their living forever—or at least until the sun went nova, some six billion years or so from now. The number was inconceivable, even to Daciana's scientific mind. Six billion years. Would they be tired of life by then? Would they welcome the sun's turning red, its swelling into a gas giant, its engulfing the Earth in fire? Or would they be living on another world by then, in another far-off star system? Surely, humans would have long perfected interstellar travel. Perhaps she and he would, indeed, live forever.

But Claire—that is, Lukas's love for Claire—had complicated her vision. Daciana had tried to coax him: he was young, he would get over her and she him, in no time. Plus, Claire would grow old and die, whereas he would remain young and vital; and no, they would not give her the Gift, Daciana could not allow it. Where would that leave me, she thought. I never settle for being second best.

Daciana *despised* Claire Delaney.

She pondered the course of her revenge. She remembered reading that if an organized crime family wanted to punish someone who had offended them, they might choose not to kill the offender but his family instead, making him live with the knowledge, the guilt, and the pain for the rest of his life. There were rumors that the Mafia had killed President Kennedy to punish his brother, the attorney general, for his attacks on organized crime.

Maybe this would be the perfect method for dealing with Claire. Kill those she loves the most; make the murders appear random … to everyone but Claire; feed her paranoia; draw the killings out over time; make her suffer.

She would exempt Radu Jones from her list. She actually liked him, they shared the same ancestry, and she knew he had always liked her. It was a fact: a person might kill an animal for food or sport without any regret at all, but that same person would never intentionally kill a pet.

Daciana sat upright, seized by a memory of her first love's ingenuity: of a unique and exquisite method of execution, one that would last day after agonizing day before the condemned drew a final tortured breath.

Yes. Once she had dispatched Claire's loved ones, she would use this technique to dispatch Claire herself. The prospect thrilled her even more than letting her live with her guilt.

She nodded and licked her lips.

She would take it slowly; she would bide her time.

After all, she had all the time in the world.

* * *

William Harding Parr, Jr., was born prematurely on Halloween, and his doting parents immediately nicknamed him Boo. He was tiny but healthy, with skin the color of a mild summer's tan, dark blue eyes, and Cupid's-bow lips. His mother referred to him as a heartbreaker-in-training. The only time they heard him cry was when he was hungry; otherwise, he slept.

Instead of taking maternity leave, Rowena plunged back into work. With Radu Jones's permission, she painted her office walls a light shade of blue, then installed a crib in one corner. She printed out a sign which read NURSING, which she taped to the door at appropriate times to prevent potential visitors' embarrassment.

Rowena and Bill were not regular churchgoers, but they both agreed that Boo should be baptized. His devoted godparents were Radu Jones and Claire Delaney.

With the exception of its newest five-pounds-and-growing-by-the-day addition to the staff, life at Jones Publishing continued as usual. Claire had convinced Gene Franks to submit a collection of his columns in the *Press* for publication. And Radu Jones was seeing Daciana Moceanu regularly every weekend. When Rowena teased him about his becoming a stud at his age, he assured her their relationship had been more mutual companionship than sexually intimate. Although he felt, confidentially, that it might be subject to change at some later date.

* * *

On Monday of the second week in November, Radu Jones called Rowena and Claire into his office. He served them sparkling water and poured a glass for himself.

"Is this good news, Ray?" asked Rowena as they took chairs.

"I hope you'll see it that way," he replied. "I won't string you along. I've sold Jones Publishing."

Rowena's glass stopped inches from her mouth. "What? But this is your life, Ray."

"It was," he said. "But my doctor has advised me to retire, and—"

"Your heart?" Ro interrupted.

"My heart ... and also the desire to see more of the world than Boston. I intend to inform the rest of the staff at a meeting after Thanksgiving, and introduce them to the new owner, a widower named Morgan Williams. He's a British multimillionaire whose parents named him after, of all things, a racing car. He has continued the tradition in naming his three children: Royce, Aston, and Bentley. Bentley, by the way, is a girl."

"And I thought 'Rowena' was odd."

"Mr. Williams is buying the company basically to give Bentley, his middle child, a business of her own to run. He assures me she has always been interested in publishing and will serve as a conscientious steward of Jones Publishing. Aston has a family and and career of his own. Royce is the baby of the family, and, according to his father, has yet to chart a course for his life."

"I don't know what we'll do without you at the helm," said Claire.

"I don't know what we'll do without you, period," added Rowena.

Jones smiled. "I'm not out the door yet. Bentley won't be able to take the reins until December first, so you're stuck with me for another couple of weeks at least. And I've already allocated the usual Christmas bonuses in a separate account, which you, Rowena, will control. As for my not being 'at the helm,' I do intend to drop by now and then, but more importantly I hope to see you all socially whenever I'm in town. You are, after all, the closest I have to family." He sipped his water. "Family by choice, not by chance."

Rowena lifted her glass. "To your retirement. May it fulfill your every aspiration."

"Hear, hear," said Claire, conviction absent from her voice.

They drank.

"There's more," said their host. "I have instructed Mr. Williams to in turn inform his daughter that you, Rowena, are currently the managing editor and will remain managing editor. She will not 'clean house,' as they say. Anyone on staff who is let go for any reason other than unethical or illegal activity will receive a year's severance, including benefits. Does that sound fair?"

"More than fair," said Rowena, still stunned by the news.

"Oh, one final thing. I've rewritten my will, and—"

"Ray, that's your business, not ours."

"Rowena, it is very much your business. I want you to be the executor of my estate."

"Wow. I can't believe this."

"And aside from stipends to Emma, Benjamin, and the staff at work, you are the sole beneficiary. Each stipend will be different, based upon seniority. Except for yours, Claire, which is a bit more generous." She blinked. "I'm still the boss, and I'm exercising the right to break my own rule. But Rowena, you will make sure that every distribution is made privately, and that each includes an enforceable confidentiality statement signed by each employee. I don't want to be party to any in-house sniping."

"Wait. Wait. Wait. What exactly did you mean about 'sole beneficiary'?"

"I mean that my house and everything in it will be yours—and Bill's, and young Bill's, of course. Mine is a lovely neighborhood in which to raise a child—or children—and there will be more than enough in your bank account to pay the real estate taxes, confiscatory though they be." He sipped his drink. "Or, you can sell it and do what you will with the proceeds."

Rowena sagged in her chair. "I still can't believe this. You can't be—"

"Serious? I am. You joke about how you would pursue me if you weren't already married to Bill, but I am sincere when I say that I love you, my dear, as I would my own daughter. Plus," he said, "I'll be damned if I'll turn over what I've worked for all these years to the great state of Massachusets."

* * *

Upon learning that Gene and Nina would be joining Claire for Thanksgiving weekend, Radu Jones insisted they all join him for dinner, along with Rowena, Bill, and Boo. "Daciana will be there, too, and I know she'd be happy to see you all again. She was positively buoyant after our first dinner together."

* * *

Thanksgiving dinner proved to be another culinary triumph—or as Bill referred to it, a gastrogasm. Benjamin had soaked the turkey in brine a day before roasting it. He enhanced the stuffing with sausage meat and chunks of apple. And Emma had made pumpkin, mince, and pecan pies, her specialties. They served the meal promptly at one o'clock, in order that they might join their son's family in Cambridge for their own Thanksgiving weekend. Nina had begged Benjamin for his turkey recipe, and Gene did the same with Emma. Mince pie, he said, was his favorite, but Nina turned up her nose at it. Every time he mentioned mince, she'd inform him that the OB Diner was right down the road.

The camaraderie around the table was evident, with even Daciana (wearing red today instead of her customary black, but still sporting that strong perfume) participating, drawing Bill into the thick of the conversation with questions about his work, how he'd met Rowena, jokingly asking if they'd enrolled Bill Jr. in Harvard yet. She made a fuss over the baby ("My little pork chop, I could just eat you up"), and, after explaining she was unable to conceive but had always wished for children of her own, asked if she could feed him his Gerber version of turkey and vegetables. Rowena, beaming, was all too happy to oblige.

Even Claire began to warm up to her boss's ladyfriend. She'd engaged Gene and Nina in conversation about his book, which she'd actually read ("Writing my dissertation was the hardest part of my doctoral studies; I don't know how you can write so well"), and she applauded the relationship they shared with Claire ("Family is the most important thing in one's life").

They sat around the table like living images drawn from a Norman Rockwell painting.

After they'd finished dessert, Nina stood up to start clearing the table—the least she and Gene could do, she asserted—but Daciana stopped her. "You are our guests," she said. "Radu and I will take care of this later."

"Agreed," said Jones. "Now come with me to the living room for an after-dinner drink."

Daciana's words weren't lost on any of them. Claire thought, "*Our guests? Later?*"

* * *

At eight the following Monday, Benjamin and Emma returned and went into the kitchen to prepare breakfast for themselves. The kitchen was spotless, everything put in its proper place (except for the load in the dishwasher, ready to be emptied). There was plenty of turkey left for sandwiches, and as they ate they reflected on how fortunate they were to have Radu Jones as an employer. They were both past retirement age—in fact, Benjamin was earning a very satisfactory pension from his days as a chef in one of Boston's finer restaurants—but retirement frankly didn't suit either of them. When their granddaughter was a baby they often babysat for their son and daughter-in-law, and that kept them both busy and happy, but now she was in school, and the couple's need to feel uesful sent them back to work. Mr. Jones—they would not call him by his first name, even though he had urged them to—was wonderful to work for, undemanding and generous, and as they finished their meal they both agreed, for the umpteenth time, that life was good.

They topped off their bacon-and-eggs breakfast with a cinnamon bun, and Benjamin brought the dishes to the sink. "I'll make a list of what we need from the store, Emmy," he said.

"Want me to empty the dishwasher?"

"No, you get started on the rest of the house. The kitchen is mine."

Emma went through the downstairs rooms and decided the dusting would be a matter of a-lick-and-a-promise. It looked like Mr. Jones had decided to surprise them and make the house sparkle for their return. A lovely surprise, she thought. She went upstairs.

Benjamin had just put the last of the dishes away when he heard the shriek.

* * *

Claire and Rowena (she'd left Boo in the care of the receptionist) arrived at the house moments after the police. Rowena's had been the second call Benjamin made. The coroner told them Benjamin and Emma had already identified the body, and there was no need for them to see it.

"Not *it*," Rowena said. "Him. We want to see *him*."

The detective urged them no, but the coroner—seeing their obvious agitation and Claire's ashen expression—allowed them into the bedroom, so long as they touched nothing.

Radu Jones lay on his back in the center of his king-sized bed. He was nude, his legs splayed, arms out to the side. There were deep scratches on his shoulders that traveled down his chest. But what seized both women was his face. His eyes were bugged out, his nostrils flared, his mouth wide in a silent scream.

"He didn't die peacefully," remarked the detective superfluously, as the crime lab photographer shot flash pictures with his digital camera.

The coroner bent over the scratches. "They're not enough to kill him, and they appear to have been wiped clean," he said to the detective. "See, there's sweat on his face and shoulders, on his belly, too. But no moisture at the wound sites." He looked closer. "And his genital area has been cleaned as well. Ladies," he said, "I want your word that everything I've just said is confidential. We will not tolerate any leaks."

"Understood," said Claire. She and Rowena backed off to stand in the corner. They exchanged looks as the coroner continued his preliminary exam. The detective turned to them. "Do you have any idea who was the last to see Mr. Jones alive? The housekeeper and cook said he had a houseful of company when they left. Were you among them?"

"Yes," sobbed Rowena as tears flowed down her cheeks. "It was Thanksgiving. Ray—"

"Excuse me, Ray?"

"That was what we called him. Mr. Jones. Radu was his given name."

"I can't believe this is happening," whispered Claire.

"Can you give me the names of the people who were here?"

"Yes. Wait, wait a minute." She pulled out her cell phone and speed dialed. "Nina? This is Claire. Where are you? ... Well, turn around and come back. Can you find Radu's house? ... GPS? Okay, here's the address ... No, I can't tell you over the phone. Just get here fast, but don't break any speed limits." She said to the detective, "Gene and Nina Franks. They were staying with me for the weekend. They're on their way back to Jersey now. Or were." The detective wrote down their names along with Claire's and Rowena's.

"My husband's name is Bill Parr, he works for Fidelity in town. He was here, too, and our baby."

"And one other," said Claire. "Daciana Moceanu."

"Who?"

She repeated the name and spelled it for him. "She's a professor at Criterion University in New Hampshire. I believe they were either romantically involved or on the verge. All of us left the house together, but Daciana stayed back to help Ray clean up the dinner dishes and get the house in order. Emma and Benjamin had the weekend off, and Ray said he wanted the place spic and span when they came back today."

"Typical of him," added Rowena.

"So this ... professor woman stayed on. You're saying she was the last person to see the victim alive?"

Rowena said, "We can't say that for sure. We just know she was the only one here with Ray when we left."

* * *

After Claire and Rowena went downstairs to sit with Emma and Benjamin, Gene and Nina arrived and upon hearing the news offered sorrowful hugs all around. Meanwhile, the detective placed a call to Criterion. When he got hold of Professor Moceanu, she asked why he wanted to see her, and why this afternoon. When he told her it involved Radu Jones, she asked if everything were all right, and he replied he needed to speak with her in person. She replied she would cancel her evening class and be there as soon as possible.

The body was removed and taken downtown. Rowena, Claire, and the Frankses stayed, commiserating around the kitchen table with Emma and Benjamin when Daciana arrived, visibly upset. Her first words were, "What's wrong? Is Radu all right?"

"Professor Moceanu?" came a deep voice from behind her. She faced the tall, heavy-set man who flashed her his badge. "I'm Detective Hannam. Would you care to sit down?"

"Thank you, I'll stand. What's this all about?"

"Ma'am, Mr. Jones has died."

She clutched her throat. "No. But I was just with him—"

"For the whole weekend?"

"No, no, not the whole weekend." She glanced at the others, lingering for a second at Claire. *Damn,* she thought, *I forgot the perfume.*

"But you were the last person to see him alive?"

"How can I know that? When did he die? Was it his heart? He had a heart condition."

"That's something we're working on, ma'am. An autopsy will determine the cause of death. He died sometime over the weekend, that's all we know for now. His body was discovered by his cook and housekeeper sometime after noon."

"Horrible." She pulled a handkerchief from her purse and dabbed her eyes. "Horrible, horrible."

"Can you tell me what happened after the dinner guests left on Thursday?" The detective was jotting in his notebook.

"Of course. Radu wanted to surprise Emma and Benjamin when they returned from the weekend by making the house neat and orderly. So we took care of the dishes and—and—" She took deep, halting breaths and wiped her eyes again. "Anyway, when the last load was in the dishwasher—"

"And what time would that be?"

"I have no idea. It was dark, that's all I remember."

"Go on."

"I drove back to my home at the University. I teach biology and specialize in genetics. I needed the weekend to work on my students' final exam. There are always new discoveries being made in the field, which means that unlike, say, professors of English, I cannot rely on final exams from previous years. And in answer to the question I'm sure you were about to ask, no, there are no witnesses at the University to corroborate my story. They were all enjoying the Thanksgiving weekend. I was alone in my office." She choked. "While Radu was here, dying, alone."

Detective Hannam nodded and made another note.

Daciana looked at the others. "What happens now?"

Rowena said, "Well, Ray has named me his executor"—*executrix*, thought Claire, then mentally slapped herself—"and I guess tomorrow I'll call his lawyer and find out what his wishes were." She looked at the detective. "I guess we'll have to wait awhile for the autopsy results, right?"

"I'll keep you informed, Mrs. Parr."

PART FIVE
DALE

Chapter Seventeen

Radu Jones's will specified no viewing, no funeral, just a simple memorial. He had chosen cremation, in a simple cardboard coffin. His ashes were to be placed in the least expensive urn and stored or scattered wherever Rowena Parr deemed appropriate.

A memorial service was held the following Saturday, December 3, in Radu's living room, with the staff of Jones Publishing and their families and Gene and Nina in attendance, along with Benjamin and Emma. They wanted to cater the reception themselves, but Rowena wouldn't allow it. A magnificent floral spray stood in one corner, with a note of sympathy from the family of Morgan Williams. Detective Hannam made an appearance to inform Rowena that the cause of Jones's death was a massive heart attack. She said she would contact the cremation service on Monday.

Afterward, over hors d'oeuvres and drinks, Daciana announced that she would be accepting a position to teach at Monmouth University. "Too many bad memories here," she explained, "and the University has been courting me for a year now." She sighed. "It's good to feel wanted."

Rowena said she understood and wished Daciana well. Gene and Nina told her Monmouth was just up the road from them in West Long Branch, and that she was welcome to drop in for dinner any time. Claire said nothing. She was thinking back to when last she saw her; or rather, smelled her. Her scent then had been subtly familiar, but at the time Ray's death had monopolized her attention. Today Daciana was wearing her customary perfume, Eau du Pungence.

Daciana placed her hand on Bill's upper arm to get his full attention. "Bill, I have been reading that Fidelity is one of the best mutual fund companies. Would you agree?"

"Well, seeing as how I work there I'd have to agree whether I really did or didnt. But I do. Why?"

"I have another two weeks to get my house in order before moving, and before I do I would like to set up an account, through you."

"That's very flattering, but you can do it all on-line. You wouldn't have to drive down here to Boston."

"But I want you to be my, what, financial advisor. I value your opinion, and I value confidentiality. For all my supposed intelligence, I have never set up a retirement account. Never had the time, and never even thought about retirement. Gabriel, being more practical, had what they call a 403(b) account, and there is also his life insurance from work. I'd like to invest the proceeds in a retirement account of my own. May I consult with you—not here, of course, not now, but in your office? Say, in a week or so?"

Bill said, "You remind me of my father's best friend."

"How so?"

"My father had a high school education, and his best friend was our family doctor. They had their love of the Sox in common, and they enjoyed sailing in the doctor's boat. But when it came to buying a car, the doctor was like a babe in the woods."

"A babe in the woods?"

"For all his education, he didn't know how to haggle for a car. But that was one of my father's hobbies. He thought car salesmen were predators—except that they didn't even belong on the food chain—and he loved making them squirm. Sometimes he'd go to a showroom just to bait the salesman; then he'd walk out, feeling like, well, like a mongoose who had just killed a cobra. Anyway, when the doc wanted a new car, my dad struck the best bargain—he told me later he had the salesman sweating—and then, instead of signing the papers, he called the doctor from the showroom and told him he had a deal."

"Interesting. But certainly, the doctor could have afforded to pay full price."

"He could. But my father hated to see him get taken. See, the doctor always refused payment for our family's medical treatments, and this was my dad's attempt at some kind of payback." He chuckled, discreetly. "Plus, as I said, messing with the dealer was his favorite hobby."

"So we have a deal then? I can see you?"

"Of course. I'd be happy to help."

Rowena, holding a restless Boo, said, "Why do you have to go to the office? Bill, can't you set things up for Daciana at the house? Say, after dinner sometime?"

Claire, who had been talking with Gene and Nina, overheard and nearly coughed out her seltzer.

Rowena went to change the baby's diaper, and when she came out of the bathroom Emma stopped her. "I don't mean to upset you, Mrs. Parr, but there's something maybe you should know. We told the detective, and he told us to say nothing to anyone. Please tell me it won't go any further." Intrigued, Rowena agreed. "You know how I found Mr. Jones, in his bedroom. Naked." A bit of color crept into her cheeks. "I am very uncomfortable telling you this, Mrs. Parr. But Mr. Jones had a drawerful of pajamas in his dresser. He changed them every day. I laundered them and put them away myself. So my question is, why would he go to bed, you know, without wearing anything?"

* * *

Rowena and Bill Parr lived in a quiet suburban neighborhood composed of modest one- and two-story homes. Theirs was a ranch style three-bedroom, two-bath home, with the master bedroom on one end of the house and two on the other. Now that they had a baby, Rowena found the arrangement unsatisfactory, and she and Bill decided to put the house on the market once Ray's estate had been probated. His four upstairs bedrooms were all adjoining and more spacious, as well. Bill could set up his own private office in one of them instead of using the spare bedroom as he now did. And as for their sleeping in the same room in which Ray had died, whereas others might shun it, they were more practical than squeamish. Ray wouldn't have wanted the room turned into a memorial for him.

Daciana came for dinner a week after Radu's service, December 10, a Saturday. She brought her financial records—only the ones she wanted Bill to see: the tax records from her University work and her savings account. It amounted to their regular deposits plus Gabriel's IRA and a death benefit of three and a half times his salary.

Rowena had invited Claire to join them, but she'd begged off.

After dinner, Daciana insisted on bathing Bill Jr. and putting him to bed. She played with him as if she were his favorite aunty, and he giggled as she tickled him and smiled as she kissed him goodnight.

Bill looked on happily. Too bad she's moving, he thought. Boo's really taken a liking to her. He thought back to Claire's Morticia remark. Daciana was certainly slim, and she did tend to wear black, but she wasn't funereal-looking in the least. Plus, her manner around not only himself and Ro but also with the baby dispelled any reservations he might have had. Daciana, were she to stay in New England, could easily become a family friend. He thought a lot of Claire, but he was just as happy she couldn't be here tonight.

As Rowena monopolized the dining room table with paperwork relating to probate, Daciana and Bill retired to his bedroom office—the one in which the late and unlamented Ronny Music had slept for a week last summer—to work out the best investments for her IRA. Later the three made their goodnights, with Daciana noting her only regret about relocating to New Jersey was the fact she would be so far from her newfound friends … and their beautiful baby boy.

* * *

At two o'clock Sunday morning Rowena awoke. Her body's clock had adjusted for Boo's nocturnal feedings, and she reflected he wasn't awake and crying yet. She had taken to feeding him a spoonful of baby cereal before bedtime, and it seemed to be working toward his sleeping through the night. She tiptoed into the baby's room intending simply to observe him, sleeping the sleep of the angels, his rosebud lips curled up ever so slightly at the edges of his mouth.

The nightlight cast a yellow glow over the bedroom as Rowena entered.

The first thing she noticed was the cold. The December air was wafting in, the curtains puffing. She always left the window cracked at the bottom for fresh air, but Bill had installed a sliding bolt on either side of the sash to keep it in place. The bolts were broken and lying on the floor under the window. The window was wide open. The screen had been torn apart.

Crying, "No!" she dashed to Boo's crib, praying in panic, only to find her worst fears come true. She wailed and wailed and couldn't make herself stop.

Bill, still groggy, stumbled into the room. Rowena threw herself against him, her fists beating against his chest. He found the light switch, and when he turned it on he began wailing, too.

* * *

Mr. Dale Keegan

P.O. Box 180
Thurmont, MD 21788
Monday, December 19, 2005

Dear Dale,

Sad news to report, I'm afraid, ironic that it had to follow such a lovely Thanksgiving. Claire invited Gene and me to spend the holiday weekend with her and her friends in Boston. Let me tell you, they couldn't have been nicer. Claire, of course, you've met. Then there were her friends Rowena and Bill Parr and their baby, Bill Jr. We were fed like royalty at the girls' boss's house, along with his lady friend, a professor from Criterion University up in New Hampshire.

Then, on the Monday after Thanksgiving, Mr. Jones, Claire's boss, was found dead in his bed. Claire told me he had a bad heart, and doctors say he had a heart attack. I don't know if he belonged to any church.

But Dale, it gets worse. Claire called yesterday to tell us Rowena and Bill's two-month-old baby boy had been kidnapped. It's been a week, they've heard nothing from the kidnapper, and the police are stumped. They've called in the FBI, of course. Claire says Rowena and Bill seem to take turns blaming first themselves and then each other. They're understandably devastated. Mr. Jones's successor has told Rowena to take as much time off as she needs, and that she and the other editors—Claire is one of those, you'll remember—would shoulder her load until she returned.

I'm sorry to be the bearer of bad news, dear, but I knew you'd want to know. Gene is beside himself. Even though we only met the Parrs that once, well, you know his empathy quotient. I guess that's what made him such a good teacher. Made you a good teacher, too, much as you tend to put on a stoic front.

I don't know what your assignment with the government is, naturally, but as usual you're welcome to visit any time you can. To Gene you're like a brother, but to me you're more like our third son.

Love,

Nina

* * *

Dale sat across from the base commander, the only person on board who knew what his covert role was. She put down the letter (did they still make typewriters?) and stared at him. "What do you think?" he asked.

The CO turned her head and looked out the window of her cottage, thinking. Rain and sleet were pelting the windows, the fallen leaves making the asphalt roadway slick as an ice rink. Dale's parka hung on a coat tree by the front door, dripping water onto the slate of the entryway. A fireplace managed to take the chill off the room. The pair sat facing each other in swivel-mounted, upholstered barrel chairs, each clutching a steaming mug of tea.

"What's your take? You've been to Boston and examined the evidence."

"True. After the family friends left, my team and our FBI counterparts moved in."

"Family friends? The people mentioned in this letter?" He nodded. "And?"

"Lauren, if there's a direct connection here I can't see it. There are similarities to the other murders, but the evidence is inconsistent with Claire Delaney's MO."

Dale Keegan was the only enlisted man on base who could call Lieutenant Commander Lauren Bachmann (the gold oak leaf insignia on her uniform was equivalent to a major's rank in the other services) by her first name. "The look on the man's face suggests trauma. The scratches are consistent with those on the other victims—the length, the distance between them—but not nearly so deep."

"And no DNA either, which is a first."

"Right. Whoever it was, was careful."

"Could it still be the Delaney girl? The one whose DNA is on the glass you filched? Maybe she changed her MO."

"Definitely not. The police report says she went home after dinner and spent the rest of the weekend taking our friends Gene and Nina sightseeing. They didn't head for home until Monday morning, and by that time Mr. Jones was already dead. Again, the wiping down of the body doesn't fit Claire's MO. She's never covered her tracks before."

"So to speak?"

"So to speak." He took a breath. "Which means there could be another one out there."

"Her DNA was in the wounds of last summer's victim, your former colleague."

"Ronny Music, yes. Along with that of a wolf. The same wolf— that is, Claire Delaney in wolf form—who colluded in killing the career criminal on the AT. Public service, I'd call that one. But that's two killings in two years, which hardly makes her a raving lunatic." He sipped his tea. "My team surmised that she and her boyfriend saw the street punk kill the campers and decided to do unto him as he'd done unto them. Which is understandable, considering that in their human form they probably wouldn't have stood a chance of bringing him in peacefully."

"So the girl is definitely a—I can't even say the word."

"She's either the word you can't say, or she has a pet wolf. One she got into the fun house in Seaside without being noticed. And put in a red dress. Neat twist to the Little Red Riding Hood story."

Lauren put her mug down on an end table and picked up a pencil. She held it in both hands between her thumbs and forefingers, turning it over as she turned over the facts in her mind.

"The funeral."

"The professor. Zeklos."

"Uh huh."

"Refresh my memory."

"I stood apart, remember. But from my vantage point, I judged Claire was very upset. We know her boyfriend killed him, but her DNA was nowhere in the professor's wounds. I'm sure she's as much in the dark about why he did it as we are."

"They found his car, right? And the body?"

"The body, but no head. He was in a landfill under about a ton of garbage. Whoever put him there had to do some pretty deep digging. Lauren," he said, conviction in his voice, "I've met her, and in my opinion I don't think this girl is a werewolf by choice."

"In the movies, none of them are."

Lieutenant Commander Bachmann stood and walked to a wall map. It was tacked over a map of the base, which was more decoration than reference anyway. All personnel stationed here, right down to the mess cooks, knew every inch of the compound as well as their own names, ranks, and serial numbers. The overlay was of New England and the New York metropolitan area, with red-capped pins indicating the three known kill sites: the Appalachian Trail in Massachusets, Criterion University in New Hampshire, and Seaside Heights, New Jersey. She reached into a desk drawer and pulled out another pin.

"You might want to make that a different color," Dale said. "And maybe add another pin. The baby's disappearance I think is more than a coincidence."

She put two blue-capped pins in the Boston area. "Can you believe two reasonably sane people are talking seriously here about— okay, I'll say it—a werewolf? Maybe even two werewolves?"

"When all reasonable possibilities have been exhausted …" he quoted.

"And you still believe she could be an asset. It's only your word that's keeping the powers that be from taking her in and taking her out."

"I know. I appreciate that. But Lauren, consider the possibilities if we could recruit her."

"You think she could be a floater. Like you."

"I can't be a hundred percent sure, but I think she has potential if she's willing to work for the good guys. And not give in to her wolfish side. At least not until it's called for."

"Naturally, my dear Dale, you nominate yourself to be her handler."

"Naturally."

"I'm still having trouble grasping the concept of a person's changing into a wolf. No one has actually seen her turn, right?"

"No one who's lived to tell us about it."

"Well, maybe it's time to bring her in. Without panicking her, of course. By all means, don't do anything to antagonize her." She stared into his green eyes. "Why don't you take your government-issue puddle jumper and, um, put a tail on her?"

"So to speak?"

"So to speak."

* * *

In the Parr household, Christmas was a time of grieving, not giving. Presents for Boo, bought before Thanksgiving to avoid the rush, remained wrapped in his closet. His crib stood as his parents had found it, except that the blankets had been removed by the forensics team. Bill and Rowena didn't exchange gifts. They skulked around the house like automatons, barely speaking, eyes hollow, faces devoid of expression. Bill had been given emergency leave for the rest of the year, but he wished he could return to work, just to get his mind on something other than the pain. Rowena and he both knew the longer Boo was gone, the less were their chances of ever seeing him again. They barely ate, rarely slept. And Rowena spent most of Christmas Day in Boo's room. Bill Senior didn't join her there.

Their parents had arrived immediately after the kidnapping and did whatever they could, but they couldn't stay forever. Daciana Moceanu showed up a few times to offer whatever comfort she was able. Claire was the most stabilizing influence, at least for Rowena. She was with them every day after work, giving her updates on the office doings, frequently ordering in Chinese or pizza and making sure she ate it. She was afraid her friend was starving herself.

It was Claire who brought them Christmas dinner from Boston Market and again forced the couple to eat. They both were beginning to look cadaverous. That night, at the time she would normally put Boo to bed, Rowena mumbled to Claire, "If he's not coming back, at least I hope he's in a loving home."

The tears came again.

Chapter Eighteen

Bentley Williams had been a godsend to Jones Publishing. Late thirties, married, a natural delegator, she fit into the table of organization as if she'd been there all her life. Ray's loss was a tragedy, but Bentley's presence throughout December was a blessing, and everyone in the company knew it. That was the good news. The bad news (for the staff, that is; fantastic for Bentley herself) was that on New Year's Eve her doctor had confirmed her long-hoped-for pregnancy and, because of delicate health issues, he'd ordered her confined to bed rest for the first trimester at least. Which meant when Rowena returned to work in January, Bentley would be on leave and her baby brother Royce would have temporarily taken over the helm.

Before she left, Bentley had given Claire an assignment that would take her out of state. Gene Franks had informed Claire he was beginning a memoir, and when Bentley learned of it, she told Claire to take a few weeks, more if necessary, to visit Gene in New Jersey and "kind of look over his shoulder. Give him the benefit of your expertise on the spot. Teach him the difference between a memoir and, say, an autobiography. His first book is still in print, and the compilation of his newspaper columns is doing well. Gene's one of our rainmakers, and we want to pamper him. Besides, he and his wife both love your company, am I right?"

On the third of January 2006, Claire visited Rowena at home and told her the news. "Will you be okay while I'm in Joisey?" she asked, forcing a smile.

"Sure, don't worry about me." She kissed Claire on the cheek. "I'll be fine, sweetie. I'll have to whip the new guy into shape, and that'll give me something at least to keep my mind occupied. We've decided: we're still going to move from this house into Ray's, you know? I think it'll be best. For both of us."

She didn't say they would be sleeping in separate rooms.

Claire hugged her. "You're my best friend, Ro. Whatever I can do, you just call me. If I weren't going away for the next few weeks, I'd be helping you move."

They embraced for a long time as tears trickled down their cheeks.

* * *

The first thing Royce Williams did upon assuming control of Jones Publishing was to have the door to his office, the glass-paned one Ray had put in storage ages ago, rehung. And it was kept both closed and locked. He never held an introductory meeting with the staff, and he spent much of each day staring at the laptop computer on his desk. He never asked Rowena if she'd heard any news about Bill Jr., never asked how she was coping, never showed compassion toward her at all. But he did leave her alone for the most part, basically turning all decision-making over to her, which kept her busy if nothing else.

She did notice Royce staring at her whenever he walked past her office to the break room—which was frequently—and some of the young women on staff confided they felt uncomfortable around him. She tried to soothe them by reminding them when Bentley came back, Royce would be gone. One said, "I live for that day."

Meanwhile, Rowena and Bill had moved into Radu Jones's house, now fully titled to them. Their own house carried a For Sale sign, and they'd told their realtor not to bother them, just accept any reasonable offer. Rowena set up one room with Boo's crib, changing table, and dresser, along with his toys.

The answering machine was always on. The only calls came from their parents and friends—and occasionally Detective Hannam, just to confirm his team was still working on the baby's disappearance but had nothing new to report.

Nina's letter to Dale had been accurate, based upon what Claire had told her: husband and wife were growing apart, and neither knew how to bridge the growing gap between them. Bill spent more hours at work, and Rowena found herself doing the same. After all, what was there at home for them any more?

It was after hours one day, when Royce had left earlier than usual, that Rowena found his office door ajar. There was no arguing with herself about the ethics of what she was about to do. Plopping herself into his large leather chair, she woke up his sleeping computer and found herself on a pornography page. No surprise there. But what shocked her was when she dug into his e-mails and found he was making deals with adult video companies for short story compilations based upon their most bizarre fetish films: bondage, transvestite/transsexual, gay and lesbian, all manner of intercourse (some she'd never heard of), all manner of body types. The stories would include photo illustrations from the videos.

One e-mail message was from his father who was on a camera safari in Tanzania. It stated Mr. Williams had arranged for Royce to attend a management seminar being held in Chicago next month. He had enrolled him from Africa via the Internet, but he'd leave it up to Royce to arrange for his tickets. Then she noted the airline tickets on the credenza, along with a hotel brochure. She swore, put the computer back to sleep, and left the office, leaving the door as she'd found it. Thinking about what she'd seen kept her up most of the night. At least this time, it wasn't solely due to thoughts of her son.

* * *

The next morning before work, Rowena pulled out her cell phone and called Claire in New Jersey.

"We're being turned into a porno publisher!" she said without preamble as soon as her friend answered.

"What? Calm down, girl. What's going on? Any word?"

"Please don't ask again. If word comes in, you'll be the first person I call. You know that."

"Sorry. I just—"

"I know, forget it. Listen, Claire, you're not going to believe this." She told her about Royce's surreptitious dealings. "Then, get this, his dad made arrangements for this douche bag to go to a management seminar in Chicago. Guess where his airline tickets are for. Clue: not Chicago. Try Freeport, Grand Bahama Island."

"Son of a bitch. Douche bag is right. What hotel, do you know?"

"What does it matter?"

"Just curious."

"Lucaya Beach Resort, right on the ocean. Starting next week, for seven days. Damn, girl. From what you and the others here said, his sister was fantastic. This guy's a human torpedo as far as the reputation of Jones Publishing is concerned. And *human* is being generous. Why are people like him alive, when—"

"Easy, now, I know where you're going."

"My turn. Sorry. Listen. Pray for a tsunami."

* * *

As soon as she broke the connection, Claire told Nina she had an errand to run and directed her to crack the whip if Gene wasn't slaving away on his computer. Nina said she would, and Claire said she'd be back before dinner.

She drove the Golden Goose to the nearest travel agency and had the clerk check the availability of rooms at Lucaya Beach. She was in luck. The hotel reported three last-minute cancellations; she could have her pick of rooms. The agent gave her a brochure on the hotel, which Claire stuck in the pocket on the side of her purse and promptly forgot about. She could study it on the plane.

Claire knew what Royce Williams looked like; she'd seen the family photographs on Bentley's credenza. She drove back to Nina and Gene's and told them that she'd have to leave them next week to meet with another client, but then she'd be back to review Gene's MS. Busy, busy, busy, she said. But better to have work than be looking for it.

Meanwhile, Dale had tracked Claire's movements through her credit card activity, and he'd followed her to New Jersey. Today's latest hit was unexpected. He contacted an associate, and after receiving the information he needed he flipped open his cell phone and booked one of the last two rooms at the Lucaya Beach Resort.

The Bahamas welcomed private pilots, and private pilots welcomed the ability to fly to an island paradise—just sixty miles off the coast of Florida—and bask on the pristine beaches for a weekend before returning stateside in time for work on Monday. Airstrips dotted many of the islands, but only a handful were suitable for commercial aircraft. Dale estimated if he left Allaire in the morning while it was still dark, he could make West Palm before sunset, weather permitting. Next morning he'd rent a life raft from the fixed base operator, file his flight plan, and fly the four-seat Cessna to Freeport. From the airport, English-style double-decker buses were available to shuttle tourists to the hotels in Lucaya.

* * *

Gotcha, Claire thought. You little slug. Royce Williams sauntered around the hotel as if he were visiting royalty. He made demands of the concierge rather than requests: more towels for his room, extra shampoo for his bathroom (he was shaved bald, for crying out loud), extra pillows for his bed. Claire heard the whispers of the wait staff actually begging the maitre d' to sit him anyplace but at their stations. For four days she'd observed him, noting every afternoon at around three he would retire to a chaise alongside the hotel pool, ogling the women guests from behind reflective silver lenses. Tomorrow she would make her move.

* * *

"Hi, there, you must be Rowena Parr," said the woman, extending her hand. "I'm Bentley Williams. And yes, you're surprised to see me. May I sit down?"

Rowena shook her hand and gestured toward a chair. "Sure, please. It's good to meet you. But it's February. Aren't you supposed to be home resting for the next, what, month at least?"

Bentley sighed. "Not any more, I'm afraid."

Rowena put a hand to her mouth. "Oh, dear, I'm so sorry. I didn't mean to be flip. Is there anything I can get you? Water? A glass of scotch? Just kidding about the scotch, by the way. Damn, I'm being flip again."

"No, no, please, it's all right. Believe me, what happened to me is … well, how does one say it? Okay, I'll be blunt and hope you understand. Of course, I was crushed when it happened, but at least I never had the opportunity to meet my child. I cannot imagine what you've been going through this past couple of months."

"Seven weeks and four days," Rowena said. "I'm very much aware of time these days."

"Listen, whatever you need, you let me know. Claire has told me how close you two are, and that's enough endorsement for me. So I mean it: anything. Now," she said, "back to business. Have you heard anything from my baby brother in Chicago? I told him to check in with you every day during his lunch break, see how things were going."

"My God, you don't know, do you?"

"Beg pardon?"

"Now it's my turn to be blunt and hope you understand." She told her boss everything, from Royce's skipping out on the management conference to his contacts (and contracts) with porn merchants. "I hope I didn't upset you," she said when she was done. Bentley's expression was unreadable.

She shook her head. "You didn't upset me, my brother did. My expectations *for* him were far different from my expectations *of* him. Don't mean to be hanging out the dirty linens, but I warned our father he would never grow up. I told Dad he was wasting his time trying to find something Royce was suited for. But fathers and sons, you know." She saw the look on Rowena's face. "Oh dear, I'm sorry, I didn't mean ..."

"It's okay, Ms. Williams. No kid gloves around me, please."

Bentley stood and extended her hands palms up. "Look: no gloves. I know we're going to work well together. By the way, I suppose it was Royce who had Mr. Jones's office door reinstalled?" Rowena nodded. "First thing, it's coming off again." She extended her right hand. "Oh, and by the way, my name's Bentley."

Rowena shook her hand. "Call me Ro."

Her boss arched an eyebrow. "Better than Ishmael."

* * *

Bill Parr didn't come home for dinner that night. Rowena barely registered his absence until near bedtime. Working late again, she thought. Or in a bar drowning his sorrows alone; she'd smelled liquor on his breath a few times. So long as he didn't get stinking drunk and pass out on a Boston street, it's death below zero out there. Alcohol may make you think you're warm, but it actually thins the blood and makes you more susceptible to cold. Bill knows this; but I wonder, does he care?

She walked into Boo's room and stared at the empty crib. "I hope, wherever you are, whomever you're with, they treat you like the wonderful little boy you are." Tears pooled in her eyes, as they always did when she stood here.

Rowena retired late, and Bill still hadn't shown up. Tomorrow she would call his office. Who knows, maybe he just decided to sleep in the lounge. Could've done the decent thing and called her, though.

During a break at work the next morning, Rowena called Fidelity.

"No, Mrs. Parr, Bill hasn't reported in today. As a matter of fact, he didn't return to the office yesterday afternoon. He said he had a lunch meeting with a client. When he didn't come back, everyone just thought the meeting had lasted past quitting time and he'd be in today waving a hefty new IRA... No, Mrs. Parr, he didn't say who the client was, we didn't think to ask. And we are so sorry hear about, you know ..."

* * *

"Mrs. Franks, I simply must have this recipe for your pot roast. I have never, and I mean that sincerely, never tasted anything so good."

"Daciana, you are too kind. My name's Nina, by the way, I've told you that before, and don't you dare call the guy sitting across from us Mr. Franks. Took me a couple of decades to break him in, I don't want anyone undoing all my work."

Gene said, "I told her that pot roast wasn't a company dish, but she insisted."

"It's too cold for namby-pamby meals," Nina said. "A freezing cold night like this, you need something hearty, something that sticks to your ribs."

"Right you are," their guest agreed. "And yes, thank you, I will have some more." Nina happily slid another slab of meat on her plate. "So. Tell me about your family."

Gene said, "Our older son is a surgeon in New York. He and his family live in North Jersey, a lovely old town called Ridgewood. Our son the doctor, as some people are wont to say. But not us, of course."

Nina added, "Of course. Our other son is a computer engineer. He and his family live in Pacific Grove. That's in California, near Monterey Bay. Every time we visit Gene insists we go to the aquarium. He never gets tired of it."

"Do you fish, Daciana?"

She looked at him with interest. "Only in the seafood market, I'm afraid. If I catch a fish, it's because the fishmonger throws it across the counter at me." She said, as if in afterthought, "Surely you don't fish in these cold winter months, do you?"

Nina said, "Believe it or not, he does. Gets up at some ungodly dark hour, wakes me up with his futzing around getting dressed, then grabs his rubber waders and fishing rod and trudges off to the beach. He's usually the only one there. If he's been a good boy, I might take him a Thermos of coffee after I get up for good."

"What could possibly make a person do that in the middle of winter?"

"Stripers, mostly," Gene said. "The big ones come closer to the surf then, within casting distance. They bite on clams. It's the only time I fish with bait," he pointed out. "Usually I cast lures. It's more sporting to fool the fish and catch 'em than to feed 'em first and then catch 'em. Don't you agree?" She nodded, appearing rapt. "The cold water makes the fish more sluggish, I guess, and they don't tend to want to chase a lure when there's that succulent clam just lying on the bottom saying 'Eat me.'"

Nina got up and collected the dinner plates, gratified that Daciana had eaten multiple servings of meat, more in fact than both of them put together. Where does she put it all, she wondered. She's like Claire in that regard.

Daciana leaned across the table toward Gene. "Tell me more about your fishing. Has our mutual friend Claire ever fished with you?"

"Whenever she visits, we try to get a day or two in the surf. She was born and raised here, you know."

"I didn't know that."

"She used to surf cast with her father. Now her parents are gone, so I kind of stepped into that role. Which, by the way, I don't say lightly. She told me so herself awhile back. It's a huge honor; at least, that's the way I see it."

"As would I, Gene, as would I."

"So, Daciana," said Nina as she brought two pies—apple and pumpkin—to the table, "how do you like living at the Jersey Shore?"

"I find I'm liking it more and more every day."

* * *

Having taken care of the Royce situation, Claire woke up the next day around noon, refreshed and ready for brunch and a swim. Over a double order of sausage and a cheese omelet in the hotel dining room, she wondered how Rowena and Bill were coping. At least I've solved one of her problems, she thought.

She wondered again what had happened to her own morality since Lukas had turned her. Hunting game, running through the forests, bringing down a deer—or even smaller game, for that matter—had exhilarated her. But after her first human kill, the wife beater she'd picked up in the bar, she'd felt massive guilt. His family was no doubt better off without him, she told herself for the thousandth time; she and Lukas were doing the world a favor by taking out the trash. But the question always lurked in the back of her mind: Who says? Who judges? And how, ultimately, would she be judged?

With Ronny Music, she had acted out of vengeance for the way he'd treated Rowena—and for who knew how many other women he'd seduced or tried to. She assumed his life insurance through the school would keep his ex-wife and kid (he'd never even identified his child by name or gender) in the black for a while. She remembered pondering whether he too had deserved to die; and whether she deserved to die as a consequence. But she'd felt a bit better after a good night's sleep in his condo. She had been meticulous about washing the bedding and wiping down everything she'd touched, and she'd tossed his key in a Dumpster at a rest area on the Garden State Parkway on her way back to Boston.

Royce Williams, though: his was the first kill she'd actually relished. She took delight in seducing him, leading him on, making him lust for her, and then letting him see her wolf's face and registering ever so briefly—no opportunity to scream—the grim reality of what was about to happen. That last part reminded her of a deer's eyes when it knew that it was doomed. Royce was prey, and for once Claire delighted in being the predator.

But if she were the predator and humans were her prey, how did that speak to her own humanity? *I am human*, she thought. I am. She started when she heard someone speak to her.

"All alone by the telephone?" The voice was deep and smooth, and the man who produced it was darkly handsome. As he stood by her table, obviously waiting for an invitation, she gauged him to be in his late forties or early fifties. He wore a loud shirt over a pair of Bermuda shorts (but no knee-high socks and loafers, thank goodness for that), and he appeared to be in good physical condition. His lips were full, his nose slightly bent as if broken once, his eyes dark. He sported a full head of black hair graying at the temples. Claire looked up and smiled.

"No telephones here, I'm afraid. Their use is discouraged. After all, you come here to get away from civilization, right?"

"Uh huh. No clocks either, for the same reason."

"Time doesn't exist in paradise." She gestured toward an empty chair. "Care to join me?"

"Thought you'd never ask." He sat and offered his hand. "Carmine Randazzo," he said.

"Luanne. Nice to meet you, Carmine. You traveling alone?"

"Afraid so. I'm a confirmed bachelor, here on holiday."

The pale band on his ring finger marked him a liar. Randazzo the razzle-dazzle artist. Claire looked around the dining room. "No televisions either. The whole world could have changed while we're away, and we'd never know it."

"Uh huh. I'm in Fox News withdrawal."

"Fox, huh? I'm more partial to CNN. I think Wolfie Blitzer is cute. And wolves have it all over foxes, by the way."

"Gee. If I'd known you were partial to Wolf, I'd have grown a beard, just for you."

Claire sipped her coffee. "No need. You look fine just the way you are." He showed perfect teeth as he smiled. "Carmine. Like red. Color of blood, right?"

"And also the name of a dye used in food coloring. Which, by the way, is made from beetles." He assumed an exaggerated professorial expression.

"Talk about a non sequitur. You're kidding, I assume."

"Not kidding. It's squeezed from beetles found in Central and South America and the Canary Islands."

"Okay, and you know this wonderful bit of trivia because?"

"I'm a chemist. International Flavors and Fragrances, Union Beach. That's in New Jersey, by the way."

Claire almost said she knew full well but checked herself.

"I've got a nose for fragrances and an eye for beauty," he continued. "One of my hobbies is growing orchids."

"Really."

"In fact, I travel with some of them."

"Do tell."

"Uh huh. In fact, only yesterday I met a lovely young woman in the bar, and when I told her about my orchids she asked if she could come up to my room and see them."

Claire sipped from her glass of ice water, sensing that this was going somewhere.

"So I said sure and took her up to my room. When I opened the door, she was nearly bowled over by the heat. Orchids were everywhere.

Well, wouldn't you know, she cursed me out, did an about face, and stormed down the hall."

"Okay … and the moral is?"

"The moral is, you can't lead a horticulture."

Carmine's teeth virtually sparkled, the result of professional whitening. Claire wondered what her dentist would say if she told him to whiten her fangs.

"Hello, Luanne?"

"Oh, sorry. That was cute, Carmine. For a moment there, I thought you were going to invite me to see your orchids, too."

He lowered his eyelids. "As a matter of fact, I was. Make that I am."

She sipped her water again, holding the glass to her lips as she stared into his eyes. She could smell his lust; it flowed from him like a wave onto the beach. It completely blotted out the peppermint on his breath. An easy kill, she thought. Another cheat-on-your-wife turd. She could do a Royce-type encore tonight on the beach.

The predator inside her liked the idea; but the human hated it. No, she would not let Luna loose. Not this time. Somewhere deep inside, she hoped not ever again.

"Mmm," she murmured as she shook her head, "I don't think so, Carmine."

He seemed about to pursue his point when he looked over and behind Claire and swallowed. Standing abruptly, he said, "Nice to meet you, Luanne," and walked away.

"Luanne? Who's Luanne?" Dale Keegan sat in the newly vacated chair.

* * *

"Busted," said Claire, shocked to find the Army sergeant sitting across from her a thousand miles and more from home. "What are you doing here?"

"Taking a few days' vacation, just like you," he said. "So who's Luanne?"

"Luanne? Oh"—think, Claire—"that's just a name I use if someone I don't know comes on to me. It's a quirk. Some cultures say when someone knows your name he owns you, or something like that."

"So is Claire your real name?"

"It is. But you don't own me."

"I doubt anyone could. And that's a good thing."

"Another good thing, Sergeant Keegan. As Costello once said to Abbott, I'm not as dumb as you look. So, why are you really here?"

"Okay. I'm monitoring you."

"Meaning?"

"For Nina," he said, easing into the fabrication he'd rehearsed. "From the beginning: I took a few days' leave and flew in to surprise Gene and Nina. I telephoned them from the airport, and Gene said I'd just missed seeing you. When I got to the house, Nina said she was worried, that you'd diddy-bopped out of there with what she thought was a cock-and-bull story about needing to see a client. Totally unlike you. To skip town all of a sudden like that."

"Nina's a very perceptive lady. But how did you know where my, uh, client was?"

"If I told you …"

"Oh, wait, I remember. I had a brochure from the hotel stuck in a side pocket of my purse. Nina must have seen it."

"Well, there you are. You found me out." Inwardly, he was grateful he'd learned not to sweat or in any other way show emotion under interrogation. Because he'd had no idea how well the "If I told you" escape clause would work.

"So, how long have you been 'monitoring' me?"

He looked at his watch. "About five minutes now," he lied. "Got in late last night and crashed. Why I slept so late today; I'm normally up early."

Claire exhaled, unaware that she'd been holding her breath.

"And what will you report to Nina, mister monitor, sir?"

"That I saw you meeting with a gentleman I assumed to be a client. That she had no reason to be concerned."

Claire smiled at him. "Thanks. I've been having some personal issues lately—"

"Nina told me about your boss and your friends' baby." He leaned forward, his face earnest. "I am very sorry, Claire."

"Thank you."

"I was on my way to the beach, thinking I'd find you there, when I spotted you talking with that guy. I didn't know if you were with him or not, but when I overheard him invite you to his room, well. Sammy Sleazebag."

"And what, pray tell, if I'd accepted Sammy's offer?"

"Then I'd really have to kill you." His grin was disarming, but his words carried an edge.

Claire laughed and flared her nostrils, taking in his scent. No pheromones. The guy must be gay—which would really be a waste. "I feel like hitting the beach myself. Join you?"

* * *

Invigorated by a long swim, the two lay on a pair of beach towels beneath the afternoon sun. Beads of salt water dried on their skin. They had reapplied sunscreen, their only physical contact with each other when they smeared it over each other's backs. Claire wore her turquoise bikini, Dale a pair of plain gray boxer trunks.

"Can I ask you a question?" Claire said, turning on her side to face him.

"Sure. Can't guarantee an answer, but ask away."

"It's personal."

"Go on."

"Not that there's anything wrong with it … God, I sound like Seinfeld. And I hated that show. Couldn't relate to any of the characters."

He laughed softly. "No, I'm not in the 'Don't ask, don't tell' program, if that answers your question."

"I didn't mean to pry."

"Yes, you did, but it's all right. If I were you, I'd think something was 'different' about me too." He turned serious. "I was engaged to be married once. Her name was Mary Rebecca Andersen, she was a junior accountant for a major investment firm. She was taking night courses at Monmouth for her CPA. We met in the student center during a break."

"Somehow, I don't think this is going to turn out well. She gave you a Dear John, and you were so heartbroken you re-enlisted." Dale shook his head, and Claire saw a flash of pain. "I'm sorry. Didn't mean—"

He went on, as if she'd said nothing or he hadn't heard. "Mary Rebecca—she used both names, I loved that—lived in Freehold and commuted to New York every day. She worked on the eighty-eighth floor of the North Tower of the World Trade Center."

"Oh, my God."

"And on a beautiful late-summer's day in 2001 she died."

"I'm so sorry."

"She got outside somehow, along with a couple of her colleagues whom we'd occasionally socialize with. They waded through the flooding in the main concourse, bumping into body parts floating in the water, smelling the stink from people's entrails. No sooner did they get outside to safety when the South Tower began to fall. They ran, and when they finally were able to stop and regroup they noticed that Mary Rebecca wasn't with them. She was found days later. All they had to identify her with was DNA evidence."

"Oh, Dale."

"When she didn't call me by the end of that day, I knew she hadn't made it. I decided then and there all I wanted to do was kill terrorists. Uncle Sam took me back, but as an independent, what we call a floater. Not a rogue, you understand, not some James Bond type, but part of a team of military, paramilitary, and civilian contractors. We go where we're needed and answer only to the President."

Claire cocked her head. "Aren't you supposed to keep that last part a secret?"

He met her eyes but didn't answer. Something passed between them that made her suddenly want to change the subject.

"I have another question." Claire fingered the long pale scars on his arm, scars which matched the ones on his back and belly. She remembered seeing, when they'd been surf casting with Gene, what appeared to be scratch and bite marks about his body. "Can you tell me how you got these? If you don't have to kill me afterward, that is."

He closed his eyes. "It was in Khost. Afghanistan."

"Where you said it was cold, if I remember correctly."

"Winter in the mountains is beastly cold." He took a breath. "It was so cold, and game so scarce, that some of the wolves actually came down from the mountains and started preying on villagers."

"Wolves? In Afghanistan?"

"Asian wolves. Bigger and fluffier than their American cousins."

"Fluffier. That's a funny way to describe them."

"Well, I don't have the same way with words you do. Their fur is thicker, I guess I mean."

"Go on."

"Our assignment had nothing to do with wolves, but I thought it couldn't hurt if I set up a post some nights. Figured if I killed a couple of man-eaters it would go far toward winning the villagers' hearts and minds, you know? Maybe gratitude wold get some intel out of them that they weren't otherwise eager to share."

Claire nodded, but he didn't notice. Somewhere inside him, he was reliving the experience.

"I set up a blind when the moon was growing full to get the best light. First couple of nights, nothing. Then on the third, something jumped me from behind. I never heard it coming. Didn't have the chance to shoot it, no room to maneuver my rifle. I spun around and grabbed it by the throat. We were eyeball to eyeball."

"You're telling me you went hand-to-hand with a wolf?"

"Hand-to-claw, more like it. His teeth caught me a couple of times, too. His hind claws went for my gut. I think he was trying to turn a six-pack into a twelve-pack. Maybe eighteen, now that I think of it."

"That's not funny."

"It wasn't at the time. I must've gotten my Ka-bar out—that's a combat knife—although to this day I don't remember how; I'll credit the Man Upstairs for putting it in my hand. Anyway, I shoved the Ka-bar into the wolf's throat."

"Ugh."

"Is right. It was on top of me, and I almost drowned in its blood. I know I swallowed some. It was like drinking liquid copper, but at least it was warm."

Claire ran her fingertips over her pentacle. "Was there only one wolf? I thought they hunted in packs."

"Fortunately for me, this one didn't seem to know that. A rogue, they called it. I still dream about it sometimes."

"You must hate wolves now."

"Not at all. This guy was just doing what all animals do. Including humans. Trying to survive. Actually, I've always thought wolves were beautiful. Still do."

He opened his eyes and looked into hers. "I think you're the only civilian I've ever shared that story with."

"Uh oh. Now you will have to kill me."

"I don't think so." He turned his body to face hers and asked about her tattoo.

"Your tone tells me you don't like it."

"Just old fashioned, I guess. The way I see it, the human body is the closest thing in God's good creation to being perfect. It can't be enhanced by poking holes in it or sticking ink under the skin. To me, it's like drawing a mustache on the Mona Lisa."

Suddenly Claire felt self-conscious. Part of her wanted to snap back that everyone's entitled to his opinion, no matter how provincial, but now wasn't the time to come across as glib. She realized she liked this guy. And she reflected on the fact that despite the urging of her adolescent friends years ago, she had decided never to pierce even her ears; it was clip-ons or nothing.

"I've offended you."

"What? No, just thinking. Short version, I'd had too much to drink. My then boyfriend and I got matching tats. Dumb."

"No, impulsive."

"That's a nicer way of putting it, thanks."

"Claire. Remember at the airport, when you told me you wanted a ride in my airplane?"

"I do, very well." She frowned. "Wait. Don't tell me you came down here in that. You did, didn't you?"

"I don't like depending on the airlines, and I don't like following someone else's schedule. Plus, I don't want to give up control of my fate to someone I don't know, no matter how well trained that person is. But to tell the unvarnished truth, flying your own plane is just plain fun."

"No pun intended?"

"Sorry. Didn't even know I'd made one."

"So, getting back to your airplane ..."

"I'm itching to get back and spend a couple of days with Gene and Nina. Would you like to fly right seat?"

"Let me think about it for a while Dale okay?" she said, making the sentence come out as one word. "When are we leaving?"

"How about tomorrow?"

She nodded. "I've had my fill of fun in the sun, I think. Tomorrow it is."

"Good. Set your alarm for oh-dark-thirty. We'll head out by dawn's early light."

"Downright poetic," she said, noting he hadn't suggested they spend their last night here sharing a room.

* * *

His name was Harvey Fish. He was a graduate student at Monmouth University, and when he saw the new genetics professor he did everything he could to be appointed her teaching assistant. He didn't know how much older than he she was, but it didn't matter; she was hot with a capital H. And the thing was, she seemed to like him from their first meeting. He couldn't help wondering what she'd be like in bed. She was built for speed, not comfort, and he knew he could get lost in her coal-dark eyes and long black hair.

Dr. Daciana Moceanu: what a lovely, exotic name.

Sometimes when he was teaching her class while she was scheduled to be in her lab, the professor would sneak into the back of the auditorium and stand against the wall, looking not at the students but at Harvey himself. When he noticed her, he could see her mouth turn up at the corners. She would stare at him until just before the period ended and then slip out again. The only one who knew she'd been there was Harvey.

She told him one day that she was a widow—he'd known that from talking with others—and confided she sorely missed the company of an intelligent, sensitive man. He summoned up his courage and invited her out to dinner, but she said it would be too indiscreet; why didn't she just come to his apartment later in the evening for a drink and see what developed from there? And when he croaked a yes, she swore him to secrecy. After all, she was new to the university, and she couldn't afford faculty room gossip that could easily find its way to the dean's office.

She arrived at ten, the hour they'd agreed upon. She wore a long black overcoat that tied at the waist, thin black leather gloves, and black stockings and pumps. Her hair was up, her eyes shaded, her lips dark red, nearly maroon. Harvey got two glasses and prepared to uncork a bottle of wine, but she placed a hand over his and shook her head. Instead, she told him, her voice a purr, to sit on the sofa, that she had something she wanted to discuss first.

He sat, and she stood facing him. With her hands still encased in the gloves, she untied the sash and let her coat fall to the floor. But for the gloves, the stockings, and the pumps, she was naked.

Harvey found it hard to catch his breath, she was so stunning. She asked if he'd kept his pledge of confidentiality. He nodded dumbly as she smiled and knelt on the sofa beside him. His hand found a breast and squeezed it gently. He brought his mouth to her hard brown nipple as her hand slid down his body to rest on his groin. She brought her other hand beneath his chin and tilted his head back. She kissed him and sent her tongue into his mouth. Then she began kissing his cheek, ran her tongue into his ear, kissed down his neck. She opened her mouth around his Adam's apple and held it there. She felt the vibration of his larynx as she heard him ask why she'd stopped, he loved what was she doing.

She spread her jaws wide, wider than was possible for an ordinary human being, the skin of her cheeks stretching like rubber. Her fangs, hinged like those of a rattlesnake, swung down and made delicate contact with Harvey's neck. She drove them deep.

Then she tore out his throat.

"Does that answer your question?" she asked sweetly, as his body convulsed and blood shot from his neck as if gushing from an artesian well.

Chapter Nineteen

Dale met Claire in the lobby of the Lucaya Beach Resort just as the sky to the southeast began to turn purple. A cab—if you could call a rusted ten-year-old Chevy with a missing front fender a cab—was waiting outside, and they tossed their gear into the trunk. The driver, who had been old when the Chevy had come off the assembly line, veritably flew down the left side of the road to Freeport. Claire was grateful they made it to the airport alive.

Dale carried both their bags to the Cessna. She could've carried them both herself, but she let him be a gentleman and didn't refuse when he picked hers up as well as his own. He unlocked the baggage compartment and stowed the soft-sided bags behind the rear pair of seats. Then he opened the door, turned on the master switch, lowered the flaps, and activated the navigation lights. Thus began his pre-flight inspection.

A metal step on each side of the cowling allowed him to climb up and check the fuel levels in the wing tanks with a penlight. "I had them topped off when I arrived, but thieves with siphons have been known to exist." Claire followed him as he checked the ailerons, elevator, and rudder, eager to learn what he was doing and why. For Dale, this was routine; for her it was the beginning of an adventure. She could almost feel the adrenaline. The last thing he did was untie the ropes that held the wings and tail in position on the tarmac.

Dale had Claire sit in the right seat, fasten her harness, and close the door. "Push the locking handle forward," he said after he'd climbed into his own seat and closed the door on the left side of the plane. He flipped open the window on his side, and produced a small clipboard with a Velcro strap that he fastened around his right thigh. He made some notes and checked his watch. "Right on time." He scanned the area in front of the plane and called, "Clear prop!"

Dale cracked the throttle, pushed the fuel mixture control all the way in, and turned the key. The propeller turned and the engine caught, filling the cockpit with noise. He closed the window and latched it, then handed Claire a headset and pulled out another one for himself. He radioed ground control for taxi clearance, motored to the edge of the active runway, and rechecked the engine, flight controls, and instruments. When he received takeoff clearance, he taxied into position, fed throttle, and told Claire she might want to look out the rear window.

The 172 rolled almost leisurely down the long, wide runway and veritably danced into the still morning air. Through the split rear window, Claire watched the runway drop away. "We'll climb to as close to ten thousand as this baby can go," he said. "That way, there's only about a ten-minute window where if the engine quits we won't be able to glide to land."

"Oh, that's reassuring."

"Life raft's on the back seat, see it?"

She looked down and nodded as Dale pressed a button on the yoke and activated his flight plan. She heard him and the controller perfectly through her own headset. The air was smooth as silk, which Dale advised wasn't the norm. "You get bumps in the aerial highway, just as you do on the ground. Enjoy this. Oh, and hold onto the yoke on your side of the plane with your left hand. Left hand only. Let the right one relax."

"What are you doing?"

"Giving you your first flight lesson. Put your feet on the rudder pedals. Don't worry, we've got dual controls, I won't let you crash. Mainly because I don't want to die either."

Dale explained the yoke, which Claire thought of as the steering wheel. Pull to go up, push to go down, turn to go left or right, simultaneously pushing the rudder pedal in the direction you want to go. Simple.

Right, she thought, as in her hands the plane began rising and falling in arcs. "I feel like I'm in a dolphin show!" she complained. "And I'm Flipper!"

Dale said, "Claire, everyone should have a porpoise in life."

"No fair! I can't hit you."

"Use your fingers to make adjustments. Very slight movements."

Eventually Claire managed to maintain a reasonable semblance of straight and level flight, and soon the coastline of Florida was visible over the glareshield. "Now what?" she asked.

"Now I think I'd better take over."

"Good thing. My hands are so sweaty that they're about to slip off the steer—the yoke."

They landed and cleared customs. Dale returned the overwater gear he'd rented, and they returned to the plane. In less than an hour, they were airborne once more. They stopped for fuel at Myrtle Beach and Norfolk, and then headed north over the western side of the Chesapeake Bay. Their flight took them over the Rappahannock River, the Potomac, the Patuxent, and finally the Severn at Annapolis. Dale had Claire bank the plane left.

"Aren't we supposed to go east? The ocean's over there, you know."

"We have to stop at Frederick first. I need to check in at my job."

"What, is this like take your daughter to work day?"

"Something like that. But you ain't my daughter."

The winter darkness was upon them as Dale landed and taxied to a hangar. He told Claire to pull back the fuel mixture knob to shut down the engine, then he turned the key and master switch off and opened the door. "I'll get the tanks topped off, and then we'll go. Why don't you hit the coffee shop, get out of the cold."

"Excellent idea," she said, shivering as she fished her coat from her duffel. "What a difference a day makes." Indeed it does, she thought. Now I know what I'm going to do with the money Ray left me: I'm going to invest it in flying lessons.

* * *

Dale walked Claire from the coffee shop to a nondescript gray sedan with government plates. They got in, and he drove away from the airport. She asked if the soldier had a Hummer as his personal car. He shook his head. "I have a theory: any guy who buys a Hummer is a G.I. Joe wannabe who never grew up; a guy who never had the stones to serve in the military but likes to pretend. I don't need to pretend. And I don't feel the need to impress others."

"Aha. So, where did you say you're taking me again?"

"I didn't say. We'll be heading north on Route 15 for about a half hour. Then we'll leave the highway and drive into the woods for awhile. Sorry if this sounds like cloak-and-dagger stuff, Claire. But if you're nervous, there's a pistol in the glove box, in case you think you might need it to protect yourself in the deep dark forest from the Big Bad Wolf."

All right, Claire thought. That was too weird. She opened the glove box, saw the .45 model 1911 semi-automatic, and looked back at Dale. "No thanks, guns scare me. I'll just have to put myself in your hands. Put my safety in your hands, that is."

They turned off the highway at a town called Thurmont and drove along a winding road, up the mountain slope. "Dead man's curve," Dale noted as they rounded a negatively-banked turn. "They say they'll build it up some day, but I understand they've been saying that for years."

"Who are 'they'?"

Dale shrugged. "Who knows?" Soon the sedan approached a dogleg turnoff where a U-turn could be made. Just past it she saw a sign, illuminated by a single street lamp: "Catoctin Mountain Park, Camp Number 3. U.S. Government Property. No Trespassing." Dale turned right onto a narrow road and drove past a tall cyclone-type fence with barbed wire strung along the top. Just beyond it stood a sentry's shed, and in front of that, bathed in a floodlight, stood a man wearing a camouflage utility uniform under a bulky field jacket. The eagle, globe, and anchor emblem stenciled on his breast pocket identified him as a Marine. He wore an olive-colored utility belt that held a holstered pistol at his right hip.

Dale stopped the car and greeted the sentry. He motioned with his head and said, "This is Miss Delaney. I assume the skipper notified you we'd be arriving."

The sentry leaned down and looked inside. "Good evening, ma'am. I'm Lance Corporal Prosper. May I see your ID please?"

Claire handed him her photo driver's license. He checked the likeness and seemed satisfied. "I'll just keep this in the gate house until you check out, Ms. Delaney. This lets the next sentry know you're on board." *Also means I can't leave by any other way but the main gate,* she thought.

"That's SOP," Dale said. "Standard Operating Procedure. Are we cleared to go, Corporal?"

"You're cleared, Sergeant Keegan." And leaning down once again so Claire could see his face, he said, "Welcome to Camp David, ma'am."

* * *

As a confused (as in overwhelmed) Claire Delaney was being photographed, issued a temporary ID pass, and eating dinner (a grainy and gamey venison version of meat loaf) in the chow hall along with some thirty discreetly ogling Marines, a couple of hundred miles away Daciana Moceanu sat in her rented shoreside home dining on what was left of Harvey Fish. She had brought thick plastic builders' bags with her last night, and by midnight she had filled them with most of what she hadn't eaten. Having drunk her fill, she used a sponge mop to sop up the rest of the blood. Her gloves remained on the whole time. She cleaned out his refrigerator, including the shelves, and stacked the bags inside—all but one, the one she would take home for leftovers. Life was good, she mused. But undead was even better.

* * *

On the same day: *From an island retreat to the President's retreat,* thought Claire as Dale walked her from the mess hall to the base commander's cottage. It was too dark now for her to appreciate the narrow asphalt trails flanked by tall trees and wood-sided cabins. And too cold, too. The air seemed to bite through her coat. She had already surmised—and Dale had confirmed—that they wouldn't be flying to New Jersey tonight, but he'd said he would get her there in a day or two. Nina and Gene, he reminded her, wouldn't be expecting them back before then anyway. His tone was casual, but Claire sensed something was not right. And she knew if she asked, he wouldn't tell her.

"We're going to see the base commander," Dale said as they walked. "She's a woman, by the way. No glass ceilings here."

He explained that everyone on board, from the Navy Seabees who built and maintained the base to the Army soldiers who handled communications and the Marines who stood guard, had a Top Secret White House security clearance and were absolutely devoted to their duty. Anything else about the place, he said, he would save for later.

They approached the wood-shingled cottage, and Dale knocked on the door. It opened immediately, and Claire got her first glimpse of the camp commander: a woman in her mid to late thirties, medium height, shoulder-length chestnut hair, wearing a Navy officer's utility uniform that had been tailored to her trim figure. She also wore a belt and holster, a holster containing a pistol that looked to be a match for the one Dale had in his glove box and the one carried by the sentry at the main gate. The commander offered her hand.

"Lauren Bachmann," she said pleasantly. "Come inside; it's freezing out there."

She offered them coffee in mugs emblazoned with the Presidential Seal and sat them in her rustic living room, where a fire blazed in the hearth. Claire perched on a sofa and Dale and Lauren sat in barrel chairs facing her. She felt as if she was about to be double-teamed. The officer's eyes drilled into hers.

"Claire, we'll get down to business first so we can dispel any doubts as to what this is all about and what we hope you'll agree to."

"I'd appreciate that. I expected to be in New Jersey by now, but Dale surprised me. I'm not sure if it's a good surprise or a bad one."

"That depends upon whether you agree."

"You're not going all *Mission Impossible* on me, are you?" Claire put the mug on a coffee table in front of the couch. She tried a tentative smile, but the others remained stone-faced.

"In a way, we are, because impossible is what I thought you were until Sergeant Keegan here brought me the facts."

Claire shifted uncomfortably and pushed herself back on the sofa. Her eyes darted from Bachmann to Dale and back again.

Dale said, "Claire, we are among the few people in the world who know you're a werewolf."

The hair stood up on the back of her neck; but she tried to maintain a calm façade, especially in light of the fact that Bachmann's holster flap was unfastened and her right hand, resting on the arm of the chair, could easily draw the pistol. The commander's gaze was steady, but her expression wasn't hostile. Claire said, "What makes you think something as stupid as that? There's no such thing—"

Dale said, in a quiet but authoritative voice, "No games, Claire. Your DNA was on the glass I took from Gene and Nina's house. It matched what we found in your victims' wounds. To quote you from yesterday morning, 'you're busted.'"

Claire nodded to Bachmann's pistol. "Got silver bullets in that thing?" Her expression was sardonic.

"No. But I do have Sergeant Keegan. Besides, I wouldn't shoot you inside my house. Too messy, in more ways than one. The sound of the shot would attract the Marine guards, and I'd have some serious explaining to do. Besides, I don't expect we'd need to use extreme measures. Am I right?"

Claire felt naked before them, totally exposed. "You've been following me, haven't you? I thought you looked familiar when we met at Gene and Nina's. I remember now, I saw you at Gabriel Zeklos's funeral. You were standing by a tree, away from the rest of the group." He nodded. "Right. And your visit to Gene and Nina's when I was there wasn't a coincidence, was it?" He shook his head. "When I first saw you at Lucaya it raised all kinds of red flags, but somehow you managed to lie your way out of it. I think it's because I liked you, and I thought you liked me, too. I wanted to believe you. Now I find that—that what? You've been manipulating me for years?"

"I liked you, too, Claire, I still like you, but the mission had to come first, and I had to be objective." He added, almost under his breath, "It wasn't easy."

Lauren leaned forward. "Claire, there are people in our cadre who want you terminated as a clear and present danger. Dale's voice is the only one at the moment speaking in favor of keeping you alive."

"How about your voice, Ms. Bachmann?"

"Me, I'm on the fence. Claire, know this: we're not your enemy if you're not ours. And I'm going to get us some refills now." She left the room to fetch the coffee pot.

Claire took a breath and looked at Dale. "Explain. I'm all ears. Not pointed ones, at least not yet."

He folded his hands and tented his index fingers against his chin. They reminded Claire of a church steeple. "As a Ranger during my first enlistment I trained in a lot of different fields, but I was particularly drawn to forensic science, how it was used to tie murder victims to their killers, things like that. After my release from active duty I earned my education degree with a double major in criminal justice, and during my brief teaching career began graduate courses at Monmouth. Where, as you know, I met Mary Rebecca." He returned his hands to the arms of his chair.

Bachmann returned with the pot and refilled their mugs. She put her mug on the coffee table next to Claire's. The flap on her holster was fastened now. "When we got word of the killing of that punk on the Appalachian Trail—"

Claire felt the tears as memories returned and lowered her head as she tried to hold them back. Lauren offered her a tissue. She looked up; the camp commander's hand was inches away from her mouth. "Not afraid I'll bite you, Ms. Bachmann?"

"Take it. I told you, we're not your enemy. By the way, if you're Claire, I'm Lauren."

Claire wiped her eyes and blew into the tissue. "Go on then … Lauren."

"The forensics people found four sets of DNA in his wounds: two human, two wolf. The anomaly was brought, as a matter of course, to the attention of the White House. It was huge. And it had huge implications."

"Dale told me he answers to the President. Which I guess is the reason he's based here."

"Dale is one of those rare agents who operate under the direct auspices of the White House," Lauren confirmed. "He works across federal agencies but is largely independent. In uniform, he's a staff sergeant, virtually anonymous, which is how we prefer it. Gives him credibility with the troops and lets him tap into their mood and morale. But make no mistake, he's got more rank than any general or admiralty grade officer when it comes to doing the President's business."

"I'm impressed."

"So am I," he said. "Sometimes I wonder if that guy's really little old me. But back to business," Dale continued as Lauren sipped her coffee. "When the professor was killed, we found only one wolf's DNA match in the wounds. Your missing boyfriend obviously killed him, for reason or reasons we don't know." Claire remembered the visual confirmation Lukas had himself been killed.

"Knowing you and he were romantically involved, the powers that be sent me to keep an eye on you. And yes, Gene and Nina provided an excellent opportunity for us to 'coincidentally' meet."

"You must know then that I'm the one who killed Ronny Music."

His expression revealed nothing. Then: "That's right. All due respect for the dead, I shed no tears over that one. I was well aware of his history … 'n stuff."

They shared a brief smile while Lauren wondered what the inside joke was.

Claire had the impulse to tell Dale that Ronny and Puglio weren't her only victims. But she held it in check. "Why didn't you take me in right then? That was, what, seven months ago?"

"Believe me, more than one person wanted me to. Not just take you in, but find a way to terminate you—with extreme prejudice, as they say in militaryspeak. Can't have werewolves running around free, after all. The fact everyone thinks werewolves don't exist made you even more dangerous."

"So why didn't you, what, *terminate* me?"

"I wanted to see if you had become more predator than human, to see if the wolf had grown more powerful than the person. I didn't believe it had, but I had to be sure. In the Bahamas, I intended to set myself up as bait, and see if you would attack me or not. Unfortunately, someone else beat me to it."

Claire frowned. "How—"

"Night vision binoculars. I wasn't sure what you were doing with that guy on the beach until it was too late to interfere. Plus, based upon your unexpected and sudden departure from Jersey, I figured you had a purpose in mind, that this guy wasn't just a random kill. Am I right?" She nodded over her coffee mug. "All right then. You can tell me your reasons another time. Seven months between kills didn't make you a raving serial killer; more like a vigilante or a one-woman star chamber. Anyway, when I heard you turn down the opportunity for another easy kill yesterday, that guy in the hotel dining room, I figured humanity had come out on top. Which made me very happy, by the way."

"In spite of my alter ego?"

"Not because of it, that's for sure. But if you take advantage of our offer, you will need to be in total control of that part of your identity."

"I can do that," she said, perhaps a little too glibly. "Okay, so what's this 'offer' you have to discuss?"

"That's simple," answered Lauren. "The President wants you to work for him. For us."

"But … I already have a job."

"Not any more. You'll have to resign."

"And if I don't?"

Lauren looked at her matter-of-factly. "That should be obvious."

"Come on. You mean you'd—?" Neither said anything. "You really would, wouldn't you?"

"There's your choice, Claire," Lauren said. "Work for the good guys or, well …"

"Or you'll keep me in a private zoo, or kill me, and have your research people dissect me, and see if you can use my DNA to create an army of werewolves dedicated to truth, justice, and the American way. Am I right?"

Dale said, "I think you've been reading too many unsolicited manuscripts."

Chapter
Twenty

On the walk back to their quarters from the base commander's cottage, Dale told Claire of how he'd been appointed to his present position. Whenever the President is arriving by limo, he explained, the motorcade has to cross a couple of mountain streams spanned by small wooden bridges. In preparation, a Marine is assigned to each bridge to check beneath it for plastic explosives. Then he stands on the bridge when the motorcade crosses—insurance that he performs his duties thoroughly.

On one occasion a Marine crawled under his assigned bridge and found a tiny antenna sticking out from between two boards. He saw that the plastic itself had been wedged into the cracks between the boards and painted to look like dirt that had fallen through the cracks. The sentry radioed in to the guardhouse, the officer of the day contacted the Secret Service, and the motorcade turned around in Thurmont and headed for Frederick. The President helicoptered in from there. It had been too close for comfort.

Dale, meanwhile, who had been administering advanced combat training to a small detachment of Marines, found the would-be assassin's trail and tracked him to where he was concealed, in a hidey-hole he'd dug in the woods. That man was now reposing in Guantanamo Bay. No, Dale replied to Claire's question, there's a reason you never heard of it. Everything relating to Camp David is classified Top Secret.

When the President's chopper landed at David that day, he joined the Secret Service when they debriefed Dale. He liked what he saw and heard. And later he called Dale back to Aspen and offered him the opportunity to join a special team of operatives, consisting of both civilian and military and beholden to no other agency.

* * *

The Marine barracks occupied the right side of a U-shaped single-story building. On the left side were the individual rooms for staff noncommissioned and commissioned officers. A bump-out behind the base of the U housed the chow hall. The whole building was based upon function rather than form, but Claire found the aesthetics hospitable, in a rustic way.

She stared out the window of her room in officers' country, across the hall from Dale's. The black of winter's night was absolute, and on their walk to the barracks she noted realms of stars she'd not seen since her nights hunting in Francestown. Even the light of the all but full moon wasn't enough to wash their brightness out. The mattress on her steel bunk was surprisingly comfortable, thick and firm. The wall locker was spacious enough for the clothes she'd brought with her to the Bahamas. The head (she'd started when Dale told her there was a head adjoining her room, until she reminded herself that in Navy lingo, *head* meant bathroom) was small but functional, with a stall shower but no bathtub. *What did you expect*, she thought, a jacuzzi?

Claire walked the few steps from the window to her bunk and sat. Her eyes were fixed on the blank screen of the television across the room, but her thoughts roamed. Some choice they gave me, she said to herself. Play ball or be killed. I could run away—Dale and the commander must've been certain I wouldn't, they didn't even post a guard at the door or window—but even if I tried, how would I do it and where would I go? The fence was too high to vault, even in wolf form, and I'm sure there must be sensors somewhere to alert the roving patrol that passed us in a Jeep as we walked back here. In a way, their apparent negligence was a nod to her own intelligence.

As a wolf, I could bolt through the front gate before the sentry could have a chance to shoot me, but once out, then what? I'd freeze to death once back in human form; therefore, I'd have to carry my winter clothes in my teeth, and wouldn't that be a sight. Oh yes, and stop in the gatehouse along the way to snatch my driver's license. Hel-lo.

Claire stood and went into the head. She'd laid out her toiletries earlier and brushed out her hair before reaching for her toothbrush. *So assuming I did get out,* she thought, where would I go? Where could I go that they couldn't find me? Not Boston, for sure.

Which brought her to thoughts of Rowena, crushed by the disappearance of Bill Jr. She had seen Ro and Bill drifting slowly apart, something she couldn't quite understand. They should be supporting each other, not blaming each other or whatever it was they were doing, retreating into their own private hells. How will Ro take my leaving, when she needs me for emotional support, and without so much as a word of explanation? "Top secret, Ro, you understand." Right. That'd go over like a pregnant pole vaulter.

Claire lay in her bunk with the lights out, between cold crisp sheets and covered by a warm wool blanket. Her eyes remained open. At least Royce Williams is dead, she thought. He won't drag Jones Publishing into society's dung heap. I wish Bentley luck with her pregnancy, but I wish she were back at the helm. She closed her eyes and thought of her career, suddenly cut short. From a life of promise to the promise of life—but only if I do as I am told. Wow, I sound like a caricature of some World War Two Nazi. I vas only vollowink orders ...

Sleep overtook her.

*   *   *

"Sleep well?" Dale asked as they walked to the chow hall. The morning was bright and made the winter world outside her window look as crisp as a fall apple.

"Surprisingly, yes, considering the sword of Damocles is hanging over my head."

"Yes, well, I can't deny that. I wish I could, though, if that makes any difference."

"None whatsoever."

The chow hall was clearing out as they entered and picked up their trays. The Marines nodded toward Dale, who was dressed in a sharply creased utility uniform with black metal staff sergeant's stripes pinned to his collar points. As they acknowledged him, their eyes jumped to Claire. Pheromones there, she noted through slightly flared nostrils. As in raging. Probably slim pickings for them down in tiny Thurmont.

They ate a hearty breakfast ("So now I can say I've chowed down on the dreaded SOS—and it's actually pretty good."), returned to their rooms for their winter coats, and stepped outside between the left and right wings of the building. It was 0730, and the Marines were conducting guard mount in preparation for the new day's shift. The uniforms on each of them looked as sharp as Dale's, and their lieutenant inspected the men's rifles from all angles as if his moves had been choreographed in ballet school. He nodded toward Dale as the pair passed and returned the soldier's salute with a subtle wink Claire almost missed. Boys. Do they ever grow up?

Dale took Claire on a walking tour of the camp. They passed a swimming pool to their right, and beyond that a tall water tower with a small shed abutting it. On they walked down the narrow road they'd driven in on. Near the gate he directed her to a road that forked to the right, at the end of which was a large grassy field and a building labeled Field House. "Not an athletic field and not a field house," he said. "Landing pad and hangar." They returned the way they came and took a road to the right past a parking lot on their left. "That's the guard house over there next to the motor pool area. We'll swing by Hickory on our way to Aspen."

Hickory Lodge was the recreation hall. Like the other cottages, all named for trees, Hickory was single story, but it had a basement which housed a two-lane bowling alley. Topside were a movie room, a small bar (slopchute, Dale called it), and in another room an old pinball machine, a relic of the past. On that room's paneled wall hung a giant black and white photo of an aircraft carrier, with the legend identifying it as the *USS Boxer*, site of the first jet landing on a carrier, by Navy Captain E. P. Aurand. Dale noted that Aurand was promoted to the admiralty and served as Naval Aide to President Eisenhower.

They walked outside.

Claire said, "We learned about Eisenhower in history class. Ancient history class."

"Very funny. A friend of mine was one of Ike's Marine guards here back in the day. He's long retired now and lives in Pennsylvania, not all that far from Ike and Mamie's Gettysburg farm. We see each other occasionally."

"You know him how?"

"He was one of my teachers. Kind of inspired me to want to teach."

"I had one of those, in seventh grade. He inspired me to major in English in college."

They paused a few moments, each reflecting, their breath misting before their faces.

"Okay, on to the Big House."

"Which is?"

"Aspen, the President's lodge. You'll see a Marine walking guard around it, probably one of the more boring posts in the camp."

"But one of the most important ones?"

"They're all important. Let's go."

They strolled past small guest cottages, all wood shingled and weathered gray. The trees loomed large over all, and ice sheathed their bare branches. "It's so quiet here I think I can hear my blood circulate," said Claire. "Well, maybe that's the wrong way to put it, considering ..."

"Here's Aspen."

The road curved left, and the trees gave way to a vast expanse of grass that led down a slope to the woods beyond. A small golf course dotted the now brown greensward, and a drained swimming pool bordered a flagstone patio.

The house itself was a large ranch design that angled slightly in the middle, as if built to complement the curved contour of the roadway. A trellis, now bereft of vines and flowers, reached to the roof. Across from the house was a small iced-over pond.

As they stood there, a Marine walked around the corner with his rifle slung from his right shoulder. Seeing the two, he stopped and swung his rifle to port. He relaxed when he saw who it was. "Morning, Sergeant Keegan. Morning, ma'am."

"Morning to you, Private Larkin. Mind if I show Miss Delaney around the Big House?"

"I've been advised you're on your way. No problem."

"I heard your mother's not doing well. I thought she was in remission."

The young Marine slung his rifle. He looked to Claire as if he still belonged in high school. "She was," he said.

"Operative word *was*?"

"Afraid so."

"You know if you need to go on emergency leave, Lieutenant Pace won't hesitate to grant your request. He told me so himself."

Larkin looked relieved. "Thank you, sergeant."

"Family's important."

"Yes, it is."

"You carry on, now."

"Aye, aye, sir—sergeant."

Dale walked Claire around the back, on the upper level of the patio. "That rock garden below was Mamie Eisenhower's. She took great pleasure in it. Ike put in the golf course." They walked down two steps onto the lower level.

"That was a nice thing you said to the guard."

"Thanks."

"I thought the different services hated each other."

"Not so. Rivalries exist, that's true, but everyone knows we're all in this together. I might also mention the super-hawks you see in the movies, the 'shoot 'em-all-and-let-God-sort-'em-out' types, they're only in the movies."

"Why did the guard call you 'sir' back there?"

"Private Larkin is fresh out of boot camp. At Parris Island, I'm told, recruits even have to call the water fountain 'sir' when they salute it and ask permission for a drink. Fountain's been there longer, see, and it has seniority."

"Oh, boy."

"So the 'sir' habit is pretty hard to break. But they manage."

"What's that shed on the grass over there?" Claire asked as they continued on the patio's lower level. "It looks like the one next to the water tower."

Dale thought for a moment. "Whether you accept the President's offer of employment ... I guess it makes no difference. The sheds lead below. In the event of attack, the President will be able to take charge of operations from underground. The tower is filled with emergency supplies to last over a long siege. It only looks like a water tower. On purpose."

"You're talking underground bunkers here?"

"Command post is more accurate. And there are more than this one scattered around the country."

"When can I see what's down there?"

"When can we get your commitment?"

Claire studied Dale's face for a long moment. "It's obvious. What choice do I have, after all? The only thing is ..." She explained about her relationship with Rowena, about the loss of Bill Jr., about the strained relationship between Ro and her husband. "She needs me, Dale, she really does."

"Does she know what you are?"

"You've got to be kidding me. She'd freak."

"I think we can accommodate you for awhile. I don't know of any emergency situations—"

"Superfluous," Claire corrected. "An emergency *is* a situation."

"Seventh grade English teacher, huh? Remind me to thank him some day."

* * *

Lieutenant Commander Lauren Bachmann, USN, was speaking on the red phone in her quarters. "Yes, sir, she's agreed to come on board. Sergeant Keegan will vouch for her. He feels her predation is controllable, and he believes she has great compassion and loyalty." She listened. "The FBI is already working on her security clearance. Aside from the fact that she's a werewolf—or a metamorph, as she prefers to call herself—she seems to have an unblemished record. Not even a traffic ticket … Keegan will be her handler, yes sir. He'll put her through a boot camp regimen to instill the proper discipline and train her in every skill he himself has. Oh, one more thing, sir." Lauren had to grin. "Delaney wants to come in as a staff sergeant right off the bat. Not for the pay, but because she doesn't want Keegan to outrank her … Yes, sir, that's what I thought, too: You go, girl."

* * *

In West Long Branch, the absence of Harvey Fish from his classes and duties at Monmouth University did not go unnoticed. It was Professor Moceanu, in fact, who officially advised the campus police of her missing TA, and she who displayed the most horrified reaction when the police reported what they'd found in his refrigerator.

What Daciana didn't know was after the police completed their preliminary investigation, a forensics team with Top Secret credentials swept in and performed their own analysis. In five days—Claire's first full day as a guest at the President's retreat—the results were hand-delivered to Camp David.

Lauren called Dale and Claire to her cottage and handed them the results. "This happened while you were TDY in the Bahamas," she said to Dale, "which is why you weren't called in on the team." She turned to Claire. "Looks like you're not alone after all. Dale suspected it, but we couldn't be sure until now. It seems there's another one of you out there."

Claire clutched the arm of her chair with one hand and reached for her pentacle pendant with the other. She wanted to scream.

Chapter Twenty-one

"I love cooking for you, Daciana," said Nina Franks. "You have such a good appetite, I wonder where you put it all."

"Am I being a pig?" Daciana asked.

"Not at all, dear. I love that you love my cooking. Gene takes my cooking for granted, I'm afraid."

"Then I confess," she said. "I have a hollow leg."

Gene laughed. "You must have; it would show anywhere else."

"Mister Franks, are you ogling me?"

Nina said, "Now there's a word I haven't heard in awhile. Ogling. My."

Gene added, "Daciana, when I stop 'ogling,' you can throw dirt in my face." She frowned. "Because I'll be dead."

"Gene loves to window shop," confessed Nina. "But he doesn't buy."

"I've never felt the need to."

"Flatterer."

Daciana said, "Well, you may ogle me all you like, Gene, I'm honored."

They finished dinner and Nina went to the kitchen to get their dessert, a concoction she'd devised years ago: balls of raised dough coated with melted butter, sugar, and cinnamon, pressed together and baked in an angel food cake pan. Her older son, the weisenheimer of the family, had called it "that famous Old World delicacy, shushkataniabopnik," and she'd seen no reason to change it. Daciana laughed at the name.

Nina dropped the cake from the pan and drizzled over it a glaze made from confectioner's sugar. Daciana took a taste and informed her that if this was what was served in Heaven, she wanted to die, right now.

Over coffee, Gene mentioned he'd be getting up before dawn tomorrow to do some surf casting. "Set the alarm for four, Mother," he said, and Nina told him to set it himself, she'd be in the other bedroom so when he got up this time he wouldn't disturb her beauty sleep.

Daciana looked at her watch. "Goodness. If you're getting up early, I'd best be on my way. Besides, tomorrow's a working day—for those of us who must still work." Over their protests, she said good night and drove away.

"Lovely lady," said Nina.

"That she is, love, that she is."

* * *

Gene was awake five minutes before the alarm went off. After a brief trip to the bathroom he slipped on his longjohns and insulated socks and tiptoed to the kitchen. He made himself a cup of instant coffee and wolfed down a large chunk of shushkataniabopnik. Still savoring the raised dough's sweetness, he went out the door to the garage, where his ski bibs, jacket, and rubber waders hung on hooks. He put those on, along with a knitted ski cap, and opened the small refrigerator in which he kept his bait; for today, large chunks of clam. Rather fool 'em than feed 'em, he mused for the nth time, but on frigid February days you have to go with what works.

He tossed the bait into a plastic bucket, where it joined a small tackle box and a fiberglass sand spike. With hat and gloves donned last, he grabbed the bucket in one hand and his rod in the other and left by the side door, taking satisfaction that his stirrings hadn't wakened Nina.

He clumped down to the beach and put the bucket down near the ocean's edge. The surf was up this morning, perfect for drawing the lunkers close to shore. He stuck the spike into the sand, slipped the rod's handle into it, and with hands now free baited the hook. He walked through the tiny clouds of his condensing breath and waded into the surf, where he cast his bait out, overhand, just as Claire had taught him. The line formed an arc in the moonlight as the bait and pyramid sinker sailed past the nearer breakers and splashed into the sea.

Gene backed out of the wash and stood next to the sand spike. He reeled in the slack line, and when he felt the tension from the sinker's dragging across the ocean bottom he stuck the rod handle into the spike, leaving his hands free. He looked left and right, scanning the darkness for any other signs of life. He was utterly alone. Guess I'm the only fool in town, he said to himself. Back in the day, I'd resent having to get up at the crack of dawn to go to work. Loved the kids, hated the hours. Swore when I retired I'd sleep in every day until noon. That got old quickly, now, didn't it? Now when I'm not fishing I'm writing, and I do the best of each in the early hours. Even when I'm fishing, standing here waiting for a bite, mentally I'm writing.

Nina will come down with a Thermos in an hour or so, and I'll be ready for a shot or two of coffee by then. Real coffee, fresh, not that tasteless instant crap. She might even bring down a plastic bag with more of her raised dough. It just doesn't get any better than this. Or, as my son the West Coast computer geek observes with implied envy, retirement doesn't suck.

The silence was punctuated only by the crash of the surf, the soft susurration of the wash as it crept up the beach and receded into the next wave. From somewhere over the dune, Gene heard a car door close. *Another idiot like me*, he thought, slapping his hands together. Should've put hand warmers in my gloves. Always forget those, always forgot 'em when I was skiing, too, and my fingers froze like icicles. Never learn, will you, Franks?

He jumped when he felt the soft touch on his shoulder. "Good morning, Gene. I thought I'd find you here."

When he caught his breath, he said, "Daciana?"

"Hello."

"Hello yourself. What are you doing out here?"

"I don't have to be in class until ten, so I have time to come down and see what the attraction is." She looked from side to side. "It is beautiful this time of morning, isn't it? So alone, so peaceful, so serene."

The moonlight made the skin of her face seem paler, her eyes darker. Her long hair draped over the dark overcoat she wore. "Are you ogling me again, Gene?" she asked playfully.

Gene chuckled. "Daciana, you could make a happy man feel old." She frowned. "Get it? A play on words: You could make an old man feel happy, get it?"

Her smile returned. "Oh, of course."

"What a pretty smile you have."

"Said Red Riding Hood to the Big Bad Wolf."

He looked down, slightly embarrassed he might actually be flirting with her. But she knows I'm harmless, he assured himself. Maybe she's flirting with me? No, those days are long over, Franks.

"Wha—? Daciana, you're barefoot!" Her legs too were bare. What was wrong with this girl? He looked into her eyes, and she tilted her head to one side, regarding him, her expression pleasantly bland. "Barefoot's for summertime. You can't come out here like that in weather like this. You'll catch your death."

Daciana dropped her coat to the sand. She stood before him naked. "Not I, Gene," she said. "But you will."

* * *

The sun was brightening the eastern horizon, sparkling on the waves, making rainbows in the whitecaps, when Nina Franks walked onto the beach, carrying a Thermos. When she saw the hunched figure on the sand, she shook her head and quickened her pace. If he was going to sit down, he should've brought a beach chair, the old fool. Probably didn't want to make two trips, what with all the other stuff he had to carry.

His back was to her, and the bait bucket was obscured by his body.

She saw the rod tip was twitching, an indication that something was nibbling at the bait. Gene should be holding the rod, waiting for the right moment to set the hook, but he wasn't moving. Asleep? Seagulls, a dozen at least, congregated around him, screeching and darting, screeching and darting, then flying away with bits of what Nina assumed was bait hanging from their beaks. She quickened her pace, and the bait bucket came into view. It was untouched; the gulls' attention was on Gene himself. She couldn't see anything of him but his jacket, ski cap, and waders.

She walked around to the front of her husband and stopped dead. A pair of seagulls fled from the jagged-edged hole in his abdomen and flew off, squawking back their indignation at having their meal interrupted. Nina dropped the Thermos and screamed.

* * *

In Boston later that morning, Rowena Parr was in Bentley Williams's office, the wall-mounted television tuned to a cable news channel with the sound muted, just as it had been when Ray was in charge. She sat on the sofa and watched her boss hang up the phone on her desk.

"Nothing," Bentley said. She had been speaking with the manager of the Lucaya Beach Resort, where she'd called an hour earlier and asked to be connected to her brother's room. She was ready to read him the riot act over the phone and tell him not to come back to Boston, ever. Maybe his father would continue to coddle him, but not his big sister, not any more. "When I got no answer the first time, I asked to speak with the hotel manager. He made some inquiries of the staff, and he tells me the maid reports his room looks untouched since she cleaned it a few days ago." She shook her head. "A pool attendant mentioned the last time he saw Royce was when he was chatting up a blond woman poolside. Actually, the attendant was staring at her, too—she was evidently quite a looker—and wondered how she could be interested in someone as, well, as ordinary as Royce."

She walked to the front of her desk and sat on its edge. "He probably hooked up with this bimbo and is staying in her room. I left word with the manager to have him call me as soon as he sees him. I can't wait to chew his ass out."

Rowena commiserated: "My daddy would say you should chew around his ass, and let it fall out by itself. No disrespect intended." They shared a brief laugh.

Bentley ventured a gentle inquiry: "I suppose you haven't heard ..."

"Nothing. Bill hasn't come back, and the police can't find him."

"Listen, I've said this before, but it bears repeating. This is a job. Family comes first. If you need time—"

"Thanks, Bentley, thanks a lot, but I need the job now more than ever. You understand why."

"I do."

The television screen showed a reporter dressed in winter jacket standing on a beach. Behind him was a group of people working behind poles stuck in the sand strung with yellow crime scene tape. Rowena barely noticed until a graphic popped up on the bottom of the screen: Author slain.

"My God," she whispered when a photo appeared in an inset. Bentley turned to look and asked what was wrong. Rowena said, "That's Gene Franks."

* * *

The same broadcast was beaming into Lauren Bachmann's cottage at Camp David. The base commander had been readying herself for a personnel inspection of the Seabees, more a mere formality here than it would be, say, on shipboard. These people could teach her a thing or two about being squared away. Even in the President's absence, they looked as sharp as Washington Marines on parade.

She heard the reporter's voice as she was adjusting the jacket over her blouse; and when his words sank in, she turned her full attention to the screen. When the remote ended and the studio chirpers came back on, she snatched her phone from its cradle and called the guardhouse.

"Corporal Smithson? Lieutenant Commander Bachmann. Sergeant Keegan and Miss Delaney are training in the woods out the back gate. I want you to send the roving patrol to retrieve them and bring them to my quarters, pronto."

* * *

The Methodist church had to open its recreation hall and string up speakers there in order to accommodate the overflow crowd that arrived following Sunday services for Gene's memorial. Nina, looking frail, sat in the front pew with her two sons and their families. All were in various stages of stupefaction, as if locked in a nightmare they couldn't escape.

In the row behind them, Claire sat next to Dale, and Rowena sat next to Daciana Moceanu. Filling out the nave and rec hall were Gene's former students, from high schoolers to young men and women in uniform and older adults with children of their own. No greater tribute could their teacher have imagined.

On the altar stood an urn.

One of the sons (dazed as she was, Claire found it hard to keep their names straight) offered the first eulogy, in which he mentioned his father had wanted to go to medical school as a cadaver after his death: "After years of using visual aids, now I'll actually be one." But he never got the chance. Everyone understood: there hadn't been enough of Gene left for students to dissect. Instead, his ashes would be mixed with the sand at the shoreline at low tide and carried out to sea with the ocean's flow and ebb. The son concluded anyone wishing to share memories of his dad was welcome to take the lectern, and a line formed along the aisles on both sides of the nave.

Claire had been surprised to see Daciana at the service—she'd forgotten the professor had relocated to Monmouth—but Rowena had not. Daciana had been calling Rowena once a week asking about Boo and had expressed surprise and regret when she learned that Bill Sr. had gone missing as well. She held Rowena's hand throughout the service.

"Listen," she told them after a reception in the church basement. "I rent an old beach house in Long Branch, two stories tall plus an attic. It has four bedrooms, three of which are empty, and I insist you all stay with me. Mr. Keegan, that includes you." The three looked at each other. Daciana added, "Nina's sons and their families will be filling up her house, she doesn't need more confusion, and besides … "

Rowena said, "We've already booked rooms, Daciana. I'm going to be bunking with Claire, and we have to get up early tomorrow to head back to

Boston. I could only come down for the day." This hadn't been the time for Claire to tell her differently.

Daciana considered. "I didn't mean to upset your plans, Rowena, I understand, that's all right. But will you at least do this for me? After my husband Gabriel … died, after the funeral and reception, a few close friends from the faculty came to the house, and we sat and talked for awhile. It meant a lot to me." Rowena lowered her eyes and nodded. "Might I ask you then, as friends of Gene, to come to my house for a brief period of quiet conversation? I didn't know him nearly so well as you, but I did consider him a friend."

* * *

"It's a winter rental," Daciana explained as they entered the large old home that fronted the boardwalk and beach. "These houses rent for almost nothing when the summer is over, just to keep them occupied, and then go for exorbitant rates during the summer season. During the summer, I can be vacationing elsewhere and return in time for fall."

They stood in a dark, high-ceilinged living room with wainscoted walls. The wallpaper above the yellowed pine was a faded buff color crowded by a pattern of green vines. A large-bladed old fan dangled from the ceiling. Its vanes were still. The air inside was also still and close. A worn brown rug covered most of the dark hardwood floor. The furniture was massive and overstuffed. An old furnace in the basement groaned as it blew hot air through vents in the floor, heat that quickly rose and left their feet cold while making their faces warm. Claire tried to shut her nostrils to the musty smell, without success. She wished the professor would turn on the fan.

They sat, and after an awkward silence Daciana began the conversation with her memories of the dinners Gene and Nina had invited her to, of Nina's exceptional cooking. Dale volunteered the collegial relationship he'd shared with Gene, a professional friendship that had turned into a personal one. Claire related her history with Gene, from reading his first manuscript to his and Nina's later roles as her surrogate parents. This seemed especially to please Daciana.

Rowena sat silently, then after the others had spoken she recounted she had only met the Franks once, at last Thanksgiving's dinner. She'd thought them charming and remarked about their easy and comfortable relationship with each other.

Daciana sat upright and chided herself for a poor host. "I want to share with you a toast. To Gene." She looked at Claire. "It's non-alcoholic, I know you girls don't drink. It comes from an old Romanian recipe my mother passed on to me. Natural fruits and berries, with some spices to make the drink less cloying." Rowena asked if she could help. "No, dear, it's already made. I keep it on hand for when I come home from work. You sit; I'll be back in a minute."

When she had gone, Dale looked at his watch. Claire nodded. "It'll be dark soon," she said, "and we need to get back to the hotel. We have some things we have to discuss before you head back, Ro."

"Before I—you're not coming with me? I figured we could convoy back."

Before Claire could answer, Daciana returned with four plastic tumblers, each a different color, on a tray. "I'm sorry I have nothing more elegant to offer the drink in," she said as she put one on the end table next to her chair and then crossed the room to the others. "As the house came fully furnished, there was no need to unpack my crystal ware."

The drink was dark and thick and smelled sweet, with a tang that was unfamiliar to Claire's wolf-sensitive nose.

Daciana sat in her chair and raised her tumbler. "To Gene. A devoted husband, an inspirational teacher, and a wonderful friend."

They drank. And as Daciana watched, smiling, the others' eyes glazed over, the tumblers fell from their hands, and they drifted—no, plummeted—into unconsciousness. Daciana raised her own tumbler again and said, "To me. A clever manipulator, a cunning avenger, and a mortal's most dreaded enemy." She downed her singularly untainted drink.

* * *

Bitter cold seeped up through the concrete floor. Two low-wattage light bulbs barely pierced the shadows of the basement. The tiny windows were painted black. Three steel chairs had been bolted to the floor forming in essence three ninety-degree compass points. Another chair, this one cushioned, stood at the fourth point, but it had not been bolted down. This was the one reserved for Daciana, who stripped off her own clothes as she had those of the others. Modesty was of no concern to her. Being naked in front of humans was no different from being naked in front of one's pet animal. It meant nothing. But to the others, ah, their mutual nakedness would be most disconcerting.

Dale occupied the chair to Daciana's right, Rowena the one to her left, and Claire the one directly opposite Daciana herself. All three were cuffed to the chairs at wrists and ankles. Their heads drooped forward. And all three were unconscious. A large plastic bucket stood next to Rowena's chair.

It was time to wake them up. Daciana delivered a vicious slap to each of their faces. Their eyes fluttered as their cheeks turned red, and when they regained consciousness and realized where they were they struggled to get free. But their struggles ceased when they heard Daciana's laugh, which instead of being soft and friendly had grown brittle and dark. She returned to her chair and crossed her legs, leaning back in a casual posture designed to infuriate them all the more.

"I've been preparing this little surprise for quite a while," she said. Nodding toward Dale, she added, "Your seat I originally intended for Nina, but I can deal with her later." Dale fought his bonds again but was unable to break them. Even if his arms could have stressed the links of the chains to the breaking point, his legs had no leverage.

"I like your spirit, Mr. Keegan," said Daciana. "Claire, I've had your cuffs silver plated. Do they burn? Being what I am, I'm impervious to silver, by the way."

Claire said nothing. What burned was the hate in her eyes.

Dale said, "What are you doing, and why are we naked?"

"Do you object, Mr. Keegan? I should think as a virile male the sight of three beautiful female bodies would be quite … stimulating." She looked between his legs. "Perhaps you're a homosexual?" His face flamed, but not from embarrassment. She stood, pacing from one captive to the other. "The reason is, I like humiliation—in others. When I was a child in Wallachia, criminals about to be executed were stripped naked and paraded through the streets. Citizens used to ridicule them and throw sticks and stones; the more charitable ones threw rotten food. By the time the prisoners reached the town square, they were almost ready to welcome death—except for the fact they knew their deaths would be lingering and even more painful. Isn't that charming?"

Rowena whimpered. "What's going on? Daciana, what are you doing? Why are you doing it? We're friends, for God's sake."

"We're certainly not friends, and certainly not for God's sake. You're a naïve fool, Rowena, as I will illustrate shortly. Meanwhile, I suggest you look at the bucket next to your chair. It's to catch your blood, and when I've drunk my fill I intend to dine on your internal organs. As wolves and other predators do. Then tomorrow I'll proceed to Mr. Keegan, who was a delightfully serendipitous surprise. And why am I doing this? Ask Claire, it's all because of her."

"Monster!" Claire shouted as the others looked at her in shock.

"This is true," Daciana admitted to Claire. "In fact, I am even more monster than you." She turned back to Rowena. "When a person lives forever, she tends to embark upon certain … projects … to pass the time, to amuse herself. Your friend here offended me with her unconditional love for Lukas Ehrlich. Who was by rights mine. I made him."

"Liar!" seethed Claire. "His parents made him what he was. He inherited it from them."

"What's going on here?" whispered Rowena. Daciana ignored her.

"But I made him more than what he was. He owed me his allegiance, his unswerving loyalty. Instead, he gave it to you. Which is why he needed to die and why I need to punish you for making me kill him.

"Besides," she continued, "punishing those who have wronged me gives me a certain sublime pleasure. So I have decided to kill the ones you, Claire, love most. That's why I killed Gene. And why I will kill Nina once her sons have gone back home. Claire, you won't be available to see me kill her, but you will know it, and that will have to suffice."

Rowena whimpered, "You bitch. You filthy, conniving bitch. I was your friend."

"You were my prey."

"What *are* you?"

"My late husband referred to me as a hemophage—but now I'm also a shape shifter, in Gabrielspeak a metamorph, and in the vernacular a werewolf—just like your friend Claire over there."

Rowena shook her head as Claire muttered, "There's no such thing as—what did you call it—a hemophage."

"I used to think the same about werewolves. All that morphing on the molecular level, it went totally against my training. But then, do not caterpillars morph into butterflies? That's at least as radical a change as human into wolf. But in my case, there's no need for change." She leaned close to Rowena, her face inches away. She opened her mouth. Her jaw dipped radically low, like a pit viper's. A pair of fangs swept down on their organic hinges from where they rested against the roof of her mouth. No delicate needles, these; they looked more like slim, tapered tusks.

Rowena shoved herself back in the chair and screamed.

"But wait, Rowena, it gets better. Watch." Coarse black hair sprouted from Daciana's naked body; fingers turned to claws; and her face projected into a snout. Her breath blew rancid in Rowena's nostrils.

"Stop it!" Dale shouted.

Daciana returned to human form. "Ah, another country heard from. I was beginning to wonder if the cat had gotten your tongue." She laughed as she made a connection. "But no, the wolf will get your tongue instead."

"Burn in hell, bitch," muttered Claire.

Daciana turned to her. "And what about yourself, Claire? Aren't you a bitch, too?"

"I'm not like you."

"No, you're not. And you never will be. I'm going to see to that."

"You not only killed Lukas, but you killed Ray Jones, too, didn't you?"

"Oh, no," whispered Rowena.

"Oh yes. That was an unfortunate accident. We were in the throes of lovemaking, you see. Our first time together. I was riding him, losing myself in our coupling, and ... I felt myself begin to change. It was totally unintentional. Poor Radu saw what was happening and died of fright, while he was still hard inside of me. I did not want him dead. I liked him, after my fashion."

"I guess you blame me for that, too."

"No, I blame Lukas for not warning me the change could happen like that. Oh, which reminds me, did your beloved boyfriend inform you of the cross you must bear, to borrow a hackneyed phrase?"

"What are you talking about?"

"No, he didn't. I knew he wouldn't have. Do you remember his telling you that his parents were dead?"

"So?"

"Do you know what killed them?"

"He didn't say. He just told me he was an orphan like me. I didn't press the point."

"They died of old age, Claire. Yes, old age. While they were in their late forties. You see, after your first metamorphosis, your body's aging process begins to accelerate. Because you are equal parts human and wolf, your wolf body wants to age seven years for each one of yours. But your human body opposes that, and so it works out a compromise. You were made about four years ago, but during that time you have aged about twelve years. Lukas's first change, he told me, was when he was eighteen. When he met you, at chronological age age twenty-four, he was more like thirty-six."

Claire was staggered. "That's why I thought Lukas was in his thirties when I met him. That's why I found a couple of gray hairs the other day in the Bahamas."

Rowena said, "The Bahamas? When were you in the Bahamas?" Again, no one acknowledged her.

"My late husband was working on a way to retard and possibly reverse that aging, which is why he and Lukas were so close. And it was probably why Lukas hesitated to tell you about it. He knew Gabriel was close to a cure, and when he had it he could administer it to you, as well as himself. Until then, he saw no need to add another element to your anxiety. Such a sweet boy."

Daciana leaned close to Claire's face. The perfume was wearing off, and Claire picked up the scent she'd detected in the woods the night she found Lukas's flayed tattoo nailed to the tree. The professor said, "You remember the day you and I met. That was the day that I turned him, and he turned me. And what a couple we made! Unique in all the world!" Her face darkened. "But no, he had to ruin it. All because of you."

"For love of you," Dale said softly. "You're not to blame for anything, Claire. You have to know that."

Rowena looked at Claire. "I'll say it again. What were you doing in the Bahamas? I thought you were with Nina and Gene."

Claire looked downward. "I went to kill Royce Williams, because he was killing Jones Publishing. And I killed Ronny Music because of what he had done to you."

"You ... killed them? Claire, you?" Her friend nodded. "Please don't tell me how." She turned to a grinning Daciana. "Oh, God. It was you took my son, wasn't it?"

"And your husband, too. You may thank Claire again."

Claire sucked in a breath, and her voice cracked. "Bill's gone too? You never said—"

"But if it's any consolation," Daciana interrupted, "I was quick. Bill didn't know what hit him ... and your baby didn't know what bit him." She licked her lips. "Young ones are the sweetest, you know. It's like the difference between veal and beef."

"Noooooooo!" Rowena wailed until her throat burned. She lowered her head, her despair now a soft keening that threatened to empty from her mind whatever sanity remained.

Claire shouted, "Listen: I didn't want to be this! When I met Lukas I was a normal, screwed-up, college senior who only wanted a job, and a boyfriend, and a future. I got the job, I got the boyfriend ... but I lost my future. I *hate* what Lukas did to me. I hated it then, and I hate it now. I hate what I've become; I hate what I am! Why do you have to kill my friends? They didn't do anything to you. I'm the one who deserves to die. Kill me!"

"How very noble of you, Claire. Nobility is such a waste of potential, wouldn't you say? Rest assured, I shall kill you, young lady, I shall. Not here, though, not now. I've something special planned for you."

Her smile never traveled to her eyes.

Chapter Twenty-two

It was Monday, and like any other Monday, normal people went to work. Daciana Moceanu, who was not normal, also went to work. She greeted her fellow faculty members with uncommon good cheer. Her thoughts drifted back to the two perverts at Criterion who often shared their breaks in the faculty room with her. Did their blood taste different from that of heterosexuals? Probably not.

Over the course of centuries, Daciana had experimented sexually with women, but she found the experience ultimately unappealing and only feigned pleasure in order to get her partners to let their guard down, which made the kill ever more gratifying. She was like Gene Franks in that regard, she mused, when he told her he preferred fishing with artificial lures: it was more sporting to fool the fish than feed them before reeling them in.

Her human side, or whatever remained of it, liked Gene. Nina, too. Salt of the earth types, they were. Rowena was pleasant, too, and certainly beautiful, what with her mixed-racial genetic blend. Bill, though, he was a prize worthy of mounting on a wall. Or mounting, period. Tall, good looking, beautiful smile, and charming in a rather pedestrian way. After they had finished lunch on the day he disappeared, she had asked him to walk her to her car, and he was too mannerly to deny her. The air was freezing, but her smile was warm.

Parking in Boston was always a challenge, and Daciana had managed to find an empty space in an alleyway behind a guest house that had seen better days. She unlocked the door and faced Bill tentatively, lips parted, eyes half-lidded. She touched fingertips to his cheek and saw his expression grow into one of confusion as he returned her stare. She could smell desire in him. He shook his head no, but her fingers beneath his chin brought his lips down to hers. Bill shivered, and not because of the damp cold.

Bill's arms wrapped around Daciana's waist, and then he broke the kiss and pushed back. I can't do this, he'd said, and she smiled and said it was all right, she had seen his pain and only wanted to comfort him. She placed her palms against his cheek and saw tears in his eyes.

Then she snapped his neck.

Daciana opened the car's trunk and dumped Bill's body into it. She carried him effortlessly, thanks to her newfound strength. She drove to the woods outside Francestown and carried his body to the spot where she'd killed Lukas. She wasn't hungry, she'd eaten a substantial lunch, but she was thirsty. She took off her overcoat and draped it over a branch. Joining it in short order were her skirt, blouse, and bra. It wouldn't do to have blood on them, for more reasons than simple sanitation. She lowered herself to her knees, swung her fangs into place, and sank them into his neck.

She had to suck hard, because his blood was inert; it wasn't being driven, after all, by a beating heart. If she wanted more, she'd have to open him up.

Daciana extended a talon, tore through Bill's diaphragm, reached inside, and ripped out his heart. She took the aorta into her mouth, tilted the organ up, and drank. When her thirst was slaked, she cocked her head and studied Bill's face. Oh, what the hell, she said to herself, morphed her head into that of a wolf, and split his skull between her jaws. His brain tasted especially sweet.

She howled once, twice, three times, and then put on her clothes and walked away. The wolves and carrion feeders would take care of the rest.

* * *

The basement stank. Daciana had kept her prisoners manacled, for exactly the same reason she had stripped them: humiliation, for the shame of having to void their bowels and bladders in the presence of others and then forced to sit in their own waste. The cellar was also unheated, and the prisoners' breaths fogged in front of their faces.

As Dale listened, Claire told Rowena how she had met Lukas, how he'd turned her, how they'd hunted, whom they'd killed together and why. Righteous kills, Lukas had called them, and she had found some small comfort in that, enough to assuage her conscience at least in some small part. Rowena's teeth chattered as she listened, not only from the cold. Her face remained blank.

Finally she whispered, "Were you ever a danger to me or my family?"

"Never, Ro, never." Tears formed in Claire's eyes. "I loved you all. But because of me, because of *me*, your family is dead."

"Stop it. You're not to blame, not for any of it. God, I've never known a friend as … as *pure* as you." She shook her head. "Even if you are—I can't even say it. But Claire, I've seen that bitch outside in broad daylight. I've seen her eat Benjamin's roast beef, which he'd infused with garlic. She was in church yesterday, and seeing the cross had no effect on her. What's going on?"

Before Claire could answer, Dale said, "She did mention her being a child in Wallachia. That's the region that abuts Transylvania's southern border."

"There's a real Transylvania? It's not something from a Bram Stoker novel?"

"They're both part of today's Romania. But what jolted my memory is the prince of Wallachia during the fifteenth century was Vlad Tepes"—he pronounced it *tsepish*—"otherwise known as Drakula … a name that means son of the devil."

"And otherwise known as my lover." Daciana walked down the stairs. "Didn't know I was home, did you, children? I can be very quiet when I want to be." She was dressed in black woolen slacks and a white translucent blouse. Her feet were bare. "Good pronunciation, Mr. Keegan, by the way. Most Americans would pronounce his name *teeps*." She sniffed. "My, does it stink in here! Oh, dear, look at you three, all fouled in your own piss and shit. How thoughtless of me not to give you bathroom privileges."

"Fuck you," growled Claire.

"Many a man has, and many more have tried. For those … it didn't go so well. After all, six centuries is a long time to be abstinent. For your information, know that Vlad, the *voivode* of Wallachia, was not a Bram Stoker villain. But he did love the blood, oh yes. And he taught me to love it, too. I was in my thirties when he was killed, still a young woman, still attractive—in fact, just as you see me now." She pirouetted and curtsied, like a child, but the glee in her face was not that of a child at all. "And Claire, like you I was turned by a man. A man who, like yours, was ultimately unfaithful and had to be destroyed. Isn't that ironic? We have something in common."

Rowena glanced from Daciana to the bucket beside her chair. The vampire noticed.

"Oh yes, my dear little Afro-Asian hybrid, the bucket. We'll be getting to that soon. Sooner than you'd like. But first—" She sat down in the chair she'd occupied last night and crossed her legs. She looked as if she were preparing to lecture her class. "Now that Mr. Keegan has brought the subject up, it seems the perfect time to tell you what I've planned for you, Claire."

"I can't wait."

"Ah, but you can wait. That is the beauty of it. Listen. In the days of bear baiting, the bear didn't know it was going to die, and therefore had no fear of what the day would bring; but you do know you're going to die, and the beauty—for me—lies partly in your anticipation. When I was drawn under my prince's spell—and he under mine—he sought to impress me with an exquisite—and dare I say original—form of execution. Now, I had been to his garden of stakes and seen the men and women impaled there. Their groans and cries of pain as the weight of their bodies forced the stakes up into their innards was delightful, indeed, and I wondered what could be even more so."

"*Were* delightful, bitch. Thought you were college educated."

"Oh, you're being funny. Even with death facing you, you summon the strength to be sarcastic. I like your spirit, Claire, I really do. But I digress."

Daciana paused, her eyes focused no longer on the prisoners but on a scene from long ago. "Vlad had a prisoner brought in and thrown at my feet. It was a man who had offended me with an unchaste remark, and for that he needed to be punished. The guards took him to the courtyard, where a horse had been tethered. Standing next to the horse was Vlad's favorite executioner, and as two other guards held the horse still, the executioner slit its throat. When the horse fell, he slit its belly, and Vlad made the prisoner scoop out its steaming guts with his hands. Then the guards bound him and shoved him into the belly of the beast. They took hooked needles and thick twine and sewed the horse's belly shut, leaving only the prisoner's head exposed. Then they made a pillow for him with a pile of the horse's intestines and Vlad directed his retainers to relieve themselves on the prisoner's head. Within seconds he was covered with flies, the big, black, biting kind. And as the horse's body decomposed over time, the man's body inside rotted along with it. Slowly and, oh so, painfully. My prince was right. It was exquisite, and he did it all for me."

Rowena murmured, "You are so sick. How could I have thought you were a friend?"

"Practice, dear, centuries of practice at the art of deception. Which brings me to our dear friend Claire here. After I dispatch you and her handsome friend here, Claire and I are going to take a little ride, I in the driver's seat, she in the trunk. No, dear, don't think you'll have a chance to escape, not with a tiny dose of curare in your body, which I've appropriated from the University. It will paralyze you, but it will not kill you. So: We are going to drive to your old hunting grounds in New Hampshire. I will bring down a deer and do to you what Vlad had done to the prisoner. It will take many days for your body to decompose, and I shall be there, watching, the whole time. Once you're dead I shall dispatch Nina, as promised, and at the end of the school year I'll transfer to another college. I'm tired of these cold winters. I thought New Jersey might be warmer than New Hampshire. The South appeals to me now."

Silence hung in the room.

"Claire? What do you think of my plan?"

It was Rowena who spoke, through clenched teeth. "Shut your foul mouth, and kill me, bitch. Get it over with. What have I got to live for now?"

"Ah, yes, Rowena. I think it's time to let Claire see the next of her loved ones die."

Daciana shrugged out of her clothes and draped them over the back of her chair. She smiled, almost sweetly, at Dale and Claire, then walked to where Rowena sat, her dark eyes defiant. Daciana lifted Rowena's chin, exposing her neck, and extended her jaw as her fangs fell into place.

In a final act of hatred, Rowena spit into her face.

Daciana laughed and lowered her head to Rowena's neck. Claire turned her head.

Rowena screamed.

The wolf pounced.

* * *

The sudden force smashed Daciana's head into Rowena's, knocking her unconscious. Daciana fell to the concrete floor, rolled over, and staggered to her feet. Before her, teeth bared, stood a huge wolf, brown with green eyes, and she had a flash of the shaggy beasts she'd shot for sport on the Russian steppes a century or more ago.

Claire sat in her steel chair, still imprisoned by the cuffs around her wrists and ankles. She snapped her head to the side and saw that Dale's chair, and the manacles which had held him, were empty. She saw the wolf leap again onto Daciana. The woman struggled against him, tried to snap at him with her fangs as she drew her knees up to try to push him away.

"Idiot!" Claire muttered to herself and began to morph. Her wolf's legs were thinner than her human arms and legs, and she was able to slide them free, as Dale had done. But Dale!

There was no time to think. Daciana was trying to change into her wolf form, but panic prevented a full shift. She pushed against Dale's throat, her own claws digging into his fur searching for hide to tear. His saliva dripped onto her face, which was still human but for her jaws and those fearsome fangs. She wormed her lower body free from beneath Dale's brute weight, and her wolf legs began to form. She slashed with her hind feet and clawed them into Dale's belly. He yelped, and he fell onto his side, whimpering, his guts exposed.

Something seized Daciana's own belly. Claire! But the silver!

No! Daciana had actually believed those superstitions about werewolves; hadn't given them a second thought. A split second was all the time she had to think before she felt the agony of her own belly's being torn apart in a wolf's iron jaws. She shrieked, a cry half demon, half wolf.

But she could heal, her kind could do that, so long as she could fight these two off. She redoubled her efforts to free herself, tearing into Claire's flesh as she pushed against her.

Claire drew back, ready to disembowel Daciana. But she stopped as if she'd run into a wall. The wolf's belly began to close. The wound, her intestines quivering behind it, was knitting, impossibly fast. Claire stood immobile, staggered, staring as the flesh closed and bonded. Daciana laughed—a cackle that turned into a howl.

Claire drove herself into Daciana, her head knocking her antagonist backward against the cinderblock wall. Daciana was shifting shape again, randomly, as if she were not yet in full control of her metamorphic abilities. Or maybe it was panic she felt as Claire fastened her teeth into her belly and dragged her to the floor. She gave a twist of her head and a superhuman pull, and Daciana's guts spilled out along with the flesh that covered them.

Daciana, still in quasi-human form, scooped up her innards from the concrete floor and tried to gather them into her body. Claire darted her head toward Daciana's own, and the centuries-old beast opened her hideous mouth and extended her fangs.

But Claire was not interested in biting through Daciana's neck; instead, she fastened her own fangs around her head. Daciana's last sight was the inside of a wolf's mouth, of the yellow teeth, the slippery tongue, and the tunnel that led to its gullet. The wolf bit down, hard, and bone crunched. Brain matter spilled out.

Still Daciana writhed—whether purposeful or reflexive, who could tell?

Claire shoved her muzzle into Daciana's belly, probed high, found her heart, and tore it away. The writhing stopped.

Holding the heart in her teeth, Claire ran to where Dale lay on the floor, barely conscious, his shaggy body ripped raw, his intestines pink against the dirty gray concrete. He turned his head toward her and tilted it back, exposing his throat, wordlessly begging her to have mercy and finish him off quickly. Instead, she spit out the heart, changed back into human form, and told him to open his mouth. She forced the heart between his jaws and commanded him to drink. As he chewed weakly, Claire shoved his intestines inside his body and rolled him onto his back.

She waited.

Dale obediently chewed the heart, its chambers burst, and blood flooded his throat. He swallowed, and in moments he began to gather strength. As Claire watched intently, his wound began to close. Sixty seconds, maybe a few more, was all it took.

When she saw Dale turn onto his side and attempt to stand on all four feet, Claire ran back to Daciana's body and lapped up the beast's blood from the floor and from her cranial cavity. She looked down at her own wounds and watched as they too closed up.

As Rowena enjoyed her merciful unconsciousness, the two wolves that were now more than wolves feasted on Daciana's body and brain. When their hunger—and their vengeance—was satisfied, Claire returned to human form. Dale looked at her, his head cocked to one side, stark fear in his eyes for perhaps the first time in his life.

"Change," she said. "You can do it. Make your body human the same way you made it wolf. It's tough at first, but you'll be able to do it. You're not a prisoner in there. Think, Dale!"

Gradually, the wolf became man, a man who lay on his back weeping like a child. "I used to have these dreams," he said. "Nightmares about the wolf that nearly killed me. But I never dreamed that—that I—"

"It's okay," said Claire, kneeling beside him, cradling his head to her breast. "It's okay."

Dale let himself be comforted, gave himself over to it. He was not ashamed to cry. Some might call it a weakness, especially in a soldier like him, but privately he saw it as a strength, for it exposed his inner emotion and dared the world to make of it what it would.

Rowena shook her head and slowly returned to consciousness. She mumbled something inarticulate, then looked down at Daciana's remains and retched, directly into the bucket by her chair.

"It's all right, Ro. You're safe. She's dead. For real."

Rowena sobbed, the detritus from her stomach dribbling down her chin. "Don't give me the details. I never want to know the details."

But she knew she would have to.

* * *

The keys to the handcuffs were in the pocket of Daciana's slacks. Claire freed Rowena, and the two climbed upstairs to the bathroom, Dale behind them. Standing together in the shower, the women ran the hot water tank cold—and then felt guilty that they'd left no hot water for Dale.

He grinned weakly, still recovering from the psychic shock of his discovery about himself, when Claire apologized. "It's okay," he said. "Since I've met you I've become used to cold showers."

"Why, Dale," said Claire. "Do my sensitive nostrils detect pheromones?"

Epilogue

TWO YEARS LATER

Mr. & Mrs. Dale Keegan
P.O. Box 180
Thurmont, MD 21788
March 18, 2008

Dear Claire and Dale,

I brought my little Smith-Corona portable with me, because Gene always told me my handwriting was as hard to deciper as the Rosetta Stone. It doesn't take up much room in my suitcase.

So sorry I couldn't attend your wedding, but as you can see from the postmark I'm halfway around the world. You wouldn't believe how beautiful fall in New Zealand is. I'll send photos when I get duplicate prints made. Digital cameras still aren't my style.

Our sons and their families insisted after I sold the house in Manasquan that I come to live with them. Isn't it sweet, they want to share me: six months in California, six in New Jersey. I told them I would, but only if they'd let me use their homes as a base when I'm not traveling. They seem happy with that. Their wives and I get along really well, and I just adore the grandchildren.

I'm going to send you a little wedding present from New Zealand—don't worry, it won't be a pet kiwi bird. When I'm back in New Jersey, perhaps you can fly in, and we can get together. Good grief, I sound like Ronny Music there, don't I?

I still miss Gene and suppose I always will. The first year after he died, I was in a drug store walking by the greeting cards when I remembered it would be his birthday in a week. When I realized I would never again buy him a card, I broke down right there and cried my eyes out. The manager was very kind, though. She had seen this kind of behavior before, she said.

I'm reminded, too, that you told me Daciana Moceanu was behind Gene's killing, as well as several others, and that you've "taken care" of her. I know enough not to ask for details. Thank you, my dears. As for that woman, there are no flames in Hell hot enough to punish her for what she's done.

Oh dear. That's not very Christian of me, is it?

Love to my "other children,"

Nina

* * *

A man and woman stood by the back gate of Camp David, he in casual civilian clothes, she in utility uniform. They watched a pair of wolves playing in the woods, chasing each other around the trees and through the shrubs. The male, larger, darker, and the shaggier of the two, leaped upon the sleek blond female, and they rolled over and over, nipping and yipping like puppies.

"Hard to believe they're dangerous, when you see them like this," the man said. "And Sergeant Keegan—who would have known that he was a—well, the same as her?"

Lauren Bachmann—Commander Bachmann now, her gold oak leaf insignia replaced by a silver one—repeated to him that no one had been more shocked than Dale when he found out, and she further assured him these two could perhaps be the deadliest covert weapons in America's arsenal.

"But they're no danger to us, right? I mean, they're not going to eat us up or anything, I assume?"

"Believe me, sir, they're in control." She took a breath. "At least that's what they tell me.